ARCTIC SMOKE

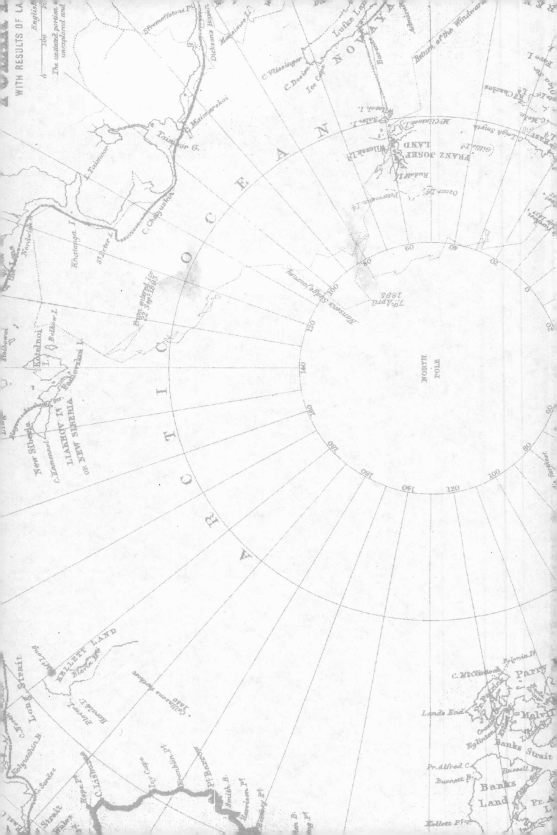

PRAISE FOR *ARCTIC SMOKE*

"UNLIKE ANYTHING ELSE OUT THERE. NOUNS PUSH AGAINST
VERBS IN WAYS WE'VE NEVER SEEN."

—**Mike Resnick**, Hugo Award-winning author
of *Kirinyaga* and *Santiago*

"*ARCTIC SMOKE* IS A PUNK ROCK FEVER DREAM. LIKE
BRUCE MCDONALD CHANNELLING ANNA KAVAN, SCHROEDER'S
PROSE HOTWIRES YOUR BRAIN AND TAKES YOU ON A
SURREAL JOYRIDE THROUGH ARCANE CANADIANA."

—**Greg Rhyno**, author of *To Me You Seem Giant*

"A WINTRY AND PSYCHEDELIC ELEGY TO THAT SPECIAL
ALBERTAN BRAND OF DESPAIR. AN ABSURDIST PUNK-ROCK
ADVENTURE THROUGH COUNTER-COUNTERCULTURE'S MOST
OTHERWORLDLY SPACES. SCHROEDER WRITES WITH URGENCY
AND GRACE, VIVIDLY DESCRIBING A ZOMBIE CAPITALIST
WASTELAND WHERE THE STRANGE BECOMES FAMILIAR AND
THE FAMILIAR STRANGE. READ THIS BOOK."

—**Mike Thorn**, author of *Darkest Hours*

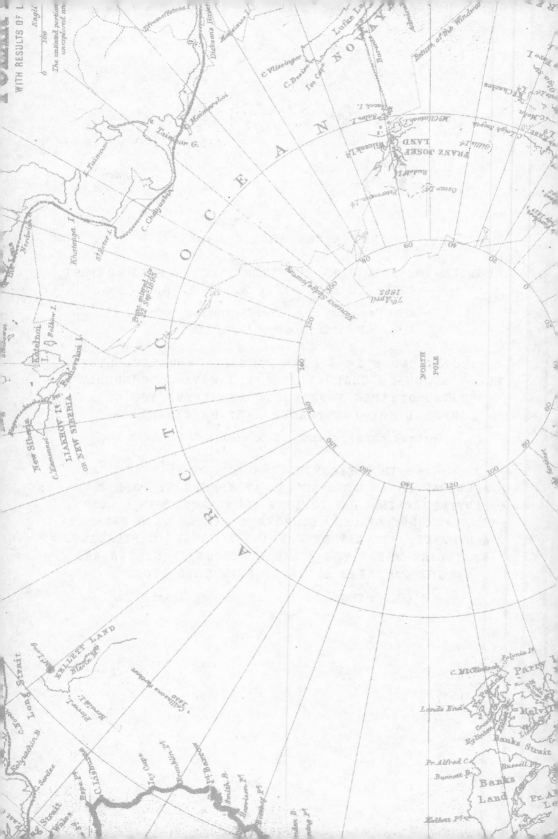

ARCTIC SMOKE

A NOVEL

RANDY NIKKEL SCHROEDER

NeWest
Press

NeWest Press wishes to acknowledge that the land on which we operate is Treaty 6 terri-tory and a traditional meeting ground and home for many Indigenous Peoples, including Cree, Saulteaux, Niitsitapi (Blackfoot), Métis, and Nakota Sioux.

Library and Archives Canada Cataloguing in Publication

Title: Arctic smoke / Randy Nikkel Schroeder.
Names: Schroeder, Randy, 1964– author.
Identifiers: Canadiana (print) 20190075074 | Canadiana (ebook) 20190075082 | ISBN 9781988732701 (softcover) | ISBN 9781988732718 (EPUB) | ISBN 9781988732725 (Kindle)
Classification: LCC PS8637.C5757 A73 2019 | DDC C813/.6—dc23

Board Editor: Kit Dobson
Cover and interior design: Michel Vrana
Author photo: Nathan Elson

NeWest Press acknowledges the Canada Council for the Arts, the Alberta Foundation for the Arts, and the Edmonton Arts Council for support of our publishing program. We acknowledge the financial support of the Government of Canada.

#201, 8540-109 Street
Edmonton, Alberta T6G 1E6
NeWest Press   www.newestpress.com

No bison were harmed in the making of this book.

Printed and bound in Canada

1 2 3 4 · 21 20 19

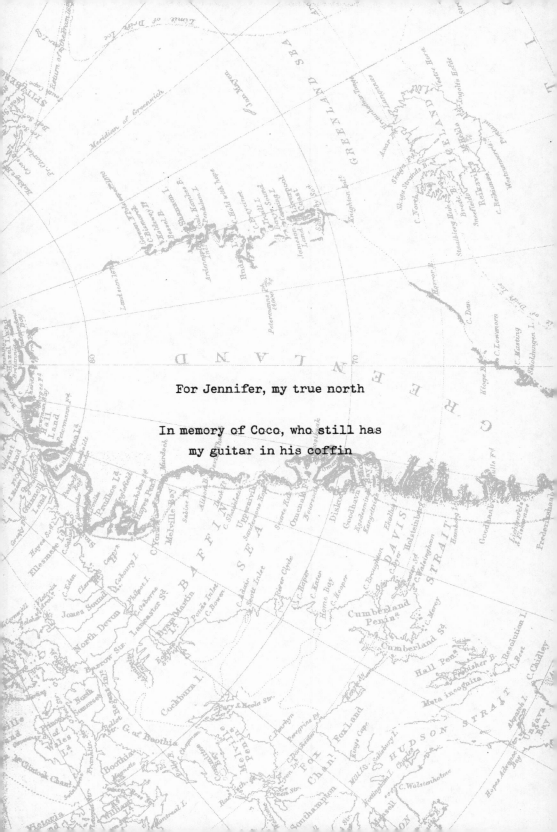

For Jennifer, my true north

In memory of Coco, who still has
my guitar in his coffin

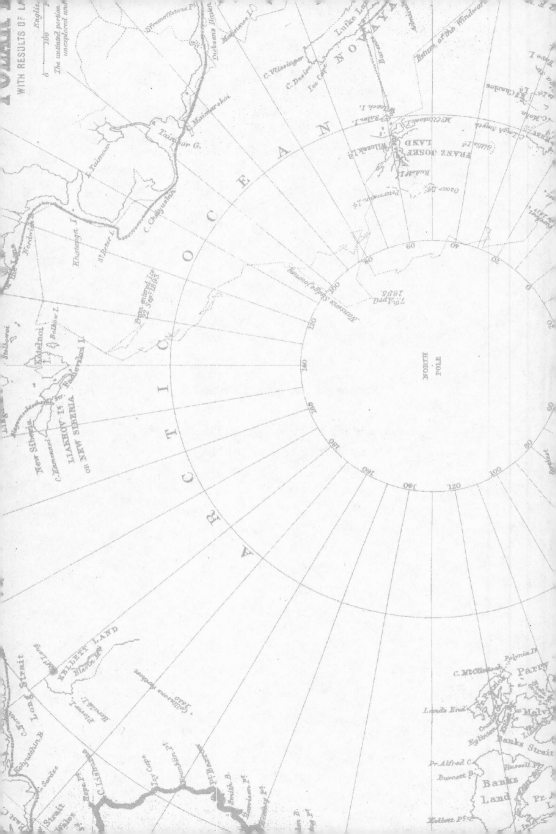

Over the last few years a great evil has been
descending over our world.
—Former Prime Minister Stephen Harper, 2015

PRoLOGue

The Marquis Hotel has a century of murmur in its bones. Tales, too—inhaled at twilight by hissing vents, circled through hallways and hidden rooms, exhaled at daybreak. Downtown Lethbridge crouches under the edifice, toking its secret histories: the coal baron and his paramour, the runaway pastor's daughter, the felon on the lam—clandestine meetings, illicit love, voyeurs known and unknown—Mormon bishops, gamblers, whores.

The Marquis is over a hundred years old, ancient history on the Canadian prairies. By day its fading brick reaches to the sun, slate shimmering reds and greens, stonework cooled by shadows. At night the Marquis casts a spell: its pinnacles slice and crack the moon's light, then strew it in peppercorns across the tangle of gardens, while starlings gather on pitched rooftops to watch. Windows gulp the remaining moonbeams; behind the glass, fires spark and dwindle in the hearths.

Townfolk say an entire floor has been closed long as anyone remembers. Ghosts, demons, murder—depends who tells the story. Some say two brothers came down from the High Arctic in the Roaring Twenties, stayed in the Marquis a whole year. Haroot and Maroot Darker, both eccentric, both in love with some Japanese woman inexplicably named Zurah. When she fled northward with a new lover, a white knife thrower from the carnival, the brothers' eccentricity turned to madness. Room One Thirteen, people say, demolished, sprayed with blood, but who killed whom? Some old Lethbridge folk tell the story differently, cackle over dark rum Cokes or burnt black coffee in taverns grimed with failing light. Insist the brothers did not die—*could* not die—for they were dark angels cast from heaven to wander earth, to feed on malice, to tear apart the bonds of love.

But the story can never really be told, because no thread is ever lost: every hard choice and chance encounter weaves the tale out of itself—stitching, whirling, snaring—forever knotting and unspooling at the same time. So the angels may still haunt the hallways, but who would know? For the Marquis has lost its voice to carpets, drapes, and pictures—to thick coverlets and layered dust.

The century is about to turn.

PART ONE

ALL THE OLD

HAUNTS

Canada is a vast and empty country.
—Former Prime Minister Stephen Harper, 2005

CHAPTER ONE

BLACK mETaL

Lethbridge, Alberta, Canada. The late 1990s—

Black Metal. Death Metal. Nü-metal. Hardcore.
Lance Armstrong in, Wayne Gretzky out.
Economic psychosis. Terrorism.
Grunge out, rave in.
Hoodies, chinos, bombers.
Quiffs and buzz cuts.
Paul Bernardo.
White people.
Modems.
Suicide.
Drugs.
Joy.
Snow.
A freak autumn blizzard blowing off a frozen moon. North winds rattling streetlights, howling glassy streets, air cold enough to crack its own molecules.

Kenneth "Lor" Kowalski sat wreathed with chill in an otherwise warm Marquis Hotel room, head tilted forward, eyes wide and unblinking, breath delicate. Snow crystals wove up the window at his elbow, ice knitting itself against glass, collecting shadow and spinning out twinkling patterns of light.

He shivered.

His guitar began to ring with overtones, light strumming its harmonics. Lor sat, salt stinging tonsils, tears on his lip and tongue. He let them sting. Just sat by the window in the darkened room, a universe pocked with a thousand stars.

·"Damn freezing out there," a whisper from the shadows in the corner, the clink of ice cubes in a glass. "Supposed to be El Niño this year. Get you a drink, sir, something to chase the cold?"

"No." Lor wiped a tear. "Thank you."

"Just clear away the dishes then?"

Lor paused a moment. He scraped a fingernail across the window, shaving off curls of frost, squinted at the shapes melting on his knuckle.

"Something troubling you, sir? Maybe a woman, lost love, lost time? An unwanted birthday, perhaps?"

Lor started, but ignored the question.

"Birthdays are the time for communion and community. Family, sir."

Lor touched the frosted glass. "Did you hear that?"

"Hear what?"

"The overtones. The music. Do you see the stars?"

A sniff from the shadows. "I don't hear anything. And I can't see the stars from here."

"Not ... those stars. The ones in this room."

"No, sir. Sure about that drink?"

Lor sighed.

From the shadows a man emerged, cloaked in baggy black uniform and brimmed hat, like a priest or cunning witch hunter. He stopped his cart near the window and bent forward, eyes hidden beneath the brim, remaining features speckled with moonlight.

"Sometimes a birthday is a dangerous thing," he said.

† † †

Three weeks before his birthday Lor fled north from Underwood, Montana, chased by a vague, relentless horror. Twenty-nine years of uncertain rebellion, he thought, bad sons returning home to kill the father. An ill-considered adult life, lived always in the moment, always in opposition to some real or imagined System, now coming to collect the rent.

But who was the landlord?

For six years he had scuttled Underwood's underground, playing with every post-punk band that mattered: Greasy Skank, The Peace Dogs, Molly Vomit—awake in late-night taverns, facing nameless lovers in strange beds, crouched beneath the covers or his wrinkled jacket, living on Twinkies, Slurpees, and cigarettes.

It occurred to him that he was a cliché, ready for yet another report on counterculture clawing the seamy undersides of zombie capitalism. Lor believed it. Here he was, dragging whatever shit he could into the light where it could be kicked and scratched to pieces. He itched to rip corporate logos, fire rocks at software execs.

"If you can't see it, you can't tear it up," he told nascent and stray black metal legend Bård Guldvik "Faust" Eithun at a deeply unlikely chance meeting in the woods outside the Grimwater Theater one Christmas Eve. "We're clinging to the underbelly," said Lor. "Exposing the lies." He spit. "Lies. Mystifications!"

Faust put away his knife.

"What about God?" asked Lor's current girlfriend, a pale Norwegian Catholic, after posting his bail for harassment and hauling him to her apartment to wash up.

"You *know* there is no God."

"Are you some kind of satanist?"

"Ridiculous."

Lor himself became a minor punk god when he smashed an entire collection of vintage guitars onstage at the Fleetwood Forum. They weren't his; they belonged to some French Canadian black metal band called Trône du Sorcier. Lor beat up a university music reporter for a backstage pass, then crept ratlike through the tunnel past security and one protective keyboard tech to the stage, where he began the systematic destruction of a '57 pearl Strat, a sunburst Les Paul with rosewood fingerboard, a pink paisley Tele, and a polished black Hentor rumoured to have once belonged to Alex Lifeson of Rush.

The show went on. So well, in fact, that Trône du Sorcier incorporated an increasingly bloody staged version of the destructive act on subsequent tours. Lor was dragged off by The Man, in a routine by now familiar.

Watching himself on the local news, wrestling the white policewoman, so soon after his twenty-ninth birthday, he realized that each year the routine became a little more like a corporate logo. A little more like something to be ripped off, then burned.

. . . Faust?

† † †

Ice.

Snow morphing to freezing rain halfway between clouds and pavement. Rooftops hammering, streets dancing a violent sheen of translucent spikes. A darkened city, a delinquent moon.

Lor lay on the bed, listening to rhythms. The old clock on the nightstand, the storm's rumble, ice cubes in a glass.

"Do you have it, sir?" The whisper from the shadows.

"Nope." Have *what*, exactly?

"You've touched it, sir. You've touched it, and now *he* will want it back, and you must bring it to him."

Lor raised himself to his elbows and stared into the shadows. "Just who are you anyway?"

"The night bellboy. The concierge. The room service waiter. I have many names." He leaned out of the shadows, hatless. His pupils were huge. "Tell me, tell me—do you *have* it?"

"What are you called?"

"I have many names."

"Yeah, man." Lor sat up on the bed. "But what's your *name*?"

The clock ticked. Between beats, deep silence. After what felt like a century, the bellboy spoke again.

"Do you have his powder from the Museum of Evil? Because he is definitely going to want it back."

CHAPTER TWO

THe muSEUm OF EViL

One of Lor's Underwood girlfriends was a bleach-skinned Lutheran, an old friend's ex-wife. She informed Lor he was a victim of the Weird.

"The Weird?" Lor said.

"God gives us our sense of place, our sense of order. You, being an atheist, are experiencing disorder and strangeness. The Weird."

Lor snorted. "Order comes from a good hard look at the shit around me. The Weird? Fuuuuck. That's just too many drugs and the stress of my birthday coming."

"I doubt it."

"What have I done with my life? Smash stuff. I'm seeing things, losing sleep, getting 'cid flashbacks."

"Thought punks stuck to speed."

"Hey." He bit a Twinkie. "I *know* who I am."

"Really? That's what Franklin used to say."

Next morning, while his girlfriend was at work, Lor thought about her ex—Franklin—his old bandmate.

"He was a bit like you," she had said. "Always pretending he didn't like company, didn't need anyone's comfort."

"Don't have to tell me."

She did anyway. Oh yes, Franklin: so full of bullshit boys' tales, all sins of the father stuff to justify his own bad behaviour and family neglect.

Elaborate, ridiculous, fanciful lies. Like the one about his great-grandfather, the Padre or whatever, who had killed himself on his birthday by jumping from the Wind River Bridge. A symbolic act, according to Franklin, a totem of despair. Pretentious, irresponsible, self-pitying bullshit.

"Do you know the old Museum of Evil down in Sevens?" she said.

"Never been."

"Who has? Anyway, Franklin used to lie that his great-grandfather had built it after coming back from an Arctic journey, in which he had seen things that no human ever should." She laughed. "Melodrama right out the ass."

"Yeah. Exactly."

"Actually," she said, "that museum was built by Canadian evangelists who came down from Alberta at the turn of the nineteenth century. Pale émigrés from Old Europe: they set up a huge tent revival, across town from some travelling circus, to combat the wicked shows and general atmosphere of paganism with the clear cool word of God. One of the evangelists painted oils of the circus performers, then exorcised the paintings right in the revival tent. Meanwhile, in a mirroring twist, the circus was performing perverted puppet shows based on the most freakish tales in the Old Testament."

"And who won this showdown?" Lor hoped it was the circus.

"Well, nobody," said the Lutheran. "Went on for months, one long hot summer, finally the Canadians missed home so much they packed up and headed back north. Circus was gone the same morning."

"Tremendous." This morning, Lor missed his old friends, Franklin and Alistair, in a way he hadn't felt for years. It surprised him.

He dug out an old map of Underwood. Here it was—Sevens District, Rotten Belly cul-de-sac, the old Museum of Evil, closed for half a century. What better trip for a hot summer's day, an ironic journey into the magic kingdom of memory?

† † †

"Dead flies cause the ointment of the apothecary to send forth a stinking savour."

"What?" Lor sat up in bed and glared at the shadows.

In the half-light he could see the bellboy, caught between stars, pale as a crescent moon. "Ecclesiastes, sir." The bellboy read from a hotel Bible. "It seems to dramatize your present state of mind. Yet you must press on, and bring his powder back to him."

"You're starting to sound like my Lutheran ex."

"Will you continue north?"

"What are you talking about? Who's *he*?"

"Chapter two," the bellboy continued. "Therefore I hated life; because the work that is wrought under the sun is grievous unto me."

"Okay." This was getting more and more like that freaky fucked up drug-dream back in Underwood, everything he was here in Lethbridge to escape.

"Chapter six: For he cometh in with vanity, and departeth in darkness."

Lor peered into the room's darkness, spied a glass jar of bright, ice-like chunks, resting on the cart. The chunks were translucent, glinting green and blue highlights. Something familiar about their iridescence.

"I'm getting a little tired of your oracular horseshit," Lor said. "Don't you have work to do?"

"Work?"

"Yeah. There's a snowstorm in the middle of autumn here. Snow piling up in front of the hotel." Lor got up from the bed and walked to the window. "This town. Even the seasons don't make sense."

"Chapter three: To every thing there is a season."

Over in the shadows the green and blue highlights winked out. The jar disappeared.

† † †

Lor took the Sevens bus to Rotten Belly, the last stop, out where the grass burned and the trees withered. At one time Sevens had been a thriving residential district, now a geography of broken hope. Almost a ghost town, still cleaving the city's borders. Old houses peeled in rows, mainly uninhabited, late Colonial with faux Old World details. Some housed front-yard trailers, blocked and rotting beneath old man willows and poplars. The Museum of Evil itself was a sandstone Romanesque at the end of the lane, trimmed with turrets and brownstone, wholly inappropriate for its time and place. The door was open, unbarred. Lor entered without incident. Grinned. The Lutheran was going to love this.

Inside, it was so hot he shut his eyes. When he opened them, wiping the sweaty sting, he saw that the radiators were all on, leaking steam and boiling water, clunking and bubbling as if the word summer was entirely forgotten here. He mopped his hair. Had he smoked this morning? No. Those rads really were humming, must have been for years. All the paint was blistered, the laquer, the varnish. Even the floor was bumped and bubbled.

Shit, wow. Lor grinned, walked through the steaming hall.

The first room was straight out of a Euro Victorian boy's tale, filled with skulls, pickled toes and fingers, stuffed crows. Long knives, dried orchids, bright bottled liquids. He laughed out loud. This was exactly the kind of place that would have fired Franklin's imagination. And Alistair's too, for that matter. Lor missed them both.

Next room. Books—stacks and stacks, shelf after shelf, a moth's kingdom of dust and dim light. Lor paused. Where was this penumbral light coming from, since there were no windows? Well, whatever. He knocked over a few books, checked the titles. Again, a boy's delight: satanic Bibles, alchemical tomes, long-forgotten religious texts like *The Book of Ozahism*. Even a gigantic opus on puppetry, some weird old-world volume called *Casey and Finnegan's Wake: A Tayle on How Divers Angels from Heav'n Fell*. Obviously bogus, made to look old. Lor chuckled. He should have called his old friends, invited them back for a family reunion, with this museum the first stop on the itinerary. But they were long gone. Franklin for good.

A third room. Paintings. Thick oil on canvas, mostly northern landscapes, frozen barrens and icy skies, a tendency to abstraction. Lor seemed to recall that Canadians loved this stuff. He was more partial to the realistic portraits on the north wall of the room, mainly snow-skinned circus folk in various poses of calculated perversion. He liked especially the boy with the knife, who stared out with a defiant look of hatred, longing, and compassion.

Lor stared back. His toes began to burn. He looked down, saw boiling water had oozed from the rad to scorch his running shoe.

"Jesus!" Rubber steaming.

He saw something else on the floor. A splotch of sparkling green and blue powder. He forgot the paintings instantly, stooped to take a closer look. Somehow the powder shimmered, produced its own luminescence. The radiators hushed.

"Shit," Lor whispered. Couldn't get enough air in his lungs. "She is going to *love* this."

He reached, touched. A bright tingle thrilled up his arm, like the first tongue of fellatio.

"Shit!" He snapped back his finger, gulped a deep breath. His lungs filled with metallic tang.

All of a sudden he didn't miss his old friends at all—boyish lunatics, both of them—in fact, Lor was glad they were gone, glad he hadn't seen them in years, glad he'd never see them again. God damn, he was twenty-nine, he'd had his fill of gleeful adventures and mystifications and freakish New Age pathologies, had his fill of the Lutheran too, come to think of it. And this museum—*shit*. Completely ridiculous, he hated it. What a dumb-ass monument to boyhood fancy, everything a punk despised.

He ground the powder to the floor with his boot. Time to go.

Outside, an old woman and young girl watched him from the weedy walk, both sallow and Caucasoid.

"Good afternoon." The old woman adjusted her shawl. "You're our first visitor today."

Lor sniffed, stalked for the bus stop with toe still burning.

"We can provide a guided tour," the old woman called.

"Are you lost?" the girl added.

Lor turned. "Shut your fucking cakeholes," he said, surprising the woman, the girl, and—most of all—himself.

He was about to apologize, but there was the bus.

The Weird hit him that night, at an all-ages show, where he was playing with an ad hoc hardcore outfit, composed of former members of The Stinging Nettles, Greasy Skank, and Phantom of the Pop Machine. In the middle of an out-of-tune cover of PiL's "Fishing," he saw flies buzzing in a dark cloud above the drummer's head. He swung his blue guitar at the cloud, hitting cymbals, knocking over his guitar stand, cracking the drummer's knee. The drummer kicked in his own bass skin and came at Lor with the hi-hat, smashed him on the head. Flies peeled off in squadrons and went for Lor's face, angry as bees, buzzing into his darkness. Last thing he saw was his own finger, still tingling, still sparkling with a dab of that museum powder.

Powder?

ONE FOR SORROW

Soon after the museum, Lor began shedding friends. He had no explanation. He started watching a lot of videos alone. He walked to the other side of the street. He ignored his phone.

"You've frozen inside," said the Lutheran. "All your unguarded parts like toys and tools in a summer snowstorm."

"Nice," he sneered.

"Dear Lord." She was horrified. "Did I just sound like Franklin there?"

Lor walked alone that night, after their first real knock-down fight. He couldn't figure out why he was suddenly so malign and anti-social. It sure felt good.

"You've got to shake this jitterbug loner nonsense," the Lutheran had said. "I've already done this tour with Franklin, don't need to do it again. So, here's the final offer: come to church with me tomorrow. Learn to listen and be still."

Lor wasn't much for final offers. Minutes later he stood in a still pool of streetlight, gazing at an arborescent greenstrip. He found himself walking into a darkened wood.

The centre of the wood broke to a small clearing, lit with drops of moonlight. He felt a hush, a thickness pressing down on his head and toes, as if something was waiting to happen. It was hard to breathe. His heart bopped. His chest pinched. He stepped in, gasped.

A tall Japanese woman crouched under a tree, her face framed by a jumble of waist-length hair. She looked familiar. One of the paintings from the museum? She grinned, peered into his eyes, then raised a finger to her lips and pointed upward.

Slowly, Lor looked to the treetops. High above, hundreds of wide-awake crows perched in the branches, basking in the percolating moonlight. None moved or breathed or made the slightest cackle or caw. It was a tightwound church of silence.

The speckles of light began to jitter. The crows blurred. Lor's legs elongated, and he teetered forward. He shifted his eyes down in order to regain his balance, then glanced back at the tree.

The woman.

Gone.

Same thing for his girlfriend, next morning.

† † †

"A drink, Lor?"

Lor watched moonlight dice through window frost and crawl up his arm in radiant splinters. "What happened to sir?"

"A good name is better than precious ointment: chapter seven."

Lor clamped his teeth. "You won't tell me yours."

Silence. Then, "Some names shall be covered in darkness: chapter six."

Lor scratched frost from the windowpane, feeling ice beneath his nails. What was it with this town? "I used to know a guy who would never tell his last name. Played in a band with him a whole year, right here in Lethbridge. Never knew his last name."

"Well. I see you don't need a drink to loosen your tongue."

"I lived here. Played with the psycho and a friend who ran off to Vancouver. A long story." Lor twisted back to the nightstand, opened a drawer, plucked a picture.

It was grainy, slightly out of focus. Shot against the sandstone of a Lethbridge post office on a clear summer day. Lor, smiling, bearded back then, framed by two tall and slender men, one with ponytail, the other with prematurely greying hair.

"Franklin and Alistair." Lor sat on the bed. "Og's missing, the bass player. Lost him to speed."

"Car accident?"

"Amphetamines. Last I heard he was in a Calgary hospital being treated for full-blown psychosis."

"And this...." The bellboy brushed his shirt audibly. "This *Franklin*?"

"The one with the grey hair. The psycho."

The bellboy floated over. "So. Your mentor in premature grey."

A flash of blue and green iridescence in the shadows. Lor's stomach tweaked. "How do you know he was my mentor?"

"You served a kind of apprenticeship, here in Lethbridge."

Lor shifted, folded his arms. "Yeah. Maybe."

"And now: regrets. All is vanity and vexation of spirit: chapter one."

"How do you know all this?" Lor said.

No response.

"Put the goddamned Bible away."

Silence.

Lor stood and invaded the shadows. "Maybe a birthday is a dangerous thing. But dangerous to whom?"

"Don't touch me," the bellboy said, raising the Bible. "*That* you would certainly regret."

† † †

Three and a half weeks before his thirtieth birthday, Lor asked his latest girl-friend, a Wiccan of Welsh descent, not to touch him anymore. The sex was getting too close, too warm. He even had a set of her keys.

She was so angry she chipped his tooth with a pool cue. "Do you even believe in the spirits of love?"

He retreated behind the pool table. "I'm an atheist."

"Then why aren't you fucking an atheist?"

He fingered a pocket. "Maybe you should be fucking a witch."

She gently laid down the stick. "Maybe you should feed your spirit."

"I don't have one."

She was already leaving.

"At least I know who I am!" he called.

That night, in his drummer's apartment, Lor sat crumpled asleep beneath a bent hi-hat. His guitar began to speak: not the jealous blue guitar, the un-faithful black one. Run, it chimed.

Toward morning he heard Christmas bells, faintly at first, then louder, an approaching sleigh in the night. The ringing gradually pulled him out of his dream, into the first rays of sunlight, where he sat cramped beneath the hi-hat, desperately jingling his ex-girlfriend's keyring.

† † †

Aye aye aye!

"What's that noise?" Lor asked.

"A bird on the windowsill."

They faced each other tensely in the shadows, Lor with fist clenched, bellboy with picture in one hand, Bible in the other.

"What's a bird doing out in this weather?"

"Bird things."

Lor peered from the shadows, focused on the window's bright halo.

Aye aye aye.

"I've got to see this shit."

Aye aye aye.

His guitar exhaled as he passed the stand. Bits of light pumped through glass, dappled his arm. He heard the Bible drop.

Aye aye aye.

Lor rubbed frost from the window, pulled back a bit of curtain, looked out into the night. On the icy ledge sat an enchanting black and white bird, poised, balanced by a long tail, chattering at the storm. The bird cocked its head, fixed Lor with a glossy eye.

Aye aye aye!

Lor's heart jumped.

"Holy shit. What is that bird?"

The bird shook itself and flapped its wings. Feathers caught moonlight; tail and wings glittered briefly, iridescent blue and green, just like that powder back in the Museum of—

Aye aye aye!

The bird flapped from the sill and flew at the storm.

"What is that bird?" Lor wheeled toward the shadows, stumbling. "What's it called?"

"Sir?"

"I want the name of that bird."

"You must already know it."

"We don't have that bird in Underwood."

"I realize, sir. But you've also lived *here*."

"Yeah, yeah, I was a little less tuned in in my wasted youth." Lor strode back out of the light. "The name?"

A sigh in the shadows. "Magpie, black-billed. Pica pica. Member of the corvid family, whose most notable members are the crow and the raven and all the European variations: the jackdaw, the hooded crow, with its white cloak and...."

"Magpie." Lor stopped in the middle of the room, still speckled with light. "Beautiful bird," he whispered.

"Well, then." The shadows whispered back: "Two for mirth. Six for the Devil's own self."

"What?"

"Seven for a journey. Which I now implore you to take. I do implore you with the utmost solemnity."

"More Bible verse?"

The bellboy scratched his shirt. "An old English counting rhyme. One can predict the future by counting magpies. Seven magpies for a journey."

"Only one here."

"It's the sign, sir. Take the powder north. Do not ignore your quest."

"Superstitious horseshit." Lor stared down at the floor and noticed the small hotel Bible, opened to an unreadable section of Old Testament. "What's one for? One magpie?"

A pause. A return to whisper.

"One for sorrow."

CHAPTER FOUR

BRiNG iT BACK

Lor sniffed himself to sleep for two nights, crouched beneath the hi-hat. He couldn't name his misery. He missed the Wiccan, superficially, along with all his other shed friends. But it went deeper, down to secret places that expressed themselves through symptomatic romantic failures. On the third night he collapsed in sheer exhaustion, next to his new girlfriend, a Buddhist with skin white as hotel sheets. She reached for something on the dresser.

"Do you like it?" she held up a crystal globe full of water and snow. "Shake it, you get a blizzard." She shook. Snow whirled. "My daughter's."

"*Daughter?*"

The Buddhist was already asleep. Lor gently pried the snow globe from her fingers and replaced it on the dresser. Then he re-lit one of her candles and tucked himself in. The window rattled open and gushed night breezes, snuffing the candle, flapping light cotton sheets. Lor moaned once, turned over.

He sat up in bed. He was a boy. His heart was ticking like an old clock. The room was soft with snow, the ceiling swept with stars. He coughed fog and pulled the covers to his neck, away from the sleeping woman.

At the foot of his bed lay a snowbank imprinted with a snow angel. In Lor's ears, a chorus of windchimes.

Let me touch you .... Unvoiced words in his head, filled with rain and delicate blue.

No, he tried to tell the angel. He drew the blanket tighter.

The angel lifted, peeling from three dimensions. It grew and grew, pouring into itself. Lor looked away, squinted at the snow's luminous imprint, covered his ears against running water, cracking ice.

The room polarized. The bed elongated toward a blasted wall, bricks and twists of rebar. Beyond the wall, gigantic night: sky choked with burning stars, trash fires at the bottom of a lake.

Let me touch you, just as you touched part of me.

No way, mister.

Bring it back to me. Make me whole again.

The boy shuddered under the covers and searched for the speaker, but found only the woman sleeping next to him, coated with hoarfrost.

The room darkened. The angel floated from behind, over the bed, mercury dropping its wake.

What do you want? Lor clutched the covers.

The angel hovered at the bed's foot.

My spirit wants to touch you.

Touch? No.

The angel flickered and leaned forward.

No! The boy dived beneath the covers.

The bed disappeared from beneath him, and he was inside the snow globe, looking out from the dresser top at a giant's bedroom. The angel now a thousand feet of towering dark, studded with sundogs and coruscations, iridescent blues and greens.

It floated toward him.

Lor screamed. His lungs filled with water.

The angel reached down from the skies and plucked the snow globe from the dresser. Lor stumbled as his crystal world floated up toward the sky and stipple. Then suddenly down, down, as the angel dashed the snow globe to the floor. Lor saw, for one eternal second, each scratch in the polish, each scuff, each accelerating whorl in the woodgrain.

Bring it back. Bring back my powdered heart.

Then the world smashed.

Night air surged in. Water surged out. Lor was carried away in a snowy river, over the woodgrain, under the bed, back into the sheets.

He blinked.

"Lorne?" said his new girlfriend, deep inside her dreams.

He shuddered, opened and closed his eyes.

"It's Lor," he said, finding his voice.

After a few minutes of paralysis he realized he was soaked.

"Shit!" he whispered.

He rolled out of bed and crouched, pulling his wet hair.

"Oh, shit."

He clutched himself tighter and tried to breathe, deeply, droplets pooling beneath him. He stood, then crouched against a tidal head rush. After the wedges of light stopped spinning his head, he wobbled to his feet and looked about the darkened room.

The angel was gone. The wall intact. But the snow globe was not on the dresser.

No. Fuck. Ing. Way.

He crept around the bed and knelt. Sure enough. There, on the floor, a shattered globe, leaking water and bits of ersatz snow in a tiny river rushing under the bed toward some lost baby sea. The igloo and its inhabitants were vanished into the night, drowned, saved, who knew.

Lor knelt, shivering, for a long time, listening to his girlfriend's breath and the drip of water off his wet skin. He felt all the discrete worthless moments in his life compact and ignite. In his stomach, up toward his throat.

Enough, he thought. I am out of this shit. Not another birthday in this town.

He remembered sleigh bells and reached for his pants, pulling out the Wiccan's keys, kissing them absentmindedly. He towelled off, dressed quietly, then packed his black guitar into its case with a bank card, toothbrush, and grainy photograph. He left his last girlfriend to her dreams, walked nine blocks, and stole her car.

He fled north, across the Wind River Bridge and through Sevens, hitting Grinteeth Road at almost twice the speed limit. Then north on the 15, stopping once in Butte to gas up and throw up. In Black Rocks, between swaths of national forest, he bought a sandwich; he gobbled through Helena, felt it churn his stomach as he rolled down the window west of Hauser Dam, puked it out in bits and pieces all the way to Great Falls.

After a restless night in a Great Falls parking lot, something drove him north again. He cruised to Shelby, then cranked it up and headed for the border, all the way north to Sweet Grass.

What was that dream? He must have taken some psychedelic and forgotten about it, hidden it from the Wiccan. He sighed. Yes, that was it, a forgotten psychedelic, he was going to have to quit that shit.

He parked for an hour next to the crossing, tried to clear his head. Failing that, he got out to walk and buy some smokes. At the duty-free store he sent a postcard to an old friend in Vancouver, scribbling his story in elliptical sentence fragments. Why had he done that? Never mind, would probably never arrive anyway. Puffing a Lucky Strike, he drove north again, crossed the parched grasslands of the border, and entered that strange vast land named Canada.

† † †

"I ask you one last time," the bellboy said. He picked up the open Bible and placed it neatly on the cart. "What is the cause of your sorrow, the source of your vexation of spirit? You will never finish your journey in such a mood."

"Spirit?"

"That seems, to me, precisely the word."

"You seem to know everything. Why ask at all?"

The bellboy leaned on the cart, creaking the wheels. A chunk of curtain loosened and swept across the window, blocking light, pouring more shadow. "Happy birthday. Thirty? Time to go."

"Thirty, yeah." Lor bit a nail. "It's ... how did you know my birthday was *today*?"

He took a step into the shadows, winced as his fist pressed a ragged cuticle. He felt the guitar at his side. Overtones tickled the hairs on his calf.

"A birthday should be a cause for joy, as should a journey's beginning." The bellboy reached to the bottom shelf of the cart and pulled out a fat green bottle. "Why not try for some cheer? On the house, chilled."

Cold drafts circled Lor's wrist. He noticed the jar of blue-green ice chunks, re-appeared.

"I don't need to be reminded of my birthday," he said. "I'm not going on a journey. I don't need a drink."

"There is no good reason for—"

"Get out."

Wind rattled the window. A guitar string snapped.

"Enough bullshit," Lor said, kicking the cart into deep shadow. It hit the wall. Dirty dishes crashed, ice cubes spilled to the carpet. The bellboy dropped his bottle.

"Sir, I must ask you to refrain from such—"

"Out of here."

Lor kicked the champagne. Somehow the cork popped. The bottle spun across the carpet, shooting foam.

"You've wasted an expensive hotel wine, not to mention these carpets."

"Carpets!" Lor pulled his guitar off the stand and threw it at the shadows, heard a musical crash as it hit the cart, a twang, more breaking glass. Ice crunched beneath his feet. He retrieved the guitar, raised it over his head, smashed down into the splintered ice, hitting the nightstand behind him, reeling backward.

"This is not only expensive, but, for a punk musician, very much clichéd." The bellboy grabbed the jar of glittering chunks and stuffed it in his coat.

"S'that right? Here's more cliché for you."

Lor swung behind his head and ripped down the heavy curtains. They hit the floor with a *whump*; the room lit like a galaxy. Lor doubled over at the light's centre, leaning on his splintered guitar.

"One more," he said, out of breath.

Then he raised the guitar and cranked it, smashing down, unearthly chord jangling. Chips of wood and finish blew off, clinking glass before spiralling to the carpet.

"My last guitar," Lor gasped.

It was the black guitar, the wise but capricious one. It finally came apart at the neck bolt, the way the blue one had the night of the flies, back in Underwood. Lor held up the broken neck, dangled the fractured body from a remaining string.

All the light gathered and rushed inward. Lor dropped the guitar and fell into a cold mash of ice. He was out of guitars. Out of energy.

After a long silence the bellboy shuffled in the corner.

"Well," he whispered. "I'll be going. But we *will* meet again."

† † †

On the final stretch to Lethbridge, the plains swept from Lor's eye to the pale blue horizon, sun baked, endless. Mesmerized by distance, velocitized by the perfect line of the highway, he crossed the Milk River, where berries dotting the coulees were turning to autumn orange, where towns dotting the map had names like Drinkwater and Smoke Hill.

At Indian Head, hidden birds chattered at him. Aye aye aye, but he paid no attention. He was magnetized north, pulled toward the only place in Canada he had ever known, drawn past high and wide signs for Antelope, Rainbarrel, Stony Beach, through tall grasses, under spacious clouds, over trickling prairie streams and rippled hills. He stopped at sundown, by a creek bed where all the moisture had evaporated to hot winds.

Why hadn't he ever noticed any of this before? He stepped from the stolen car to piss on a cactus, warmed by an exploding sunset. His pee sizzled; his thoughts scattered. Minutes later, he was speeding to Lethbridge, a site which held a secret and seminal meaning. Franklin's town, the town where Lor's punk had started, and so, the town where the Weird must have started.

But by now Lethbridge must be free of punk and weirdness. Everyone and everything he had known there was gone: dead, lost to drugs and madness, vanished to either coast.

That was good. That was *great*.

That was exactly what he needed: the same geography, but all the layers peeled, stripped to the fossils. Then he could see clearly. Because deep beneath these sun scorched hoodoos and thirsty riverbeds were bones. And Lor's own bones remained in Lethbridge, somewhere, bleached clean by ten years of wind and sun, ready to give up their secrets.

He smiled at his own wisdom. Friends and lovers got in the way of clarity and sanity. Love in all its varieties was an invocation of chaos, the Weird, for God's sake. Why had he bothered with so many girlfriends? Better to cut the ties.

I'll avoid the old haunts, he thought, inspired. I'll find some hotel I've never been inside, downtown, in the old district, where I can forget that batshit Underwood drug dream, and the Weird will never find me. I'll crouch beneath the buildings, hide from this sky, let things reveal themselves. That's it. Downtown, out of sight: the Marquis Hotel.

He cranked it up, cruising through Windy Butte and Crow's Bluff, blowing bits of memory out the tailpipe, leaving them to mingle with dust, grass, night.

PART TWO

FAMILY REUNIONS

Our security agencies work with each other
and with others around the globe to
track people who are threats to Canada.
—Former Prime Minister Stephen Harper, 2013

CHAPTER FIVE

A WALK iNsTEAd

When Serendipity Hamm was a young girl, she had her very own dark angel. A ceramic Gabriel, stained with India ink, blowing the horn of judgment. Sooty Gabriel lived at the very top of a precisely over-stacked toy chest, fixed in the north corner of Seri's room. In it, toys and books lived in a carefully maintained hierarchy: angel and Barbie in heaven, Slinky and Frisbee on middle earth, a purgatory of puppets and costumes, finally an underworld of picture books. And at the very bottom, perhaps in Toy Hades, her favourite—an enormous, lavishly illustrated hardback of C.S. Lewis' *The Silver Chair*.

She looked at the pictures almost every day, especially the one of the wicked Green Witch, whom she found more interesting than Barbie or dumb old Gabriel. But getting to Narnia meant an almost daily unpacking and repacking of the toy chest, always in the same meticulous order.

"This toy chest of yours." Her Granny Finnegan sat in the window seat and stretched the Slinky across her lap. "It's like a sedimented library."

"Are we going to the liberry?" Seri looked up from the Green Witch, then frowned at the neat pile of toys.

"No Seri," Granny said. "I'm just wondering why you put your favourite book on the bottom and the toys you never play with on top."

"Oh that." Seri closed Narnia. "Well, the book is the biggest, so it has to go down low. The books can bend a bit. But the angel is all funny-shaped, and he's got the wings, and he won't bend at all."

"Should he bend, Pepper?"

"An angel shouldn't get so hard."

Gran laughed, but Seri didn't know why. It wasn't a joke.

"But Potatoskin," Granny said. "It takes you so long to take everything out, then put it back in."

"I know." Seri looked down, scratched at the book's cover.

"Don't you want more time to play?"

"Yes."

"So why don't you put your favourite books at the top?"

"I tried, Gran." She looked up, squinted at the sun. "I tried so hard. I can't do it. It makes me feel all funny."

"Like what?"

Seri paused. "In my stomach. Like I have to go to the dentist."

Gran laughed again. "That's called anxiety, Pumpkin." She leaned forward. "Here. Where in this sediment does the Slinky go?"

"In the middle. Slinky can bend real good, so he won't break."

"Clever girl," Gran said. "Let me help you." She slid from the window seat and bent until her knees cracked. "See? All going to the right place. You show me."

Then Gran's eyes got a funny look, like when Aslan was disappointed. "Ah, Pepper. You're too much like your father."

"Oh." Seri hadn't thought of Dad since Ricky's birthday. It made her feel dried out, until she remembered that Dad was coming back, if she only wished hard enough.

"Damned preacher," Gran muttered. "Lost his toys."

"Toys? He never even liked toys, Gran."

Gran paused to consider the children's Bible in her hand. "Faith and hope. But come, these are too heavy for a child."

"When's he coming back?" Seri let the Slinky cascade from her hand.

Gran closed her eyes and sighed. She whispered something to herself, then looked at Seri. "Honey, he isn't coming back."

Seri leaped to her feet, tumbled into her Grandmother's arms. "I'll *never* run away! I promise."

They clasped for a long time. It felt like the whole afternoon. Seri nuzzled at Gran's neck, making herself smile. Because whatever anyone said, she'd wish hard enough, and Dad would come home.

"So," Granny Finnegan said, later, when the toys were packed tighter than treasure. "Tomorrow would you like to read *The Silver Chair* again? Or play with the angel for once?"

Serendipity tugged at a meaty cheek. She squinted at the window glazed with sun.

"Granny," she said, finally. "Maybe we could take a walk instead."

† † †

Years later, Intelligence Officer Serendipity Hamm drove a company car toward the vast prairies of southern Alberta. It was a province she did not know or understand, with such wide skies, such strange acres—Windy Butte, Broken Rock, Blackie—towns and cities named with a kind of dusty magic.

Her car, an ancient grey four-door Pontiac from the unmarked fleet, neatly fulfilled the Canadian Security Intelligence Service's ongoing and particularly Canadian mandate to appear less interesting than it actually was. One mile from a new assignment, somewhere west of Crowchild Trail in Calgary, the tires went to sleep. Seri lost control of the car, which skidded through an intersection onto a snowy boulevard, then stalled and died.

"Darn this freaky blizzard." She pulled the repair manual from the glovebox, climbed out, cracked the hood. This was no battery or starter trouble, wrong noises for that. More like a loose vacuum hose or broken wire.

"Lovely." Seri frowned. The hoses and wires were fine, but the engine was unfamiliar, all strange angles. She flipped a few pages in the manual. Here. Something called the ECU could apparently run a diagnostic. But where was it?

"Goodness." The contraption wasn't even in the engine, but under the passenger seat. That made so little sense, like keeping your favourite toy *outside* the toy chest. Seri climbed back in and dug the ECU from under the seat, then whistled. The thing was so small, so smooth, just a box. What kind of miniature tools did you need once you snapped it open? She checked the manual, shook her head. You couldn't even get at the workings. The diagnostic involved display codes, switching modes, erasing memory.

"Gosh." She plumped the box on the seat and fished her antique pocket watch, stroked its face. Here was an analog beauty, all the springs and wheels. How different from that ECU, that realm of hi-tech ghosts.

"I could use a few angels right now." Seri smiled, cheeks dimpling. Perhaps three heavenly messengers, dressed in overalls, speckled with grease. But there was only one angel she knew in Calgary. Swallow your pride, she thought, grabbing her cellphone from the dash.

"And darn this freaky blizzard." Her hands were cold, but her gloves were far west in Vancouver, neatly folded atop Granny's hearthstone. She dialled with numbing fingertips.

"Hullo?" A Newfoundland accent, crisp hints of Japanese, and a clean French finish.

"Anselm," she said. "Gosh, glad you're in town."

"Serendipity Hamm?"

"I just had a little accident with your car."

A pause and a slurp at the other end of the line.

"I'm fine," Serendipity said. "Just stalled."

Another pause and slurp. "*Secret Agent* Serendipity Hamm?"

† † †

The last time Seri had seen Anselm was two weeks earlier, back in Vancouver, the day she received the mysterious letter. When she read it, she got so nervous she caught insomnia, and spent half the night perched on her bed, eating peaches in the dark. In the morning she flinched to see peach stones strewn across the bed and carpet. She plucked one from the pillow and studied it, disgusted by the cracks and peach meat stuck between. How much folded space in a pit? So convoluted, like a brain. She gathered and tossed them, then peeled the juicy bed sheet and went for breakfast.

Over tea and oatmeal she studied the mysterious letter again. What to do? Rooke, her old CSIS supervisor, wanted her to quit the service proper and come work for a special task force. The request was vague and unusual. Why a *letter*? She half thought it was a joke. But then, if memory served, Rooke was fully legitimate, with a clean and distinguished record.

First thing after breakfast, Seri biked in to the office to ask around, see if anyone knew of this secret branch or Rooke's secret mandate. But nobody had even heard of Rooke. She made a few phone calls. No luck. So she sat down at her desk during the lunch hour to pray and read the Bible.

Rising from forty minutes of fruitless prayer and meditation, she biked to the library. But, after hours in the Government Documents, she still had no answers. This whole episode was unfolding with such a lack of definition and order. She needed something certain, one true thing, a rock on which to build her decision.

By teatime she knew her choice. "I'm not going."

Granny Finnegan sipped a Pilsner and crunched a pretzel. She cleared her throat. "Seri. I think we both know what's happening here."

"I will not leave this family."

Gran swished her bottle. "He's not coming back. You *will*."

"Can't do it." Seri ground a pretzel against the tabletop.

Gran plunked down the beer. Foam bubbled over the lip. "You were five, Serendipity. Do you know what he said when he left? To your mother and me?"

Seri shrugged.

"He said that God had lost control. That the only things left were evil," she pinged the bottle, "and chaos." She folded her arms. "You going to let that stand?"

Seri stayed silent.

"You going to let him win?"

"I won't leave," Seri whispered. "I can't."

Gran snorted. "Never heard you say that before."

Seri plucked another pretzel, nibbled the end.

"Look at it this way." Gran slugged the last of her beer. "If your faith is genuine, if there is order in this world, then you're coming back. As certainly as he isn't."

† † †

The next day it rained. Serendipity packed quickly and neatly, but found too little room in her suitcase. After minutes of careful figuring, she removed her skipping rope, her folded gloves, and a box of tampons to make room for a chain reference Bible, Dante's *Divine Comedy*, an advanced philosophy text, and Saint Augustine's *Confessions*. She put them on top. When she was done, she packed a lunch, took the last peach in the fridge, and set it momentarily on the hearthstone.

"Well," she said to Gran. "Now I'm truly a fundamentalist in motion."

"A what?"

"Fundamentalist in motion. Like you told me all the time when I was a little girl."

Gran laughed, grabbed for the peach. "No, Tomato. I said a fundamentalist in your *emotions*."

"Emotions."

"Your head," Gran tapped peach to grey temple, "worries that life is chaos. But your heart refuses to believe it." She replaced the peach on the hearthstone. "And that's why you're leaving."

"You can tell?"

"Oh, Pepper."

Mum and Gran drove Seri to the office, for a quick goodbye party. The current branch supervisor, Anselm, loaned Seri an ancient company car, gave her a detailed map and a pair of phone numbers.

"If you're driving through Calgary," he said, "you might give me a call. I'll be there in a week."

Seri drove all the way to Clearbrook with Gran, along to visit an old friend in a retirement home. It was lovely, spending the last hour together. When they were about to part on Clearbrook Road, Gran leaned in through the passenger window.

"I want you to have this." She handed Seri a beautiful antique pocket watch. "In case you're not back for your spring birthday. It belonged to your grandfather, Reverend Finnegan."

Seri loved it at once. She waved at Gran, shuffling across the street to the retirement home, then looked down at the gift. Silver, with intricate detail on the casing and a delicate chain. When she glanced up again, her granny was almost at the home door. Seri backed the car quickly, zipped open the window for one more goodbye.

"Goodbye!" she called.

Gran turned on the walk and waggled her finger. "Not goodbye," she chided. "Never goodbye again. Always *see you soon*."

Seri smiled at the old game.

"See you soon," she said.

She drove off, hoping it was true.

† † †

The drive into the Prairie Region was uneventful, except for one night in Lethbridge, in that creepy Marquis Hotel with the empty elevator that kept ringing and going up and down. Just below Seri's window, in the hotel gardens, a coven of children had tended a bonfire all night long, and in its chaotic light performed a puppet show. The fire cracked and sizzled, but the children made no sound at all, and no one came to shoo them home: not parents, not police, not hotel staff. Who would deliberately come to a city filled with such perceptible, distilled weirdness? Seri hoped it was her first and last visit. She rose early Saturday, sped to the city limit on Highway X to Calgary.

Why did Rooke pick *her* for this promotion?

She had liked her old desk job at CSIS. Analysis, collecting, and collating perishable information used for threat and risk assessments in Ottawa, crunching unclassified information, ordering the chaos. The old job was systematic and time sensitive. It had symmetry and closure. It was nine to five, coffee and lunch.

She stopped at a drugstore in High River, bought sugarless gum and a postcard of three magpies in a willow. She started the Pontiac again, noticed a cough in the engine, noticed the sky: dark cumulonimbus clouds squatting all along the western foothills, rolling north as far as she could see. Looks like snow, she thought. Maybe I should get a hotel just to be safe. She booked into the Bluebird Motel, hoping for the storm to exhaust itself. The blizzard blew in at noon and went into hysterics by evening, convulsing across the prairie and rattling the motel windows all night.

Unable to sleep through the racket, she read till first light, rotating the Bible and the logic text. In the wee hours after midnight the rotation suddenly struck her as absurd. She was wise enough to know the importance of dialogue between oppositions, what Granny Finnegan called the *dialectic*. Serendipity's whole heritage was dialectic, gosh sakes. Both sides of Mum's family were obsessive and pugnacious in their worldviews, the Finnegans priests, the Caseys engineers. The Hamms were diplomats, alchemists of dialogue. But Seri often struggled to see logic in the Bible or sacrament in the logic. Often she just craved fundamentalist certainty.

In the morning the highways were still icy, lit with watery sun. The car coughed once and started. Meeting with Rooke at eleven-thirty, boot it and pray. She bit off half a gum stick and wrapped the other half neatly, putting it in her pocket. Who argues with God? No one.

She said a small prayer and stepped on the accelerator, blowing worries out the tailpipe to mingle with snow, ice, light.

† † †

Pierre Anselm Kanashiro was tall and thin as a hickory wand. He had the casual stare of one who travelled often enough to have never really been any-where, the service's most itinerant investigator. He dressed in white shirts, bow ties, and black jeans. Claimed to be nondescript to the point of oddity, but knew better. Claimed to belong to the oldest Japanese Canadian family in Newfoundland, but acknowledged with an eye twinkle that you knew better. He was sipping a Tahitian Treat Slurpee, which Serendipity thought a funny thing to do on a snowy day.

"Well-o, Ms. Hamm," Anselm said. "Didn't expect to see you again. That was a good going-away party. Good pumpkin pie."

Serendipity watched the tow truck winch the Pontiac. She grinned at the screeches and clanks, delighted to see that engine chained and dragged by something as tactile and mechanical as a tow truck.

"Why doesn't the service get some decent cars?" she said.

"Such-o?"

"El Camino, Duster, Dart."

"You were born in the wrong century," Anselm said. "You're an Enlightenment rationalist, eighteenth-century man. Like a sip?"

Serendipity removed a half stick of gum from her pocket and deftly peeled the paper. "Does anyone know how to reach Rooke?"

"Nobody's seen this Rooke in seven years." Anselm sipped the last of the Tahitian Treat, crushed the cup, and dropped it to the sidewalk. "And nobody really ever *saw* the man anyway, know what I mean? I've wondered whether he's a figment of our imaginations."

Seri chewed hard. "Someone knows something about his secret branch. The letter was totally official."

"Mucho strange-o."

Serendipity leaned down to pick up the cup.

"As for T.F. Rooke," Anselm said, "still alive and working the regions, that is a scenario I can't even *imagine*."

"I'm not looking for imagination."

"Hey, never knew the man." Anselm twisted his bow tie. "Goodbye Seri. Keep both my phone numbers. Perhaps we meet again."

"Wait a minute," Serendipity said. She checked her antique pocket watch, Gran's gift, then stuffed it in her pack's pocket. "Can I borrow another car or something? I'm late."

"Sorry, the Pontiac was a personal loan. In terms of official policy you are completely out of my jurisdiction. According to the memo, I don't even know who you are anymore."

"Can you at least give me a ride?"

"Who are *you*?" He smiled.

"Please," she said.

"Sorry. Appointment. Could give you bus fare."

"Gosh, Anselm. That's harsh."

So she shouldered her pack and walked north on Crowchild Trail, into the storm, toward an address she didn't know and a promotion she doubted, to knock on the door of a man she hadn't seen in a century.

tEN BOtTLes OF COKE

Lor stared at the ceiling, dreaming of bellboys. The radiator pinged in polyrhythms. Outside, wind shrieked from torn cloud, littered the streets with snappy branches.

Oh man, this escape wasn't working, was it?

Lethbridge was every bit as weird as Underwood. Lor felt a swell of claustrophobia, walked to the window, pressed his fingertips against the bitten glass.

I gotta bust out of this snow globe, he thought.

Minutes later he was clipping down the steps of the Marquis, out into the chill, where supercooled drizzle glazed textures of brick, bark, pavement. He stopped to catch his breath, lungs freezing. The sky roared down at him. He choked.

Jesus Christ, how could the horizons pin down that much sky?

He looked out over London Avenue, and it was wide and long as the Mississippi, chugging toward that endless blue reservoir. He coughed, tried to catch his breath. He needed to walk, get lost in the streets, washed clean, remember? A block to downtown, where he could lose himself to hardy shoppers and vagabonds. But though the streets were strange, they were uncomfortably familiar as well. All the eyes this morning were intimate, lingered on him for long seconds, took the measure of his thirty years. Who *were* these people?

Two Japanese electricians with laughter in their eyes, carrying a ladder. Wasn't Lethbridge a destination for displaced Japanese Canadians in the Second World War? Hutterite women in handmade dresses and polka-dot kerchiefs, ruddy faces, language he didn't understand. That bum with two hotdogs and one tooth. What was his name again? Skeleton Tim, something. Those girls with the Chicago Bulls caps. Blackfoot Nation. But Blood or Piegan? How would he know?

They all had a whiff of familiarity. Acquaintances? Somebody's brother? Old lovers? People who used to come see the band, back when Franklin ruled the local counterculture—strung it together with punkish bon mots, wound it tight with the force of his temperament? Lor wanted to flee the streets. He needed breakfast: settle the stomach, settle the mind.

He stepped into the Kresge's. His glasses fogged immediately, but he knew each step to the diner bar, where you could once get two eggs, hash browns, toast, and a small Coke for a dollar ninety-nine.

"Hi sweetie." A reedy voice. "Where you been?"

"Just out." He shrugged, mounted a stool at the speckled counter, removed his icy glasses. His vision was cloudy, but he noticed whiskey-pored codgers and a bearded Hutterite, Lethbridge archetypes at breakfast. Somewhere an old radio squawked Max Webster's "Beyond the Moon."

"Still a dollar ninety nine?" he said. "Still sub coffee for Coke?"

Everyone looked at him like he was nuts.

"What do you think, sweetie, the price is going to go up? Only been ten years. But jeez, that coffee for Coke is gross. This is breakfast."

The Hutterite laughed, while a glazed branch screeched on the window glass. Wind whistled over bricks and frost-heaved pavement. A sheen of glittering snow shook from the roof, pixelating the morning air.

Lor heard sizzle and the smack of a plate. He put his glasses back on, grabbed a chunk of brown toast, dipped into runny egg.

"What do you mean ten years?" he said, mouth full.

The waitress turned, leaned into the counter. Lor knew her immediately, the stub nose, the amazing beehive hairdo.

"Where *you* been eating?" she said. "Skipping breakfast?"

"No." He swallowed thickly, gulped hot coffee to melt the glob in his chest.

"You getting the band back together?" she said. "He was in a band, Jake, good band."

"*Jah*, nice." The Hutterite nodded.

Lor put down the coffee and pushed the plate, fished some coins from his pocket and tossed them to the counter. He stood and stalked to the revolving door.

"Hey," she called. "Still have my number? Hey Lorne."

He did glance back once, as the door spun him into the cold. The Hutterite was already shovelling into Lor's unfinished breakfast, while the waitress stared like a moon-drunk fox.

Lor crossed the street quickly, headed into Stubbs Pharmacy. He could feel Franklin's presence in these bricks and tiles, sum of the town's old ghosts. Franklin would know how to outwit the Weird. But the real Franklin was truly vanished.

"Something for the stomach," Lor said to the druggist. "And can I get over-the-counter sleeping pills?"

The druggist handed him a creased white packet with the drugs inside, then cocked her head and fixed him with a single indigo eye.

"You look familiar," she said. "Do I know your family?"

"Don't have a family."

He hustled down icy walks, towards the Marquis, guzzling pink liquid from a plastic bottle. His stomach bunched and knotted.

Franklin. He'd have some good ideas about what to do. He'd have—

Lor stopped. He was in front of Danny's, an independent grocer. Who can explain the vagaries of memory? Here Franklin bet him a cube of hash, bet you can't drink ten bottles of Coke in a row, ten years past, almost to the day. Lor drank the ten bottles, then squirted puke into this very gutter.

Slowly he pushed the door and entered to the same old sound of bells, to the same old perfume of sweet tarts and hockey-card gum, to the same old creaking tile. The geometries were all unchanged. Behind the counter, the same ageless face, Danny they called him, though his real name was Kwang Sok, the same cigarette behind the same left ear, perhaps *really* the same cigarette, ten years unsmoked, the same popbottle glasses, same blowfish eyes, same crinkled eyeskin.

They looked at each other. Lor could hear his own heartbeat.

Danny nodded.

"Ten bottles of Coke," he said.

Lor ran from the store. All the way back to the Marquis and up the stairs and into his room, where he gulped two sleeping pills, then four, then waded through the wreckage to collapse into oblivion.

† † †

A tapping at the door.

Lor awoke to a thick tongue and a dark room. He tried to rise, roily with the lingering stupor of sleeping pills.

The doorknob turned; the door creaked inward. A tall pointed hat poked in, followed by a wide brim and long white face. A scarecrow in a fringed jacket shuffled through the doorway, carrying a wooden chest. He removed his hat, loosing a long tumble of silvery hair gathered in a ponytail.

"Lor." A crackly voice, not unfamiliar. "Hey man, it's certainly been a long, and, if I may hazard a guess here, *consequential* time since we last spoke, fraught with happenings y'know?"

He grinned. White teeth floating in the dark.

"Don't speak to . . ." Lor tried to swallow, ". . .ghosts." He reached for his glasses, knocked over the old clock on the nightstand, breaking its glass. "What are you doing here?"

"Perhaps a more interesting, a more enchanting question, is what exactly *you're* doing here, back in Canada, in small-town Lethbridge, wi' this storm on top of our heads and nothing to do, really, in terms of both entertainment and the so-called job scenario, and the Man, in the guise of a fat little domestic hoodlum in a city cop's outfit, at every street corner 'n donut shop breathing down the neck of anyone with hair over the ears or for that matter growing out the ears, or a pierced body part whether that be schlong or nutsack or lip or nipple or clit, or, hell, even *shit*. . . ."

"What do you want?" Lor reached down to grab the fallen clock, forgetting its broken glass.

"You summoned me here," the scarecrow continued. "By postcard. And I travelled as the crow flies, over seven—"

"Shit!" Lor dropped the clock, blood dripping from his fingers.

"Hello . . . ." The figure dropped to a crouch. "Now this is truly fuck-o'd, shipmate, 'cos there's crushed ice all over the carpet here, and it's sponging up your blood."

Lor closed his eyes. "Still frozen?"

The scarecrow paused. "This here's the Crimson Slurpee. Symbol of the small ice, amigo."

Lor felt a few beads of narcotic exit his brain. "Small ice?"

The scarecrow cuffed the busted clock. "Popsicles, frozen dinners, ice jars in basement bars, all that shit that kills your spirit: cellphones, video games, barbecues. . . ."

Lor threw his legs over the bedside, brain-surfing chemicals.

The scarecrow opened his wooden chest and removed a bottle. "The cause of the world's disenchantment is this fucking 'fridgerated life-sapping suburboididity, this small ice." He took a swig from the bottle and spit it on the ice chips, then flared a match and dropped it.

"Yeah." The ice burned, blue and bleary yellow. Baby wildfire skittled over the carpet.

"Fire and ice," the scarecrow said. "Suburban version: Nintendo nights and hemorrhoids after sixty-nine years on the couch watching *Brady Bunch* re-runs, dig?—fridge stocked with ice from the chain of corner stores that— Ho-lee shit!—are precisely the same wherever you go, right down to the pimple-faced kid mopping the aisle floors in a brown vest just itching to get home and watch some stoopid porn with his buddies Mike and Matt and Mario between periods of *Hockey Night in*—"

"Stop!" Lor felt all the narcotic rush to his stomach. He stumbled from the window, head suddenly clear. This can't be happening, he thought, grabbing heavy curtain. It's just some creepy Lethbridge dude, some gaffer from the Kresge's, some hobo, some schizo. It's Japanese Elvis, Crazy Legs, Falcon Eddy....

He threw open the curtains and turned.

"Oh God," he said.

"Lor." The scarecrow threw up his hands.

"Alistair Grimes." Lor bit the inside of his cheek.

Alistair Grimes? *Here*? His old bandmate, his old life—all coming to roost, and you had to run full speed just to stand still. Lor sat on the floor and put his head in his hands.

"Jesus Murphy, Lor, see you haven't lost your taste for smashing guitars."

"You sound like Franklin."

"Ahhh, Franklin." Alistair gently stroked the bottle's neck. "Franklin didn't go far enough. Now you and I...." He grinned. "We will. I have a plan. I have a proposition."

"Get out." Lor rose to his feet.

Alistair chuckled, sat back on the chair.

Lor reached for the broken guitar neck on the floor. Still dizzy, he teetered and fell into the bloody ice.

"Lor, what'n the fuck—"

Lor crawled through ice, hands and knees smearing red. He snatched a glass from the carpet and threw it at Alistair, but his aim was whacked. The glass pinged the radiator, cracked. He wobbled to his feet, wiped his hands on his shirt, then headed for the door.

"Where you going, *compadre*?"

Lor pulled open the door, lunged into the hallway. He stumbled down a narrow hallway to the stairs, smelling a century of food, smoke, sex. Two steps at a time.

Alistair Grimes? *Here*? Lor wasn't even standing still in the tide of memories. He was washing back into the Weird, and Lethbridge was wrong, all wrong, bones not bleached at all.

He ducked into the arcade. It was mainly full of kids at ancient video games. But one lonely pinball pinged to nimble fingers, while the machine lit a vaguely familiar face—a tall Japanese woman, middle-aged, long braid. Game called *Treasure Island*. Dancing pirate skeleton, cutlass between its teeth.

. Lor backed into an unplugged game and ebbed to a squat.

"Amigo."

Lor turned. Alistair, still carrying the chest, still wearing the pointy hat.

"C'mon, amigo," Alistair said. "Look at me."

Lor shook his head. His shoulders slackened.

"You sent me the postcard, 'migo."

"Shit."

Alistair squatted next to him. "I know the cure for your disenchanted state."

He opened the wooden chest. Black paint and lacquer, deeply grained, carved with moons and stars.

"Here." Alistair removed a map tube, magnifying glass, and bottle of Jack Daniel's. He unscrewed the tube and pulled out a frayed map, then unrolled it on the chest. Lor could see a mass of white, some pale blue on the paper.

"North," Alistair said, grinning. "Want a drink?"

"I don't drink."

"We go north. Far north, into the Canadian Arctic, to the big ice." He pointed at the map, tapped a finger up to the top. "Where we drive life into a corner and see what stuff it's made of." He twisted off the Jack Daniel's cap. "Drink?"

"North?"

"Arctic."

Lor shivered, brain filled with sky and vast plains of snow. He folded his arms and rocked himself. "I hate the Arctic."

"You been?"

"Never been because I hate it."

Alistair picked up the bottle. "The Arctic is the *source*, man: the noumenal, the land of dreams and visions."

Lor dizzied. "Why are you here?"

"Why are *you* here?"

Sometimes there are no good answers. What to do? He couldn't return to Underwood, old girlfriends, that bit about the stolen car. But there was no way in hell he was going to the Arctic, all that ice, that light, that sky. With Alistair? No way.

Alistair tapped the wooden chest. "My friend?"

Lor tried to smile. "Why won't you leave me alone?"

Alistair grinned and shook his head.

"I'll hide," Lor said.

"I'll find you."

"I'll leave."

"I'll follow you."

Lor recoiled against the wall. "I'll kill you."

Alistair laughed. "Somebody will." He reached into the wooden chest, then whispered, "Look at this."

"So?"

It was a small unvarnished box, a mouse's coffin.

"It's *his*," Alistair whispered. "He asked me to keep it safe."

"Who?"

"Jolly Jesus, *Padre*, who d'you *think*?"

Franklin.

"See, dude," Alistair continued, "one time, in Underwood where else, he convinced me to 'company him to this place called the Museum of Evil." He grinned. "Yeah, kid you not on the name. So we went, reason being, he was so lonely for his family, who ran the place, like, in the fuckin' sixteenth century or something."

Lor massaged a temple. More fairy tales.

Alistair whispered through his grin. "So the place is hotter than Milton's hell, and we find all this heavenly wiggin' stuff, I'm talking real freak-o, like Wicca, pirates, and Freemasonry ... you ever been to this place?"

"No," Lor lied.

"And one of the items is this li'l box. Now, to be honest—I can admit to this in the full wisdom of adulthood—that box siren-songed us with some fuckin' heavy-duty, magical, uh, *magic*. Me'n him had a little tussle over it—you listening?"

"No."

"Actually, we fell over a few radiators, knocked a few tables. You'd think we would have spilled whatever was inside." He tapped the box. "I'm getting to that. Anyway, he kept the box at the time, and I was a little, er, you know, jealous. I even offered him my hat in trade. Remember how he was always begging to try on my hat?"

"No." Lor dug into the temple. Alistair was actually getting worse with age.

Alistair shifted in his squat. "Here's the bewitching part, 'migo. Years later, in Lethbridge, he gives the box to me, asks me to keep it safe. And," his knees cracked, "do you know what was inside this magical mini-casket?"

"Shit."

"No, little dude." Alistair opened the lid. "Not shit."

"Well?"

"Look."

"I don't see anything."

"'Xactly. *Nothing*." Alistair closed the empty box. "There was nothing in it." Leaned back, folded his arms, raised his eyebrows.

Lor closed his eyes.

"*Empty*, dude! The guy was bugshit over an empty box, do you see?—the *space* man, the noumenal, the presence inside the absence. It's his last sign: we're s'posed to go north and finish the expedition."

Lor looked up. "Maybe he just emptied it."

Alistair stared back, eyes smooth, brow unlined, as if a child had just suggested a mustard ice cream cone. "It's *empty*, 'migo." Said with compassion.

Lor smacked the wall and stood. Alistair rose with him, voice soft. "You're on the horns of a dilemma, friend. Tell you what: for now, practice with us, lend us your good ears, your rhythm—"

"Practice *what*?"

"This northern expedition. It's a musical tour, see? I'm getting the band back together, to complete Franklin's quest."

Lor slumped.

"Rehearse with us until we depart," Alistair continued, gently. "And I'll leave you be, promise. Mid-November, we scatter to our respective journeys, and God help to ease your soul."

Lor was silent.

"*Compadre*: surely you have the patience to put up with an old friend for a few weeks?"

After a long pause, Lor said, "Is Oggleston back from rehab?"

"Fuck no. Sans Og too."

Lor stared at his old companion.

Alistair took a pen from his pocket, scrabbled digits on the peeling bottle-wrap, then handed Lor the bottle. "You call me when you change your mind. You got a phone?"

"No. I—"

"Hush!" The scarecrow shook his long legs and picked up his chest. "When you're ready. Till then, *punchinello*." He strode from the arcade, into the crystal evening.

Lor looked at the number. Unfamiliar, of course.

"A crow!" yelled an attendant with broom held high. A squawk in the rafters. Guns, roars, explosions.

"Oh yeah!" the Japanese woman cried, as the pinball machine began to ring up numbers.

Lor headed for the door.

The skeleton lit behind him, like a Christmas tree on Halloween.

†††

Lor lay on the hotel floor. The more he thought of the Museum of Evil, the more he was not going to call that bastard Alistair. But, by some Möbius logic, the more he resisted, the greater the urge. Finally he grabbed the Jack Daniel's and reached for the old phone on the nightstand.

Seven rings and Alistair answered. "Hey, *gaucho*. Man, didn't take you long to mull over the deal, while I just heard the damnedest sermon about—"

"Al. Who's all going to be rehearsing?"

"Haven't finalized the details."

"Anyone I know?"

"Not exactly, *hombre*, but I'm trying to convince Franklin's kid brother, Fatty, 'cos he's a wicked white jazz percussionist, what I hear, and—"

"Franklin's *brother*?"

"You heard me. The kid is just zonko, like, madcap."

A long pause.

"What do you mean?" Lor said.

"Well, the kid's all that, and wigged out too, from the stories. 'Parently he carries around a guitar case, 'cept there's no gee-tar inside. Some say it's full of dead flies, some say a shitload of blue powder."

"*Powder*?"

"The kid is spaghetti. Nuttier'n a box of Turtles."

"Powder?"

"Powder, cowboy."

Lor listened to his breath pumping, felt a thin sheen of sweat slicking the space between his fingers and the phone. He thought of the powder, spilled on the museum floor back in Underwood.

"Okay," he said. He could not believe he was saying it.

"Okay what?"

"I'm in. Just for a few weeks. That's the deal, right?"

Alistair let loose a barbaric yawp.

"Well awl right pirate," he said. "You *sure* you never been to the Museum of Evil?"

CHAPTER SEVEN

A mAP iN THe ASHEs

I should really be in church this morning, Seri thought, checking the address on the mysterious letter. She stood at the walk, staring at a gingerbread mansion layered with snow, frosted with ice. The main door was open. Inside, walls had been knocked out, space carved by rows of gloomy cubicles, a vacant desk to the right, a phone with a blinking light.

Seri sighed. Already skipping church, already making compromises. She vowed to do better.

"In here," a voice from an office to the left. "Everyone is gone for the weekend. That you, Serendipity?"

She entered the office. "Hello, Mr. Rooke."

"Theodore, please, as this is not so much the continuation of an old working partnership as the inauguration of a new one. Ted, actually. Ted will do nicely."

Seven years had done nothing to soften his looks—bluff cheekbones, black crew cut and white Van Dyke beard, the lovechild of Colonel Sanders and Morticia Addams. If Serendipity's memory served, his behaviour was also typical in its oddity. He perched on an enormous glass-topped desk, legs hung over the side, fingers feeding pictures to a small ashtray fire.

"A dry picture makes good kindling, Seri. Have a seat. Wait, let me move my briefcase ... don't touch it. There. How was your journey?"

"Fine. Thanks. Gosh, interesting office."

"Yes, it's not mine. You and I, we have no office to speak of in our natal program of law enforcement." He smiled. "We don't actually exist."

"We aren't law enforcement."

"We are." He chewed a mint.

"CSIS is a civilian agency."

"We're not CSIS, Seri."

"What are we?"

He stared at her. He had a piercing stare.

"Seri, I'm going to ask you to look into the glass on this desk, as if it were a wishing well or pond." He fed more pictures to the flames.

"Ted?"

"Indulge me. Yes, that's it, straight down, letting go and giving in to the illusion of depth."

The desktop was deep brown and wood-grained beneath the glass, overlaid with flickered reflections from the ashtray.

"Seri, CSIS has a lot of rules: no police powers, an extensive warrant process for intrusive measures, an advisory role. Even SIP wears a straightjacket most of the time."

"Special Intelligence Projects?"

"You've heard of them."

"I've heard *rumours*."

"Believe them. Each branch, regardless of coverture, operates within the same set of parameters. But *rules*, Seri. Sometimes rules make things a little dark." He fanned the flames until they smoked out. "Rules are like mud at the bottom of a well."

He dumped the ashes onto the desk and spread them with his hand. Serendipity coughed.

"One could draw a map in the ashes," he continued. "Like this. Carefully tracing lines of probability across the mud. Like ... so."

"Ted, what are you doing?"

"Indulge me." He raised one ashen finger. "Rather like a Buddhist sand painting, isn't it? Puts one in mind of the ephemeral nature of existence."

"Ted?"

"One *could*. But why engage in half-measures? Careful now, move back a bit."

He leaned down and blew the ashes off the desk with one breath. Several clung to her skirt.

"There," Rooke said. "Clarity right down to the bottom. A crystal ball."

"Clarity?" She shook her head. "The ashes are gone. There's nothing left to clarify."

He blinked rapidly, looking bewildered, as if his entire edifice of certainty had just been blown away, itself made of ashes. Slowly he tightened his jaw, stood, and pointed a finger down at the desk.

"Bang." His voice pitched slightly higher, paced slightly quicker. "See? With clarity, law enforcement becomes a bit like shooting fish in a barrel. The Chinese have a word for it: *wu wei*, which, roughly translated, means the ability to act with clarity and economy, without wasted effort. Like the snow-laden tree that bends rather than breaks."

"That's some nice symbolism, for sure. But a little spooky, don't you think?"

"Look: the fish swim, as they must. They are never themselves visible, but if you are very still, you can see their shadows on the bottom. You must simply wait patiently for those shadows."

She tugged her cheek. This was some twisted Zen. "I'm here for a new job."

"But." He leaned forward, crunched the mint. "You're also here to be renewed. As am I."

She shrugged. "What's our mandate? What do we do?"

Rooke stared at her. Slowly, deliberately, he put the ashy finger into his mouth and sucked.

"What do we do." He pulled out the finger and appraised its cleanliness. "These are wayward and desperate times, Seri, populated by so many lost souls, so many punks, most of them searching for something to believe in. But a punk can never be renewed."

"How would we know? We were never punks."

His left eye blinked. He quickly reached to steady it with his cleansed finger. "Too many among us are lost and hungry." He slowly lowered the finger to trace against his lapel.

"Punks, you mean?"

"We're all out to kill our past."

He leaned forward and peered into her eyes. "We're all out to sprinkle a little angel dust across our memories."

Seri looked down at the floor. Ashes sparked the carpet.

CHAPTER EIGHT

THE SiLVeR CiRcLE

A perfect winter evening. White snow, black sky, bright crescent moon. Except it was October, and Lor would have preferred autumn's reds and yellows. He stood at the hotel window. At least that freak storm was over, the world restored to stillness, the sky restocked with stars. He put down the phone and sighed, then lay diagonally on the bed.

A rap at the door startled him.

He got up and stumbled to the light switch, flicked, opened the door. Some short Caucasian kid with orange dreads, seventeen, eighteen years old, holding a watermelon.

"Yeah?" Lor said. The kid just walked in, humming. Lor immediately noticed the eyes. Small, round, glassy—like the scary porcelain doll in a grandmother's attic.

"You are?" Lor said.

"You!" The kid's voice was high.

Lor suppressed a chuckle. "O-kay. What do you want?"

The kid sat down and produced a plastic knife and spoon, then sawed around the melon and broke the whole thing open. "I've come to take you down to the Crystal Room. For the band meeting."

Lor watched the kid spoon the melon's flesh. "I see. You belong to Alistair's gang."

"My girlfriend knows him." He slurped, choked, coughed seeds into his lap.

"Who's your girlfriend?"

"You!"

"What's the Crystal Room?"

"A conference room down the basement floor." The kid's mouth was already stained to the chin. "First we have to drive over to DanDee's and pick up some pop and crackers."

Lor stared at the juice trickling to the kid's collar. "Okay. Why not."

"Let's go," the kid said. "You going to wind your watch or pee?"

"Who's eating the melon?"

"You!"

Man, that was one high voice.

† † †

"What did you say your name was?" Lor said, as they wobbled down icy roads in the kid's four-by-four, chilled air pouring through the windows, warm air blasting from the dash. Lor recognized Cutbill Street, winding through the oldest neighborhood in Lethbridge.

"Fatty Core," the kid answered.

"Franklin's brother!" Lor clapped his hands on the dash. "That your real name?"

"Yeah."

"Really?"

"No."

Fatty skidded the Jeep to a halt at the corner of Ashmead Street and London Road, in front of a Chinese grocer. An unzipped crescent moon hung over the steep shingled roof. Inside Lor bought a pack of Lucky Strikes. Fatty got a Coke, crackers, roll of tape, and two popsicles. He pressed against an ancient freezer, chest puffed, till his nipples were hard enough to peck a keyboard. Then he wandered to the checkout and said, "Is it cold in here?"

Lor chuckled.

"What is your real name?" he said, minutes later, as they tottered back up Cutbill.

"Fatty."

"Liar."

"Hey, I don't make up the rules." The kid yanked a bouquet of nosehairs from one nostril. Eyes watering, he turned on the radio, fiddled. The dial hit static, and some faint vocal music crackled beneath, Celtic perhaps, something about a tower and frozen skies.

He stomped the brakes. The Jeep skimmed a patch of black ice and stalled. Fatty, heedless, twitched the dial back and forth, washing static from speakers.

"Damn," he said. "Damn. Did you hear that song? Did you hear it? Where did it go?"

"Well ... yeah, I heard something," Lor said. "Sort of distant."

Fatty looked down, scratching his head and breathing deeply. Then he punched off the radio and started the Jeep. He drove almost all the way back to the Marquis in second gear, stumbling and surging up Apple Hill, then coasting down a mirror-slick Corvette Boulevard.

There were no more words. Only the *glug glug* of foamy Coke, bottle rolling on the dash.

† † †

Ding.

The elevator doors opened.

The Crystal Room was silent. In one corner, a bulging couch. In another, a coffee table. Seven silver chairs circled the room's heart. The elevator rolled up the west wall, empty, bell sounding at intervals.

"Bad wiring," Fatty said. "Like me."

A row of lit candles flittered. Spiky shadows from hanging spider plants danced on the walls. The air smelled like spiced earth, baked squash, or something.

"So," Lor said. "What's your real last name? Not Core."

No answer.

"I want to know. Your brother, Franklin. Wouldn't ever tell his last name. Strikes me as kind of psychotic."

More silence.

"Fatty?"

Lor turned, but he was alone. Candles guttered, shadows twitched. He sat in a silver chair, while the phantom elevator dinged and creaked upward. Where was everybody?

Patience, he thought. Identify the problems, deal with them one by one. It was all clear now. He had to get out of the damn hotel, away from the bellboy, then hang on until Alistair left town taking the old life with him.

Lor lit a Lucky Strike.

"Care for a drink, sir?" someone whispered. "Something to chase the cold?"

"Shit!" Lor jerked, cigarette spitting ashes, and peered into the shadows. Spied the outlines of a cart and a brimmed hat.

"What are *you* doing here?" he said.

"Don't forget your journey."

The elevator dinged and rolled downward.

"Something to eat, sir? We've got *Zwieback*, roasted corn, a tureen of pumpkin soup."

A doorbell rang.

"Would you get that?" the bellboy said. "North wall."

Lor rose and walked to a large wood-grained door with a brass knob. As soon as it cracked open someone pushed inside, as if expected. It wasn't Alistair, but a hefty white man in a green hooded jacket.

"Alvin Ballooni, at your service." The man unzipped his jacket and hung it on the wall. "Soundman. I run the board."

The bell rang again. A thin kid pushed through, seventeen, eighteen, with dark hair and a rain cape. He was carrying a five-string bass, pegs sparkling with frost.

"Oh, I see you've started," the kid said, spying Ballooni's jacket. "I'm Jerome, my friends call me Rusty."

The new kid sat next to Ballooni. They spooned pumpkin soup out of steamy china bowls and bit into *Zwieback*, faces flushed with candlelight.

The bell rang. A grunge girl in toque and flannel, baggy black denims. "Gawd, a real throng," she said, peering in and blinking.

"Natasja!" Ballooni called out. "Come over, have some soup, couple of these *zwee-bucks*. Natasja, from the production company."

"Lor Kowalski," Lor said, offering his hand. His eyes were starting to dry out. How many people were in on this damn thing?

Natasja grabbed two *Zwieback* and a cob of corn wrapped in foil, dripping butter. She perched on a chair-back and blinked into the candlelight. The elevator dinged. The doorbell rang. A thirty-ish white woman, with multi-coloured hair extensions and a T-shirt that said *Anonymous Was a Woman*. Fatty followed with his grocery bag and half a bottle of Coke.

"Look who I found out in the Jeep," the woman said. "Had his radio up full blast, twiddling up and down the satellite."

"He's been doing that a lot lately." Rusty waved.

"You Lor?" the woman asked. "I'm Dawn Cherry, manager. I'll book the tour and do logistics."

"Cherry?" Lor said. "That Irish?"

"Old stage name," she said. "Old act called Coach's Daughter. Get it?"

"I do not get it."

"It was sad and sulphurous satire."

"M-hmmm." Lor returned his gaze to the room's centre, where Natasja was reaching into a tub of ice and handing out bottles of Lethbridge Pilsner, which Alvin Ballooni opened with his teeth. These Canadians were....

He couldn't think of a single word.

"Who wants 'em?" Ballooni said, spitting caps.

"You!" Fatty on the carpet, feet in the air, bicycling and farting. Natasja chortling, butter running down her chin.

I'm hooking up with the damned circus, Lor thought. Even as a boy he had hated the circus.

Someone rapped loudly. Lor opened the door, just as the latest guest knocked again with an umbrella top. Alistair, in tall hat and silver scarf, with his wooden pirate's chest.

"Lor. Hey man, I guess I'm a little late, looks of things, I mean we seem to have quite an assemblage, a congregation—"

"Get in here, windbag," Dawn Cherry said from the circle of silver chairs.

"Windbag?" Alistair squinted.

"Yes." Dawn Cherry turned to Ballooni. "That's the windbag I was telling you about, back from the West to drag us all north to enchanted places."

"You're not coming," Alistair said.

"Nothing new there," Dawn Cherry said.

Alistair tapped the wood. "That was never my fault. Hello, Dawn Cherry."

"Wo," said Fatty, grinning.

There was a long pause, in which the candles fluttered nervously. Then the elevator opened, a yawn, and closed, a gulp, as if to swallow the silence and transport it north to some enchanted place between the floors.

Ding, ding.

† † †

Alistair stood, like a preacher, inside the silver circle.

He unrolled his map on the wooden chest and pinned it with a magnifying glass and a *Zwieback*. "Ahem. Ten years ago, Underwood, Montana. Fatty's bro', Franklin, 'twixt his own desires and the influence of this li'l enchanted box," he pulled it from the chest, "has an inspired idea. He shares it with me 'n Lor, kids at the time, and we get his drift." He winked. "Lor?"

Lor sighed. This was an old routine.

"He smuggled us all into Canada," Lor said, as Alistair tapped his umbrella on the map. "Where he suspected we might illuminate for ourselves the mysterious truths of experience. That's a quote."

"Oh, it's *more* than that, amigo. We were taking our li'l punk band out of the suburban sprawl and into the wilderness, said wilderness being this very town of Lethbridge, Canada, Franklin's birthplace, where the lack of context would force us to look into the heart of things, to discover the very pith of life. Lor?"

Lor was silent. He shuffled away from the throng, toward the coffee table.

"How do you know if you're anti-establishment," Alistair continued, "with the Man hanging around your neck day in day out? No. You have to light out for the territory, drive life into a corner."

"Your life is all corners," Dawn Cherry said. "Without corners you've got a vacuum."

"Exactly," Alistair said.

"I used to have an Auntie Establishment," said Fatty. "She loved to stick the old vacuum right up—"

"See, amigos," Al said. "In the empty wild, with no authentic culture to set the limits, who do you rebel against?—get me?—like, will our energies turn in on themselves? Dissipate? Don't you want to know?"

Lor shuffled further, eye suddenly fixed on greens and blues in the table's grain.

"What happened to Fatty's brother?" Ballooni said.

Alistair's eyes bugged, then squinted. Dawn Cherry groaned.

He went mad, Lor thought. And if *he* could go mad, was there any hope for the rest of them? And where was he now? Because if anyone would still know what to do here, mad or not....

Alistair rapped the chest-top. "The point is, Franklin had a good idea that didn't work out." He looked around, nodded. "And the main problem was his vision, which was too small. I mean, *Lethbridge?*—sure, a town north of the 'Nited Snakes, but still, hardly the wilderness we need. And he knew it."

Lor crept still further from the silver circle, toward the coffee table.

"That's why I propose to continue Franklin's project," Alistair continued. "'Cept this time we go all the way, and trek into the *real* territory, I'm talking the Canadian Arctic here, the islands." He lit his pipe and blew a fragrant cloud. "How do you keep your punk up there in the white?—'cos I'm talking almost to the *North Pole*, man. The social means nothing up there, it's all myth."

A pause, punctuated by Fatty munching cracker and Ballooni breathing through clogged nostrils. Lor tugged at his collar. The elevator gave two quick dings.

Then a whisper in Lor's ear. "Perhaps, sir, you will get more myth than you bargained for." The bellboy.

"You are so supremely full of shit, 'Stair," Dawn Cherry said. "The north ain't *empty*. There's a plenitude of the social up there."

"Eskimos and stuff," said Fatty.

Dawn Cherry snorted. "You don't call them *Eskimos*, you opprobrious twit."

"I don't make up the rules." Fatty polished off the last drips of Coke and spewed a long sonorous belch.

"Actually, you do," Dawn Cherry said. "Lemme school you: the Hare, the Dogrib, the Yellowknife. The, uh, Tutchone …."

"Them the ones that carve up the soap?" Fatty burped.

"Christ, Fatty," Dawn Cherry said.

"There are many cultures in the North," the bellboy said from the shadows. "Not only the Inuit, but the Dene, the Aleuts, the Netsilik, the Iglulik, oil workers, government, frost demons, tourists."

"Lot of people," Lor said.

"Lor?" Dawn Cherry gave him a flinty stare.

"I myself have returned once from his kingdom, the land of the ice and snow," the bellboy said. "That is *my* little box."

"That's *his* box," Lor said.

Natasja blinked. "Who?"

"Hey superfreak," Dawn Cherry said to Lor. "You going to join us or just sit there talking to yourself?"

"You went up north?" Lor said to the shadows. "How far?"

"Farther than you can imagine."

Alistair, who had been smoking and watching with what looked like amusement, rapped the top of the wooden chest. "Actually," he said, "where we're going there is, as I promised, no culture at all, because—dig me—it's a bona fide, notarized, certified wilderness."

"A what?" Natasja said, blinking.

"A deserted island." Alistair grinned. "Actually."

…frost demons?

† † †

Fatty made a bong. He planted a lighter tube and hollow pen in the plastic Coke bottle, cutting holes with a penknife. Then he covered the lower tube with foil, poked holes for a sieve, and filled the bottle with ice. Dawn Cherry handed him a bag of weed, which he poured out and began to slice with the penknife.

"So where's this island?" Ballooni said.

Alistair grinned and leaned deeper over the map.

"Right here, amigo, floating in the high Mackenzie." Alistair paused suddenly and began to tap his finger. "Eh?" He moved to extreme close-up. "What the *fuck*?"

Ballooni vented smoke. "It's not there."

"It was there this morning." Alistair straightened.

"So you're going to an island that ain't even there?" Natasja was at the bong, sucking hard.

Alistair fell to his knees and peered through the magnifying glass. "Fuck, I *know* it's there, saw it just this morning."

"Good going, Merlin." Dawn Cherry wrestled the bong from Natasja. "Perspicacious as Odin himself."

The room was clouding. Lor dug at his fingernails and inhaled great thunderheads of weed smoke, which floated over from the silver circle to dump narcotic rain on the coffee table. He needed to move, get out.

"Bong?" Dawn Cherry called to him.

He shook his head. No point. The *room* was a bong.

"The island *does* exist," the bellboy whispered. "You will return there."

"Return?" Lor said. "Never been."

Alistair dropped the magnifying glass. "Whatever the case, amigos, we journey to Foggy Island, site of a punk festival at which we play the main stage." He quickly rolled up the map.

The room hazed, white smoke twitched with seams of darkness. Lor lit a smoke and kneeled over the glass-top, running fingers through the grain's blue whorls.

"Here's your ticket north, sir." The bellboy dropped a small glinting packet to the floor and vanished in shadow. "Don't forget the powder."

Lor felt a chill at his knees and gazed down, then dropped his smoke. Frost blossomed across the floor. He looked up to see Fatty scoop the glinting packet.

"Check this." Fatty held the packet to the light. A tinfoil ball. "Somebody dropped a fat-load of drugs."

"Throw it away," Dawn Cherry said.

Fatty ignored her, popped it in his pocket. Then unwrapped two half-melted popsicles, bright pink goo stringing from stick to paper.

Lor rubbed the frost, felt a sting of distant wind chimes on his fingertips. Candlelight sparkled on the spit-shined length of Fatty's popsicle.

"Let's get this straight." Natasja looked at Alistair. "I'm producing a tour to a place that ain't even *there*?"

"It's there, 'migette, it's there, and we could, like, *see* it if that fucking popsicle wasn't clouding our spiritual vision."

"Lord." Dawn Cherry snorted. "Your irrational hatred of treats."

"So where's the island?" Natasja said.

Frost skittled to the corners. A candle laughed. Voices getting distant now, echoes across a prairie night.

"Here." Alistair.

"Where?" Natasja.

"Nowhere." Dawn Cherry.

"Aroooo." Fatty howling like a coyote.

Lor reached up to the rim of the glass-top, raised himself, looked down at the table. It was snowing inside—sky raining flakes, drifting up to cling on the underside of the glass.

"Sometimes a birthday is a dangerous thing." The bellboy loomed at his ear again, whisper dry as autumn leaves, breath smelling of warm pumpkin.

Lor tried to pull away his hand, peered into the upside-down world beneath the glass. He rose to one knee and gulped a panoramic snapshot of the Crystal Room, where Natasja stood with hands on hips, where Fatty bounced on the couch, where Ballooni blinked at a broken bong, where Alistair smushed a popsicle in the ash tray, where candles guttered out of control on dancing wicks, and the elevator chattered its doors, burping smoke, dinging over and over.

These Canadians were just....

Just....

Lor inhaled once and fell into the table. For no clear reason, the last thing he imagined was a snowman laughing wickedly, way at the bottom, down in the snowy sky.

CHAPTER NINE

CHASING THE DEVIL

"So, Ted. Why did you pick me?" Seri brushed ashes from her skirt. A few smudged.

Rooke slithered from the desktop, straightened long legs till he stood over her. "You're in excellent physical condition. Quite a figure, actually." He tapped the desk with a finger. "Plus you have a degree in pharmacology, specializing in narcotics." He licked the finger. "Perfect."

She looked up at him. Her skirt was ruined.

"Punks," Rooke continued. "We are hunting punks."

"Yes. Why me?"

"Hunting them with all the energy and intelligence we possess." He strode around the desk and dropped into the swivel chair. "Because they cannot fix themselves. Jesus said—"

"*Jesus?*"

"—if thy right eye offend thee, pluck it out."

Seri leaned forward and put her elbows on the desk. "Jesus said, 'Judge not, that ye be not judged.' Besides, what's Jesus got to do with anything?"

His head snapped toward her. His neck cracked. "You know the Bible?"

"I did a triple degree. Pharmacology, geography, *and* angelology."

Rooke leaned back, massaging his neck. "Well. How ambitious. Then you'll know the angel religion Ozahism, which teaches that one must judge if one is to find redemption."

"Except for my final humanities project, I concentrated more on the pharm and geo. Is that a highly symbolic religion?"

He glared. "Do you know the teachings of Zaron, in which the symbolic figure of the knife thrower cuts all the bonds of love?"

"I probably studied it." Seri looked at her smudgy skirt. "What happened to *wu wei*, the snow-laden tree that bends but doesn't break?"

He pulled a long breath through his nose, glaring at her. "There are many religions, more than you know. I have tried all of them."

She laughed. He didn't.

Seri was a little rattled. "Okay. All? Did none of them work for you?"

Rooke looked quickly down, tapped his finger three times on the desk. Then he raised his hand to stroke his beard, his eyes roving inner space. After a few seconds his eyes returned. He bit the inside of his lip, then smiled.

"Seri, there is work I must do. You are going to help me. We are the hammers of God." His smile stiffened. "Whoever that is."

† † †

"Never trust a man with too many layers," Seri's Great-Grandma Casey would often say, before her death at the age of seventy-three in a rock-climbing accident.

Granny Finnegan always disagreed. "A bit of mystery and misdirection in a man is never unwelcome. It gives spirit and dimension, puts him somewhere 'twixt hell and heaven."

"Hell and heaven?" Grandma Casey said, one rainy Thanksgiving. "Devil of a comment for an ordained minister."

Granny Finnegan plucked a bit of turkey from between her teeth. "It's called the *dialectic*, dear. Do well to remember it."

"Mumbo-jumbo." Grandma Casey neatly peeled a baked potato. "What do you think, Seri?"

Serendipity gulped cranberry and shook her head. She was dating a youth pastor at the time, if it could be called *dating*. They spent much of their time sublimating at the rock-climbing gym. They drank a lot of tea. They kissed three times a week.

He would not open his mouth.

He would not speak in tongues.

† † †

Rooke yawned, covered it delicately with the palm of his hand. Seri noticed his fingers, impeccably groomed, not a cuticle out of place. He replaced the file in the top drawer and removed nail clippers from his coat pocket.

He started with his thumbnail. "How much of our history do you remember?"

"Yours and mine?"

"CSIS history."

"All of it."

"See, the problem really began with the dismantling of the RCMP Security Service back in '84." He was filing the thumbnail to a perfect crescent. "The Mounties once had some measure of power where subversion is concerned."

"That was a good thing?" She chomped a stick of gum.

"In the old days, we could go after those with threatening ideologies. The punks, the freaks, the anarchists, the whole crew."

Rooke rounded a nail's curve, continued. "Now our hands are tied. Do you know what it's like to have your hands *tied*, Seri?"

"Nope." Her mouth dried. She coughed.

"*The CSIS Act* in '84 took away many of our powers. But *The Osbaldeston Report*, in '87 . . ." He clipped loudly and dug the spike under a nail.

Seri was chewing hard, two-and-a-half sticks' worth.

"Do you know the wording, Seri? In the report?"

"Of course. Do you?"

"CSIS's counter-subversion program casts its nets too widely. Too *widely*." He sliced a nail and leaned forward. "How do you catch fish without casting your net?"

"You're using the wrong metaphor—"

"In the absence of counter-subversion, what has become our top priority, as established by government clerks?" He gently set down the clippers. "Economic security." He stroked a cuticle. "Criminal, is what it is."

"Criminal?"

"Protestors marching on Parliament Hill every second day. Dopers challenging drug laws. People on mad journeys, south into deserts or north to the Arctic, trying to 'renew' themselves." He pronounced *renew* as if he were about to vomit.

Seri flushed, looked down.

"Handcuffed," he said. "From SIP right on down. Ever been cuffed, Seri?"

"Never."

"And when we do get some juicy intelligence, we give it away."

It's called the coordinated approach, Seri thought. She looked down at the carpet. "Why are we fixating on subversion?"

"Punks," Rooke said, as if that answered the question. "Why should the RCMP get all of our best so-called ancillary information? Why should we simply fly around gathering shiny bits of foil to line someone else's nest?"

He tapped his fingers and leaned forward once again.

"What are we, *magpies*?"

† † †

Granny Finnegan played the violin for her boyfriend, Mr. Scott. He came over to the house on Friday nights, sat with hands folded over lap. She played Paganini till the strings snapped. Mum just smiled. Grandpa Hamm, from the family's other side, laughed and laughed until it was time for his medicine.

Some Fridays, Granny Finnegan would put the violin away and drag Seri out on a double date. Granny sat in the back seat with Mr. Scott while Seri's current boyfriend, Greg, drove to the bowling alley. On rainy nights, when the windows fogged, Seri would feel claustrophobic.

Greg was the youth pastor at a Mennonite church. He read the Bible to Seri and talked earnestly about the sacrament of marriage, the blessing of family. He kept his car so clean. He insisted they never pray together, because that level of intimacy could lead to a careless mistake.

At the bowling alley, Granny would have a few beers, Mr. Scott a scotch with ice. Greg would have one Coke. The pins would crash. Lights would flash. Granny would pat Mr. Scott's bottom.

It was obvious, even logical, that Greg was God's will for Seri. Greg had all the right qualities: fidelity, truthfulness, righteousness. He was like her father, the preacher she remembered, perfectly correct in his views on family and ethics. The only difference was that Greg would keep his faith, and never run away. He was even handsome, in a youth pastor sort of way.

Greg is God's will for me, Seri told herself.

It was a rainy night.

She threw the ball at the pins, hard.

† † †

Rooke slipped a compact disc into the stereo on the shelf, turned up the volume.

"Do you like Paganini, Seri?"

She nodded.

"People thought he was the devil," Rooke said. "He played the violin so fast, so hard. Somewhere between madness and brilliance."

Seri smiled. "My Granny is a violinist and a minister of God. She would say Paganini's music, played with brilliance, chases the devil."

Rooke stared, hands on hips. His fingers tightened, twisted black fabric. "What do any of *you* know about the devil?"

"Us?"

"I want you to look at this map," he said, yanking a string from the ceiling. A wall-sized geography of Canada unrolled, much like a retro grade-school map. "Look at the space, the whiteness, the vast borders. Does this look like a place that can be policed by clerks and bureaucrats?"

Seri sighed around what was now a wad of gum. "So, *what*, Ted? What is our job description? Tell me clearly."

His shoulders, held high, dropped suddenly. He looked at the carpet and held his breath, reminding Seri of her childhood playmate, Ricky.

"Ted?"

He exhaled in a whoosh. "I am not, at this time, completely certain."

"Sure you are." She turned down the stereo. "Just explain at whatever level of specificity you have."

He pulled up his shoulders, a little higher than looked comfortable. "Certainly not the usual security clearances, background checks and other assorted impotencies. Look at that map, Seri." His voice gathered speed. "Up here, at the Arctic Archipelago, the District of Franklin—look at all that *space*." He smiled, tapped his tooth with a fingernail. "Clarity, Seri. We need a bird's-eye view, a transcendent position. A roost."

He tugged at the string, and the map shivered in waves.

Seri dabbed chewed gum into a wrapper and folded it neatly. "What does all this have to do with Paganini?"

Rooke frowned. His pink tongue flicked his lips. "You think we no longer have subversives in this country?"

"Of course." Seri touched the dimple in her cheek. She uncrossed, then crossed her legs. "What's the main distinction between us—"

"And CSIS?" Rooke warmed, straightened, smiled. "The handcuffs are off. We do not get monitored by the Security Intelligence Review Committee. Not budgets, not activities, nothing. We have no intercourse with the Inspector General, nor the Solicitor General, nor the federal courts." He looked less like Ricky than anyone she had ever seen. "We report to no one."

Well, that was nonsense. Seri would find the proper channels, regardless of what Rooke did or didn't know.

"And our jurisdiction, Ted?"

"Expanded considerably. Wide-ranging discretionary powers, and, best of all, no affidavit for intrusive measures. My say-so is the only warrant we need."

Serendipity rose to fetch a glass of water, stopped, sat down again quickly. "What about due respect?"

"Punks do not merit due respect. Least of all ageing punks who should know better."

He was close now. Seri could smell soap, cologne, the spice of body odour.

She exhaled. "You seem to have it in for CSIS."

Rooke snapped a nail. "They won't let me do my work."

Dear Lord. Seri thought of peaches.

"Do we get guns, Ted?"

"Guns?" Rooke laughed, as a nail popped and spun onto the glass-top. She whiffed his cologne again, stronger this time. He grinned, teeth so white, snapped the volume up till Paganini burned from the speakers.

"No guns," he said. "That would be like bad American TV. And this is still Canada. And I am an upright man."

CHAPTER TEN

A WELCOME dARk

Lor drifted through the long hallways of the Marquis. Radiators bubbled, paint-skins peeling, heat pressing windows, windows shedding stains, stains seeping down through carpet to the underworld. Dead flies guarding the sills, the whispers of everyone who had ever stayed overnight, and the tock-tick of the grandfather clock at the hallway's end, where he hovered to stare at the broken face, then entered the heat of the bathroom and the stifled drip of corroding pipes, where the mirror was fractured, and his eyes were bloody, and he was a boy.

"Lor. Come on, man, wake up."

The ice around Lor's brain slowly cracked, letting in the blood.

"Lor. You had me worried, brother."

"Where's ... everybody?" Lor raised his head from the table. His cheek was numb.

"You were gone, man. Totally out."

Lor stood, wobbled a bit, looked about him. There was shattered glass at his feet and on his hands.

"Whoah, buddy." Alistair grabbed Lor's shoulder, steadied him. "You're a li'l mixed up there, account of some wonky body chemistry. Here, have a bun, steady you a bit."

Lor shook his head, ignoring the *Zwieback*. Then he fell over.

"Criminy," Al said. "This zany shit's what got us into this mess, this imbroglio, this, uh ..."

"I can't think." Lor grabbed his sticky forehead.

"W'fuck. You're hungry, you're high, you're in a basement, of course you can't think."

"What's an *imbroglio*?"

Alistair kneeled beside him. "My map nixed the island, you nixed the meeting, so Natasja nixed the tour. Dig?"

"So the bargain's off?" Lor looked up hopefully. "You want to be rid of me?"

"Hell no, bargain's on, and you, captain, are going to help us buy some new gear."

Lor dropped his forehead to the carpet.

"Look, 'migo, Natasja bailed, so we had to redesign the tour, meaning, far as you're interested—we ain't leaving till Christmas now. And if you don't help us get the gear we ain't never leaving."

"Oh god."

"Here, put on my hat."

It covered his head, and the brim cast a welcome dark.

† † †

Humongous Pizza Slice is seven feet from the Marquis, as the crow flies. It is always open late, because proprietors Mucciaroni and Chan both have advanced insomnia, and neither has slept since the Second World War. Humongous offers the finest hybrid cuisine anywhere for those on a budget, queer pizza creations that would never be whispered of by daylight in suburban restaurants or traditional households. And the smell.

Alistair gobbled two whole-wheat slices trimmed with bok choy, peanut sauce, and feta, while Chan giggled and Mucciaroni tossed and punched dough. Lor smoked and smoked, a chain of Lucky Strikes.

No more drugs, he thought, over and over. A mantra. Just say no. Drugs were clearly his problem, psychedelics in particular, because the line between hallucination and reality, though sound, was beginning to blur. Someone had obviously dusted that weed in the Crystal Room. No more drugs. And forget that damned bargain, too, Al was out of his mind. Lor was not going shopping for *anyone*, least of all these fuckheads.

Alistair chomped. "Weird thing was, he always wanted my hat."

Lor nodded. Franklin again.

Alistair sat on the table and told Mucciaroni and Chan the story of his project. How he had discovered a phantom website that told of an upcoming

Arctic music festival, complete with hazy visuals of Foggy Island, the festival site. How the extended text blasted gross commercialism and lazy suburban ennui. How anyone could show up and play. There was to be no producer, no program, no sponsorship. DIY writ large.

"It's going to be white chaos, picaroons, a convergence, harum-scarum, the experience of a lifetime. Mooch, who's the juicebag watching us over in the corner? Albino rhino with the thick glasses and piggy eyes?"

Mucciaroni turned. "Malachi Frump. Eats his weight in gold, keeps us open."

"So what's his gig, *machiavel*, like what's he taking notes on us or something? Hey! Taco Bell, you spying on us?"

The man closed his notebook and capped his pink pen, began to cram a wedge of cured meats and mixed cheese.

"Leave him," Chan said. "He writes for *Alberta Watch*. His mom's a famous politico."

"The razorback is eavesdropping. Hey! Take your notebook and get back to your fucking flat tax or flat earth or flat affect conference or whatever the fuck."

The man clicked open an attaché case and neatly placed the notebook and pen in their designated pockets, then folded the remaining pizza and crammed it.

"Thanks, Chan," he said, rising.

"Yeah. Come back later when these creepies are out of here."

"I will. Thanks, Mooch."

Mucciaroni nodded. Frump headed for the door.

Alistair gave him the finger. "Actually, don't come back, *babushka*, and while you're at it—subversives you say? Fuck you, that's a compliment where I come from, yeah, hope to see you again too. . . ." Alistair was far enough over the table that he almost dumped it.

Lor collapsed into his chair. Where did Al get all that energy? It was exhausting.

"See what I mean?" Alistair turned. "That's the Man, frozen in small ice."

"You're crazy," Chan said. "And bad for business."

Christmas, Lor thought. I can't wait that long.

"Get out now," Chan said, tapping the back of Lor's chair. "Maybe we let you back in another ten years."

"Maybe," Mucciaroni said.

"Doubtful," Chan added.

† † †

They stood beneath the horned moon and the buzzing neon, in gently warming air, while a rainbow of western sky cut into streaks of cloud. Lor leaned against the rail and tried to keep his eyes open while Alistair clicked a boot heel.

"Dude," Alistair said. "You really need some rest."

"I can't go back. I have to get out of that hotel. I have to."

Alistair lit his pipe. "Tell you what, starting tomorrow night you stay with me."

"I don't think so."

Alistair puffed. "Ready to shop?"

Lor slumped.

"Dude?"

"Whatever," Lor said, looking down, eyelids heavy.

"And you'll stay with me."

Lor nodded slowly.

"Chinook arch," Chan told them, momentarily popping out with a broom to sweep the remaining snow from the walk. "Hot winds coming, early tomorrow, maybe tonight. Chase the moon away." Mooch called from within, and Chan disappeared with his broom.

Lor let go of the rail and looked to the sky. "So, Al. When you went, did you ever see any, I don't know, any *powder*? Like in that little box you and Franklin fought over?"

"Powder?"

"In that old Underwood Museum of Evil. Like a sparkling dust."

"Fuck no, kidding amigo? That place was filled to the nuts with interesting stuff. Too bad you never went."

"Yeah. Too bad."

They watched the sky darken.

"Al. I have to get high."

"High?"

"Up. Off the ground. I need to walk to a view."

"Tomorrow, then."

They parted at the Kresge's. Alistair clomped away beneath a winking streetlight, pointed hat bobbing. As Lor watched, he suddenly felt a twist of fear and loneliness, like a boy heading off to summer camp for the first time.

"Al!"

"Yeah."

Lor paused, unsure as to why he had called out. "Good to. . . ." The words jammed up in his throat. "Good to. See you again, brother."

Alistair grinned. "Good to see you too, *confrere*."

The moon faded behind a nebulous roil, horns catching briefly to rip a seam through the clouds.

† † †

Midnight.

Lor took the remaining Lucky Strikes and wandered out into the night, under the overpass, through a tangled hedge, down train tracks frosted with ice and filtered starlight. The sky was streaked with chinook cloud to the west, stretched over rows of wartime houses, windows winking with domestic secrets. Who were these people, and how did they put up with the chaos of a family?

He ambled down the tracks through knee-high weeds still sugared with snow, to the pedestrian overpass. Beneath, two lovers giggled, sprinkling whispers and chemical magic. Who were these people, and how did they put up with the chaos of love? Lor climbed the concrete steps and sauntered to the centre.

His head jerked with memory. The Japanese woman. The arcade. The wooded greenstrip, the crows. Damn, the Weird was following him. Backward in time and motion, from Lethbridge to Underwood.

He bowed his head.

Far below, in the west, the city stretched to coulees, and coulees to prairie, and prairie to dark horizons. Lor focused on the middle distance: suburban twinkle, traffic buzz, the promise of seasonal days and nights. Wafting up now, the smell of pizza all the way from Humongous. Lor sniffed, taken with childhood memories of weekend suppertimes, when the world was enormous and a lifetime stretched to its own horizons.

The Weird was going backward.

The night silenced, all hushes synchronous. For a few seconds Lor heard nothing. No cars. No lovers. No urban hum. Then, suddenly, the chatter of a magpie, up long past its bedtime.

PART THREE

BROWN

ALBERTA BLUES

It is imperative to take the initiative, to build firewalls around Alberta.

—Former Prime Minister Stephen Harper, 2001

CHAPTER ELEVEN

FoUr CReATuREs

Calgary, though no Lethbridge, has its own few pockets of weirdness, braided almost secretly through the mesh of freeway snarl and corrugated suburbia. The neighbourhood of Mission is a pocket: nested between the perpetual rush hour of Seventeenth Avenue and the upscale convolutions of Elbow Drive, Mission is an entanglement of French Catholicism, working-poor stoicism, punky freakdom, and ambitious yuppiedom. Late-nineties Mission is not yet gentrified, and no gentle place.

Seri stood in front of the Ship & Anchor Pub at the northern tip of Mission, washed in gently warming air, trying to decide whether to go in early for a beer. She was not much of a drinker, but this evening she felt the need for a bit of unwinding before meeting Rooke again.

"I'll show you the kind of subversives I mean," Rooke had said, earlier in the afternoon. "They gather at a bar in Mission, like flies." His fascination seemed disproportionate. Seri wondered where the conversation was leading.

"I hate them," he had continued.

"Punks."

"Men with long hair. Men with no hair. Men with pointy hats. Surrealists. Musicians. Tall men. People who label things *quixotic* or *foucauldian* or *kafkaesque*."

Seri laughed. Rooke didn't.

"Ted. Hate is no mandate."

He seemed downcast. "They are thieves. Careless. They destroy what isn't theirs. They have faith and hope. They have plans."

"What ridiculous nonsense," Seri said out loud, remembering.

"Then come in for a pint," said an attractive young woman, chain-linked with piercings and tattoos, hand in hand with a straight-up pretty dolly.

Seri surprised herself. "I suppose I will. Is there a band tonight?"

"Depends what you mean by a *band*."

"I might call off our project," Rooke had said, earlier. "You're right. We have no mandate."

"Nonsense," Seri had replied. "I never said that. Where are your best sources of information?"

"I have a spy down south, in Lethbridge, named Malachi. He keeps a watch on the subversives."

That was more like it.

"What can I get you?"

"I'll have a half-pint ... no, a *pint* of Guinness." Seri wedged herself in a corner booth away from the knotted herds, considered briefly how some watering holes attract a disparate mix of animals. At the dartboards a gaggle of after-work secretaries tipped and giggled, watched closely by a murder of skinheads perched at the railing. A pod of assorted punks and urban vampires drifted from table to table, surfacing periodically to feed on fresh rounds of drinks, circumnavigating goths or hipsters clumped in islands. Young men hived shoulder to shoulder. Old men strung themselves around the bar, ageing monkeys calling out to each other across the canopy. Most of all, there were lots of cats, cats everywhere, observing prey with a languid dissolution, weighing the compulsions of lust against the fragility of image, nursing secrets, fading around their own smiles.

Seri was a fish out of water. She took a sip of Guinness, and began to order her world with mental notes—ask Rooke how many more nights to book in the hotel. Check into getting a vehicle. Find a local church.

"Alone, lass?"

The man was hip-to-hip with her in the booth. He must have been completely silent in his approach.

"Alone, lass?"

For a moment she thought it was Rooke, then realized her mistake. "Yes. Excuse me."

He stayed fixed against her. "I'm thirty today. My name is Og."

She checked her watch.

"What's *your* name? My name is Og."

"Serendipity." She squeezed further into the plush seat and nestled the wall.

"My name is Og." He looked down at his fingers, then smacked a hand flat on the glass-top and stared at it.

"Mr. Og." She touched the dimple in her cheek. "Let me out, please." He was unresponsive, except for a twitch in his splayed fingers.

Drug intoxication, she guessed, feeling her pulse quicken. Phencyclidine. PCP. Agitation, aggression, confusion, blank stare. Angel dust.

"My name is Og." He turned his stare at her. "Thirty years old. My birthday. *Bang!*"

His pupils were almost completely dilated, with a thin ring of ice-blue frozen around dark bulbs. His face was skeletal. Skin sores stippled his forehead.

No, Seri corrected herself. High-dose amphetamine, probably 125 milligrams, maybe more. Chronic speed misuse. High levels of NE, activation of dopamine neurons.

"Bang!" He rolled his fingers again. "Where?"

Compulsive behaviour. Suspicion. Delusion. Where was Rooke?

Og leaned close. "What's your name?" She noticed his infected gums. "Lass?"

"Will you please let me out of the booth?" she said.

"You are my birthday present." He began to scratch the glass-top of the table. Dear Lord, he was psychotic. In person, it was much more disturbing than the dry textbook descriptions she was familiar with. Maybe Rooke was—

"Bang!"

You have detailed knowledge of narcotics, Rooke had said, earlier that afternoon. We'll go after the druggies, with full force. The sellers? she had asked. No, Seri, the users. The abusers. You can never get redemption through drugs, nor through any subversive quest.

"Thirty today. Thir-teee." Og smoked, holding the cigarette like a martini and taking quick puffs while scratching the table with his free hand. "What's your name?"

It looks so different up close, Seri thought. Either her watch was fast, or Rooke was late.

"Do you like the band?" Og took a sip from his cigarette. "Your name? This table is itchy."

Suddenly she was dying to smash Og's face, bust all those teeth from their bloody pockets. Riding her swell of aggression, she shoved his shoulder, slipped under the table, and crawled across the beer-soaked carpet to the aisle.

"Bang!" he cried, kicking the underside of the table with enough force to capsize the Guinness. "Get you!"

She stood and dashed through a clump of underaged goths while Og jumped up and threw the cigarette at her.

"Hey, Og," one of them said, a young witch with a silver bone through the septum. "The hell you doing?"

Og slapped the witch and pitched forward, head swivelling. She reset herself and punched him in the groin. Two of her heftier friends grabbed his arms and pulled him to the ground.

"Go get Schuster," one of them said.

"Careful." A brawny bouncer emerged from the knotted herds. "Oggie's a handful when he's screwed up."

"Get him out of here," the witch said.

"Wayne!" the bouncer called. "Give me a hand?"

Seri stood at the bar between a soccer hooligan and an old sea captain. She clutched the rail, breathing deeply.

"What can I get you?" the barkeep said, polishing a glass.

"Nothing," said Schuster the bouncer. "She's leaving."

"No." Seri tapped her watch. "I have a meeting."

"Too bad. We have rules here. You're out."

"I didn't do anything. I have an important meeting."

He pointed to the door.

The sea captain smiled kindly. "You're shaking, lass."

"Don't call me that."

Two bouncers dragged Og past the bar.

"Bang!" He twitched violently and let his feet drag through beer swill and cigarette butts, then pointed at Seri over Schuster's shoulder. "That's my birthday present."

"Whatever," said Schuster. "You can uwrap her outside."

"No." Seri's pulse thumped in her neck. She felt faint. "I can't, I have to—"

"Lass." The sea captain tapped her elbow. "Sneak out the back door. Through the kitchen." The barkeep nodded.

Og gave her a look as they hauled him to the front door.

"Get you," he said, his pupils sponging light.

††††

Seri left slowly, hiding out among pots and pans for as long as she dared. When she finally stepped into the alley, it was deserted. She walked to the street, passed a tattoo shop, and paused to look at her reflection in the window. Behind the glass she could see samples of neo-pagan iconography, runes, charms, and creatures.

The moon, battling with encroaching clouds, granted the city a last gasp of luminosity. Light splashed down narrow roads and alleys, pooled in shop windows and snowmelt. Seri buttoned her coat. She would wait for Rooke across the street, where she could get a better view of the Ship & Anchor's entrance. She quickened her pace, humming an old hymn.

He melted out from behind the dumpster without a sound.

"So soon, lass?"

"So soon what?" Her rattling heart. An absurd answer, the kind given in moments of sudden distress.

"My birthday present," Og said. "Bang, bang."

"I have a meeting," Seri said. He was blocking the sidewalk. The Interfaith Thrift Shop to her right was closed. The road pumping with traffic. No other pedestrians in sight.

He blinked.

She turned and fled. A block ahead, the Rose & Crown Pub winked with good cheer. Laughter and the clink of glasses flowed out on softening night air. Her senses prickled: thick toaster-burn of roasting coffee, broiled potatoes from the Greek restaurant, fish and nuts sizzling on the Mongolie Grill. The Green Dragon Chinese and Western loomed to her right. Somebody opened a door and dashed a tub of hot water into the alley where it splashed against the snow and hissed in a cloud of steam.

"My biiirth-day!"

She leaped two steps at a time and entered the Rose & Crown. A blast of air, warmed by sweat and kitchen, fogged her glasses. She took them off, and was struck with an immediate sense of relief. Here was a congregation of normal people, gathered cheerfully around a roasting hearth, people who had houses and spouses, who plotted their lives across well-chosen meridians.

"Bang! A-ha!" Og loomed in the doorway, casting a long, fire-lit shadow.

She turned toward a table set with jugs of brown beer, circled by laughing women nipping at chicken wings held like expensive French cigarettes.

"Excuse me," she said. "That man is chasing me."

The laughter flattened. Four glasses lifted to five pairs of lips. An angular blonde turned to a brunette and whispered something, while a tall henna redhead jiggled her watch. Two very young women, one pig-tailed, one barretted, pointed their noses at the ceiling like synchronized swimmers; the pig-tailed one o'd her mouth and released a faraway giggle.

Og was strolling now, hips absurdly loose.

"Hello, lasses."

The henna redhead made a pop with her lips and stroked a zigzag through the condensation on her glass. She yawned. "My boss is chasing me again."

Seri backed up, knocked over a stool, walked quickly toward the back of the bar. As soon as she rounded the bar she broke into a run, through an arched doorway, into a back room low-slung with smoke, a fireplace popping. A small group of men and women, all bespectacled, sat smoking a hookah at a high table, set with one tall bottle of absinthe. Their conversation lapsed.

"Excuse me." Seri locked eyes with a silver-haired man, a fox. She noticed how small his hands were, how delicate his fingers.

"There's a man behind me ..." she began.

They stared, unblinking, with an air of casual decadence, as if they had just been discussing deviant sexual practices and stock-trading tips with equal languor. The fox smiled and pointed a finger.

"That way," he said.

Seri rushed out the back, then cut north toward the river. A crash behind her, as Og leaped through a window. She looked back once. Og shook the absinthe bottle at her, then threw it.

She ran. The bottle sailed over her head and smashed on a minivan, spraying green.

Seri zigged left.

She stopped.

A high cubed hedge blocked her way, cut with spiked iron gates. Beyond, a clutch of towers, a statue of Jesus backlit with spectral green glow.

The old Catholic mission.

"Yeeee-ah!" Og must have been sucking unlimited draughts of energy from the moon, back in orbit and unzipping the clouds with furious white heat.

Seri accelerated. Squeezing every fibre, she aimed for the hedge, struck it full-bore. She crashed through, rolled over buzzcut grass still wet with snow.

She jumped to her feet and raced for the buildings. A squat parish office. A cathedral. A sandstone convent, turret speared with green-lit Jesus.

"Ack!" Og must have tangled himself in the hedge.

Seri tracked the cathedral, eyes wide. Entrance stuck in a stone tympanum. Statue of the Virgin in canopied niche. Bell tower scratching sky.

"Bee-auty!" Og called behind her.

She rushed between the stems of a builder's scaffold, saw cathedral doors, embossed with four creatures: winged lion, winged bull, eagle, angel. Prophets or something.

What now? Angel. Sky. Up.

Climb.

She leaped, grabbed the scaffold. Then monkeyed a diagonal brace and scrambled pipes to the top. She jumped to the roof, just about slipped on pitched wet shingles.

"Lasseee...." Og blistered through the scaffolding, then vanished around a corner.

Seri crept toward the tympanum. At the roof's end she took a deep breath, then jumped. Her toes hit the ledge. Her hands grabbed buttoned bricks.

"Bang! Hell-o-ho...." Og's voice fading.

Seri swung from a brick and landed on the tier over the tympanum. She jumped, flinging her arms around the Virgin's neck. Pulling hard, she scrambled up and came to rest astride the Virgin's head.

"Sorry, Mother."

She dragged her whole body onto the canopy and out of the light, then collapsed face down, sweating.

You have amazing conditioning, Rooke had told her earlier, in the mid-afternoon. And the resolve of a prophet.

Prophet?

Seri almost snapped a finger. She was hardly acting like a prophet here, running mindlessly. More like cowardly Jonah, who fled God's purpose and ended up in the belly of a whale. More like her father, who had preached many sermons on Jonah before his own breakdown, a quick irony she never forgot.

She slapped Mary's head. Whoops. Made a fist, whispered a quick prayer, immediately remembered the four prophets below. Yes, thanks for the signs and symbols, Lord. She understood: this was a test, a small crucible, a reminder that there were also strong, steadfast prophets: Samuel, Isaiah, Elijah. Who was the fourth?

Og shuffled below. Adding apology to prayer, Seri peeped over the canopy's lip. Was she an Elijah or a Jonah? A Samuel or—

Og had vanished. In a crooked shadow below, a circus midget in a top hat and red military jacket sniffed the air. When he kneeled to snuffle the pavement, his face lit with halogen light.

Not a midget. A boy.

"Okay, Lord," Seri whispered. "Not exactly sure what your will is here." Was this some fast-flowing contingency, or another sign?

The boy straightened his spine. From his jacket he drew a small jar of ice cubes and a knife. He rattled one cube from the jar and placed it on the ground, where he chopped it to powder with the knife. He then he gathered the powder in one palm and held it to the wind. It blew south, sparkling blue and green.

He laughed.

Then he stood and followed the airborne powder across the wet grass, tossing and catching the knife. Both boy and powder vanished into a ring of dark trees.

Seri kneeled, searched for Og. No sign.

She looked toward heaven, scanning the belltower's lines where they cut the night sky. The moon was still white-hot, blistering cloud-skins. Overcome with vertigo, she looked down at the neighbourhood, houses winking with secrets, dotted along the western hills and Bow River.

Well. One lost meeting with Rooke. One blown chance to follow God's purpose. She promised to do better.

She thought of the door's four-winged creatures, and suddenly remembered that they weren't prophets at all. Each symbolized one of the Bible's evangelists. But these creatures looked more like pagan gods than saints. She stared out at the ghostly green Jesus, then to the trees where the boy had made his exit.

This world, Rooke had said. It's not what you think.

"Yes it is," she corrected. "Yes it *is*."

Across the mission, from the ring of dark trees, she heard a chunk, like a knife slicing into wood. A magpie cackled, then strangled to silence.

CHAPTER TWELVE

SMALL ICE ON THE HAT

Frozen leaves scattered in the wind.

"This is where we're staying?" Lor said.

"Yessir, amigo-san."

"This is a *church*, Al."

Alistair reached to catch a leaf. "Lookit, it's free lodging."

Plus the bellboy wouldn't be messing with his head anymore. Lor assessed the building. Red-bricked, bell towered, stained-glass windows mincing rainbow.

"It's padlocked," he said.

"Yessir, been that way for prob'ly fifteen years, since before Franklin started living here, bringing his girls'n boys—"

"Franklin?"

"Yeah, 'migo. Like, this was Franklin's *hideout*."

"Holy shit."

Alistair laughed. "Yeah. Holy shit."

"Who owns it?"

Alistair shrugged. "Who knows? This little beauty has been abandoned for years, which be why we have to climb in through the window."

"Gives me the creeps."

"You want to return to the hotel, bud?"

"No."

"Well 'en, you gets what you gets, 'n my guess is you may get to like this place, has a certain *cachet*, y'know?"

"Lethbridge." Lor shook his head, while Alistair stomped off toward the church.

"Hey, 'migo," he called back. "Technically we're not in Lethbridge—not even North Lethbridge—till this little hamlet gets annexed next year."

"Hamlet?"

"We'll be long gone, Lor."

"Where the hell are we?"

Alistair stopped and turned around, ankle-deep in a whirlpool of leaves. "Spookleton," he said, and laughed.

"*Spookleton*? That's ridiculous."

"No shit. Suits us, doesn't it?"

† † †

The Spookleton Our Lady of Grace Church, abandoned, was more cracked and cobwebbed than the set for a grade three Halloween play. And the set designers seemed to have fled, leaving all their tools scattered on the floor.

An asthmatic stained-glass window wheezed crimson over Lor's head. "Al. What are all these books?"

"Don't know, Buckshot, haven't had a chance to look."

Lor removed a dusty, dimpled tome and opened the cover. It was part of a series of books, all lined neatly in an ornate hardwood bookcase.

"What's *theodicy*?"

"Special branch of theology, vindicating God's ways to man. But mostly, a personal definition here, the special theology dealing with God's silence."

"Silence?"

"Hell yeah. His unwillingness to connect with us, his sons and daughters."

Lor put the tome back on the shelf, eyeing an older and more tattered book at the case's end. He peeled it out by the spine. A small pouch tumbled after and plopped on the floor.

Lor stared. He replaced the book. It fell sideways.

"Looks like somebody hid some small treasure in the bookcase." Alistair leaned in, set the tattered book upright. It fell again. "Maybe some of Franklin's old drugs, if we're lucky, still magically preserved and—"

"I'm finished with that shit."

Alistair righted the book again. It fell. "Well, open the pouch, *dixie*, see what we got."

"I don't care." Lor picked up the pouch by the drawstrings and tossed it to Alistair, tried again to right the tattered book. Could not. "Al. Hand me something to prop up this old book, before it falls apart."

"What's the title, 'migo?"

Lor looked. "Something about some *other* Franklin Expedition, whatever that was."

"Dude, another sign!" Alistair clapped his hands, pouch spinning around one finger. "That's all 'bout the northward journey, dig? That's the analogue, the precedent, the fuckin' *Ur-text*. Here, prop th' tome with this. We'll finish the ritual."

He handed Lor the tiny, empty, wooden box. Lor stared.

"Lor, dudette, the *space* 'migo, remember?"

"You want to part with that? I thought it was your symbolic—"

"It's a perfect fit."

Lor took the box, wedged it tight beside the old book.

Alistair grinned, nodded. Then he stilled the pouch still swinging on his finger, opened the strings. "Well, nothing in here, like, drug-wise. Just some kind of sparkle-ass blue powder."

Lor's hand fell from the bookcase. His heart knocked an extra beat. His toes tingled, his vision hollowed.

"Here." Alistair closed the pouch and threw it back.

Lor caught it. His fingers twitched; his arm hairs rippled all the way to his shoulder. He shuddered and stared, then spilled a bit of powder into his palm. It was pure granulated colour, sea-blue salted with deep emerald, exactly like the spilled grains in the Underwood museum.

Alistair squinted. "Very Neptunian."

"It's nothing, nothing," Lor blurted. "Just junk." He sifted the dust. He tubed his hand and carefully poured it back in the bag, then slipped the bag into his shirt pocket. For no good reason, he felt like punching Alistair in the teeth, then sprinting into the night.

† † †

Somewhere, a phone rang.

"Why do people go to church?" Alistair said. "Church is all about the visuals and the music, dig? Hymns, holy attire, icons, stained glass: crimson tide, deacon blues, light and sound—"

Lor crouched in the corner, stewing, tapping his pocket. His nerves were suddenly zippered, teethed, and rusty. Something jangled.

"Jesus, Al. Isn't that a *phone*?"

"Fucking-A."

"In *here*? Like an old phone on the wall, with a dial?"

Alistair shrugged.

Lor felt like he could almost taste the light, stained-glass windows pressing sunshine, squeezing the visible spectrum until the essential oils of colour beaded on his tongue. "Al. You going to get that phone?"

"The hell for?"

"Maybe it's Dawn Cherry."

"Exactly."

"Did you two ever...?"

Alistair developed a twitch in his eye. He reached up to tug his eyebrow. "So, you kept that li'l bag of Franklin's, didja, punchinello?"

"No. I threw it away." Lor reached into his pocket to make sure the drawstring pouch was still there. He turned to face the wall, pulled out the pouch. A bit of glimmering dust smoked out.

The phone continued to ring. Alistair stomped out, found the payphone behind a rotting nativity set.

"Hello," he said, after thirty rings. Muffled jabbering on the line's other end.

"Ahhh." He smiled. "If it isn't our own lady of grace."

† † †

Alistair couldn't stop smiling after he hung up. "Dawn Cherry got us a gig, so's we can tighten up 'n maybe even get that Rusty some basic chops before we leave you and march up into the White."

"Gig?"

"Gig."

"Where?" Lor felt his gut twist.

"'Member the old Carpenters' and Joiners' Union Hall in Galt Gardens?"

"How could I forget?"

"We're back."

"When?"

Alistair grinned. "Christmas Eve."

Lor frowned. "Cabaret?"

"Fucking-A."

"Fucking-A indeed. Alberta Blues."

Alistair frowned. "I sense a bit of sarcasm there on your part, buckster, a smitch of bitterness, makes me wonder: is there a problem here, 'sides your determination to get your old friends out of town?"

Lor grimaced.

Alistair shrugged. "All a sudden you seem kind of distant, *monsignor*, kind of cold, schizophrenogenic, mean, a complete one-eighty, dig? What you do, take an ugly pill?"

Lor hunched on a dusty, rolled-up carpet. He patted the pocketed pouch. "You know the problem."

"Fuck, come on, *crapehanger*, that was ten years ago. It's not even quite the same building any more."

"He lost it, man. Right on stage."

"Yeah, sure, he went batshit, so what?—nobody's seen the fucker since. And, like, when did *you* get all superstitious?"

Lor jumped up, discharging a cloud of dust.

"I'm kidding, okay?" Alistair stepped backward. "Criminy, take an Ativan."

Lor glared. "We'll be up there. *Again.* With his kid brother. That doesn't freak you out at all?"

"Sure, dude, but we need the practice. It's not like history's going to repeat itself."

"Why Christmas?"

"Just pretend it's the Pagan version." Alistair smiled. "You probably won't have to pretend."

The phone rang again.

Lor jumped.

† † †

As soon as they rode the bus out of Spookleton and back into Lethbridge, Lor began to smell glass. Bus windows. The bus was full of plump kids in striped T-shirts, most of them white, slapping the wheels of their skateboards, swinging earbuds, munching ripple chips, burping obscenities.

"Do we have to go back into town?" he said, rubbing sore sinuses.

"Yeah, *pookie*, how do you propose we do a gig without instruments? You smash the fuck out of your guitars—don't give me that look—'n god even knows whether anyone's got any sort of gear, so's, like—"

"This is going to end up a punk thing, isn't it?"

"So?"

"I've given it up, man. And why are we going to the Kresge's?"

Alistair laughed before Lor even finished the sentence.

"Well, 'migo, this is entertaining, 'cos Kresge's is the only place in this town that sells instruments. Used to be a proper music store over on Whoop-Up Drive, but some overzealous CSIS agent closed it down, rumour tells—so now you not only can but basically have to chow a greasy breakfast, get your guitar, pick up some third-rate oscillating fan made in China in the sixties, and get your bag of year-old pink Lucky Elephant Popcorn all under the same fucking leaky-ass roof." He grinned. "It's called capitalism."

The bus rattled. Lor's head thrummed. One of the juicy kids stared, bobbing in headphones, shaking a mittful of coloured chalk. Over the kid's head, a sign for Canadian Airlines: two flights north daily—Edmonton, Yellowknife, Norman Wells, Inuvik....

Lor turned to stare out the window.

"Al."

"Yeah?"

"Isn't that Galt Gardens out there?"

"Yeah."

"Where's the Carpenters' Union Hall?"

"Can't see it, *granger*, 'cos it's hidden somewhere in all that foliage. The place is treed up the hooey, ain't it?"

The park was studded with cottonwoods and tacamahacs, still green and leafy, crackled with frost.

"What's with the ice?" Lor said.

"Fuck'd, man. A cold fusion of winter and summer. 'Slike the place follows a different climatic logic, devised somewhere in its own leaf-curtained heart."

Some of the branches were still flexed with icicles, dripping to misty roots and underbrush.

"Man, that place is creepy," Lor said.

Al grinned and nodded, hat bobbing. "Lethbridge's Mirkwood."

Under the Canadian Airlines sign the kid nodded and rattled bits of chalk. But whether he was eavesdropping or keeping time with his own music would have been anybody's guess.

Right now neither Lor nor Alistair was guessing, drawn as they were by the dark pulse of the trees, steaming chill just beyond the fragrant, rattling bus windows.

† † †

In Kresge's, with the creaking floor and the permanent smell of—what was that, *popcorn*?—they saw the freak, the kind that zaps norms like a bug trap cracking flies. He had long greasy hair, beard rooted to oversized pores, a Toronto Blue Jays baseball hat decked with curly pink ribbons. Tight jeans with strands peeling over eggy hip bones, fly unzipped, cuffs dangling threads. He was being railed at by a white man in a bow tie.

The bow-tied man stopped, turned his gaze to the band, then beyond.

"Hey!" he said. "Thought I told you two shavetails to stay out of my store."

Lor followed the man's gaze down the aisle, where two punks rattled Smarties boxes. One had a crackle-red Mohawk, the other a sapphire porcupine and "Smash the State" T-shirt.

"A pox on you, Mr. Shemp," said the Mohawk, with surprising articulation. He spilled his Smarties on the floor and stomped them, then knocked over a stand of Tupperware.

"That's it." Shemp, clearly the manager, waggled a finger at the freak, then strode away. "I'll call the police. And you boys—" He squinted at Lor, over his shoulder. "Don't touch any instruments."

"Boys?" Lor said.

The porcupine gave Shemp the finger, then sauntered for the door with friend in tow. Lor gazed after them, suddenly sad. They were younger incarnations of himself, going nowhere, on a collision-course with thirty and breakdown. And for what? For a poverty of ideas: resist everything, believe nothing, smash, smash, smash. There was nothing rational about it. Who was the Man anyway? Shemp? Fuck. Shemp was a self-important twit with a vanilla wife, maybe a small chip on his shoulder. The Man was nothing. The Man was a ghost.

"Lor," said Alistair. "Come on, dude, our friends have arrived. We got some shopping to do here."

They browsed the guitars, which were, in Fatty's words, supreme pieces of shit.

Alistair tapped his foot. "Well, like, what do you propose we do, Fat-ster? Make some instruments out of balsa wood and Silly String?"

"Why don't we make 'em out of my nuts?" said Fatty.

"Too small, amigette."

"Least I got one."

Rusty, who hadn't said a word so far, suddenly yelped. The freak had snuck up behind him and pinched his ass.

Close up the freak was a delicious sight—fluorescent blue scarf around each ankle, white stilleto heels, too high for comfort, too tight, pink skin bulging at the straps. In one hand, a twisty poplar branch, ragged at the end, probably chewed off, possibly by the freak himself. He moved in close to Lor, pointing with the stick, one eye closed tight.

"You have it," he whispered. His breath was musty, not unpleasant. A bit like grandmother's attic, hinting at cobwebs, weird old-world boardgames, bright marbles.

Lor crossed his fingers in his pockets. "Have what?"

"Do not give it to *him*."

"Who?"

"Are ye all from the island?" the freak said, louder.

Alistair, suddenly grinning, stepped forward. "No, but we're on our way to an island, Methuselah, name of—"

"The House of Fog," the freak said, shaking the stick. "Where the demon dwells." His eyes liquified. "Though his spirit wanders, I am told."

Alistair laughed. "Are you crazy?"

"Ha! By your graces, if 'twer only true. Nay, I have my own reunion on the island. I am under the spell of the slotted spoon, and crave your misgivings."

"Well, you got 'em," Alistair said. "Are you sure you're not mad, grandfather?"

The freak opened his eye. It was creamy blue, without a pupil. "The soul of the world is itself mad. The question, then, is superfluous."

Alistair chuckled. "You are a delight, old man."

The freak turned to fix his gaze on Lor. He pointed the stick at Alistair. "This one loves chaos." He pointed the stick at Fatty. "This one searches for a song."

He pointed the stick at Lor. "And you...."

"Well," Alistair interrupted. "I'm sure you have some kind of fuck'd-up wisdom there, dude, but we're going to the House of Fog, hell or high water."

"Do not expect me to endorse your mystagogic apperceptions."

"Wouldn't dream of it, greybeard."

They moved off to check other gear. Lor stayed behind, momentarily root-ed to the floorboards. The freak leaned in close, jiggling the poplar wand.

"You have the scent of blue dust upon you." His breath was alarmingly cold. "He wants it dearly, every single grain. You must flee him."

Lor tried not to laugh. "The demon?"

"Nay, fool, the accursed one. The chaser and thief. The thrower of knives."

"I don't know any—"

"Flee north. Creep in stealth, lose yourself. Do not stay overlong in one place."

Lor sniffed.

"I will build a snowman, as a warding charm against him. He will not pass. I will help you hide."

"Thanks, no," Lor said.

"A snowman, do you hear?" The freak moved even closer. His knuckles whitened on the stick. "Do you fathom my counsel? The dust is a great power. He needs it to dash the fires of hate, to restore the bonds of love."

Lor stepped back. "All right, grandpa. How about I just burn it?"

The freak's knuckles cracked around the stick. "Rattlepate. Fool. It can never be destroyed, only scattered, dispersed, transferred, endlessly given away, freely or not. The demon himself cannot be made whole again."

Lor took another step back. "O-kay. All-righty."

"Hey!" Shemp, creaking along floorboards, wielding a pen. "I told you to leave the premises."

The freak closed his corroded eye. "And watch for *flies!*"

He clattered away in those wobbly pumps, wand dowsing for trouble, and disappeared behind a high stack of Lucky Elephant Popcorn and Buttercrunch.

The manager squinted after him. Then jumped and hollered. The freak had doubled back to poke that stick at Shemp's tightly clenched bottom.

"Woo!" Fatty's marble eyes popped from their lids. "Yeah!"

The freak giggled shrilly and galloped down the aisles, heels clicking like satyr hooves.

"That's it," Shemp said through clenched teeth, pulling out a phone. "We're phoning the police."

"Fuck tha po-leeese." Alistair seized the phone from Shemp's hand, then grabbed a red Ibanez Destroyer by the neck.

"Hey!" Shemp cried. "Hands off the guitar. No merchandise is to be—"

Too late.

Alistair lobbed the phone into the air, swung back the Ibanez, and thwacked a fly ball. The phone flew up and chopped into a ceiling fan, which tore free and tumbled in a plastic cascade.

"Wo." Fatty was already at the food bar, glass eyes wide. In seconds he was tossing gobs of porridge and poultry at another ceiling fan, till it rained chopped oats and chicken.

"Stop." Lor held up his hands.

Shemp flushed, quaking.

"Stop," Lor said.

Alistair shrugged and signalled Fatty with the Ibanez. Fatty wound up and threw his best chicken-leg slider, which Alistair read perfectly and smacked foul into the bra section. The guitar twanged with glee.

"Stop?" Lor said, spattered with gravy.

"I'm calling the police from my office." Shemp's voice quivering.

Alistair whistled for another pitch. But Fatty was at work on bottles of Pepsi, which he was shaking violently and spraying in sizzling arcs at a rack of old Harris Tweeds. Meanwhile, the stunned Rusty munched a fan-chewed drumstick, head tilted, shoulders drooping.

"Burger Frisbees," Fatty called.

One splatted Rusty in the cheek. He didn't blink.

Soon the walls and ceiling were spackled with grease. Wobbly prisms of flying red Jell-O. *Pock pock pock* of the guitar hitting chicken, punctuated by the odd grotesque chord or wang bar dive. Then a siren, red lights.

"Shit," Lor said. "Time to fly."

"One more," Alistair said, holding up an honest-to-goodness Celtic harp and pointing at the Jell-O. Fatty wound up and delivered a perfect strike, which diced itself through the strings and into oblivion.

Fatty stared in wonder. "Wo. Greasy gunk explosion."

"Run," Alistair said, hanging the harp gently on the arm of a mannequin. "The Man has arrived."

Lor felt sick to his stomach. There was no Man. How could Alistair persist in these delusions?

"C'mon, dude!" Alistair grabbed him by the shirt. "Less you want to go to the hooskow."

Lor ran. There was no angry wonder any more. There was no Man. Only ageing fools, rattling life's tamborine, smashing hope season after season.

† † †

"Where are we?" Lor said, breath scouring his bronchi.

"Trust me, 'migo. Run."

They hustled up a flight of steps to a heavy door, Alistair leading with long legs. He flung open the door, to sunshine and a whirl of leaves. He stomped out onto a balcony, held out his arms, reached to stay his hat against the wind.

Lor, directly behind, saw a catwalk stretching from the balcony across an alley to the Shanghai Restaurant. The catwalk was suspended, cable-stayed to a single tower, narrow, latticed, without rails.

"Shit." Alistair let his arms drop. "The fucking thing is metal-fatigued to the nuts, bro'. Take a look."

Lor looked. The catwalk was fissured and deformed, webbed with cracks all along the girders.

"Meaning?" Lor said.

"Meaning, 'migos, we have aggravated crack-growth, perpendic'lar to stresses, heading for brittle fracture."

"Least we got one," said Fatty.

Alistair turned to face them. Squinted. "Rusty, you first. Then the rest of you."

Lor frowned. "What—?"

"Now!" Alistair said, pointing across.

Rusty squeezed by and teetered across the catwalk, followed by Fatty, whistling a tune. Then Lor. He tripped just before midspan, and for a second was bent over far enough to spy each bit of garbage in the alley below—popsicle wrappers, Fudgsicle sticks, Slurpee cups.

He heard a soft thud.

"Move," Alistair said behind him. "I can hear the Man's hobnailed boots on the stairs."

Lor shimmied past the tower, then stopped.

"Shit!"

"Move," Alistair said.

Lor smacked his shirt pocket. Turned.

"Al, I dropped my bag of dust."

"Say *what*?"

Lor pointed.

"I thought you ... w'fuck it."

"Fuck you. Step aside. It's on the bridge behind you."

Alistair turned, shook his head. "Christ," he whispered, then spun to face Lor again. "Run. *I'll* get it."

In an instant Alistair was back across midspan, snatching the bag. Lor scrambled to the far side, then swivelled to watch. Alistair turned again.

"Got it," he said.

Almost had time to grin.

The girders abruptly snapped and twisted, as the catwalk buckled beneath his feet. The balcony screeched. The midspan fell away. Alistair reached up and knotted his fingers through the lattice, then plunged downward with the remaining metal, trailing blue powder from one fist.

"My bag." Lor couldn't believe he was saying it.

Alistair kicked back his legs. On the upswing, just as he released the bag, his hat blew off. Both bag and hat twirled against the sky. Then the bag hit Lor in the stomach, a perfect pitch.

The door across the alley cracked open, and Shemp popped through holding the Jell-O'd harp, followed by an enormous cop. Shemp's fly was open, sprouting bits of red underwear.

For a moment, everyone was spellbound by the spinning grey hat, riding the wind to briefly eclipse the sun. The hat sucked in a batch of leaves, then coughed them out and plunged like an angry kite.

Lor stared from the Shanghai side, mouth open, bag clenched. The cop drew his gun and pointed it at the hat.

"Constable Ratzass!" Shemp blocked the gun with the harp.

"Fly!" Alistair cried, hanging helplessly.

Lor and Rusty were mute.

"Wo." Fatty whispered.

The hat nosedived.

It splashed down in a pond of garbage and began to tumbleweed, sticky with junk—wrappers, sticks, Slurpee cups.

"Small ice on the hat," said Fatty.

"Fly!" Alistair dangled. His voice ricocheted.

They stared—at the swinging scarecrow, the monstrous cop, the rolling hat. Shemp shook the harp. It whispered a few notes in the wind and seemed to drive the cop back to his senses. He pointed the gun away from the hat and across the alley.

"Fly!" Alistair cried. "Fly, you fucking fools!"

The spell broke.

They flew.

PART FOUR

CONCERTO
DRUGGO

Tobacco is a product that does a lot of damage.
Marijuana is infinitely worse.
—Former Prime Minister Stephen Harper, 2015

CHAPTER THIRTEEN

DON'T FORGET

THE REVIVING GOD

"Sorry I missed our meeting at the Ship & Anchor." Rooke's car clumped over the Highwood River bridge, somewhere south of Calgary.

"You did?" Seri said.

"I had thinking to do."

Seri tugged her seatbelt. "I did a little soul-searching myself. Ever hear of a boy in a top hat and red military jacket?"

"Never."

They passed a poplar shattered by lightning. "Ted. Where we going?"

He didn't answer. When they reached Okotoks, the whole town seemed to be celebrating the chinook winds and the passing of snow. A garden wedding at the top of a still-green hill, shading down to a pumpkin patch. Kids fishing from a tree. Well-groomed families on the way to midweek Bible study.

"You'd think it was already spring," Rooke muttered.

"I like it," Seri said. "My birthday is in spring."

Rooke grimaced.

"Everything seems in order here," Seri continued.

"You sound like an eighteenth-century sermon."

"Ted?"

"They tended to depict God as an all powerful watchmaker."

"Nice."

Rooke frowned. "The clockwork universe is wish-fulfilling mind-rot."
"It isn't."
Rooke began to tap. "Think of what we give up in such a universe."
"Think of what we *gain*. The assurance that we can be renewed—"
"Be quiet." Rooke's knuckles whitened on the wheel.
Fine. Seri bit her lip.
Rooke released his fingers. "A few weeks ago," he said, "I set up a sting for subversives, on the web."
"Good."
"A fake advertisement for an Arctic music festival, tailored to attract punks and druggies." He tapped. "Blasting gross commercialism and lazy suburban ennui, to appeal to their mistaken sense of hope, and meaning. A web: I was the spider."
"Spider." Seri nodded. "What do you mean, *was*?"
Rooke sighed.
"So have you caught anyone yet?" Seri said.
The car slowed, rolled to a stop on the train tracks.
"So you have no taste for chaos?" Rooke said. "None whatsoever?"
Warning bells began to clang. A train hooted in the distance.
Seri gripped her seat belt. "Ted. Where are we going?"

† † †

"Yesterday I was chased by a punk. A druggy." She could play Rooke's game. The car sped, but in what direction she wasn't sure. "He was on speed, dangerous, completely, uh—" she searched for the word. "Completely wired."
But instead of jumping all over it, Rooke sighed again. His shoulders slumped.
"Ted, don't you care? I'm telling you, this guy was—"
"I'm calling it off."
"What?"
"It's over."
"What's over?"
He brushed the dash, as if it were dusty. "You were right. We have no mandate, no theatre of operations."
"I didn't say *that*. We'll find out."
"I am not in communication with any authority."
Well, that was nonsense. Seri would find out, and soon. Why were they so aimlessly driving the countryside?
"Ted. If you had seen this freak, I'm telling you."

Rooke offered a dismissive wave.

"And he was with this kid who threw knives, I think they were together. Og was probably giving him drugs too, because—"

Rooke's teeth clacked. "Who?"

Seri tapped the glovebox, wondered if there was a map inside. "The kid, because—"

"Not the kid."

"Og?"

"What did he look like?"

Seri pulled her seat belt, let it zip back. "Tall, shaved head, lots of skin sores, skeleton face. A cross tattooed on his neck."

Rooke slapped the dash. "Oggleston!"

"No, just Og. Ted, watch the road."

He turned his head. "He couldn't possibly still be alive. Are you certain?"

"Is he a friend of yours? Family?"

"Family?" Rooke began to tug his goatee, then muttered, "If he's alive, the others, too, maybe, home, south...."

Seri saw the rage, and her opening. "See. There is work to do. Identify these punks for me and we can prioritize a list of destinations. South where?" She opened the glovebox, hunted for a pen.

"No." Rooke's shoulders dropped. "We're finished, Serendipity."

"Stop thinking out loud, and brainstorm with me. South where?" But Seri could already feel it slipping away. The car slowed. Another set of tracks.

Then it was clear, God's plan for her, part of it anyway. She was sent to do a prophet's work here: to remind Rooke of his job, to supply his fire, to keep him on the straight and narrow. Of course: to keep him from running. She was Aaron to his doubting Moses.

"Ted, *listen*." But she could not remember an example of steadfastness from her own life. The more she dug, the more vacancy she unearthed. Surely there was a perfect story somewhere, a principle, a parable. Well, memory was fickle. There would be a good example in the Bible, in history, in the lives of the saints, topics she could always remember.

She exhaled, slowly. "Ted. Stop for a drink?"

"Pick your poison."

The car slowed. The train hooted, already far behind.

† † †

They stopped for tea at McCunney's in Nanton Springs, where Rooke gazed at her through a haze of Earl Grey steam.

"This is our last meeting," he said grimly.

"No." Seri bit toast and looked for jam. "Our *first*. Look, Ted. I can tell you're disenchanted. Of course I don't know the details, but I know you've lost your fire."

"Oh?"

"I imagine you feel paralyzed, or like nothing you do matters particularly. I know you feel like running away."

"Oh?"

She considered her purpose, the best way to quicken God's plan. "What you need to do is look for one true thing."

"Could you be a little vaguer?" Rooke fanned steam.

"One true thing, to hold you steadfast. One bedrock you cannot deny."

He roared a laugh, then bent backward so his spine cracked on the chair's back.

Seri flushed. "Fine." She was surprised to find herself angry.

"No, no." Rooke sniffed, composed himself. "Do go on. My apologies."

She glared.

"Seriously." Rooke sipped tea. "I'm interested. I forget. I need reminding."

She looked at deep thumbprints in her toast. "Everyone has a dark night of the soul."

"Mhm."

"So you find one true thing," she continued. "A belief, a purpose, an emotion."

"What is the most powerful emotion?"

"Love."

He smiled, foxily. Some kind of facial semaphore, coded warning: *you are someone I can disenchant.*

Seri ignored him. Steadfast, now. "Do you love Western history?"

"The Nazis had their hatred." Rooke was already moves ahead in this chess game. "And the old, dark consolations of Teutonic mythology. Two true things."

Seri paused to think.

"Ragnarök," Rooke reminded. "Heinrich Himmler."

She switched gears. "Read philosophy?"

"Me or Himmler?"

She ignored him. Here she was on firm footing, especially with the Moderns. "Descartes had his doubt. He could not deny one certainty: that there was a doubter in the universe."

"Inspiring. Makes one want to go out and do some good in this world."

"Well, we can never understand how everything is connected. That's God's business, ours is faith."

"Yes, connected." Rooke sipped, frowned as if his tea were cold. "Connected to sensual pleasures, to family, to revenge."

"Obviously you don't want to go *that* route."

"Yes." Rooke smiled. "Obviously."

Seri plodded on. "Anyway, if nothing else, Hume had his skepticism."

"As you have yours."

"No." She massaged toast crumbs in the saucer. "That's not *my* bedrock."

"God?"

Seri looked out the teashop window, at the chinook arch smudging the west horizon. This prophet's work was tricky and subtle business. Perhaps the saints?

"Augustine is a fine example," she said.

"Yes. Of what?"

She leaned into it. Augustine was one of her favourites. "Even in confusion, even in great doubt, he remained steadfast. He never lost his will, or his certainty. Augustine had his faith."

Rooke fixed her with that piercing stare. "And Aquinas his hatred of women."

She nipped toast, three quick bites. "Of course there's always a shadow side, that's what gives life its depth."

"Of course, Seri." Rooke cracked a knuckle. "Of course."

"You told me yourself, hatred can be one true thing." She immediately regretted saying it.

He smiled, almost kindly. "You do remind one. Do I need to keep you? Go on."

Time to try God's very word. "Do you read the Bible?"

"Backward and forward. Some good stories."

"Yes." She warmed. "Think of some. Job, who never cursed God, despite Satan's games. Abraham, who was willing to sacrifice his own son at God's command, and never questioned why. Jacob, who wrestled the dark angel till dawn."

Rooke beamed.

"What?" Seri spread jam with a finger.

"You wrestle him yourself."

"No. Not." She stroked the dimple in her cheek. "Exactly." What had she been saying? Oh, right. "King David, who sinned, but did not succumb to easy guilt, or break his covenant with God. All the prophets, the ones who didn't run away."

"Don't forget the reviving god himself."

"Who?"

"Seri. Come now."

"Oh." She nipped toast. "Jesus. Well, some comparisons are a little—"

"You make a great Sunday school teacher."

She felt the flush at her ears. "It's called faith. Do you think I'm less worldly than you?" The words tumbled downhill. "These sound like naïve pronouncements, naïve and tawdry, and they are, in one way they are, but they are no less true for that, as anyone who has had direct experience of grief, and loss, and ennui and existential crisis—"

"Enough." Rooke squinted. He watched her, but seemed to speak to himself. "Our reminders do sometimes come in most unexpected ways, don't they? Perhaps you are my unexpected visitor. Like Lot's three guests? Lot, as in Abraham's nephew, as in Sodom and Gomorrah? I like your word. *Ennui.*"

Seri began to blank.

"Here." Rooke smiled. "I'll continue for you. How about Satan in *Paradise Lost*? Who vowed to make a Heav'n of Hell, who constructed himself entirely of hatred, who nursed that hatred like white fire in his heart, and so made himself whole, gave himself a purpose."

Slipping fast.

He continued. "Satan, your ultimate existential man."

Faster.

"Perhaps you'll light the white fire in my own heart, Serendipity?"

Suddenly Seri couldn't help but think of Rooke as a falling angel, already on fire.

"Look," she blurted. "They may still be alive, still out there." This was risky, but Rooke was going to call checkmate soon. "Og's companions, or brothers, or whatever."

"All dead." Rooke's mood lightened and darkened at once.

"Og wasn't dead. They're punks right?" She pressed. "Worse than Og himself?"

"All dead. One way or another."

"But what if they're alive?" She unrolled her fingers, palms up. She didn't even know who *they* were.

"Yes. Do your best." Rooke's voice was bitter as strong black tea, fingers milk-white on the teacup. "Unexpected visitor."

She paused. Don't do it, Seri. Something unhealthy here—less well-lit mandate, more Pandora's box. Not worth it, don't do it.

She did.

She took a breath. "Where did they live? That's where we'll begin."

He shoved back his chair, stood, glared. Whirling quickly enough to spin the back of his coat, he strode toward the rear of the teashop, creaking the tile. He did not look back. The washroom, Seri thought, he's gone to the washroom. She heard a door slam, felt a rush of cooling wind.

Minutes passed, and he did not return.

She drank more tea. She spread more jam. It stained so red.

"Lethbridge," he whispered in her ear.

She jumped. She spun. "Where'd *you* come from?"

"They lived in Lethbridge. All of them. When they were alive."

His lips perked at the corners. But it was hardly a smile.

CHAPTER FOURTEEN

tHe TiP OF A dROWNED WiTCh

Lor scampered down alleys as cloud-shadows roared across the cracked and pitted urban landscape. Somewhere God's Q-tip factory had exploded. Cottonwoods were in mad unseasonal bloom— down his lungs, up his nose, in his eyes. He didn't stop running until he reached the northside Safeway, where he stumbled in to buy a devil's food cake, then stumbled out and wolfed the entire thing on the walk.

He stomped down Whoop-Up Drive, further north, face grimed with icing. Everything was screwed now—Alistair in jail, those two kids scattered, and what was Fatty's number anyway? Lor kicked a rock. All for a bag of *powder*?

Everything was slipping back to chaos, out of concert. All the shit was getting dragged into shadows, where he couldn't kick it any more. He couldn't see the edges, the details. He was losing the names, the sites, the *map* for God's sake.

Where was he?

Back in Spookleton.

His headache was gone, but his palm throbbed with four cuts the shape of ill-trimmed nails.

†††

Back in the church, the first thing Lor did was kick Alistair's map tube down the stairs. Then he seized the abandoned drill and pierced the wall in a dozen places, widening the holes with a punch and the hammer, finally throwing the punch away and just hammering gashes into the plaster. Picking up the upright vacuum, he aimed for a stained-glass window. Light sliced his eyeballs and burst into prisms.

He stopped, vacuum held high, biceps quivering.

What the fuck was he doing? Acting out the mulish delusions of a punk hangover, clamping creation to destruction yet again. What profound bullshit.

He fled the church into an afternoon awash with autumn smells. Leaf decay, crab apples squashed and gone to wine, river steaming to winter sleep. He collapsed high atop a coulee, beside a rotting cactus, under the cooling sun. There he sat, while crows patrolled a nearby stand of tacamahac.

I have to stop smashing stuff, he thought.

Down in the river, something grey and pointy floated by. The tip of a drowned witch.

Lor stood, leaned forward, squinted.

"Holy *shit*."

It was Alistair's hat.

† † †

A full chinook finally seeped over the Rocky Mountains and nudged the thermometer up ten degrees. Old-Time Chinook, said the Spookleton greybeards, not hot and dry, but warm and smooth. The kids came out in droves to greet it, riding bikes and go-carts. Bug-eyed boys and goggled girls, chanting, singing, armed with sticks. Over there—some crewcut redhead dragging a cow's skull through the weeds. Over there—twins riding a wolfhound, whistling strange melodies, trailing barbecue perfume through strange avenues.

A quickening. Lor felt it.

I'm going to remake my black guitar, he thought suddenly. Fix it.

He sat on the coulee till the sun was overturned by chattering stars, then rose, dusted his pants, and headed back. Cotton swept the sidewalk. He sneezed, and noticed chalkmarks on the road. Hopscotch lines in black and blue, childish spells against the coming winter.

† † †

Frontenac the violin-maker had his own gruff charms. His shop, tucked in a tight curve on Spookleton Road, reeked of resin and sausage. Frontenac himself dispensed measured doses of garlic from his mouth and pores, so fat he looked like he had been injected into his skin with a silicon gun.

Lor liked him immediately.

"Do you sell woodworking tools?" Lor asked, out for an afternoon wander.

Frontenac laughed. "No. Yes. Of course. For whom?"

"Does it matter?"

"We have no tools. Beat it."

"For me."

"In that case. Hmmph. Perhaps."

"Do you sell instruments?"

"No!"

"Whose violins are these?"

"All mine. My wife's. My brother-in-law's. Go home."

It took Lor two days of gentle prodding before he could get a decent answer. Frontenac did sell instruments, and tools, depending on who was asking, the time of day, the week. Something to do with a creepy CSIS agent who shut down music stores.

"How can an agent do that?" Lor said.

Frontenac shrugged, whistled between his teeth. "I have to eat supper now. Beat it."

On the third day Lor scraped together all his pennies and a few crumpled bills. After searching carefully over Frontenac's shelves, he scooped some pellets of hot hide glue, an old-fashioned glue pot, spaghetti tubes, and a violin-maker's knife.

"How does the knife work?" he said.

Frontenac rubbed his belly with a ham-hand. "The blade will shorten after sharpening. The handle is made of wood, see? Cut the wood away to get more blade."

"Interesting."

"Cut the knife so the knife can cut."

"Yeah. How much for the lot?"

"How much do you have?"

Lor spread his shekels on the counter-top and made a quick calculation.

"Twenty-one fifty," he said.

Frontenac rang up an ancient cash register and ripped off the reciept. "Twenty-one fifty. Go home."

††††

When Lor opened the guitar case, he despaired. The thing was trashed beyond hope. The neck was broken at the heel and split at the peghead. Some of the frets were twisted, others had fallen out. The body was chipped and cracked in many places, the pickguard cracked in half, exposing wiry shreds.

Start with the neck, he guessed.

He heated up the hide glue and checked over the peghead. Diagonal grain, too short, shitty workmanship. He worked in the hot glue and clamped, then fell into despair again. He wandered out to spend the rest of the day high above the river, close to the edge of the coulee, daydreaming of hats.

The next morning he checked the peghead, and, finding it solid, felt better. He used the violin knife to trim the dried glue, then set to work on the heel. It was cracked, but the main damage was at the bolt-holes where the bolts had ripped out of the body. He glued the cracks, clamped, and drilled larger holes for larger bolts.

No way this was going to work. How would he get the right neck angle? This thing was going to be a mutant.

He unkinked and smiled. A *mutant*. Hell yeah, why not? He guessed at the neck angle, set the action high, adjusted the truss rod as far as it would go in reverse bow. Then put all the springs in at the bridge, so the string tension would be cranked. Easy.

The frets were another problem. First he took a pair of cutting pliers and ground them flat, then tried to rip out the frets. They held, rooted to the neck's brittle ebony fingerboard. The pliers slipped. He gashed himself.

So he took a pair of long wrenches and sawed them in half, busting the saw blade. He ground the ends of the broken wrenches to make two chisels, then inserted them on either side of the frets and punched. The frets popped out like toast.

He smiled. Imagine breaking tools in order to fix something.

Inspiration hit him. Why re-fret the thing at all? He'd leave the mutant fretless, like a violin, invite those whiny smears and microtones. Hell, why not? He used the violin knife to chip out the inlays all along the fingerboard, until there were no markings at all.

Screw the *map*.

Sensing a pattern, he filled in the large body fractures with chunks of plywood and wood-dust mixed with glue. No sense trying to make anything match. No sense trying to preserve the tone. The smaller chips he filled with a mixture of glue and shredded sermon, tightly packed.

He turned his attention to the wiring. He insulated the leads with the spaghetti tubing and crimped everything, then grounded the strings by running a wire from the tailpiece to what he guessed was a suitable ground-point.

By this time he was tired of the whole process. But the mutant guitar was whispering, demanding a certain tone. So Lor rewound the pickups, a tedious task. Finally he glued the pickguard back together, screwed it on, and re-strung. He stepped back to admire.

The black guitar, the wise but capricious one, was now a reclamation project. My God, he thought, it's a Frankenstein. But how interesting that a thing could be remade to outwit its original destination. And how interesting that it still carried all the old cracks inside, almost like a skeleton. That, for some reason, just felt cool. Lor laughed from the belly, and the unfamiliarity of that made him laugh even louder. In the space of three days he had gone from smasher to fixer.

But something was still missing.

† † †

In the middle of the night the guitar fell over and hit a strange chord. Lor awoke in a nest of cushions, wondering what the mutant was trying to tell him. He got up, dressed, hoisted himself out the window, and stumbled into darkness.

The coulees were brindled with light and dark. The river carried the sky's reflections north. Lor sat. Light, but no inspiration.

On the way back he heard two magpies screaming from deep inside a gnarled poplar. In the middle of the street, in a puddle of light and blood, a third—dead, on its back, feet twitching.

Magpies, he thought, remembering the bellboy. One for sorrow, two for mirth, but what was three for?—*death*? He shuddered. High above, a pale sickle moon pressed against still-blue sky, waning out of season. Floating cotton settled in his hair. Then he heard music, and sat on the street.

This was a new experience. Music in his head, blaring right out his ears. Cotton swimming night air, glittering, green and blue.

He leaped up, pictures meshing with music. Of course—green and blue glitter. That's what that damn guitar needed, green and blue, highlights to the black.

He ran back to the church. He set the mutant against the wall and painted a thin sheen of glue over the body, then pinched a bit of iridescent powder from its pouch. He threw. The powder hit the guitar and stuck in whorls.

He fired again, spinning to his head's music. The dust spattered and sparked. The guitar danced into three dimensions. He pitched until he was out of breath, then dropped to the floor.

A witchy shadow hovered on the wall.

Lor spun on the floor, heart knocking, fingers covered with glue and sparkles.

"Who?" He pointed at the darkened door frame, to a tall figure in a stunning white hat.

"Well, fuck, 'migo, just me, back from the abyss, no less, to conspire anew with my best compatriot. What's with the sparkly fingers? You been whacking off an angel?"

† † †

Alistair perched on a high stool in the church's tiny kitchen, while the tap dripped into a sink full of ancient dishes and Lor brewed tea in a stock pot, stabbing the tea bag repeatedly with a knife.

"That hat," Lor said, twisting the dial on the stove.

Alistair lit his pipe. His new hat was even taller and pointier than the old one, with a wider brim, if that were possible. The water boiled. Lor yanked the tea bags and dashed them into the garbage, then poured into a chipped blue mug and a Styrofoam cup. He gritted his teeth and strained the tea. "Don't you always show up when least expected. What happened?"

Alistair cleared his throat. "Well, *compadre*, after you babes fled, the butterball arrested me without warrant—what else, considering the crime, duh—'n dragged me down to the Man's holding tank, fingerprints and all, where I languished for, what?—five days."

"Charged with?"

"Fuck-a-duck, who knows—violent crime against the community, obstructing a peace officer, public mischief. . . ." He took another sip. ". . . obscenity, perjury, buggery, extortion, abortion, contortions, personality disorder without mitigating factors, paperhanging, immoral performance, injuring or endangering cattle—"

"Okay, enough," Lor said.

"—conspiracy to accept bribes which incite a child to commit failure to provide a breath sample—"

"Enough!"

"Yeah. Don't forget to turn off the stove."

Lor punched the dial and poked a calloused finger at the fading orange element. "Are you on your own recognizance?"

"Nix, man, I had a bail hearing this afternoon, the judge was in a good mood, we bonded over mutual midlife crises—mine 'specially manufactured for the occasion—and he let me go taking into account my lack of criminal record."

"You have no record?"

"Nope. Well, not *now*."

"How's that possible?"

"Many strange things are possible."

"Shit."

Lor squashed his cup and ransacked through dusty shelves. He found a box of soda crackers, magically preserved.

"Who paid?" He tore the wrapper.

"Dawn Cherry."

"How much?"

"I don't know, like, sixty-nine pesos or something."

Lor munched. The cracker surprisingly crunchy. "Conditions?"

"Abstention from alcohol and drugs, remain within jurisdiction."

Lor felt his heart squint. "When's your court date?"

"Seven months hence, May, June, something."

"So you're staying?" Lor smashed the cracker to the counter.

Alistair leaned forward and pointed a long finger. "Don't worry, 'migo, I have a plan. We're heading north right after the Christmas Eve gig. Without you. I even have a harp."

"You play the *harp* now?" Lor crushed the Styrofoam cup again, threw it at the sink, stalked out of the kitchen. He collapsed into his cushions and ripped off his ancient Doc Martens. "What the hell you staring at?"

"Criminy," Alistair said from the doorway. "Talking to your guitar, 'migo?"

"Fuck off."

Suddenly the guitar made Lor sick, with its secret cracks and incandescence and cranked-up string tension. He threw a Doc at the neck. It sproinged off, E minor.

"Leave me alone," he said.

Alistair removed his hat. "Me, or the magpie guitar?"

"Both."

Alistair blew smoke rings through stained moonlight, and, for once, said nothing. The magpie guitar twinkled, still ringing with overtones.

CHAPTER FIFTEEN

A FURIOUS GOODBYE

For weeks Lor despaired of ever escaping his past. The Weird was seasonal, had always been with him. He dwelled on the looming cabaret. He threw rocks at the crow in the tacamahac. He did not touch the magpie guitar.

At night, messed up on insomnia, he would often wander to the coulees, sometimes all the way down to the river, to watch the black water sponge moonlight and float it northward. On nights when winds howled in from the Arctic, the river seemed to flow in two directions at once. Then Lor would get angry and stamp back up to Spookleton to raid the 7-Eleven, where he strangled American cigarettes and drained Slurpee after Slurpee, gulping small ice like poison was the cure.

"C'mon, amigo," Alistair would say. "I do have a plan, damn good one, promise you."

"Piss off." Another rock at the tacamahac, old crow squawking.

In mid-November the chinook blew itself out, and El Niño went to sleep. Christmas settled on the streets—white snow, red noses, sparkling blue days. Spookleton folk spent chilly evenings warming at the local bonfire, steaming chestnuts in a fire pan and drinking beer from porcelain mugs—laughing, coughing steam, hitching sleighrides with the half-soused Frontenac, who somehow reined the horse and played a fiddle while sipping a frosty winter ale.

The sleigh bells drove Alistair batty. He stood at the church window, tapping his foot, whispering curses. "Fuck off with the bells."

Lor ground his teeth.

"And, like, what the fuck is my map tube doing on the stairs, covered in dust and bootblack?"

Lor ground his teeth.

Sunday mornings church bells cracked air, and Alistair would clomp up the stairs and out the window on his way to worship. Or whatever the hell it was he did. Lor would pretend to sleep until the window slammed shut and a current of chill flowed over his cushions. Then he would get up and make his daily pilgrimage to the river, visiting the 7-Eleven to snag a warm bagel and coffee.

One Sunday he stopped by a beaver pond, nuzzled in a wildwood of silvery birch. The water's surface was iced to a pattern of overlapping spirals, as if someone had tossed in three rocks and the ripples had instantly frozen. Lor was spooked, but couldn't look away. He traced the corkscrews, first with his eyes, then with his fingers. His coffee went cold.

Dazed and confused, he climbed back to Spookleton, through the church window to his hazy room, where the magpie guitar waited.

"All right, baby. . . ."

He picked it up and strummed a suspended sixth, expecting the open strings to ring. When they didn't, he strummed again.

"God." There was no sustain at all. He'd destroyed the tone completely. He thrummed a few chords, notes drooping from the fingerboard.

"But." He shook his head.

Setting the mutant against the wall, he removed a shoe and lobbed it, gently as he could. It hit the neck at the missing twelfth fret. Harmonics pealed and hung in the air like smoke.

"Good Lord." That defied the laws of physics.

He picked up the guitar again and strummed. His own notes died, even as the ghostly harmonics from the shoe continued to ring.

"Looks like Van Halen, sounds like a fucking banjo." Alistair, from the doorway, smoking his pipe.

Lor looked up. "Looks more like the Frankenstein monster."

"Yeah, man, like the *Fran Halen Banjo*, the Frankenjo, the Ban Halen Vanjo, the, er, Mondo Vankenstein Monjo, the Bandaiden' Banjo creature for Beaujeaulais Bolsheviks . . ."

"Cripes." Lor forced a laugh.

"Even Groucho Marx had an off day here 'n there, *bello*." Alistair squinted at the guitar. "That's a mysterious tone. Like, *noumenal*, man."

"Nothing mysterious about it," Lor said. "I wrecked it, pure physics."

"No metaphysics?"

"Hell no."

"Then why are them harmonics still ringing?"

Lor palmed the guitar's neck, shut up strings, then set the mutant against the wall. A wide silence. Alistair watched smoke drift.

Lor coughed. "Been to see Dawn Cherry lately?"

"Nah. Busy."

More silence. Lor cleared the tickle in his throat. "So, what's up?"

"Nothing, I guess."

"Eaten?"

Alistair puffed, chewed the pipe-stem. "'Sup with you?"

"Not much."

"Seem a little pissed off lately, like . . . I don't know. A personality transplant. Anything in partic'lar, or. . . ."

"Nah. Just." Lor pinged the strings of the magpie guitar, above the nut where they tinkled. "You eaten?"

"Yeah, cripes, had a big-ass plate of fried mushrooms li'l while ago, a breakfast of *champignons* if you will."

"Hungry?"

"Yeah. You?"

"Left my bagel and coffee down by a beaver pond."

"Why don't we go to Humongous Pizza Slice, maybe have a three-cheese brunch, visit Mooch and—"

"No way."

Alistair tapped the pipe. "Yuck Foo's, for hot-and-sour?"

Lor paused, felt the old affection in his blood. Unable to squelch it, he nodded. "Okay." Smiled. "Yeah. Little early for hot-and-sour. But yeah."

Alistair grinned, crinkled his eyes, snuffed his pipe. Halfway out the window he said, "But no Slurpees, boy-o. I've seen the fucking slime-trail of suburboid effluvium you've been leaving lately."

Lor dropped to the ground, where Alistair put a hand on his shoulder.

"Deal?" Alistair said.

"Deal."

† † †

Lor's mind drifted for almost four weeks, scattered over snowdrifts and wind-polished ice. He watched the Oldman River steam through the valley, choked with slush. He tried to master the magpie guitar, adjusting for its lack of sustain. He wandered Spookleton streets and alleys; they were remarkably resistant to the Weird, everything Underwood was not.

He forgot his powder. He was almost happy.

Every so often he would see Frontenac, puffing, tromping across the street or buying stamps in the 7-Eleven, dressed in an overstuffed parka and a pair of filthy Kodiak boots.

"Hello," Frontenac would yell. "Not now. Busy."

Alistair was friendly enough, but preoccupied, and always off to meet with shadowy companions for even shadowier purposes, face hidden beneath the brim of that new white hat. He would often climb out the window after dark, then return with heavy parcels in the wee hours. When Lor did manage to hook up with his old friend, they would go for green tea at Yuck Foo's, to tell old stories and giggle like schoolboys.

Gradually, the tiny stage in the chapel of the Spookleton Our Lady of Grace Church filled with Alistair's midnight parcels—a Celtic harp, a weathered bass, a hodgepodge of stomp boxes and percussion—crotales, bongos, temple blocks. A tiny Ludwig drum kit.

"That Fatty is gonna love this." Alistair tapped a battered hi-hat.

Lor frowned at the gear. "All hot, right?"

"Fucking-A."

Fatty was an endless source of amusement for Lor, who especially liked the way the kid's voice would squirrel up to soprano.

"What kind of drums do you like?" Lor would ask.

"You!"

Sometimes Lor and Fatty would go to the Silver Fox Pub. Fatty would guzzle a bottle of white wine in the alley, then enter the bar to drain infinite gins with soda, and flirt with every man and woman who crossed his path. In the bathroom, he would pee standing at the urinal with pants and boxers down around his ankles, wiggling his bare ass and humming the theme from a children's show called *Mr. Dressup*. Lor, having no idea who Mr. Dressup was, just laughed and took Fatty's word for it.

One moonless night, while they navigated icy streets in Fatty's four-by-four, a few seconds of symphonic static and eerie vocals washed from the radio. Fatty stopped the truck and fell silent, fingers twitching on the wheel, eyes closed.

"Did you catch it?" he whispered.

"Catch what?" Lor shook his head.

"The kid's manic-depressive," Alistair said, later, sipping green tea from a tiny china cup. "One minute he's off his nut, the next he's down in his mouth, bummed, sucking the life out of me—like, totally zap-o."

Lor bit an egg roll. "And that guitar case he lugs around and never opens. He's wigged, for sure."

"Wigged? Fuck, he's madcapped to the nuts, bro, a nuciferous zon-koid, looking for something, all of us are, but different, hear? The kid's driven by some kooky inner demons, f'sure, bet my life on it. He's lost. Irredeemable."

But the kid would redeem himself every time they jammed. He was *that* good. Sometimes both Lor and Alistair would stop playing and watch, mouths open, as Fatty filled the spaces with syncopations or thundering quads, always dynamic and tasteful.

"It ain't punk," Lor said.

"Really, kid, you don't belong with *this* band," Alistair said.

"Least I got one." A sophisticated *pitapat* on the bongos.

Rusty, if possible, got worse with practice. His timing was atrocious. He missed entire notes. His frets bustled, his pickups buzzed, his amp barked. His tone would have sucked in the sixties; it was unbearable *now*.

"Yes," Dawn Cherry told Alistair. "My brother is going with you or the tour is off. Understand?"

"Fuck you," said Alistair.

They built an eccentric repertoire of songs, culled by Alistair from every nook and crack of pop culture: Iggy Pop, Killing Joke, Loverboy. Some Underwood Dolls, MC5, The Slits, entirely too much punk for Lor's liking.

It all sounded like shit.

"No way," Lor said, a week before Christmas. "I draw the line at Van Halen."

"Come on, amigo, you have no sense of irony. Lighten up for once."

"Forget it. Ancient stuff. Shit. Total non-punk. You surprise me, Al."

On the morning of Christmas Eve, Dawn Cherry had a surprise for the whole crew.

"Happy Hanukkah," she said, holding out a fan of papers.

"Whatsis?" Ballooni said.

Dawn Cherry smiled. Sweetly, Lor thought.

"Your whole tour booked." She put an arm around Rusty's shoulders.

"When are you guys going?" Lor said.

Dawn Cherry dimpled her cheek with a forefinger. "Aren't you going to thank me? Alistair? Any graciousness in you at all?"

"Yeah, fuck, thanks. How do we get there?"

"You," said Fatty.

Dawn Cherry cuffed him. "Fatty'll drive. As for the gear, some of my clients are driving a van to Yellowknife," she said. "Tonight, actually, right after the cabaret, 'round midnight. We can load most of your stuff in there."

"When are you guys going?" Lor said.

"Clients." Alistair glared at Dawn Cherry, eyes crowfeeting. "Some of your *clients*. Like, peelers?"

"Oh for god's sake," Dawn Cherry said. "Spare me your predictable moralizing. Live the life first. Enter the quiddity."

Lor smashed his hand against the neck of the magpie guitar. "When?" he demanded.

Everyone turned to stare at him. The guitar jangled.

"Lordy," Dawn Cherry said. "What does it matter? February fifteenth. Alistair, don't you start with—"

"No." Lor's face flushed.

"No?" Dawn Cherry and Alistair, simultaneously.

"Al, you fuckin' told me Christmas at the latest."

Alistair shrugged.

Lor felt a cuticle snag inside his fist. "And you have a plan, right? For the court date?"

Alistair stroked his chin.

"Alistair?" Dawn Cherry said.

"Oh, hell yeah, dig me 'migos, shit yeah. 'Course."

Dawn Cherry sighed.

"Listen Lor," she said. "If it's that important for you to get out of here, you can ride with my clients tonight, right after we load out. You can meet up later in Yellowknife with the rest of these assholes you call your band."

"No!" Lor's lower lip numbed against his teeth. He squeezed his shirt pocket, felt the reassuring squish of his dust-pouch. "I'm not riding anywhere. Christ, I'm not going at all. Don't you *know* this?"

Dawn Cherry stared mutely, then looked at Alistair.

Alistair shrugged. "Lor's shedding friends." He looked suddenly sad. "Just not his gig any more. Maybe never was."

† † †

Five o'clock, Christmas Eve. An early moon, buoyant in a bowl of aqua-blue. Winding alleyways paved with new snow. Christmas lights a-twinkle, strung across gingerbread suburbs. Neighbourhood pubs pouring steam and chatter and the smell of hot cinnamon into the streets.

Across from Galt Gardens, a flock of kids sang "Hark! The Herald Angels Sing" on the steps of a stone mansion. They grinned and waved—crabapple cheeks and knitted mittens, clear high voices in the evening air. A white Scottish terrier barked steam as the front door opened, and a jolly old man emerged with a tray of overfilled mugs. He spilled hot chocolate and marshmallow onto the steps, where it hissed and puffed to the delight of the carollers.

"Shitheads," said Alistair.

Lor saw a young woman stop briefly to watch, her honey hair streaked with moonlight. She seemed to sing along against some chaos or self-doubt. She had the most delightful cheeks.

Fatty turned the truck with a jerk, parked at the Galt Gardens meter lot. The headlights lit a stand of aspen before blinking out.

"Shit," Lor said. "There are still *leaves* in there."

"Yeah." Alistair's face was hidden beneath the brim of his hat.

Aspen leaves trembled in the breeze, tips lit with frost and blue twilight. Beyond the aspens, a dense weave of thicker, blacker trees.

"Jesus," Alistair whispered.

Lor nodded. "Yeah."

Fatty snorted Slurpee from a jumbo wax cup, then leaned over Lor's lap. "'Scuse me while I get my nuts out of the glovebox," he said.

He pulled out a ball of tinfoil and grinned.

"What's in the foil?" Lor said.

"*You.* Come on."

Fatty opened the door and reached into the back to get his never-opened guitar case, then sucked more Slurpee.

Lor opened the passenger door. "What's in that case anyway, Fats?"

"Yeeo!" Fatty dropped the case and bent over, holding his temples. "Slurpee head, wo."

Alistair sat, face dark beneath the brim.

"Al. What the *hell*? Let's go. Soundcheck."

Alistair nodded, slowly, and removed his hat.

Lor shut the door and peered into the gloom at the back of the truck. "What is it, man?"

Alistair pointed at the woods. "That's where he fucking lost it, bro, in there, ten years ago, right? I'm, like, suddenly creeped out to the eyeholes. Look at the trees."

Lor sighed. "This was *your* idea, Al. Your expedition."

"No, man. His. *His.*"

They stared at each other in silence. Fatty clunked outside the four-by-four, kicking back Slurpee and jiggling his guitar case.

"It'll be fine," Lor said.

"How do you know?"

Lor paused. "I don't."

Alistair grabbed the headrest and leaned forward. "What do you think happened to him? Did he die?"

"Franklin?" Lor shrugged.

"Jesus. He had no right to disappear, without a word to anyone, without so much as a forwarding address, without . . . ."

Outside Fatty dropped his case. "Whoopsie daisy," they heard him say.

"And his little brother, here," Alistair continued. "With the guitar case full of flies and the small ice and . . . what'n the *fuck* are we doing, Lor?"

Lor sighed again.

"Yeeow!" Outside the truck Fatty doubled over, fell to the snow and began to roll. "Wo, wo, wo."

Lor lit up a smoke, match flashing the gloom. He put his hand on Alistair's. It was warm.

"Come on," he said. "Brother."

Alistair nodded. "Brother."

Lor hoisted his guitar and opened the door. Just before he climbed out he double-checked his shirt pocket. He suddenly didn't feel anything *like* a brother.

Good.

The bag of dust was still there, plump with glitter, nestled at his heart.

† † †

They followed a winding path through the trees.

"This place is dark." Ballooni eyed the trees, mixing board hoisted over his shoulder.

Lor felt a slow crush in his lungs, like the air was turning to slush. This place was dark. And somehow *old*—old poplars sick of moonlight, old ice jammed in barky gashes, leaves that refused to die.

"The whole path is strung with lanterns, fool," Dawn Cherry said. "Cheery and bright."

"Yeah," Ballooni nodded. "But it's so . . . *dark.*"

Dawn Cherry sighed more deeply than usual. "Dazed, doltish, puerile, cretinous."

"Where's the union hall?" Lor watched lanterns twinkle and sway in light breezes. He wished so badly to be alone.

"At the end of the path," Dawn Cherry said.

They followed her through the trees, under waterfalls of silver light. Fatty whistled, shaking his guitar case and flipping the bellboy's tinfoil ball, bouncing it off Rusty's head. Alistair trailed, silent.

Lor's nostrils stung with poplar scent. "How long is this path?"

Alistair nodded from beneath the white hat.

"We're here," Dawn Cherry said. "It's a two-minute walk."

It had seemed like two hours.

The pathway opened to blue-black sky. At the clearing's edge, moonlit, stood the Carpenters' and Joiners' Union Hall, nut-crackered between an oak and a clump of icy black poplar.

"Yow," said Fatty. "Zers."

Someone had scattered bales of hay around the hall and lit a batch of outdoor candles. Slitted windows seeped red light across the snow, up the walls and flagpole, to a wooden angel on the roof.

"That's one creepy nativity scene," Lor said.

Fatty flipped the tinfoil ball, caught it in his elbow's crook, rolled it to his palm. "Come on. My nuts are freezing."

They followed him in, except for Lor, who stopped by a window. He could smell glass again. The lights came on inside, washing out over the trees.

Then the leaves stilled. The sky hollowed. The world stopped. No wind, no bells, no voices. Lor looked up at cold stars, and suddenly felt more alone than he ever had in his life.

"Al?" He hustled for the door. "*Alistair?*"

† † †

"Bloody blue Goddess. You guys some kind of *punk* group?" A short, chalk-skinned bald man, thin pigtail, round glasses, and fringed vest.

"Who the fuck are you?" Alistair set down a guitar.

"It's Pixie," Dawn Cherry said, from the side of the stage. "From the other band. Pixie—Alistair, Lor, my partner Fatty. You know Rusty."

"You guys have five minutes to finish soundcheck," Pixie said. "We have some expensive gear to set up."

"Who are you?" Alistair said.

"Mystic Rhythms. You're opening for us. Five minutes."

Alistair glared at Dawn Cherry. "The fuck?"

Dawn Cherry put a finger to her lips and shook her head, while Pixie un-cased a rack of effects. Two tall blonde women clattered up the stairs carrying an acoustic guitar, a mandolin, a violin.

"Twins," Fatty said, twirling drumsticks.

"Hey Dawn Cherry," said one of the twins, a low alto. "Sorry we're a little late, but ... who are *these* jerks?"

Dawn Cherry closed her eyes. "The openers. I think I told you."

"What, some kind of old school ..." the twin looked nauseated. "...*punk* group?"

"This is a folk gig," said the other twin.

"Forget it," Pixie said, unrolling a snake of bundled wire. "They get half an hour, who cares. No lights, low volume."

"Fuck you," Alistair said. "We—"

"Hey!" Dawn Cherry stepped between them. Then whispered, "'Stair, I'm doing you a big favour. Don't screw it up."

Fatty played a snare roll, a cymbal crash.

"Too loud," Pixie said.

"Least I got one. Woo." Another *ratatat*, punctuated by three loud flams. "Hey, you guys know how to play *acoustic*?"

"Dork." One of the twins snorted. "See this violin? An electric five-string ZETA, not that that means anything to you."

"More money on this stage than you'll probably make in a lifetime," the other twin added.

"I have been soundly chastened." Fatty rose to bow. "Do you play the skin flute as well, m'ladies, perhaps the bone-phone or the scrotal harp? Because if so, I have a booking for you right here between my—"

"Fatty!" Dawn Cherry turning red. "Jesus H. Christ of Latter-day Fucking Saints!"

Lor set his guitar against the amp and peeled the foil from a new pack of Lucky Strikes. People were starting to trickle in.

"That's a right bloody long walk on that pathway," said a starchy old Englishwoman, leaning on a silver cane. "We might just as well be parked somewhere in the Belgian Congo."

She was followed by a plump man with thick glasses and a camera. Somehow familiar.

Lor lit up, exhaled through nostrils. "Al, who's that guy at the door?"

Alistair squinted from beneath the hat. "That's the juicebag from Humongous Pizza Slice. That spy, Malachi Frump."

"Frump?"

"Something is not right here," Alistair whispered to himself.

"What do you mean?

No reply.

"Al?"

"Hey twins, want to go for a hoot?" Fatty, chewing a drumstick.

One twin snuffled. "You kidding us? We don't do drugs, not even aspirin."

"Enough," Pixie said, "Off the stage. There's a *real* soundcheck to do here."

Alistair looked down, shoulders quaking. He stomped over to Dawn Cherry, face hidden beneath his brim.

"...these assholes?" Lor heard him say.

"'Stair, please." Dawn Cherry unwrapped a long banner, stapler in one fist. Alistair watched her unfurl the banner, then staple it across the back of the stage.

"The fuck is that?" he said.

"Can you read?" she said.

Lor read: *Happy Hanukkah, Kwanzaa, and Solstice from the Working Class Feminist Collective.* It was a very long banner.

"*That's* who's sponsoring this cab?" Alistair said.

Dawn Cherry nodded. "Surprised? *That's* no surprise."

"I? What?" Alistair said. "You can't be a stripper *and* a feminist."

Dawn Cherry didn't bother to respond.

Alistair continued. "No, like, you're all letting the Man construct your desires, prob'ly tells you when to *come* for God's sake—"

Dawn Cherry smashed a staple into the wood and threw down the stapler. "You want a neat package, that it? Enlighten me, then."

"Wo." Fatty chewed a drumstick.

"Your language sickens me." Frump, with camera, at the side of the stage.

"Shut up," Dawn Cherry said. Then she turned suddenly to Frump. "Hey, you're the asinine bastard who wrote the 'Flaky Fringe Feminism' article for *Alberta Watch.* Who invited you?"

"Free country, ma'am."

Alistair seemed to have lost his concentration. He was tapping a foot, gazing out over the guests.

"There's a woman in a ballet costume over there," he said. "Right next to a guy dressed like a . . . witch?"

Dawn Cherry turned.

"And a fool or jester, some such thing," Alistair continued. "A skeleton, Captain Canuck with a flag for a cape."

"A couple of Gypsies," said Fatty.

"Not *Gypsies.*" Dawn Cherry sighed.

"Some creepy boy in a top hat and red military jacket," Lor added. "Or . . . where'd he go?"

"And a sheik," Alistair said. "And, fuck me, Darth Vader. A huge Orson Wellesian Darth Vader."

Dawn Cherry frowned. "Excuse me a minute while I find out what's going on."

Lor sat down on a pile of gym mats, already tired, and watched the cabaret unravel. The party was cleaving to three distinct groups, all Caucasian—uptight banker types sipping martinis, a rag of bumblebee kids on skateboards, an untidy herd of young Lethbridge rednecks. He was especially drawn to the rednecks, clotted around the drink table. There was more Spandex and hockey hair and tight jeans there than one usually saw in a lifetime.

"Play some fuckin' AC/DC!" a tall, acne-fed dude in unlaced high-tops yelled at the unfortunate DJ, who was spinning mainly Rough Trade, Bruce Cockburn, and some pretentious college fare called Moxy something.

"Feminism, my ass," Lor heard Alistair mutter.

Light flashed. Frump, taking a picture of the witch and the skeleton, mumbling about satanic feminism.

The martinis were history over by the rednecks, who sucked back regulation glassfuls for a while, then hijacked and passed around whole bottles of vermouth and gin while the bankers stared in horror.

"Beer-tinis!" Acne Boy hollered, draining a Molson from two feet into a martini glass. Meanwhile, the janitor was chasing skateboards and mixing threats with highly detailed descriptions of floor-waxing procedures, while the Englishwoman took her silver cane to Rusty, who was, Lor noticed, lit to the gills on a smuggled bottle of Jack Daniel's.

Behind Rusty, Captain Canuck and the Skeleton wrestled the camera away from Frump, and were about to smash it when Darth Vader, chortling loudly, convinced them to give it back.

"Break it," Darth said. "No. Give it back. Let the little man have his toy. Go home."

That voice, Lor thought. I know that voice, that French accent.

"It's a bunch of people who thought this was a masquerade party." Dawn Cherry, back from fact-finding. "No harm done." She gazed out over the gym. "Man, Rusty is *stinko*."

"He's whoozled up the tonsils," Alistair said. "Maybe he can actually play this way."

Lor lit a smoke. He saw Fatty bounce the tinfoil ball off Rusty's head, then off the snowy head of the Englishwoman, who reached up to scratch.

"This is nonsense," Pixie said, re-checking a rack of digital effects, frowning at the party. "Who invited these—*damn!*"

He tripped over Fatty's guitar case and just about bonked the rack over, then huffed off, looking for the twins.

Lor scanned the case. Bulky, scuffed, with broken clips. But full of flies? One clip seemed to jiggle. What the hell? Lor raised himself for a closer look. The lid popped up and slammed back down. Lor dropped the smoke on his lap, brushed it, ashes spitting.

He got up and walked to the steps. "Alistair?"

"Yeah."

"When are we on? I need to get out of here."

Alistair shook his head. "A while, 'migo. Enjoy the fucking par-tee. Sit with me."

They sat on the steps, sober, and watched everyone else get roaring drunk. Rusty, pie-eyed on Jack. Fatty, singing "Chestnuts Roasting in My Ass." Rednecks, now mixing it with suits and social butterflies, all of them flushed and wobbling, old lady cracking her stick over young drunk heads. Skeletons,

Gypsies, witches, all flashed by Frump's camera. Lor noticed Mucciaroni tickling Chan over by the snacks, sipping from a bottle of impossibly red liqueur. And behind them, glowering and sluicing a supercan of Lethbridge Pilsner, Shemp, the Kresge's manager.

"Everybody's here," Lor said.

Alistair quivered perceptibly. "Some kind of decidedly un-harmonic convergence going down, bro, can feel it in my bones, some *culmination*, y'know?"

"What do you mean?"

"S'all adding up here, like, mathematics, quadratic equations, exponents . . . a butterfly effect."

"A what?"

"Butterfly effect. Chaos theory, man, small initial conditions giving rise to catastrophic and unpredictable results, butterfly causing a hurricane. Like a movie that films itself right off its own screen."

Lor sighed. "What's the butterfly here?"

Al turned on the step, face pinched, eyes squinty. "*Franklin*, shithead, what'd you think? Franklin's the butterfly and he's whipped up, like, a force-ten shitstorm."

Darth Vader rumbled by with a casket of wine, reeking of garlic. Fatty followed on a hijacked skateboard.

"Wo," Fatty said, teetering, holding his nose. "Garth Vadic."

He turned to grin at Lor and Alistair, crashed into Darth's ample back and fell to the floor. The skateboard zipped through Darth's legs and took out a card table decked with Cheetos and popcorn balls, flipping up to ping-pong off heads and bottles.

"You're giving him too much credit," Lor said.

"Franklin?" Alistair said. "Fuck, no."

"I suppose we're on a ten-year cycle or something, doomed to repeat ourselves?"

Alistair sniffed the air, glanced left, then right. "It's Franklin's unfinished business," he whispered. "His ghost is here, 'migo, lurking somewhere, we should have never gone to that witch-fucked museum all those years ago, shit. I have made one big motherfucking mistake. . . ."

"That's flaky, bro. You can't see a ghost."

"Ergo?"

"There are no ghosts."

"I need a joint."

"Hey." Fatty, onstage, holding his back. "One of you guys crack my spine for me?"

"Got a joint?" Al said.

Fatty grinned.

Behind him the guitar-case lid popped up, then down.

† † †

They sat in a backstage room hung with a bare bulb.

"Come on, punks," Fatty said. "Let's do some."

He pulled out his tinfoil ball and unwrapped it. Inside was a clot of bright, ice-like chunks, glinting blue and green highlights.

"Oh. God." Lor coughed.

The chunks were translucent, self-lit.

"Where did you get those?" Lor demanded.

"You!"

Lor remembered—the Crystal Room, the haze, the tinfoil. The bell-boy's glass jar in the hotel room.

"We'll smoke it," Fatty said.

Alistair shook his head. "How do you know what it is, fool? That shit could be toilet cleaner for all you know."

"It's angel dust," said Fatty.

"Not on your life," Lor said. "Not crystal either. Look at it."

"It's some kind of psychedelic," said Fatty. "Come on, we'll smoke it and see."

"Forget it." Lor pulled out a cigarette. "I do *not* do psychedelics anymore. Not even pumpkin-pie spice."

Alistair leaned forward and grabbed a chunk from Fatty's palm. "Let me see." He rolled it between fingers, snorted.

"That's a hunk of crystal meth, wonderboy—glass, Kmart cocaine, clan-lab Kraft Dinner, the cheapest shit on the streets next to banana peels and old vinyl albums. You want to be sucking the glass dick, tweaking up the tits, going psychotic? We already lost a friend that way."

"Og." Lor nodded.

"So what?" said Fatty.

"So *what?*" Alistair glared. "That shit in your hand is a redneck diversion, son. Make your hair twitch and your heart race, but utterly devoid of the vision, man, ever heard of the *vision?*"

"Least I got one."

Alistair rubbed the chunk with a thumb. "Who cooked this stuff anyway? It's cold like ice."

Lor felt something dig into his appendix. "Give me that."

He grabbed the chunk and held it to the light, watched highlights spark against the naked bulb.

"It's not meth, Al."

"Ha!" said Fatty.

"Never seen anything like this," Lor said.

Except in the bellboy's glass jar.

"So what is it, junkie?" Alistair said.

Lor shrugged, offered the chunk to Fatty.

"Come on," said Fatty. "I'm making a tinfoil pipe."

Alistair and Lor shook their heads.

"Scared?" Fatty said.

Lor laughed. "I've sucked back more drugs than you'll ever *see*, Fats."

"Yeah, when you were young. Now you're old. Just turn thirty or something?"

Lor coughed on the cigarette.

"You guys are granny punks," Fatty pressed. "You guys are the Man's tight little boys."

"Fuck off," Alistair said.

"You're just like a university professor. You're a yuppie-hippie, you're a suburban—"

"Enough!" Alistair said.

"You guys are fucked. You're fakes."

"S'that right?" Alistair tapped a finger against his lap.

"Oh yeah. You've been sucked right back into the Man's hoity-toity world."

"Enough," Alistair said.

"You're like old rock stars, living in your small ice world of—"

"All right." Alistair's voice was low, threatening.

"You gonna take it?" Fatty said.

"Give me the fucking crystals, wonderboy. Lor?"

Lor shook his head.

"Come on!" Fatty said, voice pitched in the stratosphere.

Alistair tapped a chunk with his ring, broke it up into powder. "It doesn't matter. Just a little caffeine to stimulate the adrenals."

Lor slipstreamed smoke out his nose.

"Come on, Lor," said Alistair. "We'll dust the kid's shit into a cigarette, mash the whole thing in my pipe. Can't let spider monkey here have the last laugh."

"Old rock stars, wo."

"We are not *old*!" Lor yelled.

Alistair muttered to himself, face hidden beneath brim.

Lor paused.

"One hoot," he said. "That's it."

† † †

Lor's limbs are hot. His heart is cold. His extremities start to melt and flow. "Why. Am. I. So. High."

Smell of glass and crushed raspberries, fading around the edges to prickled whiffs of blue and green.

"The less you smoke." Fatty's words are bubbles, bursting in tinkles against the smell of glass. "The higher you get."

Said the bellboy.

"Homeopathic drugs." Alistair is the floating blue cartoon. His words silver smoke and glitter. "I smoke too much."

Lor looks up, mouth wide. A blizzard howls inside the lightbulb—strange, because it is always autumn inside glass. The universe is in the bulb, and the moon. The moon is made of ice, molten core exploding, seams of fire running clear to the surface to freeze and blow away. The moon's fiery heart is unravelling to snow.

"Oh?" Blue cartoon scarecrow, floating against the bulb.

So hot.

So cold.

Lor inhales Fatty's bubbles, coughs a spiculed rainbow.

So big inside the lightbulb, so much space, fire, snow, so much darkness coiled at the filament. Lor stares at white light, clears his head. Concentrate, just psychedelic, I know this, I've been here....

The door opens, the lightbulb chuckles.

"Christ's name?" Dawn Cherry. "You guys are onstage in *two minutes*."

"Oh." Lor stares at his rainbow, tries to will it away. "Oh. *Shit*."

† † †

Concentrate. Lor held the magpie guitar firmly and waited for Fatty's count-in. The neck flopped in his hands, but he willed it back.

Flash.

One-two-three-four—they kicked into "Lust for Life," cycling at two beats per minute, thick as chocolate. It's normal speed, Lor thought, they can all hear it at normal speed. Concentrate.

Flash.

Alistair stretched to seven feet, still the floaty cartoon playing bass. Where was his harp? Behind Al, the stage flowed out in waves from beneath the drum kit, gently droning, rolling, foaming. Fatty's guitar case popped its lid. Lor missed a chord change.

Flash.

That damned Frump, taking pictures from the side of the stage. Lor glared at the spy, watching plump fingers elongate on the camera. Flash, flash, flash.

Fatty's guitar case washed up against Lor's calves. The lid popped up and down.

"Chord change!" Alistair, yelling from the bottom of the sea, blue rill from his lips.

"Oh...." Lor willed the neck back to solid wood. He heard banjo chords plink from the monitor, too loud, neck slippery as a fish dipped in Vaseline. Been here before, he thought. No magic, just chemistry—wonky transmission of dopamine neurons, junk binding to opiate receptors. But why could he think so *clearly*?

"I can't stand here!" Alistair yelling inside his ear. "Exact spot where Franklin went crazy, I can't stand here! You stand here!"

The tempo scrambled. Fatty raced up over a hundred-fifty beats per minute, thwacking the snare, drum-sounds turning silver and bright metallic blue, crashing into the rill from Alistair's mouth, spray shooting at the rapids.

What the hell song was *this*?

Then red sounds, fiery threads splicing blues and silvers. A violin.

A *violin*?

Darth Vader, at centre stage, flogging the ZETA five-string like Paganini on steroids, hunched over, crushing that baby fiddle, stomping and sawing in a cloud of resin-dust, catgut flaying from the bow's tip. The ZETA was triggering some kind of demented xylophone sample, layered with backward horn sections and clots of feedback, black noise from the devil's own heaven.

The monster was a virtuoso. He loomed over the crowd, hunched under his big black cape. He marched up and down the stage, rattling the boards, riding higher and higher on the fingerboard. His intonation perfect. His tone otherworldy. He wedged up against an amp and rocked it back and forth with his bowing arm, faster, now faster, some unthinkable brew of Locrian and Phrygian scales, skipping strings, slurring, smearing, sliding, and what wicked pact could account for this, what late-night exchange with Mephistopheles in what darkening theatre?

Sounds melted, the smell of blue steam hitting burnt silver. The thrashing hoedown breached an impossible tempo, the unravelling point, notes and beats breaking their bonds and orbits.

They were knee-deep now into meandering free jazz, anti-punk, then a medley of standards. Lor stared out over the audience. At the very back, standing very still, was that boy dressed in a top hat and red jacket.

"We've *never* played this shit before!" Alistair screamed, hair white with resin.

Fatty cut the engines, and they drifted into Stéphane Grappelli, Jean-Luc Ponty—Lor had never heard any of it before, colours he'd never seen, but he was playing them. Then a stew of Hendrix, Beatles, even a few riffs lifted from Van Halen, what the hell.

"House of Pain!" Lor yelled.

Then his monitor died, along with some of the lights. Pixie was onstage, steaming, bundle of ripped cord in his hand.

"You bastard," Pixie said to Darth. "That's *our* violin."

"Oh. That so?" Darth released a great gust of garlic from behind the black mask. "It's mine. My brother-in-law's. Yours. Go home."

"Jerk." A twin wrenched the ZETA away, one string popping, others unwinding audibly, MIDIed horns and feedback zinging down the octaves. Darth chortled, bat-winging his cape.

"Off the stage," Pixie said. "Enough shit."

"Fuck you," said the blue cartoon, stomping like a sandpiper. Fatty responded with an accelerating snare roll, spitting blues and silvers now pocked with zinc and lemon pixels. Rusty continued to play in perfect time. He was wasted, in the groove.

"Off!" Pixie said.

The cartoon punched him right in the face. Pixie stumbled backward, twirled once, and hit the stage with a neon-purple clump. Darth burst into guffaws, bellowing garlic and resin, just as the twin smashed the ZETA over Alistair's head. Speakers coughed an exploding MIDI symphony.

"Look what you made me do." The twin looked about to cry, staring at the mangled fiddle in her hand.

"Let me set you up with the right amp," Alistair said, heaving his guitar neck-first through the speaker of a Marshall cabinet. The Marshall rocked back and forth, crackling, then tipped and slammed into the stage floor inches from Rusty, who played on. Fatty, flushed as a devil, rolled the bass drum at the amp and tossed a cymbal after it.

"Wo!"

"Stop," Lor cried. But they were already in mid-brawl, pops and snaps and punches all amplified through the P.A. system and doctored with delay and reverb over at the mixing board. Lor glared at Ballooni, who just continued mixing. Ballooni grinned and shrugged. "What the hell," he mouthed.

"Alistair!" Lor was suddenly cold straight, head clear and pounding. "You're already in violation of—"

Alistair looked at him, eyes wide and bloodshot.

"Too late, 'migo, too late. It's happening all over again, Franklin's ghost, all over again, ten years, too late. Save yourself." he threw a splintered mandolin out into the audience, where Acne Boy and a clump of skaters leaped for it like boys at a wedding's garter-toss.

Rusty played on.

Lor flopped down on the stage and clutched his guitar. They were all going to jail, and those assholes would *never* leave town. He glared out, quickly blinking, to the back of the gym. There, staring back, stood the boy in the red jacket. Something familiar about that smile—

Lor smelled fire. Fatty was loose, perched atop the remaining amp, setting a match to Captain Canuck's cape while the twins leaped and tried to knock him over. No! Not fire, Lor thought. It was happening all over again, exactly.

He gripped the guitar's neck, and couldn't tell where his hands ended and the wood began. His spine turned to melody. Lilac blood painted his bones: wine, violet, sapphire. He heard buzzing at his thigh. The guitar lid was wide open, leaking flies. They hummed up in a dark cloud and cruised straight for Fatty's head, now wrapped in smoke.

Flash!

Frump jumped onstage and started shooting.

"The flies!" Lor pointed. "Alistair!"

Alistair shrugged, then disappeared in a haze of blue molecules.

Out over the sea of bobbing heads, at the far corner, the hatted boy stood on a chair. He pulled a knife from his red jacket, held it by the blade, drew it back to his ear.

"Shit!"

Lor leaped to his feet, shaking. Scents of pine and cinnamon exploded. Merry Christmas, Lor, get the hell out of there. He watched the flies circle Fatty's head, angry as bees, felt a wrench deep in his gut. So the flies had followed him all the way from Underwood. So there was no longer any distance between: his old life was sparking against his new one, his Underwood now *inside* his Lethbridge.

He fled, as everything fell to pieces—fled offstage and out of the narcotic swirl, out of the pine and cinnamon into the smell of new paint, through a cheerless, jingleless, untwinkling hallway with stage props crashing down around him, under a busted exit sign, into Bible-black night, Ecclesiastes ringing in his head—one for sorrow, two for mirth, all is lost, all is vanity, crash, crack, crumble.

Christmas Eve.

†††

"This way!" The freak from Kresge's perched beneath the glowing exit sign. "Flee north from the snowman, my warding, beyond which the Knife Thrower cannot pass."

Slam. Lor tumbled out the door. A cold wind smacked his face and rushed his nostrils. His eyes watered. His heart banged up over one-hundred-forty beats per minute, thrash tempo. He ran.

"But do not touch it!" the freak called after. "Whatever comes, do not touch—"

The path zigged through the woods, roots splitting ice, leaves choking moonlight. Lor felt underbrush rip his clothes and fingers. Frozen berries fell. Poplar scent soaked his lungs.

This path, he thought. This is not the path we came in on. He almost stopped, but heard muted buzzing behind him. Then the path swiftly dipped and went silent—no buzz, no birds, no wind. A path which no bird knoweth.

Lor slipped. Fell onto his back, skidded down the sloping path, shadows rushing, underbrush catching his jacket. His spine cracked on a rock. He spun sideways and crashed into a stunted birch, unleashing an avalanche of wet snow from the branches. He lay for a second, cold seeping into his chest, then staggered to his feet. He shook the snow from his hair. He wiped his eyelashes.

The world was bright with moonlight. He stood in a small clearing hedged with tall trees, in which a ring of old stones and ashes smudged one mummified pizza, single slice missing. Directly over the fire pit, from the tip of a long branch, a staring glass-eyed dolly hung swinging from its hair.

Lor shivered. Beyond the trees was deep darkness. The cabaret seemed a hundred miles away, a hundred years.

He turned to scan the clearing's far side and felt his lungs tighten. Behind him, melting under a giant black cottonwood—an abandoned snowman, broken-down and dirty. Two poplar wands for arms, no eyes, no face. Lor took a step forward. Somewhere the drip of water, sound like the smell of dirt after rain.

A faint buzz, growing.

Flies.

The cloud zoomed over the far trees in a low black drone. Lor covered his ears. The drone faded and swelled, till the flies reached the clearing's end and banked. They made a low pass over the blinking dolly, then kamikazed as one mass into the snowman. *Pock, pock, pock*, and the hum sizzled out. Steam rose from the snow.

Lor uncovered his ears and kneeled, stared at the pied creature melting before him. An urge to touch grew. He could almost taste the texture, the knurl of pinstuck flies and cobbled snow.

Let me touch you, said the snow angel.

Lor rose, stepped toward the snowman. The cabaret was gone. Somewhere in another life, lanterns swayed and spilled silver light, mixed with camera flashes and revolving reds and blues, cop cars, voices, hell to pay. But here: here was water and moonlight, no more.

Lor reached out a quivering finger, paused, reached further, then slowly, gently, pressed his finger into the snowman's face.

Someone blew the moon out. The night went black. A crash of blues and greens seared Lor's retinas. He heard sleigh bells and laughter, the same wicked laugh from the Crystal Room. His heart clenched.

Then voices.

"—out here somewhere—"

"—he did?"

"Hey! Lor!"

"—the fuck are you, man—"

Then,

Yes. Let me touch you....

The snowman, alive in the darkness. Lor could feel it. Solid. Dense. At the centre of things.

Bring it back to me....

Light chips splintered from wickerworks of rainbow. The snowman melted to snow angel, poplar wands to honeycomb wings.

Let me touch you.... A laugh from deep down in the sky.

Lor tried to roll away, so heavy he could barely move. He lifted his head, stared at two blinding lights. Someone grabbed his shoulder.

"Lor, fuck sakes, man, we got to *fly*, cops are here and that shithead Frump's got everything on camera, and I do mean *everything*."

"Fatty?" The twin orbs brightened, grew.

"I am in serious violation of bail, boy-o, no going back now, just fucking fly."

Lor turned his head. Alistair's white brim was soaked with blood, streaking his cheeks.

"Your plan?" Lor said.

"No plan, 'migo, I just ...*fly*, man. We'll see you in Yellowknife." The hand unclenched on his shoulder. Alistair rose and fled into the trees.

Lor turned to the bright orbs, heard an opening door.

"Hey! Way to wreck the snowman, punky," someone called from behind the lights. "You Lorne?"

"Lor."

"Well, get in the van. We were about to leave without you."

Lor clambered to his feet and stumbled toward the headlights. He stepped on the old pizza. The hanging dolly brushed his face.

"Here." He felt a warm hand on his arm. "Help you up. Hurry now, I think the police are looking for you. And we have a date in Yellowknife."

The door closed. Seatbelts buckled. The van backed up, smushing whatever was left of the snowman. It felt like a violation and an invitation. The moon peeped again, illuminating a dashboard twinkling with lights, three heads bobbing in the mirror.

"You okay?" A woman. Lor could smell her rose perfume.

He nodded, then pitched forward. "My guitar, I have to go back."

"Don't worry. Dawn Cherry gave it all to us. We packed it for you, along with the other gear."

The van lurched forward. Lor touched the bag of glitter in his shirt pocket. He felt a thrill of menace at the bottom of his thoughts, as if going north was his heart's desire, and his worst nightmare. The van sped up, dark trees and shadows tumbling outside the windows.

"To the Arctic," a voice said.

Somewhere, deep in the foliage, magpies chattered a furious goodbye.

PART FIVE

EXPEDITIONS

The understanding that most Southerners have
of the North has been shaped more by romantic
imagery than practical experience.
—Former Prime Minister Stephen Harper, 2006

CHAPTER SIXTEEN

GRAINS OF WATER, BEADS OF DUST

"Let's go." Rooke broke a full hour of silence. Seri had spent the entire time in prayer.

"Yes." He pinged his teacup to its saucer. "Let's move."

Seri spilled her own tea. After two pots of caffeine, almost anything jingled her nerves. But she recognized the new resolve in his voice. That was good. She had done her job.

"To Lethbridge, then," she said. "I'll drive."

Rooke tossed coins on the table.

In the car, he turned in the passenger seat to stare out the window. In a few minutes he pulled a Swiss Army knife from his pocket and withdrew the tiny scissor, then began to trim his fingernails.

"Ted, I just stay on Highway 2, right?"

He did not look at her. "You say you love Saint Augustine."

"I never said that. Number Two, all the way to Lethbridge?"

Rooke snipped. "What about his counterpart, the gnostic Mani?"

Seri scanned for road signs. "He was a bit Zoroastrianist, a bit Buddhist. Straight south, right?"

Rooke scratched his cuticles with the scissor, unfolded one of the blades and sliced lengthwise down the nail. What was he thinking? Seri felt relief that they were moving, that she had put Rooke back on the path. The next goal was to clarify the mandate and proper channels for report. But she hated this silence.

"Ted. Mani was a heretic. Augustine renounced him."

Silence.

She continued. "The gnostic view of evil is—"

"Mani's thinking is highly symbolic and alchemical. North is the direction of light, spirit, and goodness. South is the direction of darkness, flesh, and death. Corruption." Rooke briefly looked her way. "Stay on Highway 2."

After that he would say no more. The miles roared by, and Seri realized she was speeding in increments. She began to worry: had she pushed too hard, bumped him onto a path more twisted and shadowy than she intended?

"So Ted. What is your one true thing?"

He began to scrape the hair from his forearm, pressing harder each stroke. Seri felt her bladder tighten with two pots' worth of tea. Rooke notched the blade between fingers, looked about to slice. "Are you an angel?"

"You mean, symbolically?"

No answer.

She cleared her throat. "Are you speaking in a metaphorical sense?"

Silence.

"Ted, I didn't study Mani all that much. My pharmacology and geography are solid, but my angelology and theology are actually ...." She felt herself pressing the gas. "My humanities project was mainly about angels. But not real angels, only people's beliefs *about* angels."

Still the silence. She hastened to fill it.

"I started the project with a lot of enthusiasm, but it pretty much ended up in disillusion. I had to find one true thing to get through. Can you guess what it was?"

No answer.

"Pride, Ted. Pride to stand my ground, and finish what I started, and not run away."

Still the silence. It stretched to the fringe of what Seri could stand.

Oh dear Lord yes, she had begun her humanities project with such enthusiasm. She'd been young: who wouldn't be enchanted by a heretical religious text, printed on stone tablets, found somewhere on the Arctic islands? The stones, the Pica Mithra, were supposedly found in the late twenties by two brothers, Haroot and Maroot Darker. The text supposedly described a tribe of angels cast from heaven to wander the earth till time's end. Their story was one of disenchantment and madness: under the spell of a single charismatic figure named only the Angel of Knives, they became increasingly capricious and jaded, like humans or ancient gods, and fell in love, and committed violence, and hated each other instead of God, until their community unravelled to diaspora, and all their tales became infected.

"Their leader, the Angel of Knives, still hunts for reconciliation," Seri said. "He sends magpies as his messengers, winging 'round the earth in search of the others. But the others are lost to hatred. His own wife searches for him, to kill him, meanwhile taking and casting aside human lovers as a way of maintaining the fires of her hatred."

It was nonsense, of course. The Darkers turned out to be hucksters, and maybe opium smokers. In fact, they were performers in some tiny Arctic circus that was rumoured to travel between Inuvik and Yellowknife, well-versed in the fantastic and the bogus. Seri knew the tablets would be fantastical; that much was obvious. But she wanted to feel their hard text beneath her fingers, wanted them to be a real gesture against the mundane and secular, not the invention of two entertainers.

But the detail that bugged her most, the one that alchemized to insomnia, was the Angel of Knives. Because though the angel was legitimate, and mentioned in scholastic literature, he was nameless. How could an angel be nameless? Attarib, angel of winter. Anael, angel of December. Gabriel, ruler of north.

Then Seri would put her knowledge to work, try to devise a rational explanation. Perhaps the Ad Lateran Synod of 745, which condemned the naming of angels. But none of the other names were lost. Perhaps Dante's *Inferno*, where Lucifer was frozen in a lake of ice because of his incapacity for love. But Lucifer was a fallen angel, in hell, with his own set of tales. Perhaps there was no Angel of Knives. But then again, there was, there was. Finally, up late before her oral exam and strung out on too much Earl Grey, the sensible realization that the Darker brothers were charlatans anyway, that there was no visitation, only a story. But still, still, the name....

†††

Rooke stared at the incisions he had made along his fingers and knuckles, neat clean bloodless cuts. He turned a hand, held the knife to the veins on the inside of his wrist. By the time the car reached the Lethbridge outskirts, he seemed completely empty. The whole landscape echoed—empty plains, distant cattle, distant shore of the horizon.

Seri was determined to reconstruct a mandate from what she already knew. She tried to remember what was known of Rooke, but found very little. Only his former official position as operations supervisor, his outward appearance. Somewhere there must have been a hidden infrastructure of details. But where? Rooke had always been ghostly, like his silhouette barely held together.

She suddenly missed Granny Finnegan, missed the sensuous green tangle of Vancouver, the mist and smell of sea salt. She remembered the drive from

Vancouver, how she had gazed back at darkening fields of cloud. Now, the emptiness of the prairie made her feel like dust. Endless, arid, exposed. How long before she fell into the sky?

Rooke began to breathe through his teeth.

"Ted. Do you know a good hotel?"

He didn't answer.

"How do we pay? What's our budget, our per diem?"

Rooke pressed knife to wrist. "None."

Fine. Another detail to track. She braked in front of a small independent grocer. Danny's, said the sign. "Okay, Ted. I need some information here."

Rooke put the knife on the dash and traced a nail across the bloodless cuts on his other hand. The skin pinched between his eyebrows.

"Fine."

Seri began to drive again. She only knew one hotel in Lethbridge. One creepy hotel, with a sentient elevator and an ongoing convention of shadows.

"Ted. I'm going to the Marquis."

Rooke clenched his fist, and all the cuts burst at once to trickle blood across his knuckles.

† † †

Seri gasped. Room One Thirteen of the Marquis was trashed—an overturned cart, broken dishes, green glass from a bottle. She looked away, thesn returned her gaze to the disorder. "How can a hotel rent a room that hasn't been cleaned?"

Rooke nudged a chunk of glass with his toe.

"Okay, no problem." Her stomach bunched. "We'll clean it ourselves."

Rooke looked at her, face solemn, index finger dripping blood. She recognized the set of his shoulders: he had satisfied his doubts, was about to tell her everything he knew. Her persistence had paid off.

"Just go home," he said.

"Beg pardon?"

"Thanks for the ride. Your part is finished."

"What? Ted. Damn it!"

His face flushed, rising from the neck upward. "You were the unexpected visitor, the message girl. Your message is received. Your work is finished. Now go home."

"No. Absolutely not." She shook her head, crouched, began to pick up broken dishes.

"This is not your calling." Rooke made a fist, squeezing more blood. "Can you imagine? The world is dry as grains of dust, all of us living useless lives,

RANDY NIKKEL SCHROEDER | 133

wound to the Internet, timed to pizza delivery, speeding playground zones, cruising suburbs in search of what? Another piece of microwave bacon?" He shook his hand, spraying red droplets. "The world is wafered with microwave miracles, wine to water, precious little communion. Go home. This is not your commission."

"Wrong. Wrong. It is." She stared, aware of her tongue. "As I've been saying—"

"Something still prowls this world, and more than just the brute facts of wickedness and suffering." He dragged the bloody hand through his black hair. "There is an actual *presence*, my young visitor, evil like sweet poisonous blossoms growing in the secret places, the bad wiring among the refrigerators. You have no idea. Go home."

"No!" Seri chewed her tongue.

"You do not understand where I'm going."

"God does."

His teeth clenched until they squeaked. He raised a fist, let it fall. Then turned and fled the room.

"Wait!" Seri started after him, just about breaking her nose on the slamming door.

"Ted, wait!"

He was already in the elevator. She chased after him.

He held the door with a hand. She sniffed hand soap. Under his perfect nails?

"We've already been through this," he snarled and flung back his hand, sprinkling bloody droplets. "Don't you listen? Don't you get it?"

She did. "Not hate, Ted." She thought of prophets. "Anger. There's a difference."

He took one step and shoved her. Her head snapped, and she tumbled and hit the carpet.

The elevator closed. Seri sat stranded in a hallway of snickering shadows, face pimpled with Rooke's blood. Three seconds, then she leaped up to rush down the stairs, two at a time.

"Ted! Ted!"

She stopped at the lobby door, panting. "Sir, have you seen a tall man?"

But she could not get a yes from anyone, nor find Rooke anywhere. Only his coat, abandoned like a shed skin on the lobby floor.

† † †

For days she searched in widening circles, using all her skills. But in vain: there were no clues to be found in the hotel, only bellboys slithering hallways, faint voices misting from vents.

"Did you find a coat on the floor?" she asked valets, chambermaids, night managers. The answer was always no, often chased with a lingering stare, a shoulder shrug, a shaking head. Seri should have picked that coat up immediately, before sprinting out to the parkade. Had anyone seen a tall man with black hair and a white Van Dyke? Sounds like something from a cheap horror movie. Your father? A lover? Beg pardon, ma'am, none of my business.

Rooke's car hadn't moved.

"Haven't seen him," said the receptionist. "How will you be paying?"

Seri offered her credit card, retired to clean the room. She tried to read the Bible, but her eyes flitted back and forth between columns, her finger flicked pages compulsively, and her mind wandered again and again to the dearth of clues. She closed the good book, looked out to where acres of snow unmapped beyond the moon-crazed glass.

God, your prophet needs a sign here.

She dug out her notebook and phoned the old Vancouver office, but no one was there. Next day she headed out and prowled the strange avenues.

"Haven't seen him," said the constable. "What kind of law enforcement did you say he was, again?"

His partner laughed. "No, ma'am, no branch in this town. Try north, in Calgary. What's CSIS, again?"

If only she'd had a picture. Was there a picture of Rooke, anywhere? She described, best she could.

"No," said the librarian.

"No," said the lawyer.

"No," said the minister. Worth a try, Seri thought. She thought of her old job, the dependable certainty. But right now home seemed far away as heaven. Have you seen a particular man, very intense, looks like....

No.

No.

Sorry.

The day wore on. No clues, only strange omens: broken trees, whispering children, tramps with rumoured names—Iceking, Rain Man, Skeleton Tim. Seri forgot to eat lunch.

† † †

At twilight, when the snow swirled like topsoil, she stopped at The Onion Pub & Grill to eat and watch a group of dryland farmers perform three sets of Celtic folk. After hot shepherd's pie and a long-nursed Pilsner, she stepped into the alley and pondered her next move. Something jigged at her visual periphery, something hunched and moonlit. She looked after it, but there was only dark.

She was about to return to the hotel and get out her notebook. But she stopped, looked again. There, flickering between fence posts—a kid riding a German shepherd. A boy, wearing a long black coat with sleeves dangling.

Seri shook her head, turned to go. Only in Lethbridge. But hold on: that was *Rooke's* coat. There was no mistaking the thin lapel, the silver buttons.

Seri sneaked after, stopped at an alley fork to peep around the fence. The boy dismounted at a back gate, long dark hair seaweed in the wind. He put a hand on the dog's head, then whistled, low and soft. The gate creaked and a girl emerged in a hooded coat, holding a giant pine cone. They smiled at each other, turned to climb the steep alley, dog padding between them.

Seri scrambled up to the sidewalk, just in time to see the kids dip into a thick wood across the street. She followed, then paused at the wood's edge, where a stone arch said Galt Gardens: downtown.

She plunged. As soon as the path turned, all street noise disappeared. Wind rushed the leaves. Light shimmered down in slants, snow holding the hushed greens and blues. Seri floated through a coral reef of frozen berries, over the sunken hull of a dead birch. The kids were gone, drowned.

No, there they were, up ahead, kneeling at the bole of a giant poplar, boy elbow deep in underbrush. Boughs loomed like tentacles, mist drifted from barky tangle to the treetops. Seri stooped to watch. She felt an unexpected loneliness, but it was all right, more an awareness of each cell thrumming her body.

At the tree, the girl laughed. The boy pulled a silver tin whistle from the bushes and blew a note. He was answered with another note, a high clear singing voice. Seri squinted and leaned closer. Nobody's lips had moved.

Then, out of the bole climbed a Lethbridge creature the likes of which Seri had scarcely imagined. Was it an old man or a bearded child? Seri peered. The apparition had long greasy hair, a Blue Jays baseball cap decked with curly pink ribbons, fluorescent blue scarves around his ankles, stilleto heels. And, in one hand, a gnarled poplar branch chewed to a point.

"Ye come in high fine time," he growled, yanking the girl's hair. "Now haste is among us, and the fox himself i' we tarry."

All three crunched off through the snow, down a sharply dipping path.

Seri waited a few minutes, then rose to follow their footprints. She heard music, wisps at first, then louder—some kind of ambient dub, threads of tin whistle, rattle of tambourine. She crept down the slope and paused beneath a stunted birch.

The woods opened to a small clearing, an island bristling with kids, most dancing madly, some hanging from the trees. A bonfire cracked at the heart, roasted nuts popping and exploding. Beyond the fire, a row of bikes rested against the trees, and a tribe of shaggy-haired feral kids glared from between spokes.

I hope they're not drinking, Seri thought.

Under a giant black cottonwood, a gang of brightly mittened girls were building a faceless snowman, under directions from the freak, who clapped his hands, pointed long nails, whirled like a dervish.

"Ha!" he cried. "And th' poplar wands! For without arms t'is no warding."

He jabbed his stick through the snow, unearthed a spinning clod of ice and dirt. "Fire in the belly!" He danced, kicked up his shoe. He caught it, began to pock the snowman's face with the stilleto, snow chips sparkling his beard. "By the slotted spoon! He will not pass here!"

"The Knife Thrower shall not pass!" the girls screamed. "Never, never until the snow melts!"

Snowballs whizzed the island. A shriek, and the dance shifted: they were throwing a hot tinfoiled potato, steam sizzling its vapor trail. Then toys—flying yo-yos, checkerboards, glass-eyed dolls blinking as they somersaulted the air. Seri noticed an open toy chest by the fire, still brimming with puppets and paints. A few kids held sticks to the fire and raised torches to the frosty sky.

I hope they don't burn the place down, Seri thought.

Then a sudden hush. Twigs and leaves drifted down. At the clearing's end, a leafy curtain rustled and swept open. A pizza delivery boy stepped through, boxes held high.

Seri peered, straining her eyes. Just beyond the pizza boy, where the wood thickened, where grew an unlikely thatch of Nanking cherries, a jacket lay tangled on a bush. In the moony dark it was impossible to tell its colour. But further, where the bright berries dropped, where the weeping birch gathered, a shadow crouched, waiting and watching.

Rooke.

Seri looked at her shoes, focused her eyes, rehearsed her various options. This scenario was so dense with visual information that she couldn't calculate the contingencies. Best idea was probably to sneak around the border, ignore the kids, and surprise Rooke.

"By grace!" cried the freak. He seized the snowman by the head. "This is our pillar of fire. We have well measured our time, and he will not follow us to the House of Fog. He will not pass!"

The feral kids leaped, hooting and spinning bike wheels. The music swelled. The dance fragmented. The dog began to bark.

Then, behind the snowman, behind the cottonwood, something red flashed. Seri blinked. A red jacket. A boy in a top hat and red military jacket, crouching, holding a long knife by the blade. The boy crept forward, raised his elbow, drew back the knife to his ear. He aimed at the clearing's heart with his free arm.

The fire roared high, singeing leaves. Seri's heart clenched. She rose and stepped into the clearing. "Hey, be careful—"

The fire doused. Torches sizzled in snow. The woods dimmed—the island tipped and sank to the bottom.

Seri stumbled, blind, eyeballs dry with smoke. "Ted!" She looked down, closed her eyes, forced her pupils to adjust. Heard a clatter of bicycles, a crunch of footfalls. A tidal wind swished through the woods, leaves bobbing in currents, bits of laughter washing up and trailing under the oldest lunar spell.

Seri reached and steadied herself against something cold. She opened her eyes, still prickly and dry, saw her hand on the snowman. Somehow she had crossed the length of the clearing. The entire pageant was vanished, leaving only toys and cinders and one uneaten pepperoni pizza, still steaming on the snow.

She sprinted for the clearing's edge, stopped. Which direction? Damn, where was that hanging jacket?

"Ted?"

Her feet were freezing, shoes full of snow. She looked down, saw she stood in a giant wheel of footprints, hundreds of tracks patterned in wild fractals. Most vanished at the web's edge, but not all. Only two sets were large enough to be adult. One made by stilletos. The other not.

Seri raised her shoulders, dropped them, sighed one long whoosh. Okay. No problem. There went Rooke's tracks—in fact, there was his dark coat, still mangled in the bush.

She reached down for a piece of pizza, bit until the juice trickled down her chin. Then, slice flopping in one hand, she cantered after the tracks, grabbing the coat. Behind her, the scattered toys remained still and silent, except for one glass-eyed dolly overhead, caught by its hair at the tip of a long branch, eyes blinking, still swinging.

† † †

How Rooke's tracks kept their integrity, through downtown streets a-slush with many feet, Seri never understood. Beyond that night she understood little ever again.

She lost the footprints once, near a flock of kids caroling at the steps of a stone mansion, where an old man popped out like a cuckoo to serve hot chocolate.

"Shitheads," someone said.

Seri's mind sharpened, as it always did on the hunt. Downtown clarified, humming colours, smells, voices. She stopped short at the window of a store called Kresge's, could not remember if she had followed the tracks here or not. Inside, Rooke hunched at an arborite counter, smoking a cigarette, finger tapping his briefcase. His hair was blotched with white, as if the black was washing out.

Her heart thumped as she pressed the revolving door. "Ted."

"Can't shake you, can I?" He stared at a picture in his free hand. He did not look up.

She stood behind a plump stool.

"Well?" he said. "Sit down. Thanks for bringing my coat." He hardly seemed surprised. If anything, he looked like he was expecting her. God, this man, with his whiplash moods.

"You need to explain precisely why you ran off." Seri sat. "Ted, I have just seen the most frightfully bizarre thing imaginable."

"As have I. You *know*, don't pretend."

"What *was* that? In the clearing."

He chuckled, then met her eyes. "So. Are you an angel?"

"You need to start making daylight sense, for one minute—"

"Have you been sent to help me get back what I have lost?"

These misty parables! "What have you lost?"

Rooke drew fire from his smoke. "Sent by whom I cannot imagine."

Seri checked her pocket for a pen. Time to get a list going. "Tell me why you ran. I know the feeling. I can help."

"A few questions of my own first. Consider it the interview we missed."

"Forget it."

"You have information collation skills?"

"Yes."

"Research talents?"

"Many." This was more like it.

"Analytical abilities."

"You know I do." She smiled.

"Tell me the name of the Angel of Knives." He fanned cigarette smoke with the picture.

She frowned. "Let's get back to the real questions. He doesn't have a name."

"Few angels do." Rooke reserved his piercing stare for the picture in his hand. "Why do you love them?"

Seri touched her temple. "I don't particularly."

"Seems out of character for a rational thinker to love the angels."

"Angelology does not resort to the evidence of the senses. But it *is* a system, Ted."

Rooke drew a deep draught of smoke, bit the filter. "Angels have pagan ancestors, the Valkyrie, gathering souls of the dead. They haunt the cracks of your faith."

"Nonsense." She saw a jot of red flesh on his fingernail, realized it was Jell-O.

He continued. "Who is the Lord of Darkness?"

She'd never forget that one. "Angra Mainyu." At university, she always hooked the name on a simple mnemonic: angra mainyu; angry man. The Lord of Darkness was an angry man. "Are these symbolic questions really necessary?"

Rooke folded his hands, cigarette still sparking diced knuckles. "Indulge me. I need to be highly satisfied of your rage for order."

"My what?" She smoothed her hair, straightened her shirt. Drew her pen from pocket, clicked it closed, replaced it neatly.

Rooke laughed heartily. "Good. Excellent. Are you sent to restore me?"

He seemed pleased, but without the smooth contours of simple benevolence. He did not betray himself through any grin or posture, but Seri felt his sardonic layer, in the clipped edges of the word *restore*. She prayed briefly, felt the purpose again. Rooke was angry, angry like the prophet Jeremiah. Well, not quite: not righteous like Jeremiah, but a player in God's plan here, woven as always in mysterious ways.

"God will restore you," she said.

Rooke dropped ashes on his picture. "You do realize it's Christmas Eve?"

"What? You're kidding. No way."

He sucked fire down to the filter. "One hour till midnight. When would you like to open your presents?"

She drummed her nails on the arborite. Pepperoni heartburn stung her throat.

"Forgive yourself." Rooke chuckled. "Memory is chaos. I need to know, finally, how fully you intuit the interstitial textures of reality."

"The *what*?" Rattled now.

"All the hidden cracks and crevices, the peach-stone spaces."

She sighed. Good God. "Hume again? Kant? Oh—the idealists. Never a big fan."

He stubbed the cigarette, ground ashes in a widening mandala. "Tell me more of the urban myths you learned at university."

Okay careful. Something hinged on this answer, she could tell.

"Serendipity?"

"I'm thinking." Actually, praying.

"Okay." She summoned her best Sunday schoolteacher voice. "There is the story of the mad priest adventurer, who believed that more evil walked the world than good, that wickedness could only be destroyed by stealing its heart."

"I love this. Highly symbolic."

He would.

She continued. "So he journeyed north, deep into the Arctic, and stole the heart of a frost demon, then fled with the name of God on his lips. The heart remains somewhere south, in some city after all these years, and the demon still wanders the world in search of it."

Rooke said nothing, eyes wide, mouth open.

"There's more," said Seri. "The demon is far from home, and has thinned, and lost his voice. His story is tragic in some tellings."

"Yes," Rooke whispered. She had him.

"There's more. Fallen angels also hunt for the demon's heart, for they believe it will restore them to wholeness, or love, or heaven. Depends who tells the story."

Rooke's pupils dilated.

She paused for full effect. "All of them animated by one true thing."

Rooke exhaled, like he had been holding his breath. "So they're the same angels as in your other story?"

"Beg your pardon?" Her eyes missed a blink. "I . . . hadn't thought about *that*."

She felt a little dizzy. Knife Thrower and snowman, weeks slipping by without her notice . . . God, had she been hallucinating? Infected with Lethbridge air, or earlier, with Og's delerium?

"So you have been called," Rooke said. "Despite my bad faith—"

"Hey you two." The waitress, thirty-ish woman with a beehive hairdo. "Merry Xmas Eve, sorry for the wait. Special tonight is toast, two eggs. . . ." She grabbed her hair. "Oh my goodness. *Franklin?*"

Rooke darkened, bowed his head.

"Eggs, Franklin?" Seri said, still dizzy.

"Good lordy," the waitress continued. "It *is* you. Almost didn't recognize you with the Santa beard, never expected to see you again."

Rooke pressed his lips.

The waitress grabbed a mittful of beehive. "Wow, been a long time, you got a haircut—"

"Hush," Rooke said.

"Your friend got a haircut too," the waitress said. "He still looks pretty cute—"

"Hush. No need to broadcast. . . ." Rooke paused, put down his picture, tapped the ashy circle. "*Friend*?"

"Yeah, the guitar guy who likes to smash stuff, remember how he—"

"When did you see him?" Rooke leaned into arborite, fingers twitching.

The waitress twirled her beehive. "Whul, like, couple of weeks maybe?"

"Listen to me very carefully," Rooke said. "Did he have a companion? A tall man, long silvery hair, excessively profane?"

"You bet. Silver, like on a tree?"

"*Think*," Rooke said.

The waitress mulled. "Yuh. They wrecked the store. They're roommates."

"Don't lie to me." Rooke stretched a breath. He was either twitching his fingers at high speed or shaking. Seri noticed the initials on his briefcase: T.F. Rooke. Oh, so that was it.

He crumpled his picture. Breath rushed from his nostrils, faster each exhalation.

"Yuh." The waitress nodded. Then whispered, "They live in some old church. Don't tell the police, 'kay?"

Rooke stood, knocking over a glass. "A church," he rasped. "Where?"

"I don't know. The neighbourhood with the silly name? Spookleton?"

He began to yank at his buttons, top to bottom. "Serendipity."

She surfaced, a little frazzled. "Yes."

"One more question." He turned. His eyes were bloodshot. "Is there anything—*anything* in this world—that could crack your faith, tear down its walls, uproot its foundations?"

"No."

"Think carefully. This is the one true thing."

She didn't hesitate. "No. Absolutely nothing."

"Then you are my angel." He grinned, plucked the cigarette somehow still smoking, drew fire to his lungs. "We have detective work to do, secrets to tear open."

He looked up and covered his eyes. Ash fell from his fingers to cling at his clothes. Finally, after long seconds, he dropped his hand, and the cigarette fell to the ground. "Fire up your metaphysics. We're going to church."

"Why?"

He stood. "To get back what's mine. Finally."

Seri glanced at the briefcase nameplate, and wondered at the secrets of Theodore Franklin Rooke.

CHAPTER SEVENTEEN

THE CiRCUS OF WHAT

Rooke roared through the amber lights. A truck hauling
Christmas trees screeched and honked. Seri tugged her seatbelt.
Now the fires were lit. The speed of the car excited her, implied
a destination at last.

Rooke rolled down his window, inviting a gush of chill. "Order the
angels."

"First explain that clearing back there."

"Order," he said. "The angels."

Okay. If the spooky stuff kept him stoked, she was willing to play her
part. "Seraphim, Cherubim, Thrones, Dominions—"

"Enough." He swooped lanes without signaling, skidded a corner. "Angel
of mysteries."

"Usually Raziel."

"Angels of confusion."

"Group commanded by God to descend to earth and seed chaos."

"Chaos." He tapped the dash. "Where does the archangel Michael
originate?"

"I'm not—"

"Ancient Chaldea." He clicked his teeth. "A pagan spirit, Serendipity.
Who is Nebo?"

"I don't know."

"One of the sukallin, ancient Sumerian spirits. Angel ancestors. Do you see?"

"No."

He flicked his head, eyes roving. "All the old pantheons, swallowed whole by Christianity. Toys in the attic. Assyrian gods, demons . . . ."

He stomped the brake. Tires wailed. The car shuddered, stalled.

"Babylon," Rooke said. Seri had never smelled his cologne so strongly.

She stared out the window. A dark empty intersection, enfolding them. Creaking stop signs, humming overhead wires.

"It is always windy here," Rooke said. The car rocked gently.

"Let's get moving," Seri said.

A Slurpee cup rattled across the street. Rooke took a long breath, opened the door, and stepped out. He walked a few paces, knelt. Seri heard his knees crack. He slowly traced a finger on the icy pavement, then put it to his lips.

"Ted." Seri climbed out and circled the car. "Get back in."

Rooke drew the finger from his mouth and beckoned. She crouched beside him, blowing into her hands.

"Will you hear my confession?" He giggled, then turned suddenly grave.

She was about to refuse, but God must have whispered in her heart. Rooke was confiding, building the kind of bond they'd need.

"All right, Ted." Let the esoterica begin.

He traced the ice again. "Many years ago, in a city named Underwood, my brother and I discovered a wooden box filled with a beautiful iridescent powder."

"You were boys?"

"We were men, then. We found the box at the very end of a dark cobwebbed hallway, among the apocrypha and esoteric paintings and satanic books, in an old vargueño desk, in one of its many inlayed drawers, in an abandoned building called the Museum of Evil."

"Where is Underwood?" She *knew* geography.

"My great-grandfather built the museum. I never knew him, I was not alive when it was open. I went at the insistence of my brother."

"And Underwood? In Canada or the States?" Seri wished she hadn't asked. She had never seen Rooke so earnest—or was that lifted eyebrow a twitch of dark irony? If he was misleading her, he was the best tale-teller she had ever seen.

"It's never been clear." Rooke scratched the ice, peered into the incision. "We stole that powder."

Seri laughed. Quickly snapped it off.

"My great-grandfather was a hellfire preacher," Rooke said. "He was obsessed with evil."

Mine too, Seri thought. Good, good. Another connection.

"He was obsessed with hellish powers on earth, all manner of the occult." Rooke clawed the ice. "My brother should not have made me go."

Seri wondered how to keep it grounded. "So you have a brother?" she asked.

Rooke cast her a deadly glance. "Symbolically."

Of course. "And your great-grandfather is symbolic, too?"

"I always wanted his hat." Rooke hoarsened. "But he wouldn't even let me try it on. Then, when I found the powder, and it sparkled in a hundred shades of blue, he offered his hat in exchange." Rooke coughed.

"Your brother or great-grandfather?"

"I refused. There was a scuffle. Some of the powder spilled."

A hat? Again she almost laughed, then felt the roots of her hair twitch. He was messing with her, of course. Let him.

Rooke reached up to tap his teeth, bit a finger. "Do you remember when King David first saw Bathsheba? Do you recall the...." He coughed again, began to pack snow into the ice-scratch. "The inexplicable, overwhelming lust that possessed the poor man's judgment?"

Seri fingered the dimple in her cheek. "Okay, I get it. Or Eve in the garden, or Lot's wife, when she turned back to gaze at Sodom."

"She should have run away." Voice getting hoarser.

Lightning lit up the sky. Snow sifted through the empty intersection. Wires hummed and crackled.

Rooke put down a hand to steady himself. "My brother made me go. He made me touch the powder. It was *his* transgression."

Seri rose to return to the car. "Okay, your sins are forgiven. Penance is, phone your brother and apologize."

He didn't hear. "Years later, north of Underwood, when the Circus of Quaphsiel came looking, my mind darkened, and I asked him to hide my lovely powder. And he stole it." Rooke spit the word. "In its absence I have tried every consolation, every religion, every cult. They are all empty, all vanity." He looked up for agreement, or explanation, or absolution.

Seri paused. "Sorry. The circus of what?"

Minutes later they sped the streets again. Seri drove. She was glad to see the winking tail lights of other cars, other intersections filled with traffic and humanity. "Where's this church?"

So she was working on Christmas Eve, the night before Christ's birthday? She'd have to tighten up, do better. Right now there were a few necessities.

She swerved to avoid fallen Christmas trees scattered on the road.

"Goodness. Must've been that truck." Ornament glass popped beneath wheels. Snared tinsel fluttered in vain at the night sky.

Rooke clenched his teeth. "You give yourself away with angels."

"Excuse me?" The car crunched over a pine bough.

"We try so hard to order angels," Rooke said. "But each attempt ensnares us further in the worlds of superstition, pagan folklore, until we can never claw ourselves free."

Seri didn't argue. Yes Lord, she'd do her part, though it strained every fibre.

"You are the daughter of a mixed marriage," Rooke muttered.

A subtle barb, but she caught it, even the undertow. The child of both Christian and pagan: just like Saint Augustine.

† † †

"What curious light in here." Seri's hands bunched in her pockets.

"Stained glass." Rooke's eyes cruised the chapel. "Chops up the moon."

An ancient payphone rang, seemed to raise the dust. Instruments littered the tiny stage, drew the light across their curves and angles—bongos, tom-toms, temple blocks. Rooke tightened his shoulders at the sight.

"Follow me." He ignored the ringing phone, led Seri up the stairs behind the choirloft. "The sanctum." He opened the door at the top. She heard him gasp lightly.

"What sort of devil...?" He leaned against the door, gripping the knob. His own phone buzzed in a pocket.

The walls were perforated, plaster gashing. A drill hung stabbed in the wall. The floor was strewn with cigarette butts, sleeping bags, dusty cushions.

Rooke entered, kneeled by the sleeping bags. Ran a finger over the pillows.

"He's been here." Rooke sniffed the finger, gently put it between his lips.

"Punks." Seri understood.

Rooke withdrew the finger. "I should have come earlier."

"We, Ted. *We*."

He silenced her with an X-ray stare, then rose and moved to an ornate hardwood bookcase on the wall. His phone sounded again. His lips compressed as he seized an ancient book at the end of the case and pulled it. He reached behind the remaining books, knocked them off one by one, until the shelf was bare but for a tiny wooden box. He popped the unadorned lid, fingers quivering.

He turned. Seri had never seen his pupils so large.

"Gone," he whispered.

Seri guessed. "Your powder." Must have been some animating totem.

"Insult to injury." He dropped the box and tapped his phone, fingers still shaking.

"Thief," he rasped, putting the phone to his ear. "Mr. Frump. I have evidence."

A long pause.

"—Galt Gardens?" Rooke said. "Are you absolutely sure?"

He began to furiously tap his fingers on the wall.

"—when?"

He hit the door in two long strides, grabbing Seri's arm on the way.

"Ted. Not so tight."

He stopped, looked straight into her eyes.

"It's Christmas Eve," he said. *"Again."*

† † †

Malachi Frump's face was a lumpy quincunx, bespectacled, lenses thick as ship windows. He snapped his fingers, pointed in two opposite directions. "About five people on each side of the stage when they lit the flag. Up there." He slapped the amp.

"Who?" said Seri.

"The boy with the reggae hairlocks. I have the pictures."

Rooke clicked his tongue. "Where are the ashes?"

Frump removed printed pictures from a leather zip case and offered them, fanlike, to Rooke.

Rooke waved them off. "Where are the ashes?"

Frump wrinkled his nose. "Here on the floor, I suppose."

"The Mounties didn't take a sample?"

"Only city police here. They haven't disturbed evidence yet."

Seri followed Frump's finger. Two cops stood at the stairs, both tall, a little gone to seed. Both into unfinished workouts—bunched biceps, meaty chests, skinny legs.

Rooke kneeled and wiped a smudge across the wood-grained stage. He raised an ashy finger, appraised it. "Seri." Held up the finger. "Any green or blue?"

"It's ash, Ted."

"Ash." Rooke wiped the finger along the lapel of his coat. He straightened, taut and humming as a power cable. "Who are the officers?"

"Turner and Bachman," Frump said. "Over there."

Rooke looked at the cops. His lips soured. "Give me the pictures you took, Malachi. Merry Christmas."

He strolled across the stage. "Hey, Randy!"

The redheaded cop with a checkered crew cut turned, frowning. "How did you know my name?"

Rooke smiled. "Pretty obvious, 'migo. How many of you here?"

"Two," said the blond cop.

Rooke stopped between them. Tall as they were, he had to look down at their badges. "Why only one car?"

"Just a routine misdemeanour," Turner said.

"Who's in charge?"

"Me." Bachman ran a hand through red thicket.

"You." Rooke pursed his lips. "That explains a few things."

Bachman flexed. "Who are you?"

Rooke swept his eyes across the stage, fanned the pictures. He looked down, tapped a foot. Then said, quietly, "Did you make any arrests?"

"They got away," Bachman said.

"Away." Rooke's voice hoarsened. "You *do* know what an arrest is?"

"Hey bud, if you think this is some kind of—"

"Why," Rooke interrupted, "do people destroy things?"

"Huh?"

"What motivates vandalism?" Rooke rasped, pattered pictures on his thigh.

Turner and Bachman looked at each other.

"Who knows the vandals?" Rooke continued, voice hazing around the edges.

"Wul, uh, we haven't had time to—"

"Did you question anyone?"

"We've been—"

"Do you have *any* information?"

"Wul—"

Seri smiled with satisfaction. She had lit this fire.

Rooke snapped the pictures on his palm. "I've been here two minutes and already I have photographs. How long have you two been here?"

The cops looked at each other, breathing through their mouths.

"Listen," Bachman said. "Who are you to order us around like this?"

Rooke fixed his eye, until the cop looked down.

"Do you have any evidence?" Rooke said, voice cracking.

"Evidence?"

"That's where you gather up clues in order to make an educated guess about the perpetrators."

Seri almost laughed.

Bachman continued to look down. "Wul, sir, we have this broken violin. Turner."

Turner gathered some shards of fiddle from the table. "A violin, sir. Somebody broke it."

"Seri." Rooke's voice a husky whisper. "Take that fiddle."

"Can't," said Bachman.

"You going to stop us, Randy? Tell me: any criminal records?"

"Wul, no sir, I'm a cop."

Seri smiled. Rooke touched his brow. "I meant—never mind. Now listen."

The cops leaned forward, straining to hear.

"Who do the vandals know?" Rooke said. "Who can be appropriately questioned?"

"Sir, we've never seen these guys before."

Rooke tapped his brow. "They're musicians. They'll have a manager. Which academy did you boys go to?"

Bachman rubbed his thigh.

"Randy?" Rooke's voice was almost gone.

Turner looked up. "Sir, are you with the RCMP?"

Rooke ignored him.

"Mr. Frump," Seri said. "Do the vandals have a manager here?"

"As a matter of fact."

"Good," said Rooke. "We'll find out where they've flown with that powder."

Seri grinned. They were humming now. If Rooke needed some symbol of lost beauty to keep him moving, so what? He lived and breathed in a mythopoetic dimension.

"Powder?" Frump's eyes surfaced deep-pool lenses.

"Gentlemen." Rooke looked at the cops. "Dismissed. Better to reign in hell, Randy."

"Better to rain...?"

Rooke shook the pictures.

"And don't point those guns at anyone," he whispered.

† † †

Rooke followed Seri backstage, to a cramped room hung with a bare bulb. Rooke stood at the door, flicking the bulb on and off. His head almost reached the ceiling. Seri shuffled the violin pieces in the plastic bag. Maybe they were overdoing it here. No. Let this partnership grow.

She sniffed. Some kind of narcotic hung in the air—marijuana, but something unfamiliar beneath, some smell right off the spectrum. Each sniff made her think of ice cracking. She bit the inside of her cheek, suddenly aware of her tongue, the way it filled her mouth, the places it touched her teeth, how it descended her throat.

"Ted." She watched him flick the light switch. "What's due process here?"

He scanned her with those eyes. One hand dropped from the light switch, index finger still pointed. The other drew his nail clippers from a coat pocket. He nodded almost imperceptibly at the bare bulb. Seri looked—a spider web knit bulb to ceiling, fat red cat-faced spider watching from the edge.

"This room is laced with the last strands of a former life," Rooke whispered.

She nodded. Just flow with the demented poetry.

He slowly, smoothly reached out to the web, hand poised, not a tremor. Then one quick snatch. He plucked the spider from the web, shook it, held it at a delicate pressure. The lightbulb flickered.

"Here she is. The manager." Frump, at the door, escorting a thirty-ish woman with multi-coloured hair extensions.

"Sit down," Seri said.

Rooke did not look up from his spider.

"I'm not talking to *you*, asshole," the woman said, sitting in the single chair. "Are you the police?" She squinted at Rooke, then looked up as if trying to remember something.

Rooke smiled, continued to regard the spider.

Seri felt her tongue swelling. Drugs in the air. Her mouth watered. "What's your name?"

"What's yours?" The woman leaned forward, clawing lint from a pantleg.

Rooke looked up from the spider. "This is just an interview."

"I didn't do anything illegal or immoral," she said. "Do I get a lawyer?"

"You don't need a lawyer at the moment," Seri said. Rooke gave the spider a shake.

"Her name's Dawn Cherry," Frump said, snapping a finger. "What a disrespectful joke to every decent Canadian."

Dawn Cherry leaned back, continued to snatch and flick lint from her pants. "You won't intimidate me." Her jaw stiff.

Rooke set the nail clippers between his teeth and peeled the pictures from his pocket. He shuffled with one hand, held a snapshot at arm's length. "Do you manage these people?"

"If you can call it that," she said.

Rooke chattered the nail clippers to the side of his mouth. He shuffled another picture out. Seri saw fire, blur, a man with silvery hair holding a broken violin.

"How well do you know this man?" Rooke said.

Dawn Cherry folded her arms. Rooke continued to hold the photo, fingers twitching, other hand shaking the spider.

Seri cleared her throat. Obviously, they needed a bit of work on protocol and method. She'd see to it.

"Tell us." Rooke's voice was frayed to a hiss. "Where have these musicians gone?"

"Musicians," Dawn Cherry snorted.

"See," Rooke said. "We share a disdain, an unease." He jittered the picture, moved it closer to her face. "You had a personal relationship with this man."

She dug lint from fabric, flicked.

Rooke continued. "A personal relationship. You've been infected."

"No!" Dawn Cherry reached forward and snatched the remaining pictures. She sorted them, clutched one, threw the rest to the floor. She held up the picture: some kid with natty dreads holding a lighter to a flag.

"This," she said. "This is my partner. And one of my lovers."

Rooke palmed and rattled the spider, ready to roll dice.

"And the third," Dawn Cherry continued. "Lor. He's the leader."

"No." Rooke flipped the picture in his own hand, the silver-haired man. "Don't let the one in this picture beguile you. Where he leads, others follow." He pressed the picture, till its edges almost touched.

Seri sniffed. There was something deeply personal here. But it was off the map, a faint glimmering both obscured and brightened by haze. She noted it, filed it for future reference.

"You're after the wrong person." Dawn Cherry held up her picture. "This kid's brother is the original leader."

"His brother is dead." Rooke dropped the photo, watched it flutter to the floor. He opened his fist and picked the dizzy spider, held it up to the light. Then he drew the nail clippers from his teeth, and gently, deliberately, almost lovingly, clipped a spider leg.

Seri jerked and accidentally knocked the broken fiddle. Frump stood in the corner, snapping his fingers. Dawn Cherry bobbed back and forth, picking lint.

"I don't ..." she said. "I ...."

"Just an interview, Ms. Cherry." Rooke's voice seeped back from whisper.

"How do you know my name?"

Seri chewed her tongue. Dear Lord, Rooke was good. Still needed some work as far as protocol, but she'd rein him in. Right now, things were humming.

Snip. Another leg.

"Who are *you*?" Dawn Cherry said. "What right do you have to question me?"

Rooke remained silent.

Snip.

"Special branch of CSIS," Seri said.

"I don't know anything," Dawn Cherry said, rocking. "Alistair's ideas are completely off the wall. Quixotic. I never understood him. Never."

Rooke tightened, clipper frozen over another leg.

Dawn Cherry rocked. "They've renewed some old project, Christ sakes, some old journey or something, some nonsense about—"

Rooke dropped the clipper. His hand shook around the spider.

"You were *never* part of this project." He whispered, but his voice was back, all the undertones. "Not in either incarnation. Yet you are not fully innocent, either." He leaned closer.

"You." He reached for her with the spider. "Have much to learn." Placed it gently on her collar. "About love."

Dawn Cherry shrieked, swiped at the morbid boutonnière. It fell and landed on the picture of Alistair, then brushed itself in a slow circle on its remaining legs. Frump began to snap his fingers uncontrollably.

Seri took a step back. She made a note to herself: it was going to take some extra work to focus Rooke's tactics, shape that demonic energy.

"Where did the musicians go?" Rooke said.

Dawn Cherry gripped the sides of her chair, looking down. "Who are you? What do you know about me?"

Rooke smiled. "*Look* at me. Dawn."

She stared up, eyes wet, nose running. Leaned forward.

"Oh my God." She jerked back. "Oh my *God*."

† † †

Rooke slammed the back door of the union hall. Dawn bloodied the sky.

"Ted." Seri jogged to keep up. "Slow down. We need to crunch this information."

Rooke stopped. He knelt and cleared a patch in the snow, then removed the pictures from his coat. He shuffled them, removed one, wordlessly handed the rest to Seri.

"Thanks," she muttered. "What's your feeling on this Foggy Island? A real place?"

Rooke stared at the picture, the silver-haired man with violin.

"Seri." He carefully curled the edges of the picture and placed it in the snow. "Help me."

She remembered Rooke's clever website, his snare. He was the spider. And now the flies turned out to be old friends, or was this just more symbol?

Might be a jurisdiction problem here, a mandate conflict. She needed to pause, crunch this info, get some ancillary. Yet the hairs bristled on her arm, the way they used to on those rare occasions when Greg the youth pastor had forgotten himself and kissed her deeply.

Rooke struck a match and lit the picture of the man with silvery hair. It flared and poured inky smoke.

Seri kneeled. "Okay, listen. We'll start by following this lead north. We'll collate and analyze on the fly. I'll drive; you tell me everything you know, and we'll profile these subversives."

Again her stomach twinged. She'd have to carefully delineate between the real subversives and Rooke's demonic symbols. This would take all her philosophy: the clarity and precision of Augustine.

"North." Rooke leaned forward and breathed in the smoke. Then coughed a cloud of frost and carbon. "To Attarib's country."

Seri stood, shivering. Could she loosen up her rage for certainty, burn a prophet's faith as fuel? Defer the answers with the patience of Job? She considered angels named and unnamed. How many danced on the point of a needle? How many watched her now?

Yes, Attarib. Ruler of the ice and snow. First among winter angels.

Last riddle of the day.

uNZiPPingS

Lor motored north with a small entourage of strippers who, according to their winks and hints, quite possibly shared his manager in more ways than one. Three Caucasian dancers with an act called The Penalty Box and a schtick involving referee outfits and whistles. Three peelers with the dubious names Carrie Fraser, Vandy-Anne Hellemond, and Dawn Koharskee.

"Another Dawn?" Lor said.
"We used to know a Third. Dawn Ho." Carrie giggled.
"Not funny," said Vandy-Anne.
Canadians. Lor tightened his seatbelt.
The van hummed, Carrie the pilot, Dawn riding shotgun and twiddling radio nobs in search of classical, Vandy-Anne next to Lor in reading glasses, flipping through a current bestseller on obscure Canadian puns. Sometimes she unfolded her legs across his lap and switched the bestseller for her invest-ment dossier or a battered copy of *Hamlet*. Lor pulled his seatbelt tight and watched the landscape grow hairier with trees and shrubs, as if the country aged before his eyes. He carried no baggage. Just a bank card, bag of glitter, guitar case, and memories.
Sometimes he talked.

"What are your real names?" he said, as the van travelled the narrow highway north of Edmonton, flexed all along the coiled banks of Crooked River.

Carrie laughed. "Everyone always wants our real names."

"A rose by any other name," said Vandy-Anne.

"Would be as thorny." Dawn rustled in the glovebox and found a pack of mint gum.

Vandy-Anne put down *Hamlet* and peeled off her glasses. "How fast you going, Care?"

"One-fifty."

Vandy-Anne nodded. "You know, Lor, in most religions a name gives one power over the named. You think we're going to offer you that?"

"You a Christian?" Lor said.

She smiled. Sadly, it seemed. Then replaced her glasses and opened *Hamlet*. After a spell she looked up. "The world is too full of unexpected joys for there to be no spirit world. But the world is too full of horrors for there to be a single god in control of everything."

"Argument from design," Carrie chirped from the pilot seat. "Dawnny, what do you think?"

"This gum," Dawn said. "Hard as rock."

Sometimes, after they had all booked into a hotel, Lor would go to watch his companions work. They danced at almost every dot on the map: Spirit River, Seventown, Little Smoky. At Sexsmith they didn't bother to enumerate the obvious jokes, for which Lor was curiously glad. He spent most evenings peering into his ginger ale, foot tapping on his guitar case, much to the amusement of his new friends.

"For a punk you're pretty shy," Vandy-Anne said, over pizza at a dusty taproom in Black Fly Creek. "Peel a few layers, what do you get."

Lor drained his ginger ale, fifth of the night.

"Finished with *Hamlet*?" She touched his hand lightly.

"Almost," he lied.

The next day he was bolder. "Have you worked this territory before?"

"More times than I care to count." Vandy-Anne pointed out the van window. "I know every bluff, every tree."

"Can you name them?"

She smiled. "Ironically, we just skirted No Name Ridge. Believe it?"

Lor took off her shoe, lightly rolled her toes. "And that?"

"Toad Hill. Beyond it, Khahago Creek. Oooh." Her toe cracked; she put back her head. "Khahago is Cree for raven. They've been here for over twelve thousand years."

"Who?"

Late that night they crossed the Peace River at Devil's Elbow, to a clump of small islands nesting a clutch of hamlets. Lor couldn't believe the names: Gipsy Creek, Merlin, Valhalla, Faust.

"We hit every one," Carrie said, stretching, clever knees guiding the wheel.

"Well, except." Dawn fiddled the radio nob, finding only static.

"Except what?" Lor said.

"Crazy Lake," Dawn said. "As you approach it gets darker, sounds muffle. You hear voices. Haunted town. We won't dance there for all the tea in China."

They all laughed, but Lor knew she wasn't kidding. His fingers softened around Vandy-Anne's slender foot. He held with both hands.

The hamlets were a snowball's throw from each other. Four days' combined travel lasted exactly fifteen minutes. In Faust they had a day off, with nothing much to do but watch TV. Dawn and Carrie went to the hotel lounge to try and drum up mint juleps and other rare drinks, while Lor and Vandy-Anne brought a sixer of ginger ale to her room.

"The secret to this town's name is rather unappealing." She stretched on the bed. "E.T. Faust was a locomotive engineer, and there was no Mephistopheles in his story. See? Sometimes it's better not to know."

Lor sat on the chair, smiled, sipped.

"The next town is Atikameg," she said. "Don't know the explanation for the name. An English mispronunciation, I heard."

Atikameg? Sounded like an angel's name to Lor. He looked at Vandy-Anne, and suddenly felt sickened by his own attraction to her. One of those feelings he sometimes had at breakfast with a lover, when everything abruptly tasted wrong, out of context, the flesh aware of its own futility.

"It's okay," she whispered.

He set the ginger ale on the radiator and bowed his head. Her breathing sounded so lovely.

"Lor." Vandy-Anne rose to sitting. "I'll tell you my name if you give me something of equal value in return."

"Yes," he said, and stood to go to his own room.

North of Devil's Elbow his fingertips began to feel numb. One night in Fort Lamneth, in a tiny bar carpeted with must and old smoke, he sat with Vandy-Anne to watch the last two acts. She gently stroked his fingers, turned his palm upward and mapped the lines. But when she spoke, he saw himself across a vast deserted space swished by wind and shadows, and her voice was lost.

After that, he remained aloof and noncommittal. His speech and gestures stiffened. He lost his rhythms, all the while desperate to be warm and kind.

The harder he tried to connect, the frostier he became, until he could only watch himself fail, as the space between them waxed to awkwardness. Night after night they travelled. Moonlight whitened the van, and Vandy-Anne grew distant by small turns, till the conversation waned to a sliver, and she curled up her legs and set them across his lap no more.

† † †

Afternoon darkened the Caribou Mountains. No one spoke for miles. Finally Dawn unbuckled and pressed her nose against the windshield.

"Is there a serious lack of light up here, or what?"

"'Tis the season," Carrie said.

Dawn sat back. "Where is this Bat Lake?"

"Smack in the middle of the Thickwood Hills. Three hours."

"Wow." Dawn swiped at the windshield. "Never been this far north. Bat Lake an okay town?"

Lor caught Vandy-Anne staring at him, over reading glasses. She frowned, returned her eyes to the open page. He looked down.

That night he stared back. A damp and tiny pub called the Fangoo, its timbers shipwrecked at the mossy heart of Bat Lake Inn. He sat at a pine table smelling of freshly cut pencil crayons and sucked in heavy sub-bass, ignoring rednecks yelling across the oval bar, flickers from a widescreen hockey game. His ginger ale remained unsipped, as he eyed each of his three companions in turn. Smoke thickened. His glasses grimed. The dancers doubled, skinny-dipped through hazy wavelets. He stared. He clutched his pockets.

"What the fuck you doing?" Carrie yelled in his ear.

Vandy-Anne crawled onstage to Max Webster's "Beyond the Moon," blanket ruffling, lights hollowing smoke.

"What?" He kept his eyes trained. Noticed that Vandy-Anne was wearing her reading glasses.

Carrie sat on the table. "You're a fucking pervert."

He felt a rush of sadness. Kept his eyes trained. Vandy-Anne looked at him from the stage, fixed him through her glasses. No smile.

"Look at me," Carrie said.

He didn't.

"Lor."

He got up, looked stupidly at the stamp on his hand. She grabbed him by the shirt and reeled him in, nearly burning his neck with her cigarette's cherry.

"Lor. What are you doing?"

"Watching the show."

She released him, then stalked off shaking her head. Lor glanced once to the stage, but Vandy-Anne was engaging a patron. The glasses were gone. He picked up his guitar and headed for the door, feeling like the night was frayed along the seams, his jeans were out of style, and he was leaving the high school prom he never even attended.

† † †

His room was freezing.

They opened the door slowly. He sat up in bed, noticed Vandy-Anne's knuckles, white on the knob.

"What do you think you were doing in there?" Dawn said.

He lay back.

"We don't want you to watch us any more," Carrie added.

A long pause, swell of old TV music.

"You invite me every night." Lor shivered.

Carrie laughed bitterly. "Well, not anymore, sweetie."

She was echoed by canned laughter. Lor pressed himself down into the mattress, finding it hard to breathe. He stared at the ceiling, noticed the textures of stipple, like tiny nipples. Dawn said something. Lor's attention lapsed—he missed it.

"Why am I so different," he said. "Than all the other guys in there? Staring at you."

Dawn snorted. "Some of them are honest."

Weather report on TV, something about more snowfall. The room dipped to the left. Lor's legs elongated. The mattress softened beneath him, cold sheets.

"I," he said. "Are those breasts real?"

"Oh man." Dawn sat on the bed. Lor almost slid off onto the floor, tumbled up into the stipple.

"What do you care what's real or not?" Carrie said.

"I need to hear your stories," he heard himself say.

Dawn popped up off the bed. He felt springs coiling deep beneath him.

"Man," Dawn said. "Didn't you turn out to be an asshole. And we *liked* you."

"Just goes to show," Carrie said.

Wait, Lor thought. Please. It's just. I....

"I paid my cover charge," he said. "Four-fifty, like everyone else."

Carrie laughed her bitter laugh. "Four-fifty."

"Asshole," Dawn whispered, almost a question.

They marched out, flicking off the lights. The mercury dipped.

Lor lay in the darkness, dappled with TV images, tears beading one eyelash. Canned laughter welled behind the screen, washed out in loudening waves. He clutched the remote, squashed the volume until the sound softened, softened, dwindled to silence.

He turned over and was shocked to see Vandy-Anne still sitting in the motel chair. She wore a heavy wool Mackinaw coat spattered with colourful patterns and stared at him through reading glasses. His heart clumped as he sniffed her strong cold perfume. She said nothing. They watched each other for minutes, until the TV went blank. The radiator clanked. Lor sat up, shivering.

Finally she removed her glasses, folded them neatly, dressed them in a zipped coverlet. Then unbuckled her Mackinaw and placed it around Lor's shoulders.

"They're real," she said, and headed for the door.

Lor stared after her, until the walls liquified and spilled all over the rug, and his bed floated on the swell and slowly turned toward the window. He awoke later facing the dim noonday sun.

"Shit!" He leaped up, still fully clothed, raced to the window in bare feet.

"Shit!" He burned his palm on the radiator, stepped back, peered out. The van was gone.

He ran to the door, out into the snow. The van was nowhere to be seen. He stared at the fading bar stamp on his hand, until his toes and heels burned with cold, forcing him to hop from foot to foot. He felt his pocket for the bag of glitter, suddenly remembered his guitar in the back of the van.

"Shit! Those damned...." He raced back into the room, chased by frosty winds, headed for the phone. As he reached he saw his guitar, in its case, on the bed, next to the imprint of his own body. He looked down, shook his head. Of course. He didn't have a cent of cash anyway. He had a bank card. The girls had paid for the rest, double-crossing sweethearts.

He sighed, grabbed the case, heard something jingle inside. What was this? He unbuckled the lid, opened. Four stacked coins clinked under the strings, twos and quarters. Exactly four-fifty, Canadian.

† † †

He sat on his guitar case by the curb, wrapped in the Mackinaw, and slurped four-fifty worth of coffee from the motel machine. After he had bonged his weight in caffeine he stood up and almost tumbled into the ditch. He sat back down. Where was he going to go? His future was darkening with the afternoon sky. But at least he was out of Lethbridge, away from the Weird.

A light winked on and off in the distance, some dwelling hidden by small trees. He suddenly remembered a summer morning in the late sixties, still early enough for dew and a chill in the air, twitter of birds, smell of pine, and himself, still a kid, astride the fence watching a spinning spider. A souvenir from his own life. But the colouring, the texture, the feel....

He shifted on the guitar case. What *was* the texture? Fold the memory, smooth it, stroke its fibres, and the kid was also someone else, as if Lor was at once feeling and spying on his own memories. All strange and new. Yet old. Then it seemed his life stretched back through such a tangle of experiences that hundreds of years were stuffed into his thirty, a fibre fraying hundreds of bright threads. But could those threads be woven back together? And did he want them to be? Yes, of course he did. Of course he did. The spider went on spinning.

A car honked, blasting his reverie. He looked up. An ancient blue Camaro idled in front of him, tire two inches from his foot. He stood, as the window hummed down and a woman leaned over the passenger seat.

"Need a ride?" Tall, middle-aged Japanese woman, buzz cut bleached white. Lor remembered her immediately. But her hair was all gone.

He raised his hands. "What are you doing here?"

She laughed. "*Quvianaqtuq quagapsi*. Get in, punky."

†††

They drove the winter road through Wood Buffalo Park to Peace Point Reserve, then the Pine Lake Highway toward Salt River. The blue Camaro rolled smoothly, sure-footed as a four-wheel drive. The woman said nothing, laughed gently from time to time. Lor could smell her raspberry lipstick.

"Where are you going?" she said at last.

"Yellowknife."

"Coming from?"

"Nowhere."

She laughed. Sound like a low bell, melody that turned to smoke before you could hum it back. "Ah, the laconic type. Can you form a sentence, or you just good to look at?"

He couldn't think of a comeback.

"Guess we'll find out." She extended a hand. Long, piano-playing fingers, silver rings at the first knuckle of pointer and index. "Darcilee Shimozowa. Call me Darci."

"Are you Canadian?" He sure hoped not.

"I asked for your name."

"Sure." His heart sped. "Call me Lor."

She grinned. "Lor of Yellowknife?"

"Just Lor."

"Try again."

"Of the flies?"

"Well. Got the charm turned to broil, I see."

"Turned off." Best he could think of.

"Aren't you the saucy one?"

"Nope."

"Depends what you're served on."

"Meaning?"

"Guess we'll find out."

Lor inhaled deeply. He thought of Vandy-Anne, everything he had seen in Alberta's north. "Meaning?"

"Think about it."

She opened a window, reached for a grey toque, unrolled it over her peroxide buzz cut. Her hands so expressive, a dancer's or puppeteer's smoothing ice on a snowman's head. Her ringed fingers pure music, like it was the last unrolling ever.

Lor held his thighs and stared sidelong. There was something unnatural about this woman—like her body was clustered with twice the nerves as usual. That berry lipstick, that grey toque. He looked down.

"Cat got your tongue?" she said. "Better your tongue gets the cat."

"Ha," he managed, but his mind was unspooling.

"Guess we'll find out," she said.

He blipped out, back to high school, pillows, and girls on cold winter evenings, his dad's cranberry vodka cloudy from the freezer. When fear always spiced desire, and nights were mulled with magical cinnamon-flavoured sex, and he always thought his heart would explode mid-kiss, and cyclones of blue lust whirled through the house and knocked over all his mother's furniture.

He had moved out at eighteen and never gone back.

Suddenly he missed Alistair. "Can you get me to Yellowknife? I have to meet some friends there." He drew the bag of glitter from his pocket and twisted the drawstrings around a finger, regretted mentioning his old companions.

"I'm headed there myself," Darci said. "Do you want to know why?"

Lor tugged the string, squeezed the dust inside. The scent of raspberry tickled his nose, as he nudged to the very edge of the seat and pressed against the cold window. He wasn't going to look Darci in the eye. He wanted to be back with the strippers, even after last night; they were mean, but at least they had their own kind of logic.

She laughed. "I was a lot like you once. On the same expedition."

He stole a long glance at her fingers, noticed her watch, perpetually stuck at twelve o'clock.

"Your hands don't move," he said.

"Oh, they move. You'll find out."

He looked at her face. "I mean the—"

"Watch. Yes." Her smile rapacious. "Music?"

She turned on the stereo. Strange melody rained from overhead speakers, distant violin over drums and bass. Lor closed his eyes and tried to remember Vandy-Anne's face, but could picture only her glasses. He squeezed the dust.

"Are you chased by some *daemon*?" Darci said. "You have the look."

Lor opened the pouch and poured some dust into his hands, sifted it through fingers, pressed the grains into the lines on his palm.

"My old lover used to grind a blue powder from the bones of magpies." Her voice drifted. "After he formed the circus. The Circus of Quaphsiel. Usually travelled about the Arctic, but on occasion far, far south."

"Magpies." Lor's breath quickened. "Powder."

"Yes."

"When?"

She clinked two rings. "Oh, many years ago. So long. I was once like you."

"When?"

She stroked raspberry from her lip, dipped her tongue at the reddened fingertip. "For many years I have chased a particular tribe of pure white magpies, across rivers, prairies, mountains. Even in the leafy corners of city parks and green spaces. These 'pies have no iridescence, not in any light."

"Quite a story."

"But before Christmas, in an arborescent greenstrip, in a city far south, I finally realized—" She turned to him, eyes flooded. "These white 'pies live *here*, in the Arctic."

"Here?" His heart bopped.

"There are many possibilities. Perhaps they came across the Bering Strait from Europe. Perhaps they have always lived here, in secret. Perhaps they're trying to get back to Europe. Or perhaps they're some new breed," she nodded at him, "altogether."

Lor felt a well of immense desire, somewhere outside his body. He leaned forward to flick at the glovebox handle.

She wasn't laughing now. "They live three times as long as a woman. If a nut is too hard, they'll drop it from a great height to crack it."

Crack it. He clicked the handle, bobbled the glovebox back and forth.

"They have a complex language," she continued, "rattles, gargles, squawks, coos."

He tugged at the glovebox.

"They'll pull up the lines of ice fishermen," she said. "Steal all the fish."

He tugged.

"I've watched them slide down icy slopes in plastic cups, taking turns, for their own amusement."

The glovebox plunked open and a bale of black hair spilled out across Lor's lap. He yelled, bounced up in the seat and hit his head on the roof.

"These are regular magpies," she said. "Not white. That's my hair. I kept it."

Lor exhaled, one long breath. "Your hair. Jesus."

She laughed. "I was starting to look too much like one of you. You still have the dust, yes? Keep it away from *him*."

He quickly gathered the hair, stuffed it back in the glovebox. She watched, half a berry lip turned upward. He sat back and rubbed his forehead, as the music sizzled to a hiss.

She watched him, one hand on the wheel. He couldn't stand her silence. "How long have you been chasing magpies?"

"How long." She flicked her eyes to the rearview mirror, then the road. "Longer than you can *imagine*."

† † †

Yellowknife was less forbidding than Lor expected—well-treed, civilized, nestled along the North Arm of Great Slave Lake. Darci slowed the Camaro and rumbled up Ptarmigan Road to tiny Rat Lake, where the Potiphar Hotel stubbed the hills with a matrix of columns and porticoes, sweating warm light and clinks of suppertime.

"Wait here, punky."

She pulled over to the roadside and stepped out. Lor watched her build a snowman. The open door chimed the whole time; she rose and stared south.

"A warding charm," she said, climbing back in, dusting snow from her pinkened palms.

"For what?"

"Where do you need to go?"

Lor looked at his fingers. He heard children's voices across the frozen water. "Uh. Not sure," he said. "My friends took off on me."

"Ah." She laughed. "Well then, you can stay with me at the Potiphar."

He watched a helium balloon escape a window to trail its string into the clouds. "Not a good idea."

"Got a better one?" she said, parking.

Lor tapped his foot in the lobby while waiting for Darci to book in. Kids from a birthday party darted under tables and between his legs, swirling the carpets, yanking balloons. All of them were basted with icing at lips and fingers, clutching cupcakes. High above, lonely balloons watched from the ceiling. A girl with chipped teeth stumbled in front of Lor, squashed her cupcake as she hit the floor and released her balloon. Darci's long fingers snatched it.

"Come on." Darci took Lor's arm with her free hand. "I have a room in the tower."

"Hey!" said the girl. "Thath my balloon."

The room was small but opulent. Peppermint carpets like a dream-lawn carefully cut, four-poster bed, gingham curtains that swayed to phantom breezes, though the hotel air was as still as an August afternoon. Darci bent to tug the bedsheets, releasing the balloon. Lor watched it scuttle northward across the ceiling, as he stood in the centre of the room, fists at his sides.

"So, when did you first hear about these magpies?" he said. "The ones without the green and blue."

"Or black." Darci stopped in mid-tug, turned her head slowly. "That was only a story."

She dimmed the lights and began to pull off her coat and sweater. She dropped her arms suddenly; for a moment the sleeves fell from her shoulders, and her shadow on the wall had many arms. Lor sat on the couch and looked for the balloon. Must have been behind his head.

"That's a nice coat," Darci said.

"A gift." Lor heard a pop. Not the balloon, more like a cork. Darci bent to decant a bottle of Zinfandel. Lor stared at her eldritch features, white cotton T-shirt bright as moonlit snow. She spoke. Lor tried to follow the ripple of her voice, but it had too much surface area, too many folds. He heard another pop, some kind of plastic lid.

Darci sat beside him. "Moisturize me."

He smelled the aloe in the cream.

"I don't think—"

He noticed the rough texture of her elbows.

She dabbed cream on a fingertip. "What's the matter?"

He pressed his fists together. He pulled off one sleeve of his Mackinaw coat.

"It's not like we'll meet again," she said.

"No." He wouldn't look her in the eye.

She stared at him without breathing a word. He turned to meet her eyes, but immediately looked down at the carpet. She tittered.

"What?" he said.

"Just waiting for you to ask." Each syllable stretched to a delicate tension. She stroked a finger between his shoulder blades.

"Ask what?" he said.

She smiled, a slowly brightening glow. "Anything you like. The answer is yes."

He sat wordless.

"Yes." She took his fingers in her own and drew them to her eyelids, now closed. He could feel her eyes moving beneath, smell the raspberry from her lips. She seized his index finger and popped it in her mouth. He felt her teeth first, then her tongue, licking lengthwise knuckle to knuckle. His back arched. His fingerprint became a whirlpool, all of his nerves pure light, every cell drawn by dark undertow.

"Darci." He pulled back his hands and stood. His Mackinaw flapped across one shoulder. She opened her eyes, looked up at him.

"You think I'm a fallen angel?" She bared her teeth. "Think I can't love?"

He hardly heard. The balloon was floating somewhere "No. I—"

She grabbed his Mackinaw, a bit roughly he thought.

"Sit," she said.

The balloon's shadow trailed across the ceiling. She tightened her grip on the Mackinaw.

"Sit," she repeated. "Lor."

"No." It hovered near him.

She pulled him down. He slackened his shoulder, and the coat peeled from his arm. He looked her in the eyes, but they were wrong, all wrong— twin galaxies, one blue, one green.

He snapped up, grabbed his guitar, hastened for the door. "I have to go." He broke into a trot. At the door he stopped. Darci stood in the small hallway, holding his multi-coloured coat.

"Run." Her voice husky. She held up his jacket.

Suddenly he felt hotter than ever in his life. He spun the doorknob. Fled.

"Next time I will not be gentle," Darci called after him.

He hit the stairwell, leaped two stairs at a time. Then raced across the lobby weaving through kids and cupcakes, out the door and down the street, all the way down, to the bottom of the hill, to the end of the road, where he dove headfirst into a snowman. It collapsed around him, sizzled his skin. Flies buzzed in his ears, and for a moment he thought he heard a pop, somewhere in the liquid light at the top of the hill, at the tip of the tower, as the black balloon burst at last.

†††

Children dug him out.

"Mister, you ruined our snowman. You broke the charm."

Lor felt like he had been asleep for a hundred years. "My guitar."

"It's right here." A cherubic boy, black hair combed straight back from a widow's peak. He brushed snow from Lor's face with a soft glove. "See? You're in the ruins. But everything will be okay. We have other magicks."

Lor sat up. He was nested in a pile of old maps and *Playboys* from the fifties. He reached for his guitar. A gang of kids circled him, faces flushed, eyes bright.

"Who are you?" said the cherub.

"Who are *you*?" Lor gripped the guitar case.

"Peace." The cherub lifted a hand. "I'm Sid. Sid Hoar." He circled his hand. "This is my gang."

A girl in a striped *The Cat in the Hat* snowboard cap leaned forward and offered Lor a chocolate bar, silver wrap half unzipped.

Lor shook his head. "My name is Kenneth Kowalski."

Sid Hoar nodded. He pulled a thin joint from his vest pocket, to Lor's surprise. These kids were too young, seven or eight at best. Sid Hoar lit up, offered to Lor. "Do you have a nickname, Kenneth Kowalski?"

"Thanks." Lor inhaled all the way to his toes. "No. People call me Ken."

"As will I." Sid Hoar rocked on his heels, exhaled smoke.

"Ken." The girl with the chocolate bar accepted the joint.

"Ken. Ken." Rippled softly through the gang.

Sid Hoar smiled. "Tell us, Ken. Why are you in Yellowknife?"

"I...." Lor looked at their curious faces. He searched his brain, sifting memories. No connections. The emptiness troubled him. He didn't seem to be properly dressed. Was he missing a coat or sweater?

"Why are you here?" The girl said.

Lor stared at her.

"Why?" Echoed softy from young mouths.

"I." Lor hugged his guitar. "I have no idea."

CHAPTER NINETEEN

BeHiNd tHE TReE

Sid Hoar took Lor by the hand and led him down a long and winding road. The kids trailed, whispering.

"Where are we going?" Lor clutched his guitar till his knuckles ached.

"To the Old Stope."

Lor shivered. This place was in many ways a normal city, yet somehow like the moon. Beneath the amenities and architecture hunched bones of rock, whistled by haunting winds. What could he possibly be doing here?

They wandered to the Rock, a massive chunk of Precambrian Shield at the centre of Old Town. The kids ushered Lor all the way up to Pilot's Monument, where they sat in darkness and swilled a panoramic view of the bay, crushed glass glimmering to the horizon. Lor's eyeballs quivered at the immensity. He focused on the planes and frozen barges studding the shoreline, finally looked down altogether. Then the strike of a match, the smell of lit weed. A Twin Otter roared below, and Sid Hoar took him by the wrist.

"Ken. Why do you cast your eyes *down*?"

Lor waved off the joint. "All that space. Makes me dizzy."

Sid Hoar smiled. They trudged a length of stairs pounded into knots of rock, while Sid Hoar quietly and solemnly served as tour guide.

"Wildcat Cafe." He pointed. "Pentecostal Mission. House of Horrors."

He placed his hand in the small of Lor's back. "Old Stope."

Lor saw the tree, a crooked Jack pine that reminded him of an old man, once tall, now stooped, still possessed of some barky wisdom. A croak above, and a raven alighted the treetop, where it opened its beak and voiced a harp-like shimmer.

Lor's breath snagged. He felt Sid Hoar's hand stroke his spine.

"Ken. You okay?"

Lor stared at the raven. He knelt, began to unbuckle his guitar case. "I know why I'm here."

Sid Hoar knelt beside him, whispered: "When you've lost the meaning, you can create another."

Lor removed the magpie guitar. "I'm here to learn."

He plinked a few banjo notes, then raised his head to watch the raven flap into night sky, unspooling a slipstream of arpeggios.

Lor smiled. "To learn. How to play this guitar."

"You may find your muse," Sid Hoar said. He gestured. "In the Old Stope."

"In the tree?"

"No, Ken. The Old Stope is a hotel."

"Hotel?"

Sid Hoar nodded. *Behind* the tree."

† † †

"Telegram for Mr. Lor!" said the concierge. He looked a bit like a handsome witch—beaked nose, black hair tied back, jacket festooned with tiny silver medallions. And dark glasses. Funny thing in a dark lobby.

"How can he see?" Lor asked the desk manager, Mr. Lifeson.

Lifeson leaned forward. "He has the inner vision. Like Mr. Milton, the poet."

"Telegram for Mr. Lor!"

Lifeson chewed the tip of his fountain pen. "Well, Mr. Kowalski, everything here is in order. Your room is waiting." He jingled a key. "Everything prepaid. If you could just—"

"Telegram for Mr. Lor!"

"Mr. Lee." Lifeson tapped the pen on desktop. "Really. It's quite clear that whoever this Mr. Lor is, he is either unavailable or indisposed at the moment. So if you could just knock it off."

"The telegram says urgent," said the concierge. "Must meet with you. Stop. Everything has fallen apart. Stop. Will you come with us? Query. Please rendezvous at—"

"Yes, yes, Mr. Lee. Why don't you go find Master Hoar? He seems privy to all the Old Stope's secret business."

"Very well." Lee trudged across the lobby.

Lifeson sighed and turned to Lor. "My apologies, Mr. Kowalski. While the Old Stope is often the very paradigm of indolence, things do, at times, get a little hectic here behind the tree." He handed the fountain pen. "Now, if you could just sign here and print your home address."

Lor signed. Then stopped, befuddled. "I...."

"Yes?"

"I don't think I have a home address."

"Where are you from?"

Silence.

"Ahhh." Lifeson took the pen. "Meeting a sweetheart, then?" He winked. "You have my word, nobody 'round here's the wiser." He tapped his forehead. "Why don't I give you a tour of the hotel?"

He crooked Lor's elbow and clutched with a slender hand. "Come along. The Old Stope here was built in '28. You may be curious about the seemingly anomalous Spanish design."

"Well, I—"

"Our hotel was copied precisely from a moderately famous hotel in Lethbridge, called the Marquis. Bing Crosby stayed there during his annual pheasant-hunting excursions to what must have seemed, to him, the great white north."

Lor nodded politely.

"Seventy-eight rooms, each with private bath," Lifeson continued. "Meals can be taken either à la carte or table d'hôte." He stopped, put a finger to his chin. "You may want to take your meals at the neighbouring Wildcat Cafe. Master Hoar and his gang most often do."

"The kid?"

Lifeson squinted an eye. "Mr. Kowalski. You will find the ambience here is such that fraternity and solitude are never at odds. Do you understand me? Your room."

"Thank you." Lor entered the small room and stepped lightly to the middle. He set his guitar case on the bed, slowly unkinked each finger from the handle. Then stepped back and put his hands in his pockets.

"You move as if the guitar is set with explosives." Lifeson, eyeing him from the hallway.

Lor stood silently and watched Lifeson in the mirror. Neither moved. Lifeson said no more. Just stood, an elven boy scout with red jacket and long pale hair.

Finally Lor turned and shut the door. He went back to the bed to stare at the guitar case, found he couldn't open it, not yet. There was much work to do here, much to learn. So he stared. His breath slowed until his chest barely

rose and fell. He lightly pressed palm to fingertips. At last he blinked and took
a breath. Perhaps a walk before the first lesson would clear his head, prepare
his mind. He turned, opened the door.

"Why are you here, Mr. Kowalski?" Lifeson hadn't moved a millimetre.

Lor smiled. "I'm here to learn how to play that guitar."

Lifeson pursed his lips, turned and strode the hallway. "Mr. Lee!"

Lor wheeled the other direction and wandered corridors until he found
himself back at the foot of his bed. He unbuckled the case and stared at the
magpie guitar. His eye wandered the spider cracks, the blues and greens. He
reached a finger and tapped a harmonic. Yes, this would take much work.
He filled his lungs, plucked one quick note, one spry triad, a ginger strum, a
thrum, a dash—brittle chords stacking till they snapped and fell like dust to
cold tile.

† † †

The magpie guitar did not want to be learned. It twisted each note, spit them
in a pile at Lor's feet. So Lor ripped off a piece of his shirt and scoured the
strings, up and down till they stopped squeaking. Once clean, the fretboard
had more glide, but insisted on catching his fingers between strings. He
clipped and rounded his nails, then tried again. This time a few stray notes
seeped between his fingers and hovered as a chord.

Lor looked at his hand, shook it. "I did not play that."

He fingered the fretboard again. Tried for a standard barre chord, got a
suspended seventh.

"Shit."

He muted the strings at the bridge, freed a gush of notes. He muted
harder, but the notes continued to ring, then wither. This was impossible. He
tossed the chords, went for a regular scale, but his fourth finger locked, and
the spiteful notes peeled off again. The finger kept locking until he put the
guitar down and massaged his palm. What he needed here was more warm-
up. Give himself tendinitis, fooling around like this.

The guitar went silent. Lor felt suddenly alone. Frustrated, he left the
guitar napping on the bed and headed out through the hotel lobby.

"Try the Wildcat Cafe," Lifeson called from behind the desk. "Master
Hoar usually takes his dinner there about this time."

Dinner? What time was it? Lor suspected he had missed a night's sleep
somewhere.

Mr. Lee popped his head around the corner. "Telegram for Mr. Lor!"

Lifeson dropped his head and put hands on hips. "Really, Mr. Lee—"

Lor darted into cold night. If it *was* night. The sky was dark, but the snow held a ghostly twilight, almost mauve. Lor squinted as he crunched across iced rock toward the log structure still further behind the tree. He threw open the door. A hot rush fogged his glasses.

"Ken." Sid Hoar looked up from a long table set with coffee and a basket of steaming potatoes. "You're just in time to join us. Sit. Let me introduce you more fully to my gang."

For the next few days—they seemed like days—Lor followed a pattern: solitary frustration with the magpie guitar, a walk out to the Wildcat for a bit of spirit and community. The kids welcomed him as an old friend, introduced themselves each time with poise and gravity. Blackie Anderson, Sid Hoar's main sidekick, perhaps girlfriend. Sleepy Jim, the laconic one. Jack Castle, Popeye Perkins. The twins, Dorothy and Hazel Cinnamon. Others, whose names he forgot.

They chatted. Ate. Slurped coffee. Those kids drank a *lot* of coffee. After winding conversations, Lor would scurry back to the hotel, chased by a creeping sense of agoraphobia, pulled by the enchantments of the magpie guitar.

On what seemed the third day, the guitar renewed its coyness. Lor, angered, decided to strengthen his fingers. He would sit and listen to Sid Hoar in the Wildcat, all the while squeezing a rubber ball from Lifeson's surprising stash of toys. But the stronger his fingers got, the worse he played. He began to punch the notes, dig in with the pick, finally switching to a quarter. The guitar only tossed out bloody tonal shreds.

"What exactly do you seek?" Sid Hoar peered through coffee steam.

Lor squashed the ball. "I just want to master that damn guitar."

Blackie Anderson laughed. "Everyone wants to be the master. And everyone wants a quest. But sometimes the two can't go together."

Lor squeezed. "What do you mean, a *quest*?"

Blackie Anderson smiled, buttered her spud.

Sid Hoar leaned forward. "Ken. Beyond Old Town there is a garbage dump that belongs only to the ravens. Through the dump wends a tiny river of black water. Where does it go?"

Lor bit into potato, looked up. All the kids were staring at him, red cheeks poised over coffee mugs.

"Well shit, *I* don't know," Lor said.

"Exactly." Sid Hoar dipped a finger in his coffee, then sprinkled a bit of sugar on the fingernail. "Its headwaters are unknown. What is its name?"

Lor shrugged.

"Right again." Sid Hoar sucked the sweet finger. "Ken. Listen. Next weekend we journey upstream from the garbage dump to find out."

Lor laughed. "You kids on drugs?"

Sid Hoar didn't smile. Beside him Sleepy Jim stood, put his palms flat on the table.

"Aren't you coming with us?" he said in a raspy alto.

† † †

On the fourth day the sun briefly pierced the clouds like a necromancer's eye. Lor immediately scuttled back into the Old Stope, back through the lobby—"Telegram for Mr. Lor!"—back to his room and the magpie guitar.

Again it resisted his efforts. He tried to keep his thumb under the fretboard, but it crept over and sapped his leverage. He tried to use the whammy bar, but notes vanished the instant he touched it. He flipped the guitar to check the whammy springs, noticed a sharp crack reopening across the body's back, starting at the routing and snaking up. He couldn't tell where it was going, but it reminded him of the Mackenzie River on the enormous map Sid Hoar would spread across the table, back in the Wildcat, while his gang gathered 'round to sip coffee and squint at possible quest routes.

Sid traced a finger across the map. "Ken. Where you from?"

"I'm not sure."

"Do you have any friends?"

Lor chewed a lip.

Sid stroked the paper. "Anyone you love?"

"I hope not."

"Come with us."

"No."

After that Lor rarely entered the Wildcat, and then only to nuzzle the shadows like a wallflower gone to seed. On the sixth day he tried to channel his frustration into new ways of seeing the guitar, the connections between notes, his own fingers. But the more he stared at the fretboard dots, the more they unmapped. On the seventh day the guitar folded inside out and liquified to utter nonsense. Lor felt his own sense of self begin to bleed, and stormed out of the hotel and across the snow.

"Why don't you let it master *you*?" Sid Hoar peered across the map and a haze of weed smoke, toward Lor's darkened corner table.

"You say something?" Lor snorted hot tea.

He stomped out, back to the Old Stope. If the magpie guitar meant one thing, it was his own solitude, his own freedom from these damned ageless kids and everyone else who wanted to unravel his life to chaos. Friends? He had no friends. He had his guitar.

He paused under an overhang and a brood of weeping icicles. Three ravens on the rooftop broke off their discussion and eyed him suspiciously.

"I don't care for your secrets," he said.

They blinked back. When he turned away, he saw the snow with such acuity—each flake's collected crystals, each pock of dust, the prick and slide of scrolls and needles, hollow columns, spiky dendrites. He suddenly understood the collisions that buffed each particle and tumbled them to snowpack, ice lenses, ribbed and pitted strata.

He punched up and shattered an icicle, scattering the ravens before the sky could fall on his head. He ran. Just inside the doorway of the Old Stope he slipped and fell to the floor.

"Gracious, Mr. Kowalski," said Lifeson. "That is some hurry."

"Yes." Lor stood, dusted snow from his pants, and scurried across the lobby.

"Message for Mr.—"

"Yes yes, Mr. Lee. Mr. *Lor*, is it? I think we're all well-acquainted with the name at this point. Do you think, perhaps, that it's time to give up?"

Lor ignored them and ran to his room, where he sat on the bed and tried to gather the threads of his personality. His stomach hurt. He wanted a drink. His hand shook as he opened the guitar case, reached and poked his index finger on the extra barb of string at the tuning pegs. As blood dripped, he felt the threads re-weave, bright pain.

He picked up the guitar and simply let go. At first it coughed a spangle of quarter notes. But then, to his surprise, a cadenza of controlled runs, strings attending fingers. He tried a few chords; they shimmered, stayed in place. Playing on, he found he could compensate for the lack of sustain by adding rhythmic articulations, making use of the spaces and pauses between notes. Minutes passed. Perhaps hours. He broke out of the standard blues box and began to skip across a miscellany of more esoteric modes: Lydian, Phrygian, Locrian. Chords wove and unwove. His finger bled.

"Holy shit." He put the magpie guitar down and paced about the room. "I've got it. I have *got* it."

He strode out into the hallway toward the lobby.

"Mr. Lifeson, I've learned that guitar."

A witch's head popped puppet-like from behind the desk. "Mr. Lifeson is out at the moment," Lee said. "Back soon, though. By the way, you ever heard of this Mr. Lor?"

"Never." Lor laughed. "Stupid name. Rhymes with *whore*."

He made for the doorway, intending to head over to the Wildcat. A bell rang behind him.

"Oh, Mr. Kowalski!"

He turned. Lee held up an old phone with a dangling cord. "For you."

"For me?" Lor put the receiver to his ear. "Hello?"

A long pause, the sound of distant breezes. Then the tinkle of wind-chimes and a delicate giggle.

"Hello." A blue wind-blown voice.

Lor's fingers tightened. Who was *this* shithead?

"Remember me, Kenny? I have to thank you. You've given me a voice."

Lor's knuckles cracked around the phone. He strained his memory.

"Christmas Eve?" the voice said.

"Which one?"

"The Pagan one."

Something gurgled in Lor's throat. His eyes lost focus. He blinked. His finger stopped bleeding.

The blue voice laughed again. "Lucky thing you touched me that holi-day's eve, baby, or we wouldn't be going to this party at all. Someone's been helping you hide."

Lor pulled the phone from his ear and set it on the desk. He stared at it for a second. Then grabbed it and smashed it against the wall, over and over, till chips of black plastic littered the desk.

"Mr. Kowalski!"

"Hang it up!" Lor said, already running.

"But—"

"Hang it up!"

Lor sprinted to his room and grabbed the guitar case. Then fled the hotel. As he burst through the heavy doors the ancient payphone rang behind him. He stopped, considered, then ran on, down the snow-covered rock towards the bay. Another payphone rang just a block ahead. Then another. Suddenly the whole world was strung together with payphones, each one jangling in succession.

Lor stopped by a red booth. The ringing threatened to pierce his ear-drums. He wanted more than anything to leave it. He picked it up.

"Run, Kenny," the blue voice said. "As fast as you can. Bring it back to me."

Like hell, Lor thought, tossing the phone. I haven't gone far enough. I'll keep running, to the North Pole if I have to. Then every corner had a ringing payphone—the end of every street, the edge of every walk.

He picked up again on Seventh Avenue.

"Run, Kenny. I'll break your heart."

He slid down a hill, right into another phone booth. Three ravens perched atop, chattering, framed by a pink horizon. Phones rang and rang, until Lor picked up again.

"Who are you?" he demanded.

"Who are *you*?"

He was suddenly washed away in a mudslide of memories, every detail from his recent life gushing forth—his life, his friends, his own stupid name.

"Jesus Christ," he said. "I'm late."

Coils of smoky blue laughter.

Lor's heart skipped. He was late. He had to be somewhere. He had to meet Alistair. He had to get the fuck out of here.

He began to climb back toward the Old Stope. Halfway up the hill he turned to stare at the ravens, who stared back, pondering the spectacle of Mr. Lor and his blue guitar, climbing to evade once again the wiles of the Weird.

Which now had a voice.

CHAPTER TWENTY

ROCK, RAVeN, RivEr

The top of the Rock was a tangle of strange avenues. Try as he might, Lor could not fix a single familiar landmark. The roads looked wider, longer, somehow newer. The buildings poured steam at the sky, hummed with bright light. He looked back down at the bay. Still there, squatting beneath aromatic moon and sky.

This was seriously screwed up. Where was the Old Stope?

It began to snow. He could feel the chemistry again—accretion of cloud droplets, sintering bonds in the snowpack, wind-blown dunes transforming snow to ice. But everything was transformed here. Avoiding another phone booth, he reached a ledge and gazed down into a ravine, to spy what seemed a garbage dump split with a dark seam of rushing water. His eye twitched. His fingers tightened on the guitar case.

"This has got to be a joke." Where was the Old Stope?

As if in answer, a raven rose from the mound, croaked, and flapped skyward.

Lor picked his way down the side of the ravine. The dump was wedged between rock faces, its bumpy contours shellacked with snow and speckled red. As Lor descended he saw that the red dots were plastic poppy pins, left over from the Canadian equivalent of Veterans Day.

He stopped. Yes, the black seam was a tiny river, rushing north. Some of the poppies were borne away in the current, spinning and clotting at the bottlenecks like bright blood cells.

Lor's finger prickled. He dipped it in the water, which was disturbingly warm. "This is so messed up."

He sat on an old wooden rocking chair and tried to concoct a plan. What would Franklin do? The thought surprised him. Franklin would go north in search of clarity. Franklin would spout some clever philosophy. Franklin would....

His mind looped back after a long lapse. What was he *thinking*? Oh yes, Franklin. But the thought dispersed again, and he found himself slumped in the chair, one hand dangling over the armrest, finger in the water, eye on a poppy.

God, he was so sleepy. The snow's light began to chime softly, night breezes whispering beneath. He had to get up and shake off this somnolence. He was so heavy. He felt he was splitting open from the inside out, nasal linings pulled and stretched across his head and limbs. He could smell moonlight, and cold, and the chatter of deep water over river stones. His guitar was in his lap, out of its case.

Get up. Get up, Lor. He had to meet his friends. Friends were the only handholds in a world of chaos. He touched the guitar, and the thought dispelled. All he needed was to sleep.

No. Get up. Follow the river. Find its headwaters.

With great effort, he leaned forward and replaced the guitar in its case. Then he stood and picked a poppy from the snow. Yes, it was plastic, with a pin for pricking in the back. He gazed about the dump, itself a cache of unsorted memories, holding more than seemed physically possible—a crib, broken toys, clothes strewn like an eager lover's. All twined. All covered in snow.

Lor closed his eyes. The poppies called him to sleep. What did he need to do? Oh, yes. Find his friends. Of course. He opened his eyes and felt a shadow—ravens circling the watery moon in a great black wheel. He looked away, pinched the prick-wound still fresh on his finger. The pain roused him.

He flicked the poppy into the water. It bobbed once and rushed away. He followed, running to keep up.

† † †

In the distance Santa crouched by a snowman and fished with a long pole. Lor rounded the river's crook, squinted. No—a white-bearded man in red parka, kneeling by a smoky fire. Wet fish, Lor thought.

"Sir!" he called.

The old man looked up, lifted his pole. Not a fishing rod—a long butter-fly net full of red circles. As Lor drew near he saw that the man was netting poppies from the river and casting them into the fire, where they sizzled, leaving the pins to whiten with heat. The smoke spiralled dark and acrid.

"The poppies shouldn't burn," Lor said.

"The river shouldn't flow."

"Good point."

The old man nodded. "This is black water. Best thing to hold a snowman together." A cinder-snap voice. He grunted, fished a few more poppies from the rapids.

"You built it?"

"'Course. Best thing for a warding hex."

Lor's head was cold, but he thought he understood. Some kind of homeo-pathic logic. He knelt. "Build a snowman to ward off a snowman?"

"Snowman?" The old man laughed. "No."

Lor frowned. "Sir, I think I'm lost."

"Where you going?"

Lor hesitated. "Are we beyond the Arctic Circle?"

"Not even close. Why on God's earth would you want to go up *there*? Land of the midnight sun."

"I'm looking for the Old Stope Hotel."

"Old Stope?" The old man grimaced, baring long yellow teeth. "The Old Stope burned down New Year's day, 1969."

"Burned down?"

"Yeh. They say the only thing survived was the old boiler."

Lor swallowed. "Are you sure?"

The old man stood and poked his net at the snowman. He shrugged. "Time is a loop. My memory was never as good as it used to be."

Lor rubbed his eyes. "Please. Try. The manager's name is Lifeson."

"Seem to remember the manager called himself O.P. Yates." The Santa shrugged. His eyes were a rheumy blue. "That may be another trick of mem-ory. There are many."

"Yeah." Lor stared at the fire's unnatural crackle.

"Try upriver," said the old man. "As it widens the water freezes. The folks up there have long memories. They know history," he dumped a netful of poppies into the fire, which hissed and jumped skyward, "as a line, not a circle."

Lor trudged on. The river widened, whitened to ice. The moon haloed a giant wheel of frozen crystal, and Lor understood briefly why summer was the least interesting season. Winter had it. The exquisite cinematography of the world—fine-grained, lit along streams of lean cold air, shearing light to severe angles. But did he really want to flee further north? He did not share Alistair's esoteric visions, though he wanted now to see his old friend, talk old times, spill new tidings. He wanted to outdistance this latest vision of the Weird. It was a brief anomaly, he thought. But he had to clear this magic circle to make sure. That meant finding the Old Stope, finding his friends.

Ahead the water widened. Lor surveyed the boats frozen at the shore-line—one ferry-like, another flat as a barge, some beat up as tugboats. Even some small motorboats. This must have been where the people lived. His ear keened. Nothing but silence. Then, gradually, a distant rhythmic thump.

Lor decided to try the boats themselves, but noticed signs at the river's middle. One large green, a smaller white—warnings to keep off the thin ice. He stepped gingerly from the shoreline and crept along toward the boats. The distant thump turned to a throb, almost a rumble. That couldn't possibly be the sound of ice groaning under his weight. He kept as close as possible to the shoreline. How thick did ice need to be in order to hold? He realized how unprepared for the north he actually was, how naïve, how ignorant. Again he felt the swell of agoraphobia, the crush of white skies.

The throb turned to a rumble, almost familiar. He slowed his pace, stretched his arms for balance. Yes, a familiar rumble—music, seventies, scent of....

Led Zeppelin? He stopped. Thought he heard the ice creak beneath him. Yes, "Immigrant Song," as a matter of fact, all propulsive octaves and banshee wail. He turned. An ambulance and two cars crawled the very centre of the river, followed by a black four-by-four with the Jolly Roger flapping from its antenna. He straightened, dropped his arms. The signs were actually road signs, directing traffic on the ice road.

"Jesus in heaven."

The ambulance rolled by. He recognized the four-by-four, and just about fell into the snow. It slowed. The window rolled. Led Zep poured forth at a monstrous volume.

"Holy fucking shit," yelled the pointed white hat. "Like, here we thought we missed you, and you suddenly appear, dazed and dusted halfway to white-out on the road to nowhere."

Lor stood and stared.

The four-by-four stopped. The music dropped.

"Climb aboard, amigo." Alistair grinned. "Did you get my message?"

PART SIX

fuRTheR, FaRtheR, FORWARD, BACKWARD

We are also being faithful to all who came before us, who
through great hardship and sacrifice made a quest for
knowledge of the North.
—Former Prime Minister Stephen Harper, 2008

CHAPTER TWENTY-ONE

ENds WitH The SeRPENT

Dark orange light bloomed on the horizon, as if some ancient city was on fire beyond the compass of the world. Seri stared north through the windshield, at thickets cut with icy rivers, the occasional raven rising from the mist.

"Ted." Her voice cracked. She hadn't spoken since Edmonton, Gateway to the North. "What do you know of these punks? Are we chasing old enemies?"

Rooke tapped the dash. "Old friends."

The north went on forever. Even in the car, Seri felt exposed to sky, so far from anything that could be called home. She missed Mum, and especially Gran today, and Mr. Scott's old *Planets* album, cracking and hissing on the turntable while Grandpa Hamm dozed off by the fireplace, pipe smoking, mug steaming.

And yet ... there was something seductive about this place, knowing you were so far from the hearth, from comfort, from safety. You could vanish in this world, between Jack pines and spruce, beneath dark rivers and waves of wind-polished snow. The sky could pull your atoms apart and tumble them across the barrens. The feeling reminded her of strange childhood moments—rainy winters when she wanted to jump from the seawall into the ocean, autumns when she wanted to run away beneath a giant moon.

She always drew away, pulled her foot back from that seawall. This feeling was not part of the clockwork universe. Not sent from God, not as she knew him or had ever known him.

She emptied her lungs, mind momentarily blank, and felt a turning within her, like a tongue of fire peeling inside out to reveal its bright white core. The image came unbidden. It cinched her stomach.

"You been this far north before, Ted?"

"Literally, you mean?"

She whiffed his cologne.

"So vast and empty," he continued. "One could stare at the sky and feel almost naked."

Seri cleared her throat. "Do you remember much of the itinerary Dawn Cherry gave us for her clients?"

"How could I forget? You forced it out of her."

"No! You did." Credit due, partner.

She stopped the car, pulled a small calendar from her pocket. Tapped a slow count on the wheel, counting the days. Then replaced the calendar and pulled a U-turn in the middle of the highway. An ancient blue Camaro racing the other way swerved to avoid them, honking.

"Maniac," Seri said. Then, "We'll go backward."

"Home?" Rooke sounded almost hopeful.

"Just had an idea, Ted. We'll go south, to Rat River."

He waited a long time. "What for?"

She knew he knew, but answered anyway. "To interview more strippers."

† † †

The hamlet of Rat River nested on the south bank of Great Slave Lake, directly across the waters from Yellowknife. Seri stopped at an impossibly small bar called Buster Floyd's, paper thin against a fiery skyline. A few four-wheel drives were parked at a fence. Between them, a thin young man in coonskin cap and double-breasted overcoat patrolled the lot with a picket sign.

Rooke smiled, cracked the door.

"Hello, friend." He stepped out, raising his collar against the chill.

"This den of iniquity will be closed soon." The man lowered his sign and pressed the cap back on his forehead. "Closed for good. This is God's will. This is my prayer."

Rooke nodded. "A good prayer. Where there is hope there will be judgment. The God of fire will not abide a Sodom or Gomorrah."

The man squinted. "You know the Bible?"

"Then the Lord rained upon Sodom and upon Gomorrah brimstone and fire."

"Well, yes." The man lowered his sign until it touched the ground. "The God of the Old Testament. But Jesus tells us to love the sinner and hate the sin."

Seri stepped out, leaned on the door.

"Are you a dancer?" the man said.

"Heavens." Seri laughed. "No. But we are looking for an act called The Penalty Box. Is this the right bar?"

The man rubbed his forehead. "What do you want with them?"

"We're law enforcement," she said.

"Are you against subversion and wickedness?" Rooke directed the question at the man, but looked at Seri.

"Why yes, yes." He jigged the sign upwards. "Are you?"

"It is our only directive." Rooke stepped forward, ice and gravel crunching beneath his buckled shoes. "Do you think one may be renewed through wickedness?"

"No. Never."

"What does your sign say?"

The man raised the sign. "God hates immorality." He sniffed, then added, "But don't forget he loves the sinner."

"You do good and thankless work," Rooke said. "Doesn't it say somewhere in the Bible that impurity is...." He looked up, bit his lip.

The man smiled grimly. "As the Good Book says, if the tokens of virginity be not found on the damsel, then they shall bring her out, and the men of the city shall stone her with stones that she die. God is clear on the consequences of sin." He stared at his thumb. "I will tell you where this wickedness is. But you must listen to the truth, first."

Seri shook her head. "We're in a hurry."

"That's my one bargain."

"Look," she said. "We can do this the easy way or—"

"He brings words of wisdom," Rooke interrupted.

Seri was about to jump back into this meandering conversation. But she stopped. No: let Rooke go. He had the poetry for this, sneaking to the heart of the information. She would just tromp all over it.

The man smiled. "You sound like educated people. Do you know Saint Augustine, who turned away from immorality and experienced the life-changing power of God?"

"Yes!" Seri said.

"Backwards?" The man's jaw loosened. "God's story begins with the fall, with Eve and the serpent, and ends with redemption."

"No." Rooke winked. "It begins with redemption and ends with the fall. It ends with the serpent."

The man's sign dropped to the snow. "May I ... may I tell you about the love of God?"

"Please do." Rooke was trying not to smile. It made Seri's stomach twitch.

The man planted his sign in the snow and pulled a black Bible from the overcoat pocket. He opened and read: "For God so loved the world that he gave his only son to die for our sins."

"Which god?" Rooke's heel crunched the gravel.

The man looked up. "There is only one God. The God of the Bible."

"And he has a *son*? How pagan."

The man looked at Seri. She offered no encouragement, no smile or shrug. She felt the turning again, saw the stripping tongue of fire.

The man flipped through his Bible. "I am the way, the truth and the life," he read. "No man comes to the Father but through me."

"This father." Rooke took another step forward. "You said yourself that he's different in the New Testament than the Old. But both are part of the Bible, correct?"

The man nodded.

"So," Rooke continued. "Just how many gods *are* there in the Bible?"

The man's tongue reached noseward, snapped back. "I told you. There is only one God."

Rooke put his hand out. "Give it to me."

The man looked at Seri, then offered his Bible. His fingers shook.

Rooke took the Bible, licked his finger, flipped. He stopped. "Who is this *Yahweh*?"

"Yahweh is God's name in the Old Testament."

"Yahweh," Rooke's voice low, "was the Midianite god of volcanoes. Read carefully: there are many gods in the Bible, one for each patriarch."

"Not true," the man cried.

Rooke looked up from the Bible. "Have you not heard God called *El Shaddai*?"

"Yes, but—"

Rooke raised a hand. "Isaac's god was named Fear and Jacob's Mighty One. And Moses...." His voice dropped further. "To Moses an obscure war god named *Yahweh Sabaoth* appeared in a burning bush."

"No, no, no." The man shook his head, twirled the coonskin cap. "There is only one God in the Bible. There is only one God."

"And is the Bible true?" Rooke said.

"Yes."

"Every word?"

The man nodded, wrapped a fist around the sign.

Rooke smiled, flipped a few pages. "The book of Psalms: Yahweh takes his stand in the Council of El to deliver judgements among the gods. *Gods.* Plural."

"Let me see that." The man flushed.

Rooke flipped a few more pages. "The Book of Isaiah: God splits Rahab in two, and pierces the dragon through."

"It's symbolic!"

Seri agreed. But this was a necessary puncture point. Tongue of fire peeling.

"Ah. But you can't have it both ways, pick and choose," Rooke said. "Then the crucifixion is only a symbol as well."

The young man twisted the coontail to the front of his head, began to flick it back and forth. The pub's door slammed and two stocky men emerged, pulling on their toques.

"Yahweh." Rooke dropped the Bible to the snow. "Sometimes a pillar of fire, sometimes a vagrant, sometimes a mountain deity. Sometimes friendly, sometimes bloodthirsty, sometimes compassionate, sometimes angry, sometimes impatient, sometimes insatiable—"

"No!" the man cried. "Your mind is clouded by Satan. Love is what makes everything work."

"You can get some love in there, Sammy," said one of the stocky toqued men, climbing into a truck. "Get some real love for a change."

"God's character." Sammy flicked the coon's tail at double speed, eyes roving between the men. "Love and purity, purity and love."

"And what is Yahweh's character?" Rooke said. "Murderous. Jealous. At times out of control with his own furious passions."

"He's pure, he's pure." Now yanking the coon's tail.

Rooke reached to pick up the Bible. He dusted snow from its covers, then handed it back to the young man. "Many events in your Bible are connected with impurity. Jesus' own bloodline is salted with harlots, seducers, tricksters."

The truck roared, backfired. "Get some love, Sammy," the man yelled through the open window.

Rooke continued to speak in low tones, partly obscured by the truck's roar. "Joseph marries the daughter of an Egyptian high priest. Lot's daughters commit incest with their father. Tamar seduces Judah. Ruth seduces Boaz."

The young man plunged and re-plunged the sign into snow. "These are vile acts, not loved by God."

Rooke squinted. "Nonsense. These are men and women favoured by God, favoured for their impure *charisma*."

The man flushed further. "How can you say these things? I thought you agreed that the strippers here were … I thought you said…."

Rooke smiled. "I'm telling the story backwards, remember? I'm telling it from behind."

The truck honked, spit rocks from spinning tires.

"Love, Sammy!"

"Yahweh was pure." Sammy removed his hat, revealing a head of blond quills.

"What is purity?" Rooke said. "Purity is death."

Sammy shook his head violently. "Yahweh was life. Yahweh was love."

"Yahweh was a trickster with a mean streak. Remember Moses? God didn't even let him get into the Promised Land."

"Ted," Seri said. "Come on." But she smiled. He was good.

"Think about it, Sammy," Rooke stepped forward.

Sammy stepped back, clutching the Bible to his heart. "The Bible says—I am the way, the truth and the life."

Rooke grinned. "The *Tao Te Ching* says—the way that can be spoken of is not the true way."

"Paganism! Awake from the dead, and Christ shall give thee light."

"Only within the dim and dark is true essence."

Sammy dropped his hat. "Set your heart on things above, not on earthly things."

"The spirit is not above this world, but within the flesh."

"No!" Tears in the young man's eyes. "Our conversation is in heaven, from whence we look for the saviour."

"Look not, for the net of heaven is cast wide."

Fiery pinks torched the skyline. Seri was stunned by the beauty.

Sammy tried again. "The truth shall set you free."

Rooke raised a gloved hand, fingers splayed. "Truthful words are not beautiful, beautiful words not true."

"Lies. Why have you abandoned Jesus?'

"He has abandoned me."

"No!" Sammy fled the lot, pressing the Bible to his forehead.

"Sammy," Seri called. "Come back."

"They're in there right now!" he cried. "Dancing with the devil!" He looked back and tripped. The Bible pitched into the air and spun comically, gold leaf catching sparks of light. He dove, caught the Bible, then scrambled to his feet, veered left, and sprinted down the road.

"Come back." Rooke spoke to himself. "God has forgotten us all, my friend. Nobody gets into the promised land."

He pointed at the sky, stroking the fading pinks.

"Nobody." He dropped his arm. "You forgot your hat."

† † †

Seri sat at a pine table with crooked legs and sipped orange soda through a straw. Wet wood smoked in the hearth and grimed the tiny stage, which was set with cheap flashing lights, pink and blue. Rooke leaned back in a polished wooden chair and cracked ice between his back teeth, fishing from a glass tumbler.

Seri nodded at in the direction of the stage. "Penalty Box."

Rooke smiled. Almost in good humour. "Rather a fetching pun for those whose education is sure to be somewhat ... threadbare."

Seri swirled the straw, watched the fizz. Rooke fingered an ice cube. She watched it melt, water beading along his fingernail, droplets rolling through his palm.

Three young women emerged from a back door and climbed the stage, six feet from the table. One wore a spidery pair of reading glasses.

"Hopeless," Rooke whispered.

"Even a punk holds on to hope," Seri whispered back.

"How pagan," said the stripper in the reading glasses, winking.

Rooke nodded.

"Well so what?" Seri said. "Everybody finds hope in their own way, even you."

"No!" Rooke smashed the glass against the table.

"Fine." Seri leaned back until her spine cracked. She had never heard Rooke raise his voice.

Without warning he stood and smashed his glass until it cracked in razor webs. His cheekbones purpled.

"Ted, sit down." Seri pinched her cheek. "You're ridiculous."

Rooke's old knuckle cuts reopened. Blood traced the cup's zigzag fractures, mingled with spilled water.

"His hope," Rooke's voice cracked, "is an abomination."

Fine, Seri thought. Settle down—her head snapped up. "*His*? Your brother? The man in the picture?"

Rooke shook the tumbler at her, bits of glass falling. Seri poked her straw at the soda, while the few patrons stared over pints and jiggers. Rooke let the glass fall, gazed at his bloody knucklebones.

"You done, sweetie?" The stripper with the spectacles. "Do we need to cuff you to the pole?"

† † †

During the show, Rooke composed himself by folding bloody napkins, while Seri nursed three warm sodas and steered him back with her silence. After the mandatory slow dance on the blanket, the mischievous dancer strode over to the table, still undressed except for her glasses.

"You want to talk to me," she said.

Seri nodded. "How do you know?"

"You're not here to watch the show."

Rooke put down a napkin. "Sit."

"I'll stand."

"Very well." Rooke rose to conduct his interview with the naked dancer. Seri let him go. To his credit, he never once looked down.

"How did you find me?" the dancer said.

"Your manager gave us an itinerary. We're looking for someone."

"Lor," the dancer said.

Rooke's eyebrows raised, then lowered. "Why do you say *that* name?"

"Pretty obvious someone was chasing him." She stroked her stomach.

Rooke maintained a level gaze. He tapped two fingers on his wrist. "You don't like him, do you?"

She didn't answer.

"I see." Rooke raised his gaze to her hairline. "Was this Lor accompanied by a companion, a tall man?"

The dancer stared back, silent. Then, "Yes."

Rooke's fingers tapped faster. His left eye twitched, one jolt. "Silvery hair?"

"That's the one."

Rooke raised a heel, crunched a few splinters of glass. "And do you know where these men went?"

She set her glasses on the table, then surveyed him again, looked him up and down from black hair to buckled shoe. "They went south. Back to Lethbridge."

"You're *sure*?" Fingers tapping rapidly.

"Quite sure."

Seri watched them size each other. Rooke looked more eager than he usually did, fingers snapping steadily. She was beginning to more fully understand his patterns of conversation. She realized that his cruel questions outside were directed at her, not at the unfortunate young man. Rooke had been trying to crack her faith ever since Kresge's, and this was to be a contest of wills after all, no surprise there. She was going to have to fight to keep him on the straight and narrow.

Still, Rooke's self-control, here in the bar, had been considerable.

"Will that be all?" the dancer said. "You can look now. They're real."

† † †

Seri spun the car out of the lot, sped down the road recently fled by Sammy the Christian, then turned left towards the lake.

"Ted, you were a little nervous in there, a little over-anxious."

"An act." His smile slid up over his top teeth. "Serves me well from time to time when dealing with a difficult subject."

Seri nodded. He was good, fires burning a little too hot at the moment.

Again she felt the turning within her, the wheeling flame, and this time knew it. A feeling not unlike her Christian conversion experience years ago: not a sudden jolt, not a bolt from the sky, not a weight lifted from her shoulders. Just quiet certainty. This journey was personal for her, too: God was using Rooke to awaken her, to test and measure her faith.

"It was a lie," Rooke said.

"Sorry?" She realized suddenly, with a twinkle of unease, that her own symbols were all from the Old Testament, the book of blood and judgment. What about the New Testament, the book of love and forgiveness?

"I said it was a *lie*," Rooke repeated. "That bespectacled dancer was lying. She sensed my eagerness, tried to use the force of it against me. But I was more subtle."

His skill was impressive.

"Turn around," he said. "North, toward the lake. To the ice road."

"She said south."

"So we go north."

Seri nodded. Good call, beyond her own talents.

Rooke tugged his collar, as if it were too tight. Then, abruptly, he slumped. "Perhaps we should reconsider. This gateway will be closed to us, once we pass through."

"Nonsense." Seri was already turning the car. "You outfoxed her. Now we have to move." Damn, that was too brusque. "What I mean, Ted, is I think your first instincts were dead on."

Rooke watched her, eyes tapered. He was right about the gateway closing behind. This was definitely a node, a possibility point in their journey. She needed to move him with delicacy.

She lowered her voice. "Remember when Abraham and Lot were trying to choose—"

"Oh, Serendipity." He sighed.

Opportunity slipping. She winged through possible tactics, any ideas Lord?

"Seri—"

"You know, it's funny," she said quickly. "But the further north we go, the more I wonder. . . ." This was a risky gambit, a lie. No, not a lie. It just wasn't true in the way he'd hear it.

"The more I wonder about my faith," Seri said.

Rooke's eyes flickered, like she had just re-lit the pilot light.

Bingo. She grinned. Rooke, too, smiled. Then he put on the stripper's reading glasses, roosting them at the tip of his nose.

"Now we'll see," he said.

"Ted! You stole them?"

The tongue of fire slowed its orbit, exchanging colours, paring her life— fire to snow, orange to white, apprentice to spy. She hammered the gas, and, for the first time in her life, like a joyful teen, like an angry schoolgirl, actually burned rubber.

wHAT SHARP TEeTh

Air flowed over the dashboard and tickled Lor's unshaven cheeks. His neck and jaw muscles unkinked. He hadn't realized how knotted they were. He sighed, smelled something delicious.

"Here, *punchinello*." Alistair's shoulder touched his own. "From my thermos." He handed Lor a mug foamed with emerald liquid.

Lor took it, felt his palms warm. "Where's Rusty?"

"Rusty." Alistair screwed the thermos lid. "Well, he kind of lost his way 'round Yellowknife, developed every one of the French diseases of the soul, like, all the psychic pricks and scratches whereby hope—"

"He quit," Ballooni said from the front passenger seat.

Alistair nodded. "He quit."

Lor didn't care. This band was none of his business. He leaned back and sipped, watching convection currents of light. Beyond, aurora borealis swirled the sky's deep waters, sea-greens roiling to primrose and lemon.

"You'll pick up the slack, mon amigo. We still got his bass."

"I'm not going. Come *on*." Lor swallowed the last beads of green foam. "I've got my own business. I've kept my end of the bargain."

Alistair took the mug. "What exactly is your business?"

Lor gave him a glare.

"Oh, 'course, amigo, the continued vagaries of the psychedelic, the persistent portals of madness, the spirit world come a-knocking."

A blue Camaro passed, honked. Lor shuddered. "There is no spirit world."

"Listen, mooncalf." Alistair adjusted his hat. "We'll take a detour through Inuvik, where I know a witch, old friend from Vancouver. She can look into your, er, condition, and offer some practical magic, some—"

"Forget it."

"'Migo?"

"Forget that horseshit. This is a brain chemistry problem."

Ballooni glared back at Alistair. Suddenly Lor felt enmeshed in a delicate root-system of hostilities, grown over many weeks, ready to flower.

Alistair clicked the mug on his knee. "Bet you'd come if it was Franklin's idea."

"You're not Franklin."

Ballooni snorted and turned back. "You guys are all nuts. This is a tour full of nuts."

"Shut up," Fatty whispered, steering with one hand, twiddling the radio dial with the other.

"And stop twiddling." Ballooni slapped Fatty's fingers. "There's nothing but static up here."

"Actually." Alistair leaned between the front seats and clicked his teeth around a pipe. "Some say there's a pirate radio station originating somewhere beyond the Arctic Circle, plays only the heart's desire."

Ballooni coughed. "That's the dumbest thing I ever heard."

"Shut your pie-hole." Fatty's voice barely audible.

Alistair lit his pipe and gusted a blue cloud. "Come on, rattlepates." He put a hand on each of their shoulders. "Supposed to be a kind of band camraderie here, like, a kind of family."

"How come you always get to be the dad?" Ballooni folded his arms.

Alistair laughed and sat back. "And Lor here the perpetual prodigal son. If you ain't going to join the family, sparky, where will you go?"

"Just get me north," Lor said. "I'll figure it out."

"You'll come around," Alistair said. "Meanwhile, where do we meet these exotic dancers to get our gear?"

Lor gasped. He turned to the frosty window and stared at the sky's spectral light. "They're gone."

"Gone?"

Lor watched draperies of pale green ripple in waves. "Yeah. I kind of..."

"What?" Ballooni turned, bear-hugged the seat.

"Kind of pissed them off."

"Where did they go?" Ballooni demanded.

Lor shrugged.

"Let me get this straight." Ballooni ground his teeth. "Somewhere up north there's three dancers driving around in a van, with my stagelights, PA, and a whole shitload of temple blocks and percussion?"

Lor scratched the window's frost.

"That's it, fuckleheads," Ballooni said. "My lights alone are worth thousands. That is *it*."

"I have their coat," Lor ventured. "Did."

Ballooni sounded like he was choking. "Stop the car."

Alistair leaned forward. "Now wait a minute, sticklebrick, you can't just go—"

"Stop the fucklebruckin' car."

"It's a truck." Fatty shrugged and hit the brake. Ballooni buttoned his coat with shaky fingers and kicked at the door.

"Oh, come on, amigo. Where will you go, and—the better question—how will you get there?"

"I'll hitchhike all the way back to Lethbridge if I have to." He pulled on thick mitts. "Give me my mixing board."

He reached back and yanked the board from between Lor and Alistair, then booted the door open. Chilly air rushed in as he stomped out, board over shoulder.

Alistair spread his hands. "Alvin. Come on."

Ballooni punched the door closed and walked into the headlights, then beyond, kicking up a dusty cloud of snow that wreathed and followed him.

"Wo," Fatty muttered. "Could have seen that coming."

Alistair chomped his pipe. "He'll be back. What's he going to do, like, call a *taxi*?"

New headlights shimmered through ice fog, brightened. A car crept from the mist. Ballooni, just beyond the compass of illumination, reached a hand and signalled. The car slowed, stopped. Fatty flicked on his brights.

Alistair's teeth cracked the pipestem. "Holy fucking . . . uh, *cow*."

Ballooni bundled his mixing board into the back seat of the cab, then hunched and climbed into the front. Lor squinted: a yellow car, Falias Taxi on the door. Wheels skidded, churning a snow-cloud, and the taxi inched by the truck. When the two were parallel, Ballooni gave them the finger. Lor briefly saw a string of beads dangling from the rearview mirror.

"Hol-ee shit." Alistair at his shoulder.

The cabbie reached to steady the beads, turned to glare. A woman in full niqab, posture perfect. One green eye. One blue.

†††

"Where we going now?" Fatty drove the truck at a crawl.

Alistair tapped his chin. "We still have a bass, drums, and a harp. And Lor his guitar, if he'd ever let go of it."

"No sound, no lights? No soundman," Lor said. "What kind of a show is that going to be?"

The heater was going cold. The seat digging into Lor's back, seatbelt too tight.

Alistair flared a match to his pipe. "Come on, this is the summons, the *call*, and, like—dig me now—what finer, sharper opportunity to drive life into a corner, what brighter test: we play stripped down like a crack fighting unit, filled with fire and menace, lean as wolves in midwinter, and what sharp teeth we have, the better to dig in, the better to bite your ears, dears."

Lor sighed, withered. "Is there *nothing* that gets you down?"

"And furthermore, my three, er, *two*, amigos, we'll detour to Inuvik and visit the aforementioned witch, who, as luck has it, not only has the spirit's medicine for compatriot Lor, but an entire collection of lights and sound we can borrow for the festival. She used to be in the film business."

Lor shook his head. "I'm not going."

"Still that old refrain?"

Fatty stopped the truck, cracked the door.

"Fatmeister. Where you going?"

"I got to drain my lizard."

"Me too. Lor?"

Lor shook his head.

Alistair and Fatty trotted to piss at the river's edge, while Lor listened to the radio's faint static crackle. He lit one of his last smokes, then, cold, reached forward to close the passenger door. The door was slightly frozen; he pulled hard and slammed it shut. Immediately the radio poured a dissonant wash, floating strings and eerie female choir.

"The familiar sound of Holst." The DJ's voice mellifluous. "Neptune, the mystic. Puts one in mind of the world's mysteries. Right, Kenny?"

Lor choked on his cigarette. He held his breath. Okay, this was a joke, that pirate radio station, some technophile playing an elaborate joke, and Al was probably in on it, *of course* he was in on it, there he was, pissing and laughing, him and Fatty having a good laugh at Lor's expense.

"It's no joke," the voice said. "Unless a cosmic joke, in which case it's *all* a joke, Kenny, see what I mean. How was Yellowknife? Get any calls?"

"Leave me alone."

"You're taking *away* my invitation?"

"What do you want?"

"What do *you* want?"

Lor leaned forward and snapped off the radio, so hard the dial broke in his hand. Then he collapsed into the seat, breathing heavily. He peeled another smoke, lit up, inhaled.

"Feel better?" the voice said. Lor slapped his hand to his mouth, as if he had spoken ill, and burned his palm on the cigarette.

"Truth is for young men." The voice glittered blue. "You, Kenny, are no longer a young man. We are thawing backward, you and I."

Lor's chest constricted, eyes blurring. The sky rushed at him. The truck so cold and empty. He opened the door and fell out, then jumped and ran for the river's edge, to the only community that remained, the only warmth—the sizzle of hot pee in snow.

CHAPTER TWENTY-THREE

RuSH, NiCKELBACk, And DAVid SuZuKi

Fatty's truck rolled north along the meandering Mackenzie River. For one experimental year, Alistair explained, the Northwest Territories were converting the entire Mackenzie to an ice bridge, all the way to Tuktoyaktuk and the Arctic Ocean. Lor didn't believe it. Alistair didn't seem to care. He just babbled on, endlessly inventive.

"Look how wide she is, boys, a frozen Mississippi, and we the Huckleberry Finns of winter, lighting out for the next territory, remaking ourselves on the fly...."

They often passed snowmen built on the river's edge, in various stages of thaw and decrepitude, or sometimes ice fishers, to whom Fatty invariably gave the finger while Alistair grinned and waved. At one sinuous bend, the headlights enveloped a fisherman in a long black coat, with a snowy owl perched on his shoulder. The owl turned its flat face to stare, flashing bulbed eyes. The man saw the Jolly Roger and grinned. He was missing a tooth. He gave two thumbs up. He was missing a thumb.

By February the stars vanished for hours at a time, and the sky flowed out toward a stark horizon lit with jangled pinks and peaches. Lor could not remember seeing the sun, as if it hid beneath the skyline. But the ice-bright moon stayed up for days on end, half a month it seemed, never setting, going 'round and 'round the sky, waxing and waning. When fog poured in from the groves of black spruce, Lor lost all depth perception, and ice melted to sky, and they drove only to the rhythm of snow.

"Feels like we're flying." Alistair pressed his nose to the window.

They landed for small towns, to play scheduled and unscheduled gigs, or for the occasional busload of Japanese tourists in Canada to view the northern lights. Often the bus would stop in the ice road's centre, barking exhaust, while the tourists wandered smoking in their bright red jumpsuits and Sorel boots, some with full suit and tie peeping from beneath. In Fort Manitou, Fatty landed the truck only to find the planned gig re-booked to a progressive blues band from Hiroshoma called Cygnus X-Freud, who between sets excitedly and in halting English listed as their primary influences Rush, Nickelback, and David Suzuki.

"Babylon," Alistair said, when they took off again. "Soon everyt'ing crash."

"What?" Lor snapped. "Stop that shit now." Good Lord. Sometimes *annoying* didn't begin to describe Alistair.

Beyond Fort Manitou, a ghost or phantom began to sabotage the gigs. Small acts—a broken string or drumstick, a missing amp fuse, a busted spring from Fatty's bass pedal.

"Is someone following us?" Fatty said.

Lor kept quiet. The more he thought about the phantom voice, the more he lost his sense of self. He became fearful of losing his memory again. Paranoid. Every night he poked his finger on the guitar string, to fire his nerves with bright blood. A bit more blood each time, a bit more pain.

"It'll go dark," said the manager of the tiny bar in Aklavik. She was an Inuit woman who smelled of peaches.

"*Amigette?*"

"We're going to have a power failure tonight," she said. "You fellows will have to play fast. There is nothing pure in this world."

"Indeed, no." Alistair counted them in. They slurred across a medley of punk and new wave, slopping it out. Only Fatty remained dead on, as always. But the audience loved it—mainly Japanese tourists, still swaddled in those bulky red jumpsuits, sweating, smoking.

The band sped faster, sensing collapse. Fatty rode the beat hard, while his mates struggled to keep up. Soon Lor was playing faster than he could think, running on pure instinct. His pricked finger began to bleed. The tourists clapped out of kilter, bonked their feet in syncopated stomps. Suddenly the music snapped in on itself, became propulsive and gentle, aggressive and delicate, as for about fifteen seconds the band hit every erogenous zone between the beats.

Out went the lights. Lor wiped his brow, to applause, felt warm blood on his eyelid. A match flared at the back of the bar. For an instant Lor thought he saw the peroxide buzz cut of Darcilee Shimozowa.

He almost threw up. He fumbled across the stage and grabbed Alistair's shoulder.

"Al?"

"Dude. Will you please come see the witch?"

Lor paused, flicking a guitar string. Then felt himself nod.

† † †

The thought gave him insomnia. See the witch? Ridiculous. For the next week he could only fall asleep for a few hours at early morning. He would lie awake half-dreaming of brothers he'd never had, then realize how alienated he was from everyone he'd ever known. He especially saw his tenacious distinction between love and lust come apart, all his sexual encounters not only failures at intimacy, but further estrangements from himself. Fuck, what a boring insight. So many memories here, more than he wanted to count, all with a sting.

Then each erotic whisper from the past turned bitter, some even malicious, and he knew there was no magic that could ever rejuvenate his personal history, except maybe the simple act of telling the story to himself.

† † †

Meanwhile, the magpie guitar continued to learn Lor. Town by town, gig by gig, his conception of music was rearranged from the inside out. Sounds became snowflakes. When he improvised, he could see that somewhere at the heart of each flake was just the right note. But it was so elusive. The faster he played, the further he got from the heart, spinning away until he was outside the song altogether. So he had to slow down, dig in—to time his entry with the subtle cues that flew just below his perceptions. It was frustrating, trying to catch that note. But in the attempt lay the most beautiful noise.

While the guitar continued to build Lor's insides, the sabotage continued to wreck the outsides. Patchcords crackled and buzzed. A tuning peg went missing from Alistair's bass. A skin from the drums. Fatty drove, said not a thing. Two miles from the tiny town of Tsintu he picked up a few seconds of pirate radio, and brightened.

"What you got, Fatster?"

"You!"

A few seconds of eerie female choir, then static. Fatty touched the busted knob, but the music was gone. Still, he grinned all the way into town, bouncing in his seat.

In the Tsintu Pub, Alistair shut up long enough to glare at two men in Karaca turtlenecks, both with laptops and expensive haircuts. One sipped a martini while the other took thoughtful pulls from the business section of a newspaper. At intervals he paused without looking up to argue the relative merits of Lagavulin and Cragganmore single malts.

"What the fuck's going on?" Alistair whispered. "This is what we're s'pposed to be *escaping*."

When one of the yups went to the bathroom, Fatty sneaked over to steal his phone from the bar top. He crouched beneath a stool and tapped. The remaining suit dropped his paper and picked up his own tweedling phone.

"Yeah."

Fatty coughed. "Hello, this is Sergeant McKracken of the Inuvik RCMP. Apparently you've been engaged in subtle acts of insider trading, but we're on to you, and we're on our way to pick you up to take you *down*."

"Who is this?"

"You!"

"And where's your authority?"

"Here!" Fatty jumped up, fly unzipped, authority already in hand.

Later, on the ice road again, Alistair offered Fatty hearty congratulations. "Couldn't have done better myself. Though, must say, the grand finale was a little limp, amigg...o...lee shit, is that a *minivan* behind us?"

Fatty looked back, swerved.

"Careful, Fatster, careful, or you'll get us all holy mother of Mary, is that a *minivan*?" He pounded the seat. "And a Beamer? God save us from that fucking small ice on wheels! This is the Arctic, not the suburbs, the Arctic, goddamn it, last time I heard, Lor?"

Lor was carefully slicing his finger with the sharp edge of the magpie guitar's body, drawing bright pain. He looked up as the Beamer passed.

Alistair yanked his seatbelt, let it zip back. "Look at the lukewarm Euro-wannabe suburboids, thinking their Beamers and minivans are God's reward for sound moral standards, living a life of constant low-grade pleasure, pecking shiny objects and shitting caramels." He smacked the dash. The Beamer fishtailed and spat snowy powder. "Dig me, we'll put their tepid moral vision to the test—hammer it, Fatty."

"Huh?"

Alistair splayed his hands against the windshield. "...lives that tinkle with vapid pleasantries—floor it, kid, floor it—Frappucinos, TV, weekly barbecues...."

The minivan swooped out to pass, hot on the Beamer's afterburn. Alistair shrieked and cast out a long leg, pressing the accelerator. Fatty's neck snapped back, cracking vertebrae.

"You'll kill us." Lor resumed his finger-cutting.

"They've got kids in the back seat, kids in argyle sweaters." Alistair stomped the gas again. "This is a bad dream, 'migos."

He stood, smushed his hat into the roof. "Run 'em off the road! Everyt'ing crash!"

Lor studied his blood.

"Everyt'ing crash!" Alistair jumped, banged his head on the rearview mirror. "Fatty! Smash 'em! Smash 'em! Here, asshole, give me the wheel!"

Then, magically, as if jealous *Yahweh* himself was on the side of the upper middle classes, Fatty's headlights blacked out, and the four-by-four stalled, and both sets of tail lights vanished ahead like homebound fireflies.

CHAPTER TWENTY-FOUR

PAUSE FOR A DRINK

And then a great night descended upon the world, and stayed for many cycles of the moon. Soon the three stranded companions knew hunger and thirst, growing as the moon grew, for the earth itself threw up nothing to eat or drink but for a mist that disappeared at the touch. And the three grumbled, and said: why did we ever come to this wilderness, to seek the god's own light, if it meant that we were to die so far away from home? The snow fell, but they did not know what to do with it, for though it would melt on their tongues, the more they drank the thirstier they became.

Then the tall one spit out and swore, and said: we are lost, brothers, and have been led astray. And the thick one said: a plague take this unending night, for if we could see a little distance we would at least know what was in store for us. And they both cursed the gods mightily. But the small one kept back while the other two talked among themselves, until they disappeared in the darkness and he was left alone.

Even then, he laughed. For Fox was not only the foxiest, but the shrewdest of the three, and knew that such profane conversation was likely to draw Bear in his killing humour. And he was right, for Bear did perk up his ears, and in his rage slew Fox's companions, both Beaver and Caribou, and left them red on the snow, and did not eat either, for they were a desecration. Meanwhile Fox had enough meat to kill his hunger for many weeks.

But when he had eaten his fill a gigantic thirst grew in his throat, and he fell down, and ate snow until his thirst multiplied. Then he cried out, and said: Why did I trick and eat my brothers, and despoil myself so, and how will I quench this terrible thirst? And he left the meat and wandered out across the snow, until he met King Raven at the fork of Great River.

I am dying of thirst, Fox told King Raven, and have sinned, and where oh where is one to get a drink in this white desert, where there is no water, but only an ocean of mocking ice? ·

And King Raven said: At the end of Great River the water melts, and rushes with a singing noise, and is sweet to drink. But how will you get there?

Indeed, Fox said, how to get there?

Then King Raven laughed: You cannot get there, any more than you can ever get home, for the River is time itself, and remains frozen according to its own secret devices, and moves in subtle loops that you can never know—

The boy storyteller paused for a drink.

Alistair tapped Lor on the shoulder and pointed.

"There," he said. "There's the witch. I told you so."

CHAPTER TWENTY-FIVE

HeR iNViSiBLE BEARd

An hour earlier, when they had finally reached Inuvik on the Mackenzie's east channel, Fatty had just about hit a car. A blue Camaro, by the looks of it, though it was too dark for anyone to be sure.

"We need those headlights," Lor had muttered. "Let's just find that witch before we kill somebody. Where does she live?"

Alistair paused, pushed his hat back to wipe his brow. "Well, 'migo, I don't exactly know *that*."

They rumbled down flat streets, past a Roman Catholic church built to look like an igloo, past an inuksuk, a humanoid figure built from rocks. Then stopped at the town's main junction and only traffic light, across from the yellowing elementary school, to check the payphone book. Alistair flipped: Dana something, Dana Angootealuk if his memory served, and who knew if it did. Either way, the name wasn't listed. When Lor asked if she was Inuit, Alistair said: "Scottish. Her married name. Yeah." He frowned. "She changed it. In the *1980s*." He paused to squint. "Wait a second."

Lor followed his squint across the street, where the school door posted a sign for a talent show.

"This way." Alistair herded them across the street, saying he knew the witch would be in the audience for that, it was just like her. Lor followed grudgingly. Fatty, sullen again, said not a word.

The sign named participants in bright calligraphy—Lawrence Komolov, B. Aslanov, the Qingnatuq twins—and word was a boy-genius storyteller would make an appearance, one Zephaniah Tookalook of Nunavut. Alistair asked around, and it turned out that all the contestants were from the east, from Nunavut, except for the Kuptana Family Singers, who were all sick anyway, and doubtful to show. But as far as anyone knew or told there was no Dana Angootealuk.

The show was hosted by a Quebecois woman named Jose Titus—or was it actually Juicy Tight-Ass with an accent, as Fatty repeatedly insisted? The audience scattered around the floor on some sort of enormous white blanket, sneezing a lot, many of them in blue parkas trimmed with fur. Lor stood nervously while Alistair scanned the gymnasium.

The Kuptana Family Singers did show, and sang "Amazing Grace" to the accompaniment of a strummed acoustic guitar and the discordant swells of its electric counterpart. Other singers came and went. The timing between vocals and accompaniment was generally nonexistent, but the crowd loved it, clapping in bursts at about every five or six bars. At one point two shy youngsters held hands and sang an old Nirvana song. The host interrupted them in order to give a brief talk on spirit guides.

"An animal may speak to you," she explained in that French-Canadian accent. "A beast perhaps. A bird. From afar at first. But if you are patient, the spirit will identify itself, and you will have a lot of good luck."

"The witch is here," Alistair whispered. "I guarantee it. Just her kind of thing."

Then a special treat: the host led a blind boy to the stage, the rumoured Zephaniah Tookalook.

"Mr. Tookalook," said the host, "will now tell us a story all about Fox and King Raven."

The boy sat on a stool and smiled at the audience, tall cup of water in hand. The sneezing stopped. For a moment the only sound was the tinkling of ice cubes in the glass.

"There," Alistair whispered. "There's the witch. I told you so."

The boy storyteller took a deep breath. In a surprisingly high voice he began: "And then a great night descended upon the world, and stayed for many cycles of the moon...."

† † †

From the Trapper's Pub windows the air itself was visible. The woman with emerald eyes called it *arctic haze*. Blue-white and beautiful, but made of pollutants, which somehow seemed appropriate to Lor.

The witch folded her delicate hands on the table and laughed, a sound like pale green liquid. "Did you know? I saw your brother, five years ago."

Alistair leaned in. "Franklin?"

"He passed through and begged me to exorcise him. Said he was possessed by a fallen angel. Personally, I thought it was the other way 'round."

Fatty whistled.

"So whatjya do?" Alistair said.

She paused. "That's *his* story."

"Tell it."

"Not yours." The witch shook her head. Smiled again. "I can help you all. With everything. Come to my place." She brushed thick red hair over her shoulder. "But Alistair, dear, your brothers will need cheering. One at wit's end, the other with the vacant look of a coming porn stud."

Alistair grinned. "You'd know."

She twinkled emerald eyes. "We have lived many lives."

"Come on, winchie, tell us the story of Franklin."

She tapped a finger on the tabletop. "Do you know what paranoia is, Alistair Grimes? The belief that all things are connected—one great, complicated, causal, weblike story."

"So, '*migette*. The story?"

"No," she said. Then two deep blinks. "Lor. Let's go."

† † †

Like most arctic dwellings, the witch's house was built on stilts sunk into the permafrost. But the siding was woven of many branches, giving it the appearance of a nest or eyrie, or perhaps a beaver lodge from a children's book. The chimney vented smoke.

"Dana. '*Migette*." Alistair pointed a long finger. "Explain."

At the end of the snowy lane a minivan idled next to a Beamer, both snuffling exhaust.

"Clients," said the witch. "Fetching herbal concoctions from my little store. Perhaps crystals. A book of chants."

Alistair pulled his hat deep over his eyes.

Dana clapped her delicate hands. "Even a witch needs to make a living. You don't have to come in. Go have tea across the street. Right next to that corner store. Check out the ancient porn."

"Ours?" A slight gargle in Alistair's voice.

Fatty stopped the truck. The witch pinched Lor's shoulder.

"We won't be long," she said. "Come with me Lor. Don't be shy."

Alistair pushed up his hat to check his watch. "Shit, dudes, we're running late, got to hit that festival soon."

The witch seized him by the brim. "Relax. Slow and easy, like I taught you." She laughed. "Try the chamomile and hops tea."

Alistair stared across the street, then at the minivan, then across the street again. His eyes lit, as if with some wicked scheme.

"Okay sweetheart." He grinned. "That corner store there. Would they have *paint*?"

† † †

The witch's kitchen smelled of forest. A potpourri hummed on the fridge, whispered sweet fragrance. Plants hung at levels, some almost to the floor, leaves brightened by flourescents. The whole room had a misty green complexion. A woven basket of fruit on the table, mainly pomegranates.

"How do you get this exotic fruit up here?" Lor picked up a mango, turned it in his hand.

"You wouldn't believe me. Sit. Try to relax."

She reached to insert her finger in a fern's wet potting dirt. By the flourescent light Lor noticed her light white beard, a delicate sprinkling of acne. It zoomed him back to high school, when he had suspected such qualities to be indications of extreme horniness. Hormonal hieroglyphs, he'd called them, not that anyone ever laughed or proved him right.

He crossed his leg.

She sat across the table. "Tell me your troubles."

He looked down and just stared at her hands, the fine fingers, the bird-bone knuckles and black nails.

"You're an atheist, aren't you?"

Lor nodded.

"Well. Take your time." She drew a nutcracker from her pocket and conjured a bag of pecans. She smiled. She had braces.

Crack! He watched those fingers squeeze and pluck the nut-meat. Her hands knew just the faultlines. So skilled. And she seemed so distant, such a stranger. Not like he would ever see her again, right?

So what the hell, he spilled, spilled to the rhythm of cracking nuts, right from the Weird in Underwood to the Weirder in Lethbridge, and the whole time his inner voice argued and argued, this confession is horseshit, this witch stuff is senseless, but what else was left, and what made sense in this winter wasteland anyway?

The witch laughed when he was done. "It's very simple, Lor."

He poked under his shirt and fingered his belly-button. "Can I have a nut?"

"Of course."

He reached. Lint on his finger, right next to the wound he kept reopening.

She smiled. "The world has four corners. At each point is an ancient city. Their names are Gorias, Murias, Finias, and Falias. The last hotel of ruined Falias lies just north of here. Do you believe in this?"

"No." He cracked hard.

"Good. Do you read?"

"A little."

"In the Twilight Language of Faerie, entire libraries can be condensed to a single symbol, then hidden in the cracks of the world. Rock, rivers, trees. You've been reading the world, Lor. A book of magicks."

"Uh-huh." He ruined nut after nut, cracking too hard, unable to extract much meat from the fragments.

"Have you heard a voice?"

A node of pecan stuck in his throat. Slowly, against his own wishes, he nodded.

"Who?"

"I don't know." He laughed grimly. "A devil."

"The devil exists only in a world that has forgotten the goddess. Do you have a particular animal you feel an affinity for? Maybe a bird?"

"No."

"Bet you do. Give me your hand."

She took it in her own fine fingers, turned it gently to look at the cut on his finger. Then she nodded. It made Lor angry, to see such kind wisdom, such insight—it wasn't real, could never be. Still, as her black fingernail traced his palm, he felt a real tingle fire up to his elbow, and glanced again at her invisible beard.

"I...."

"Yes," she said. "Take back your hand."

He rested his fingers on the jagged pile of pecan.

She stood and opened a drawer, drew out a small braided whip. He pulled his hand from the table and stuffed it in his pocket to feel the reassuring lump of the powder pouch.

"Start," she said, "by visualizing the wisest person you know."

He gulped, thought of Franklin.

She flicked a lighter and lit the end of the whip.

"It's not a whip, Lor. It's a braid of sage." She blew out the flame and fanned the smoke with a white feather, toward her heart, over her head, down her arms. "Close your eyes."

He breathed sweet sage smoke, felt the heat simmer down his torso.

"Count your breaths. Ten, nine, eight...."

He felt heavy.

"Now," she said. "When you are completely relaxed, visualize the goddess. She sits on a stone dais in a summer meadow full of poppies."

He thought of the witch's fingers.

"Her robe is pure red, her hair pure sunlight."

He thought of the witch's green eyes.

"She is surrounded by birds and animals. They come to her without fear."

He thought of Franklin. Then of a waitress he had slept with his very first night in Lethbridge, so many years ago. What was her name?

"See if you feel an attraction to any of the birds or animals. Does one speak to you?"

Guess he never did know her name. He thought of a dewy spider web between the fenceboards of his childhood home. Then of Alistair's white hat.

"And she releases beams of healing light, into your heart."

Alistair's grey hat floating in the river.

"Now Lor." He felt light hands on his shoulders. "If you have performed this visualization mindfully, you are ready for a ghostwalk. To find your animal spirit, if you will, and the answers you seek."

She smelled like lilacs and lemon juice.

"When you're ready, open your eyes. Drink the glassful in front of you. A concoction of poppy, lime blossom, and clover. With pure snow. When you're ready. Then walk through the kitchen, through the solarium, out the back door to the woods."

He nodded.

"Only one rule, Lor. One ancient rule: don't leave the path."

He nodded again. That knot of pecan in his throat seemed to be growing. He opened his eyes. The witch was gone.

Taking a deep breath, he reached for the glass of pale green liquid and kicked it back. It was bitter. He wiped his lips, stood, floated through the kitchen into the solarium. Music played softly, some Celtic tune about a tower and frozen skies. Dense greenery quivered in the moonlight—misty ferns, snake plants stretching, apple trees bearing real baby apples. A white rabbit scampered across the rug, weaving between clay pots. Lor carried on, through the back door, down the steps to the well-trod path. Then off the path. Of course he wasn't going to stay on the path, he was still a punk after all, damn that witch.

Beneath a trembling aspen he unzipped to piss in the snow, free hand gripping the pouch of dust. Each squirt of pee sounded like the cooing of a dove. Suddenly the potion hit his bloodstream, and it was all he could do to get himself zipped up again, before the tree itself unzipped its bark, and an ocean of hungry pith gobbled forth to paint the world.

† † †

A mist rises from the ground to water the snow. Ice constellations bend moonbeams. Smoky light drifts. As Lor walks a frozen river, the dark heavens slowly whiten, while black stars fall to splash the sky and storm seaward.

No, not the sky. The riverbed. He is upside down, walking the underside of the river, its frozen ceiling, and the stars are river stones beneath him.

Crack! The ice breaks, and he is swimming, carried by the river's rush. The water is emerald and warm as summer wind.

He tumbles down rapids, tangled with winking lights, glass globes, tinsel strings—an entire flotilla of Christmas decorations. Ahead a giant spruce grows at the river's centre, its lower boughs spastic with the rush of smashing ornaments, which crack and whip and snarl its base in a growing pile of fractured glass.

"That's right, Kenny. Into my parlour." A voice from the treetop. "Look up."

Lor crashes through the heaping shrapnel at the tree's base. Glass slices his arm, while a string of lights tangle round his neck and wiggle upward to burrow, winking, in his ears. He hits the tree headfirst, pushed upward by the river's force, hands clawing fragrance from bark. The lights unsnag and fall away, hitting the river in a series of sizzles as one by one each bulb pops and darkens.

Lor grabs for the branches and chins up. His feet dangle. Water fattens his shoes. He climbs beneath a prickly overhang, pulls himself through the wickerwork toward the tree's heart. His fingernails dig, bend back, start to peel from skin. Hundreds of feet above the river, he slips and falls. But the tree snags his hair. He jerks up, scalp yanking from skull, and bobs like a hanged man.

"Up here, Kenny."

The branches curl, hug him until his spine cracks and his eyes water. Bark grows beneath his skin; he tastes the knot and the gnarl.

Then he's inside, cruising the tree's bones. The core is enormous, full of clouds. He senses rings: year within year of bug whispers, the scent of green melody. Each secret cone and crow's joke, each drop of spring.

"Up here, Kenny Ken Ken. Come see me, we'll kick the stars from the sky."

Lor flies up at the sweet spot of light. He sees speckled stars, crows roosting on the horns of a hunter's moon. The sky begins to foam.

Not the sky.

The river.

Again.

Splash!

The water is neither warm nor cold. He is rushing with a rainbow's exhaust, lemondrop threads lacing blue infusions, violet ice and whippersnap whites.

"Ke-nneeey. Up heeeere." The voice gargles.

Lor bubbles up through the ice-hole and squirts across the river. He spits cold water and lies gasping, suddenly anxious for his pouch of dust. He tries to check his pocket, but his hand is too numb.

"It's there, Kenny. But where is the rest of it? Where is your guitar?"

Lor raises his head. He scans the trees, but sees only twigs like finger bones.

"Where is your guitar?" the voice continues. "For you have painted your heart with part of mine."

Painted ... *what the fuck*? That sounds important, but it's nonsense.

"Where are you?" Lor croaks.

"Wherever you wish," says the voice. "For who can escape what he desires?"

Lor sniffs the cold air, smells frying fish. His eye follows footprints to the riverbank, to the back of an enormous figure, cloaked, crouching at a fire.

"Welcome, Kenny."

Lor eyes the branches. No magpie.

"It's *my* voice," says the visitor, stroking a white rabbit.

"No."

"Yes. You've given my spirit flesh, Kenny. Flesh, finally. I thank you."

"I haven't."

"Oh, you have. I can't thank you enough."

Lor longs to jump back through the ice-hole and swim away. He stays on his knees, breathing hard.

The visitor reaches a stick to the fire. "Come eat some fish. Renew your strength, or you will never finish this journey."

Sparks burst. A delicious aroma fills Lor's nose. His mouth waters, but he doubts that anything in these woods can be wholesome to eat. His fingerprick throbs, a crimson cloud of pain outside his body.

"No," he says.

"You think me completely heartless? Have a little faith, Kenny. Take. Eat."

Slowly, painfully, each hand forward pressing his finger to greater pain, Lor crawls across the ice, following the footprints. Round and round the fire, breathing the broil of fish.

"Eat, Kenny. Eat."

Lor eats. The fish is delightful, zested with orange and sweet herbs. The bones warm his hand.

"Good." The visitor strokes snow where the rabbit has disappeared.

As Lor's strength returns, his muscles numb and slacken. His lungs slow, his brain dims, he begins to shiver. But it's okay, because all he can feel is his wounded finger.

"You can't touch me yet, Kenny. I am only spirit here."

"I don't want to touch you." Surprised that his lips and tongue still work.

"But you will." The laugh. "Oh, how you will touch me."

The rabbit reappears, grey this time, one eye closed in a prolonged wink.

"I'll run all the way to the North Pole." Lor's voice is thick.

"Good. I have all the time in the world, Kenny. And none, if you take my meaning."

Somewhere in the distance Lor feels his teeth clench.

"See you real soon." The visitor taps the rabbit's head. "Don't forget to bring your guitar, your painted heart...."

"Fuck you and your voice and your flesh and your fucking—"

Heart?

† † †

Lor blinked. He was in the solarium between plants, the white rabbit lazy in his lap. The song skipping, a haunting voice and melody. Wait. That was the same song that Fatty's radio—

Where once was Falias?

Does still her tower rise?

Silent old hotel stretching to the frozen skies....

He jumped up, spilling the rabbit, knocking over the snake plant.

"Dana?"

No one in the kitchen. A few green drops left in the glass.

Through the window he saw Alistair, standing in the snow, grinning, holding a spray can of paint. Lor pushed open the door.

"Step it up, amigo. Like, we're going to be late for the festival here 'cos of your little tête-à-tête."

"Alistair. Let's get the fuck out of here."

"Yeah, dude. That's more like it."

"Someone is chasing me, it's all clear now, I can feel it. Somebody is after us, old friend, someone—"

"Woaah! 'Migo. Like, when did you become Mr. Superstition?"

"Let's go, man." Lor clattered down the steps. "Where's Fatty? I swear, I know it now. It's real. Al, we got to run."

Alistair dropped the spray can in the snow. "Hell-o. What have you done with the real Lor?"

Lor reached to wipe his lips.

"Dude. You've bloodied your mouth." Alistair demonstrated, smeared red paint across his own.

The world dusted with indigo. Even the sound of Fatty's truck was blue.

"Fatty." Lor beckoned with a fist.

The truck surged forward and skidded inches from their feet, open door swinging, borrowed gear rattling. Lor shoved Alistair into the front seat and dove beside him.

Fatty fumbled between their tangled knees. "I can't get a good grip on the stick shift."

"Go!" Lor grabbed him by the throat. Fatty peeled, then hammered the brakes. Lor jerked forward and smashed his glasses on the dash.

The witch, a sudden apparition on the road, dropped her arms. "Did you stay on the path?"

"Yes!" Lor screamed.

"Just drive," said Alistair.

Lor looked down at his busted glasses, then up at the blurry world. The last thing he saw was the minivan and the Beamer on the drive, both painted across the doors with Al's spidery red script: *Fuckrs Go Home.* Then he knew. Alistair was all wrong about ice, and you could travel everywhere in the wide world and never really go anywhere, and you could turn thirty or forty or eighty and never gain a smitch of wisdom, and no matter how far you fled you would always end up gnawed and homesick for some home you'd never been to.

Lor clutched his gut.

"Foggy Island." Alistair ducked his head. "Where it all comes together. You're still in, right, Lor, still with us?"

"Go." Lor reached to grab Al's shoulder. "We finish it together."

He squeezed hard. But in his heart he despaired.

PART SEVEN

AND NOW, THE WEIRD

Evil comes in many forms and seems to reinvent
itself time and again.
—Former Prime Minister Stephen Harper, 2014

CHAPTER TWENTY-SIX

The BUSHES At THE ENd OF the GiANTS BRidGE

Seri roared across the tundra with renewed vigour, raced over
the ice road at dangerous speeds. She stopped only for fuel,
paying with her Visa. Time later to sort out expenses. Right now,
got to move.

Rooke was not helping with the info-crunching. He spent hours leaning
into the dash, squinting through his stolen spectacles. They began to stop at
the side of the road to sleep, take stock, reorient. While Rooke snoozed, Seri
sat with her notebook to make sense of the data, but all she crunched were
contradictions and questions. The more she dug for answers, the fewer there
were. She stabbed the pen at the page. The more she slept, the sleepier she
became. Why had Rooke picked *her*, again?

Sometimes, enchanted with velocity, she fell into micro-fits of slumber,
then awoke in a panic. Once, at Camsell Bend, she bobbed in a half-doze,
then started fully awake, instantly aware of Rooke's lips, how full they were.
He reached to brush her shoulder. "They've run north. It's an admission of
their guilt."

She opened the window a crack, then zipped it back up. She had missed
some vital sign along this road, she knew it. Too sleepy: this landscape made
you forget.

Of course she prayed. She read her Bible. But the more she prayed, the
more distant God seemed. The more she read, the more her Bible tumbled
out of order. So she renewed her vigour, wrenched up her concentration.

Again, the Bible's sense seemed inverse to her efforts, even at early morning. If she set her watch alarm, it went off at the wrong time. If she left it, it began to beep at seven-thirty precisely.

The next two nights she drove through, flexing her endurance. She could hardly see clearly out of herself any more. She knew what was happening. Augustine called it the *phantasticus*: a secret part of each person that roamed the world in spectral form, while the true self dreamed its experiences. Somewhere in Lethbridge—probably in that clearing—her own spirit had shaken loose, and her true body was far south, probably in the hotel, dreaming all of this mess. One more problem, then: to reunite body and soul.

No. She punched the wheel, honking the horn. Wake up. Enough was enough.

"Ted. Let's review our evidence."

He sneezed.

"Do you know where to report?" she said. "Surely you have important info in that briefcase?"

"But of the briefcase of knowledge you shall not open."

"Yes. Eve. Funny."

Rooke began to hum, a sleek and twisting melody. The car pointed straight north, as if it shared his single-mindedness. Then Seri remembered in detail how the CSIS Act strictly limited the types of activities they could investigate, strictly controlled the type of information they could collect. But were they still in CSIS? Were they still in *Canada*?

"We have to stop and get some sleep before we go nuts with exhaustion. We'll have fresh eyes in the morning."

"Fresh eyes." He squinted through the lenses.

The delay was unfortunate, but there was little choice. She stopped at a hunter's lodge on the Raven's Throat River. A single white VW Rabbit was parked outside, licence plate IML8IML8.

"A lodge with no name." Rooke tapped his teeth. "How enchanting."

Seri felt a wash of loneliness. Not her own: some empathy with this quiet lodge, cracked by years of estrangement. She gathered herself. How absurd. The lodge tilted slightly north—a trick of the light? No, it really was.

"I'll pay," Seri said.

"Foundation cracking," Rooke answered. "Rest assured."

† † †

Supper, first. Rooke sat in the lounge, sipping ice water and nipping white unbuttered toast. Three bearded men sat at different tables, each reading a section of some dated newspaper, each with a pot of stew. Seri found the silence unholy—no slurps or chewing noises, no paper rustling. The server, a great bear with the nametag Grimwater, floated about and took orders in a soft monotone, communicating mainly through a subtle lexicon of shrugs. All the steps were too steep. And the place was unnaturally bright.

Seri ate salmon, pretended to read a pamphlet stained with Rooke's ice water. Something about an underground river running backward beneath the lodge, shifting the foundations. Her mind wandered. She nodded.

"Ted. I'm going to get some sleep."

He stared up, eyeskin tightly pouched.

Halfway up the steep stairs to her room she saw the picture. A large man, squatting beneath a snowy tree, gripping a rifle. He had a pair of antlers fastened to his head in some crude hunter's joke. Eyes concealed behind dark glasses, beard stained red.

In her room, she stretched and cracked her notebook for a final look, but plunged into sleep roiled with dreams. Much later—or was it minutes?—she woke in the dark, still clothed. Where was she? She stood. The notebook dropped to the floor.

She'd been driving in her dream. They'd picked up a mad hitchhiker who looked like Rasputin, a preacher man who said they could not pass further until they accepted the grace of God. Then they were chased by RCMP, but outran him at the train tracks, where the train derailed behind. She looked back: a circus train, twisted, smoking. Disoriented clowns, angry elephants, dead midgets.

Stop. Ridiculous.

She reached for the notebook, snapped on the light. Except the RCMP. That part almost seemed as if it had actually happened.

Clenching her teeth, she opened the notebook, clicked the pen. She'd been lax and disorganized. She'd missed the signs along the road. Time to redouble her efforts.

She scratched and scribbled, crossed off and crumpled. She stabbed the pen to the page. Finally she grabbed the room phone. The Security Intelligence Review Committee had access to all information under the service's control, including expense accounts. That would be a way in—check the expense account of Rooke's special branch. But there was no answer, no voicemail. What time was it? She called the deputy director's office, was referred down to the assistant director of human resources, and somehow ended up talking to a career portfolio manager who was no help at all. The phone buzzed like she was calling from the moon. When she asked about Rooke's special branch, the manager simply hung up. She called her old office, but the number was rerouted to an RCMP detachment, and the man who answered had never heard of Rooke. All she got, finally, was a low-level clerk who told her that CSIS was no longer tracking subversives.

Seri hung up, noticed how tightly her toes clutched the fabric. She put down the notebook and drew a card from her wallet, then phoned Calgary.

"Hell-o." The line hummed, but the voice at the other end was brisk. Her old friend, Anselm Kanashiro.

"Anselm," Seri said. "I need a big favour. Information."

A long pause. "Serendipity?"

"Yes." She frowned. "How deeply into the layers of the intelligence community do you think you can penetrate?"

"Serendipity Hamm." Another long pause. "Well, it's good to hear from you again."

"Yes, yes. Anselm?" She felt a prickle in her toes.

"Before we get the information, can you tell me exactly where you are?" A tapping deep in the static.

"Why?" She remembered the RCMP dream. "I'm actually in a bit of a rush."

"Well-o. I understand that. But." He stretched a long breath. "Just a bit of an update, Serendipity. Is all I need."

"First answer my question."

"We'll get to it, soon as—"

She slammed down the phone. Dear God, were they chasing her? Was Anselm trying to track her now?

She clutched her hair, took a deep breath. Who were *they*, Seri? Who were *they*? Special Intelligence Projects? This was paranoia and exhaustion. She stood, tiptoed out to the stairs' edge, looked down. Rooke was still at his table, staring at three empty glasses, finger trolling ice in a fourth. Bearlike Grimwater floated from table to table, wiping spills.

She turned and hastened to Rooke's room.

She stared at his briefcase. Room hot, mouth dry. Hurry. Open it, Seri. Would a prophet do this? What was the sign? Surely God wouldn't give her this opportunity if he didn't mean her to take it. On the other hand, Granny Casey had taught her that the right action never depended on the situation. Wrong is wrong, she once said, don't ever use bad for good. But then Granny Finnegan said, "Didn't Prince Rilian kill the witch in *The Silver Chair*?"

Seri's hand hovered over the briefcase. Nails so ragged, really letting herself go up here in the north. Before Seri's seventh birthday, Granny Casey had washed Seri's hair and trimmed her nails so neatly, and forbidden her to go into the backyard or even look out the back door until the weekend party. But Seri had looked one day after school, too curious to wait, and saw that Mum and Grandpa Hamm and the Grans were building her a miniature Giants' Bridge, just like in *The Silver Chair*, best birthday present ever. Then, at the party, she had wound up in the bushes at the end of the Giants' Bridge with Greg, bad little Greg, years before he became the youth pastor, and he had leaned over and kissed her right on the lips, mouth sticky with icing from the cake that was baked in the shape of a rabbit. And she had suddenly thought of her cousin Ricky, and how they had watched from Ricky's treehouse as the lady undressed in the window and rubbed cream all over her breasts, and Ricky got so excited, and Seri got caught up in it, though she wasn't sure why. And suddenly it seemed like she was kissing Ricky at the end of the Giants' Bridge, not Greg, and she screamed and fled the bushes. Later Grandpa Hamm asked her if she had been in the bushes with Greg, and she said no, and saw the angel-food rabbit missing his legs, and felt so guilty for telling the lie and for kissing Greg and for spying with Ricky and most of all for peeking at the birthday present, and she began to cry, and her birthday was ruined, and for a moment spring became the season of lost hopes.

She blinked, hand still poised above the case.

Jonah would run. She did not want to be Jonah. Not that kind of prophet. Not her dad.

She took a deep breath and cracked the briefcase.

It was mainly empty, containing nothing more than five books and a large, folded piece of paper. She gingerly turned over the books. Bible, *Tao Te Ching*, the *Upinashads*, something old called *The Book of Ozahism*, something ancient called *Die Alchemie*. She opened the Bible, found it full of holes. Chapters and entire pages were neatly snipped out. She opened each book in turn, found each cut up in the same way, as if someone was literally clipping and eating the words.

Replacing the books, she removed the paper and unfolded it across the bed. It was a collage, about four feet wide each direction, spangled with scribblings, clippings, runes, and pictures, each dated with Rooke's tidy script. The collage was clearly divided into stages, almost a map. The top left corner was from ten years ago in October—Rooke's handwriting, most of it charred and slashed as if someone had attacked the words with a knife and lighter. Seri looked closely at the remaining fragments—*our quest will renew us . . . north, to Lethbridge, to test our punk spirits against suburban banalities . . . .*

Then an entry dated December 27. A splotch of green and blue powder podged to the paper. A fragment of feather, also iridescent. A cascade of doodles and icons—fire, skulls, crows roosting on the horns of a crescent moon. What juvenile madness.

Seri looked further, to January—newspaper clippings from December, news from the *Lethbridge Herald*, a story about a Christmas Eve cabaret gone wrong. Seems the drummer in the band lost control of himself and trashed the stage, burning a Canadian flag in the process. Then he disappeared. Police were baffled. The local Christian community blamed drugs and punks. A Piikani leader blamed the chinook winds, said the snow-eater was also a mind-eater for those who were too contemptuous to understand other cultures, let alone absorb the spirit of the plains landscape.

One of the clippings was from a year later, a guest column by some kid from the university, who in retrospect marvelled at the community's response to this small affair, when, after all, there were more pressing crimes committed every day. The kid seemed especially upset that everyone continued to talk about this drummer, this damned punk Franklin, who had never been found, and held some power by virtue of his absence.

Franklin. Theodore Franklin Rooke. Seri smiled grimly, stroked the briefcase nametag. She was beguiled by this new image of Rooke as a punk drummer.

She looked to the next entry. August, a year later. This one looked like a ransom note, words and letters cut from various sources and pasted together in sentences. *All hopes and faiths are ridiculous....*

September. Rooke's scribblings, getting messier, more childish—*and what magpie whispered in my ear? ... real hope by stealing the false hopes of others*—almost illegible.

It was the last entry for nine years. But then Rooke had renewed his writing, weeks ago, just before Christmas Eve. Seri looked up. That must have been what he was doing when he disappeared in Lethbridge. She scanned again the bottom of the collage. More scribblings, cramped and leaning to the left—*kill hope....*

She opened the envelope and pulled free a picture, slightly out of focus, shot against the sandstone of the Lethbridge post office. A bearded man, framed by two tall and slender companions. The one with prematurely greying hair was obviously a younger Rooke. A clean-shaven Rooke. The other one, the one with the silvery ponytail, was the man from the recent Christmas Eve cabaret. His eyes were burned out.

Seri stuffed the picture back in the envelope. She threw the envelope on top of the books and grabbed the collage, which spilled some of its blue-green powder. Brushing it from her knee as if it were hot ashes, she snapped shut the briefcase, locking it quickly. Granny Casey was right. Never mess with wrong actions, look what you might get.

But what other choice was there? No jurisdiction, no mandate, no budget, no plan. Notebook nonsense, Bible nonsense. SIP after them, RCMP on board, get her in for questioning. She was running. She was Jonah.

No, Seri, *no.*

Maybe Rooke was some kind of special agent, only acting crazy, watching and waiting for her to incriminate herself. But for what crime? Lord, Seri, keep the faith. This was God's test. Find a way.

She returned to her room and called Vancouver.

"Appleskin! I'm so glad you called."

Seri's shoulders unbunched a notch. "Gran, I need your help." She spoke quickly, tumbling out all her doubts.

Gran chuckled at the other end. "I don't often do this, Pumpkin."

Seri knew. "A Bible verse."

More laughter. "God alone is my rock, my fortress. I shall never be shaken."

"Old Testament or New?"

"Old, King David. I think I misquoted. And don't forget your Augustine, who battled skepticism with all his heart."

"Yes." Seri's stomach unclenched. Yes. Gran's voice was the thread to the real world, thin but strong, the voice of clarity and certitude.

"Potato, Mr. Scott and I are on our way to Europe in a week." Gran giggled. "Kind of a sinful surprise."

All of a sudden Seri felt so alone. "Europe?"

"Yes, darling. A honeymoon without the wedding. Granny Casey would have been so disappointed."

Seri flipped her notebook cover back and forth. "Europe's pretty far."

Gran laughed. "So's the Arctic."

"Oh, Gran. It *is*." Seri closed the notebook, traced her name on the cover. "Hope you have fun. I guess this is goodbye till then."

"Not goodbye," Gran chided. "See you soon. And keep calling. I'll give you a Bible verse whenever you need one."

Seri smiled. "See you soon."

She hung up, smile lingering. Yes, always one true thing: love. Family, see you soon and never goodbye. It was enough. Time to fetch Rooke, get him some sleep, renew the journey.

She paused on the middle stair. There he was, still at the table, cleaning his glasses with ice water. His hair was mostly white, patched with black. A wiry beard had almost swallowed his once neat goatee. As Seri stepped down, she passed again the hanging photo of the horned hunter, who, for all she knew, winked behind his own dark glasses, or stared mercilessly, or had no eyes at all. Then she realized why the lodge's light was so unnatural. There were no shadows here.

CHAPTER TWENTY-SEVEN

The HOTEL AGARtHA

"Ted, we still on course for Foggy Island?"

"I see it." He peered through his reading glasses. "Keep north, a day's drive at most."

"When does your bogus music festival pretend to begin?"

"Three days hence."

"We'll be early, waiting for them."

"Perfect," he said.

"A trap. Spiders."

"Perfect."

Seri nodded. They were partners now, set by the purity and simplicity of their goal. No junk remained, no hesitation. Speed north. Catch flies. Catch punks. This landscape cut everything to its cleanest corners.

Yet the land seemed to sicken as the day rolled by, like Narnia under the White Witch. Small thickets smouldered, still afire, trees bent and broken as if by unnatural wind or striding giants. Ravens lifted croaking to the air, heavy wings bedraggled. Stalled vehicles at the roadside, overturned Ski-Doos, some burnt to husks.

Seri's thoughts wandered to images of Rooke the punk drummer—fingers clenching drumsticks, clean-shaven face warped with concentration. Now he was full-bearded as Moses, face going crooked as his forehead pulled one direction and his jaw another.

"Ted. Something's wrong here, unwholesome."

He knocked his teeth with a spoon stolen from the hunter's lodge, turned to stare right through her. Seri noticed for the first time that his eyes, magnified by lenses, were the colour of pine needles.

She turned away. "Keep north."

He hummed a sleek and twisting melody. His front teeth were chipped. After minutes the melody disappeared, though Seri could not remember its end. Rooke stared at his picture burned with two holes—stroking it, then crushing it, then gently unfolding its creases with one hand.

When they stopped at the last station, Seri looked in the washroom mirror and started. Her face was salt-white. She was the witch, causing the land to wither, the same way Pharoah's indecision caused the plagues, the same way Satan's games caused Job's cattle to die. She splashed her face with freezing water, came to her senses. Phone Gran soon, get another verse. Gran was the live coal in her heart.

"God is my rock." Seri looked up to the mirror again.

The checkout person was a child with mismatched eyes.

"Sorry," she said. "This credit card is maxed. You a witch, ma'am?"

Seri dug her Visa. "Try this one."

The lines chuckled and whirred. The child handed back. "Sorry. Something wrong with that one too. So are you?"

"Wait here," Seri said. "I have a third in the car."

She trotted back, heart tripping, trying not to think of Gran, or God for that matter.

"Better hammer it." Rooke grinned.

"There's much trouble loose." An old Inuit woman sat in the back. "Someone's let the demons loose, forcing against nature, pushing too hard."

Seri turned, reached back and opened the door. "Out. *Now.*"

The woman smiled, eyes crinkling, cheeks pouring inward. "The harder you dig, the more dirty you get."

"Now."

The woman hobbled out. At the station doorway, the child limped forward, finger raised.

Seri turned to Rooke.

"Three," he said, still grinning.

"Three *what*, Jesus goddamn it?"

She floored the car and spun out onto the ice, seatbelt undone, still dangling from the door.

† † †

A small ship listed west, frozen neatly at the waterline. The *Ferry Queen.*

"Lovely pun." Rooke said. "Perhaps this elf knows the way to Foggy Island."

A tiny man perched a stool below the boat's stem, wearing only a white linen suit, reading aloud from a great Bible and cutting from a chunk of meat with a knife. Behind him, the boat's ghostly funnel rose from a superstructure caped with mist.

"Ferryman!" Seri stepped from the car.

The man looked up, lips bloodstained. "The island you seek is directly behind me." He spit. The spit froze before it hit the ground.

"How did you know we...?" Rooke tapped the hood with his spoon. "Thank you. Where?"

The man gestured over his shoulder with the knife. Drops of seal blood scattered, froze in pearls while airborne.

Seri stared. At first, all she could see was the jaundiced moon behind columns of fog. Then a hazy hump, a small mountain smudged with mist. The smoky pillars shifted, and the moon unrolled a carpet of lemon light to reveal the south side of the island. It seemed half submerged like an iceberg, drawing up to a small volcano spider-webbed with polygons.

"A trick of the moon," said the ferryman. "Not a volcano. A *pingo*." He pointed to Rooke. "*He* can see."

"And at the top of the pingo?" Seri pointed at the hill's summit, where a sprawling mansion pulled shapes from the night.

"The Hotel Agartha. Canada's oldest hotel. An impossibility, given the erosion and the ancient lake beneath."

Seri nodded. "And there is a festival there?"

The ferryman smiled. "A gathering. Yes."

Seri got the feeling they'd been circling the island for days without seeing it.

"Has this island always been here?"

The ferryman closed the Bible and looked down at her. "No. It floats up and down the Mackenzie, depending on the season. Come, I'll take your keys. There are no roads where you go."

"No." Seri crunched a foot in the cobbled snow. "I'll keep those, thank you."

"It's the law."

"We are the only law here," Rooke said.

Seri nodded. They were clicking now.

"Very well," said the elf. "Clearly you have missed the signs."

Seri ignored him. "Will we find what we seek?"

"What do you seek? Love?"

"No," Seri said. "That I already have."

The ferryman gobbled seal and remained silent. Finally Seri stomped off toward the island, Rooke following.

"Friend." Rooke stopped and turned. "Will you at least tell us what month it is?"

"Today is the perfect day to seek love," The ferryman called from behind the mist. "Today is Valentine's Day."

† † †

The Hotel Agartha was built of stone, inlaid with ice chips and a permanent lacquer of hoarfrost. The hotel's bulk squeezed all the oxygen from the ice until it glowed a glacier blue, blue veins between shingles, blue haze filming windows.

Seri stared through her breath fog as she climbed the pingo. The hotel was built in overlapping styles, a herd of old stone mansions. The only light was a burnished orange glow in the turret window. A murmur of smoke poured from one of many chimneys, pooling, drifting down as if too old or sleepy to float skyward. Seri had a sudden impression of animals lurking in the hotel's heart, scuttling on footpads, watching from cracks and vents.

The lobby had a strange honey odour. Sweet, but the sweetness of decay. A cheerless fire cracked in the stone hearth, fed by shingles and what looked to be an unhung door with brass knob. Seri squinted. Atop the door, as if in offering, were a smoky pillow and three sizzling apples.

Rooke followed Seri to a great wooden counter, on which a rotating fan swept back and forth, rustling an old calendar and whistling at intervals across the bottle-top of an ancient Coke bottle. Seri shivered and wondered at the fan. It was freezing in the hotel, despite the fire.

Seri tapped the bell. A thin curl of smoke drifted across the calendar page, dispersed at the fan's wind. Then a head slowly rose from behind the counter, giving Seri a start. A boylike head, but beautiful, pageboy cut and dark glasses fogged over, cigarette holder clenched between ivory teeth.

"Hello," the woman said, stretching the *o* in a luxurious sigh. "Ah." She smiled at Rooke. "You have the *vision*."

Bespectacled Rooke licked dry lips. "We're looking for a brother lost— once, now, and forever." He thrust the picture at her. She smiled. Smoke pooled beneath her nostrils.

"The man in this picture," Seri clarified. "Have you seen him? We need to know if he's arrived early."

The woman drew cigarette from teeth, clutching it between thumb and pinky. After minutes she chuckled. "It is not good to stay at the Agartha for too long." Spoken slowly.

Again Seri sensed animals, hibernating in vents and closets, dreaming of spring, white-furred and bearded as prophets.

Rooke bent his spoon against the counter's wood. "Raise a star for us in this dark landscape."

Seri sighed. Come on, Ted, drop the hogwash poetry. "Is the man here, ma'am?" she said.

"Sprinkle some angel dust," said Rooke.

"We need details," said Seri.

"Before the days lengthen," said Rooke.

"This information is time-sensitive." Seri was actually catching his rhythms.

Rooke leaned into his spoon. "Well?"

Seri nodded. "Well?"

The woman watched smoke wind between her fingers. "Would you like a room? I do not recommend more than a week's stay."

"Listen." Seri leaned into the fan so her hair riffled. "We are law enforcement. We're setting a sting for this man. He's supposed to be on this island. Soon. We need to be absolutely certain he's not here yet."

"Teleological time," Rooke added. "White time."

The woman sucked smoke and nodded. "*Today* is a rather tricky concept."

"Is this the only hotel on the island?" Seri said.

"It is."

"Can I see your guest book?"

She slid a fat book towards Seri, who opened to the latest page and ran her fingers over the signatures: John Thompson, John Abbott, Arthur Meighen, John Alexander Macdonald.... Nothing recent here. Seri snapped shut the book and pushed it back. "We'll take two rooms."

"Two is a rather tricky concept."

Seri ignored her. "Two rooms."

"We'll wait. Like spiders." Rooke smiled. A kindly, krinkly, bespectacled grandfather's smile.

The woman handed over a pair of old ringed keys, eyebrows arched beneath foggy glasses.

"Spiders," she said, blowing her *s*'s like smoke.

Seri unlocked a tight fist. How long had she been clenching? Time to get hold of Gran, grab a good verse. Or else her cord to the real world was going to be more like Hansel and Gretel's crumbs than Ariadne's thread.

"This is very important." She stepped forward. "I need a working phone."

The woman chuckled. "We haven't had a phone here in fifty years. A hundred years."

Seri clutched the lip of the countertop, glanced at Rooke, then at the woman again. "What?"

The woman exhaled smoke at the fan, so it blew back at her and streamed into her nose. "A hundred years." She shrugged. "A thousand years."

Seri breathed deeply, repeated Gran's verse in her head. "This is a hotel. How can you not have a phone?"

"One hour. One minute."

Seri's fingernails pierced the wood. "A phone, damn it. How can you not have a *phone?*"

The woman laughed, a sound like ice cubes in a tin bucket.

"This is the Agartha," she said. "We've never had a phone."

Seri coughed.

"Or...." The woman traced a finger across the fluted tip of the cigarette holder. "To be more accurate, we haven't had a phone in forever."

† † †

Seri could not remember walking through the hall or inserting the key in the door. When she heard Rooke's footsteps in the hall, she loped across the carpet and flung open the door.

"Ted."

He looked at her, but his lenses were foggy.

"Ted, we need to make our plans and set the trap."

He reached into his pocket and pulled the photograph, offered it without a word, then shuffled to his room. Seri unfolded the picture and stared at the eyeless man with the silvery hair, his body creased and re-creased. She stuffed the picture in her pocket and stepped back into her room to crack her notebook.

As the hours unfolded crookedly, the desire for Gran's voice became a restless ache. Seri climbed the winding steps up the turret to glance out across the Mackenzie, where, far below, between curtains of smoke, a blue Camaro idled next to the *Ferry Queen*. At this distance both ship and car looked like toys, gone missing from some hoarfrosted toy box. She moved closer to the window to get a better view, but a raven alighted the rail and stared at her through the glass until she turned away.

Back in the hallways, she felt Rooke's shadow looming. He hummed his melody, which vanished each time she leaned in to hear it. Soon she was dreaming in bed. Rooke was a raven, and she lay naked in the snow. He landed between her legs in a white explosion. His wings beat the inside of her thighs, and he gently inserted his beak inside her, till she could feel its hard hooked tip pressing her cervix.

She roared to consciousness, hand flinging for the absent bedside phone. She leaped up shivering, folded and re-folded her clothes, pressing the creases, over and over. She scrawled Gran's verse in her notebook, *I shall never be shaken*. But her own words appeared as arcane symbols, nothing she could interpret.

"Do you have any hidden rooms?" she demanded of the night manager, now wearing a nametag that said *Peart*. "Anywhere we can perform surveillance from?"

Smoke wafting sideways. "Perhaps you should summon your phantasm, in order to roam the ballrooms and hallways unnoticed."

"The *phantasticus*?"

"There are many names."

Seri's nails dug the counter wood. "You know Augustine?"

"Which Augustine?"

"The saint."

Peart shook her head, tonguing tendrils of smoke. "I know Augustine *Rooke*."

Seri's thumbnail peeled from skin against the wood.

Peart got a dreamy look. "He is very handsome. And so polite, even at his most driven, always *sir* this and *sir* that."

Seri's nail peeled.

"Dead now." Peart sighed. "A century. Was he a saint for his relentless pursuit of evil? You tell me."

Seri pinched down the painful nail. "I beg your pardon?"

Peart smiled around the cigarette holder. "You are following in his footsteps. Surely you know that."

"Bullshit," Seri said, first time ever. The word tasted like vinegar.

Peart winked.

"Bullshit. Horseshit goddamned lie."

"Lie. Tricky concept." Peart tipped her cigarette, blew it out like a candle. The cherry splashed to the countertop, still aglow. "You are a lover of myths and suburban faerie tales."

"Am not." Seri scanned the counter. Phone here somewhere, somewhere, what kind of hotel.

"Once upon a time," Peart relit her cigarette, one deft flash, "there was an itinerant preacher and hunter of all things wicked and unnatural, for whom the saying *hell freezes over* was quite literal, and who, following the philosophies of Mani, determined that north was the true direction of evil and so the direction of his calling, and who insisted, in typically deft fashion, that the heart was a museum of evil, and, furthermore, that this metaphor could be made flesh, enacted, in a ritualistic gesture of renewal, nay, *salvation*, in almost the manner of the Israelites of the Old Testament, for whom the physical and material act of building, of arranging, of the journey—"

"Stop!" Seri cried. "I know the story, you know I know it, I'm not sure what you're trying to—"

"Don't you want to hear the part about the frost demon's heart?"

Seri shook her stinging thumb. "Did Rooke put you up to this?"

"Rooke is trapped far south, in another hotel, in a place called Lethbridge."

Seri punched the counter. "Not Augustine Rooke!" Her thumb flared, she paused. Why travel this labyrinth? Why unspool further this crimson thread? Surely there was a verse she was forgetting, something about steadfastness, something about Elijah. She took one deep breath. "Look. Are you absolutely certain you don't have a phone?"

Peart stared at her cigarette. "I'm not certain of anything. Are you?"

† † †

Was there a mythology somewhere, a proposition, a science, a religion, a model, a folkway, a cult even, where it was told that stories themselves became manifest and visible, were made flesh, leaped fully formed or even partial and asymmetrical—a trope here, an image there—from their fractal or liminal or intersticial space, from imaginary dimensions to the real world, where they entangled themselves with experience and history, with all that was quotidian and empirical, like viruses loose or far-flung refugees to be feared and rushed home with one-way tickets to the land of dreams and deliriums, or even, alternately, finally, offered status as true citizens? There must have been something in Seri's triple degree, some tale somewhere, that knit the disparate threads of geography, pharmacology, and angelology, some paradigm that proposed or accounted for such myths, spun in dim light, given life, tracked in their migrations. A topography of mythic hallucinogens? A map of psychoactive myths?

No.

For God's sake, that was nonsense. That was a collapse of distinctions Saint Augustine would abhor, an entanglement and diminishment of the truth no prophet would endure.

† † †

Seri awoke from a fitful nap, crouched at the bed, hands folded, knees and knuckles aching. Skeleton shadows twirled across the far wall, dancing on the room's penumbral light.

"Long time," he said.

She turned to see Rooke beside her, lenses aglow, open briefcase at his side, fingers feeding a paper-fire. His briefcase was almost empty. He was burning the last of the cut-up books and newspaper clippings. His diary collage was already blackened and curled, snowing soft grey ash at the ceiling.

"What are you doing?" she said.

He smiled. "The only way to keep warm is to incinerate the past."

She unkinked her fingers. "Where's my Bible?"

He nodded at the flames. "Only one left now." He plucked his own Bible from the case. Its covers flipped, revealing slashed and severed pages ready to fall.

"Do you want it?"

She stared. "No."

"May I have my picture back?"

She handed it to him.

He smoothed the creases. "The man in this photograph is here for one reason. To destroy my powder, and, in doing so, to renew his own spirit."

"Really. Great." She was so tired.

"He's going to throw it back into the fiery cracks from where it came." Rooke slid the picture between the dissected pages of his Bible. "That's why he's here. At the punk music festival." He closed the Bible. "Where I go next."

"Ted." Seri shifted. Her knees cracked. "Get it together for once. You invented the festival. This is *our* trap."

Rooke took a deep breath and stood. He marched to the door.

Seri unkinked her aching knees. "Hold on. We have to plan this carefully." She already had her notebook out.

"Here it ends," Rooke said.

"Clarify yourself. These occultisms won't do forever."

"Here is the final entanglement of threads—"

"Whose?"

"—postponed but inevitable. The butterfly effect."

"Ted," she warned.

"The final strike of the match or roll of the snowball."

"Ted, can you shut up for once?" She clicked her pen. "What are you going to do?"

He turned, lenses clear, eyes green as a poisoned river. "God in heaven," he snatched her notebook, began to scribble, "you really do need every little thing spelled out for you."

His pen tore the page.

"Ted, no need...." She tried to imagine Gran's face, but the white tongue of fire turned inside her and burned it away. She tried to hear Gran's voice, but heard only rising wind and her rattling heart.

Somewhere a phone rang.

Rooke ripped the page from its coils and held it at arm's length.

"Clear enough?" he said. "Real enough?"

She stared. Sanskrit, Latin, runes, what were these curls and cursives?

"Shall I draw a chart?" He sneered.

What was this spider-script, this hieroglyph, this Gestalt?

"Shall I make a tidy list, Serendipity?"

Her eyes focused. She processed.

"Do you need glasses?" he said. "Read."

She did:

I'm going to kill him.

Rooke crumpled the page, dropped it at her feet.

Seri reached a hand to steady herself, found nothing, almost fell.

"Ted." She swallowed hard against the nausea. Her whole paradigm turned upside down, emptying its plans and proofs and explanations, darkening as suddenly as the clearing in Galt Gardens. She had missed the signs with fastidious precision. She *did* need glasses. She was a Sunday-school spy, a toy-box prophet, a winter clown.

She opened her eyes, almost laughed, how clear at last. This was some chase, some threesome: Seri, Rooke, and Rooke's shadowy acolyte. The Biblical parallel was indeed King Saul and prophet Samuel, but also David, the third, Saul's apprentice, replacement and nemesis. This was an unravelling tale of displacement, charisma, jealousy, rage, and madness.

She bit the inside of her cheek.

Also a tale of laxity, blindness, and torpor, Gran help her, God forgive her. But even King David got a second chance, right? Still time. Seri choked down her nausea, smoothed her shirt, summoned her fire. She strode to the door and flung it open.

"Ted. Wait. This has gone far enough."

The air chilled. The phone rang in some distant hemisphere.

She followed Rooke out, fingers flailing, trying in vain to catch the steam clouds that poured from her lungs.

CHAPTER TWENTY-EIGHT

ThE HOTEL AGarTHa

Whatever the Weird was, it now had a voice and a body. Lor wondered how far it could press into the physical world before he was certifiably insane. He wouldn't let that happen. He'd run. He'd find the answer.

Someone kept sabotaging the equipment—impossible, since they saw no one after Yellowknife. Lor just ignored it. He closed one astigmatic eye, and, with the other, watched dots of moonlight in the truck's interior, caught like summer flies between the windows.

Summer itself was a vague and distant memory.

† † †

"Now what?" Lor rapped the frozen truck door with his knuckles.

A giant fissure cracked the Mackenzie. The truck stood idling at the edge, bumped up against an overturned stool, next to a car totally whitened by frost.

"Weirditudinous." Alistair had his map unrolled on the hood. "But I can see the south side of the island from here. Hearties," he looked up and winked, "We can hoof it."

"What is *that*?"" Lor squinted at an icy hill in the distance. Fatty stood beside him, thumb knuckle glazed with frozen snot.

"Looks like a pingo, mates, though I can't explain the utter strangeitude of colours. Blue, green—Lor, kind of looks like the glitter in your pouch."

Lor squinted harder through his lenses' icy cracks. "With a circus tent on top?"

"Looks more like a haunted mansion." Alistair rolled up the map with a snap. "Come on. We travel light and lean as wolves, an instrument in each hand, a festival to play, lives to be pared down to essentials—"

"What about the mixing board?" Lor said.

"Fuck it. Come on, we'll negotiate that fissure, claw our way up that pingo and storm that mansion like renegade angels."

"What about my truck?" said Fatty.

"Leave it with the other car."

"Dingle my nuts I will."

"Who'd steal it? A fuckin' frost demon?"

"A fuckin' hoodlum!"

"You're the only hoodlum here."

"Where is *here*?"

"Fatty. My friend." Alistair grinned and pointed to the sky. "We are at the top of the world. And we are about to finish your brother's mission."

† † †

Lor felt an instant attraction to Night Manager Peart—her boylike face, the sizzle of her cigarette, the tap of her finger as she moved pawns across a chessboard.

"I like to play with myself," was the first thing she said. "Need a room?" the second. She fingered her nametag. "I do not recommend more than a week's stay."

The lobby of the Hotel Agartha had a sweet mammal smell, like someone had slopped a bunch of caramel on a hot hog's back. Various bits and pieces of the hotel were cracking in the hearth fire—shutters, couch legs, baseboards, anything made of wood. Erratic clouds of steam and smoke drifted low across the floor, settling in corners, between bookshelves, beneath chairs. Just outside the front door, a guardian snowman glistened in the dim light.

"This place is even creepier than the Marquis," Lor said.

"There is only one hotel." Night Manager Peart did not look up at her three frosted guests. "With many shadows."

"Can you tell us how to find the alternative music festival?" Alistair said through chattering teeth. "It started earlier today."

"Today." Smoke collected between her nostrils and drifted downward. "*Today* is a rather tricky concept."

"Oh, indeed princess." Alistair dinged the bell on the countertop. "Like, the trickiest, abso-fucking-*lootely*. But surely you can help us."

She moved a knight with a hand as veiny as leaves. "There is no festival."

"What?"

"That I know of."

Alistair smacked the bell again. "What the fuck you telling us, '*damoiselle*?"

She smiled, brow furrowing like bark.

Fatty, who had been poking at the fire with one toe, yelped and jumped backward, boot smoking. Lor felt himself inexplicably getting a hard-on.

"Will you need rooms?" Night Manager Peart said. "I do not recommend more than a month's stay."

Alistair grabbed the brim of his hat and yanked down. "Good fucking night nurse, *madam*, the festival is here somewhere, you just don't know it. Do you have any idea how far we've travelled, any inkling darling, any hypotheses or suppo-fucking-*sitions*? Good God!" He smacked the bell. "Get us those rooms now."

"There is only one room, with many shadows. Who needs one?"

"You!" Fatty screamed, smoky boot tapping.

"Book us, baby," Alistair said. "We'll find the festival ourselves."

† † †

In Lor's room was a frozen hearth fire, which shattered to ashes at his touch. When he looked again, the hearth itself was gone, and the walls had changed from blue to green.

"There is only one room," Night Manager Peart said later. "With—"

"Yeah, yeah." Lor clutched the lip of the burnished counter. "With many shadows. What kind of place *is* this?"

It was hard to stay awake in the Agartha. Conversations were slow, stretching themselves so thin you could see through them. Sometimes he would realize that he'd been standing in the same place for hours.

"An hour." Night Manager Peart flashed him an ivory smile. "An hour is a tricky concept."

"How did you know I was thinking—"

"You just said so."

"When?"

"An hour ago."

"I did?"

"You."

"Me?"

"I. You. Me." She fingered a chess piece. "Tricky concepts." She dragged the piece across the board. "It's easy to split yourself. Checkmate. Damn!"

Again Lor felt a sexual attraction to Night Manager Peart's boyish features, to the set of her hands, which moved as if she were always holding fruit. He leaned over the counter and grabbed her by the shirt.

"Who is the phantom that chases me?" he demanded.

"Which one?" She removed his hand from her shirt with cold fingers. "All the secrets of life will be revealed to you, in time, by God himself."

"Really?"

She twirled a pawn. "No, not really."

He clenched his hand, unclenched. "Can we ever leave?"

"Yes."

"We can go back?"

"Of course." She knocked down a queen. "Less than a century ago, a holy traveller wandered this way, and, after a terrifying adventure, returned to southern lands unscathed."

"So he was okay?"

She considered. "No, not really. He is still simmering with regrets and the desire to set things right."

"You know him?"

"He was always so polite. *Sir* this and *sir* that."

Horseshit. "What kind of adventure?"

Peart lit a long cigarette. "North of here, where the night gathers, he wrestled with a dark visitor."

"What do you mean?" Lor crossed his toes inside his shoes.

"A creature of ice and shadow." She drew fire. "They wrestled the entire night. Then, at dawn—"

"There is no dawn here."

Peart squinted. "This is a *story*." Exhaled smoke. "At dawn, the holy man stole the visitor's very heart, and fled south with it. But his story did not end there. Back in his own home, the man was increasingly distracted by his talisman—infected, let us say—until his love soured, and his own family abandoned him and.... Well, do these tales ever end well? He kept the stolen heart secret. Kept it in a tiny box carved from the bark of the old tree."

"Which tree?"

"This one." Peart smiled, rolled up her sleeve to show a patch of discoloured skin, much whiter than the rest.

What horseshit. "Sounds like a folk tale," Lor said.

She twirled the cigarette. "To us, your lives are all like folk tales."

"Who are *you*?"

"All is connected. There are many stories. There are many rooms."

Behind the hotel, Lor found a single tree, its bark skinned in strips to reveal the silver beneath. He peeled off his bent glasses and smashed them against the trunk. The lenses popped out. He hung the twisted frame from a branch.

Back in the lobby, Night Manager Peart had beaten herself at chess once again. Her skin glowed silver. She flicked the fallen queen, squinting through Lor's mangled glasses.

† † †

Lor sat on his bed and poked his finger with the magpie guitar's strings. But this time his awareness seemed to drain with the blood. He poked another finger, then another, but could not clot his bleeding sense of self. He poked all four fingers and his thumb, and played the guitar, squeezed the neck until there was blood everywhere. By this time he hardly knew who he was. He reached for the bag of glitter and tried to stanch the cuts with it.

Suddenly his fingers clenched around the pouch.

That fucking *dust* was the problem! Of course. He'd been holding the dust the whole time at Inuvik, during the vision, the whole time at Yellowknife. It was in his pocket the whole Happy Hanukkah cabaret, it was all over the magpie guitar. The Weird had smuggled itself out of Lethbridge in a pouch.

He glared at the dust, seething with attraction and repulsion. Standing, he threw the pouch into the nightstand drawer and slammed it shut, then kicked the nightstand for good measure. He grabbed his guitar and made for the door.

He never wanted to see that dust again.

He wanted to open the drawer, pick up that dust, and never let it go.

† † †

Lor entered a room scented with ganja, saw Fatty slumped in a chair, Alistair bent over him. They had a fire going in the middle of the floor, burning rolls of toilet paper, a cube of weed, the closet door.

"So cold." Alistair tossed the last of the toilet paper into the flames. It turned to ash in seconds.

When the fire dwindled, Alistair began to take apart Fatty's drum kit and roll it into the fire. With each tom popping, each cymbal sparking, he added his own bass guitar, then produced a harp and added it to the flames.

The fire ate a hissing groove across the bass' twelfth fret; the neck buckled, scissored and stroked the harp's strings; the harp snapped, each string striking a drumskin. The fire played a concerto, transmuting rhythm to smoke, an offering to the ceiling gods.

"It ain't punk," said Alistair.

"No," Lor agreed.

Alistair pointed at Lor's guitar. "Now. Your own sacrifice."

Lor felt a rush of love and rage. He hugged the guitar tight to his breast. "Don't touch it."

"Amigo. We're *dying* here."

"Fuck off."

"We'll take it."

"I'll kill you both."

Alistair sighed. "This is an imbroglio of sorrows." He put his hands on Fatty's shoulders. "We have news."

Fatty's jaw clenched. His teeth squeaked.

"Tell 'im," Alistair said.

Fatty did not look up. "Fondle my nuts."

The fire began to play a jig.

Alistair turned to Lor, said, "Fatty's been sabotaging our gigs. He's our boy."

"What?" Lor pulled the guitar tighter. The fire vamped, cracked out a rhapsody.

Alistair giggled. "It was the only way he could kill his pain, his terrible cry of the heart. The kid has been desperately chasing a song all these years, never catching it. It's been driving him mad, says it even has a *smell*, f'you can believe it."

Fatty sniffed.

"This amigo is truly his brother's ... er, *brother*."

The fire broke to a smoky lullaby.

Alistair clomped a boot. "Like, the little dude heard the tail end of a song on the radio, years ago, or somebody singing, dig? And—how do you explain the vagaries of mystical experience?—he's been searching for it ever since, always just out of reach, just out of earshot, somewhere in the distance, beneath the static—"

"Fuck off," said Fatty.

Alistair grinned. "And now he keeps hearing someone hum snatches of that mel-o-dee, in the next room, in the hallways.... Deep down, the li'l shit is really ...uh, *deep*."

Lor freed a hand and put it on Fatty's shoulder. "What's going on?"

"You." Said without feeling. The fire dwindled for an intermezzo, then crackled between blues and bebop.

Alistair tapped his boots. "Can you hum a few bars for us, amigo-san?"

"Dingle my nuts."

"Fatty," Lor said. "How does the song go, man? We may have heard it."

Fatty looked up, lip between teeth. He exhaled, took a breath, started to speak, stopped. The fire began to die around a florid arabesque, singing whiffs of bitter smoke.

"Hum it, Fatster."

Fatty hummed one note, coughed. He tugged one ear, then the other. Stuttered two beats, clicked his tongue, fell silent. He looked like he would get up, but slumped instead. He stared at his own crotch.

Alistair nodded vigourously. "Yeah, man. The relentless elusiveness of the ineffable."

Fatty sat, motionless.

"Hey. Dude."

Fatty an ice sculpture.

Lor leaned down. "Fatty?"

Fatty spoke, voice a cracked whisper. "Kiss my piss."

The next morning he was gone.

† † †

"Well," said Alistair through blue lips. "Truck gone, no way back now."

"Franklin could have found this damned festival," said Lor.

"If only he were here now."

"If only."

The ashes from the fire briefly revived, glowing with the sounds of a distant hootenanny.

CHAPTER TWENTY-NINE

ALL TABLES ARE COVERED IN VOMIT

"Stop, Ted. It ends here." Seri almost tumbled into a wall mirror funhousing the Agartha's remaining light. Her fingers twitched; she was dying for a phone. Rooke plunged into the hallway shadows, long stride navigating curves and corners.

"I created him," he called back. "I'll destroy him. This is not your journey."

"You wouldn't even be here if it wasn't for me." Seri's breath sandpapered. She passed a room in which two people were obviously making rough love—bedsprings creaking, door rattling, a whip or cracking belt.

"You can't renew yourself through destruction," she called to Rooke. "Give it up."

"Don't lie to me."

"Destruction is a tricky concept," Peart croaked from a darkened alcove, where she perched upon an overturned armoire chiselled with gargoyle motifs, fingers flourescent with sticky stars. She laughed, a clink of frozen moons. "We are in a Fimbulwinter. We are waiting for the end."

Seri sped to catch Rooke, who had vanished behind a corner. "Ted, enough! I'm putting an end to this."

"Really?" He stood waiting. "How?"

"Your quest is over."

"Lovely! Will this be a citizen's arrest?"

"We're going back south."

He grinned. "Will you call down a choir of angels?" He snapped two fingers. "Oh! Perhaps your darling grandmother will help you, send up a magical Bible verse."

"How did you...?" She felt a roar of rage. "I'm alerting hotel staff, right now."

"Have you seen any?"

"I'm calling the spymasters at Internal Security Division."

"Will they know me? Send them my love."

"I'll call the RCMP."

"How?" He dangled his cellphone.

She squeezed the coins in her pocket. Her toes bunched in her shoes. Dear God, open a path here. This was like punching fog.

"Yes, pray." Rooke shoved her, loped into the shadows. "We'll see how powerful your watchmaker is."

The hallway dipped, went dark. Seri followed what appeared to be tiny running lights that winked all along the joint between walls and floor. The hallway opened to a luciferous lobby. She squinted, saw that the lights were actually snowflakes, dicing through a cracked window to swirl and curl across the hotel's spirit breezes.

In the eye of the blizzard stood Rooke, gnawing a fingernail, clutching his Bible, path blocked by of all people the freak from the Lethbridge clearing. The freak stared through greasy bangs with one good eye, toe tapping, stiletto heels squeezing pink feet. He had Rooke pinned with a ragged walking stick.

"Let us pass," Rooke said.

"Ha!" The freak jiggled the stick, stuck out his tongue to catch the snowflakes. "So that ye may visit the island? An island, yes, but which island: Serendip, Patnapida, Prince Edward, Hades itself? Nay, such are the islands of lost souls. Especially Prince Edward."

"This is Foggy Island." Rooke said.

"Nay!" The freak cracked his own head with the stick. "This isle is named Azoth, and has no fewer than seven directions."

"You stare with Odin's eye, old man."

"As do you." He tapped Rooke's glasses with the stick. "Yet I care not a whit for your malapropic convolutions."

Rooke took a step backward and raised the Bible. "I seek a thief. "

"If you follow this path, you will end hither in a forest of Christmas trees, by the fog of the river. Perhaps in the arms of your own dear brother."

Rooke started. "What do you mean?"

"The one you seek is at the tip of the island."

"This man is going nowhere," Seri called.

They ignored her. Rooke's fingers quivered on the Bible.

"Who *are* you?" Seri said.

The freak let his stick descend. It tapped the tiles. "Once I was of the House of Darker."

Rooke clapped the Bible. "Where is the path? Where is the brother?"

The freak cracked his own head again, then clubbed the floor—*tock tock tock* —breath shrieking from nostrils.

"Old man, where is the brother?" Rooke yanked a white scarf from his pocket and wrapped it around his own neck.

The freak covered his corroded eyeball. "Say *brother* no more. Your whispered incantations put me in mind of my own family, for whom I bear eternal hatred."

"Where?" Rooke demanded.

The freak considered. "Once we bore only love," voice wisping. "Only love. But the thrower came between us." He spat. "The thrower and the master himself."

"This thrower is your brother?"

"He is a knife thrower. His plans will fail."

Rooke's face stiffened. He stepped forward, wagging the Bible till shreds and pages swished from between covers and floated to the floor. "Where is the one *I* seek?"

"I have told you."

Rooke bit down on his index fingernail, then yanked hard and pulled it right off. He turned, strode past Seri, finger dripping, white scarf flapping, lips pulled to a grin.

"Ted." She grabbed his shirtsleeve. "Don't listen to this madman."

"Jeremiah the prophet was mad." He brushed off her hand. "Oh—you mean *insane*?"

"Ted. Stop. Think."

"You still here?"

Back into the dark hallway, pricks of snow flitting like fireflies. Joists and floorboards creaked, as if the hotel was an old galleon shifting with the tide. The walls brightened, and the hallway broke to a frozen tearoom honeyed with moonlight—fine bone teapots and snowy scones, some half-eaten, atop mahogany tables laced with Irish linen, studded with icicled jam pots. Wedgewood cups and saucers. Walls papered in silk, an oriental rug stormed with wild designs, turned up at one corner, tassels bedraggled. A room long abandoned, a century-old tea party preserved in ice.

Seri shivered.

Rooke stood between skirted chairs and an abandoned tea service, mumbling at his open Bible. Behind him, an enormous yellow moon hung at the picture window, its daffodil glimmer brightening a cabinet lined with china figurines.

He hummed a few bars, then sang softly in a luscious tenor: "Now God be with us, for the night is clo-sing, the light and darkness are of his dis-pos-ing . . . ."

Seri paused. His voice was so lovely, she almost let him go. "Okay Ted. That's the benediction."

"Shhhh." He reached down to tug at a skirt. "This room is designed to resist obscenity."

Seri reeled for options. Her words were grotesque in their inadequacy. What other leverage did she have here?

Rooke sang, with growing vigour: "Before Jehovah's aw-ful throne, ye prophets bow with sacred joy, know the Lord is God a-lone, he can create, and he destroy."

Seri clasped her hands. Lord, a sign please?

"How about Psalms, little prophet girl?" Rooke held forth the Bible.

She saw it was the one of the few sections not slashed to bits.

"King David's book." He licked a finger and flipped a page. "I will make my arrows drunk with blood." Flipped another page. "Happy be he who takes their little ones and dashes them against a rock."

"Out of context," Seri blurted.

Rooke pointed out the picture window. "Look for once. There *is* no context."

"You want to live by the Psalms?" Seri saw a glimmer of hope. She briskly stepped into the tea room. "I'll quote you Psalms—All the paths of the Lord are mercy. Sing unto him a new song—"

Rooke sang. "Guide me O thou great Je-ho-vah, pilgrim through this barren land." He winked. "Come, little prophet girl, sing with me. Ladies only on the second verse."

Heat cascaded Seri's cheeks, beneath her collar, between her breasts. "Cease from anger, forsake wrath."

Rooke clapped his hands. "Don't get mad, get even."

"The Lord is my shepherd."

"You are a sheep."

She dropped a fist, knocked a frozen teacup. "Ted. Jesus Christ."

"He can't hear you. He's busy throwing snowballs at the angels." Rooke sat on the table. "So. Our hands are no longer tied."

"Stop toying with me."

"Are you a toy?" He fingered the white scarf.

"Listen to me! I know what's going on here, I've been watching you—"

"And I you!" Rooke clapped. "Oh, dear little believer."

"I've been watching you since—"

"A watched kettle never boils. Psalms chapter zero."

"You're mad!"

"Is this my tea party?"

She stepped back.

"Don't go away mad." Rooke rose from the table. "I love you." Chased with an acidic laugh.

"Ted, you've lost it."

He stepped towards her. "We are all lost! Psalm 21:12."

"My God. Ted."

He looked at her. "Oh, Serendipity. Couldn't you think of a *single* woman prophet?"

Seri felt a sudden empathy, as he stared at her, gnawing his nail-less finger. For the first time ever he seemed fully present, like his gaze wasn't piercing her, but seeing her, really seeing her, all expectations dropped.

Then her stomach seized. In his presence she also felt the shadow of absence, the places where Rooke held himself in utter distance. Dear God, maybe there was no communion in this world, only endless manipulations. She tried to think of a rationale, an explanation, incantation, anything.

Rooke laughed. "He despairs of escaping darkness, Job 15. Or she."

Seri clutched a frozen teacup. "Ted, don't give in to this. Psalm 51: He will wash you whiter than snow."

"All tables are covered with vomit. Isaiah 28."

"Renew a right spirit within me, it's the theme of the Psalms, don't you see?"

"Which Bible are *you* reading?"

She tightened on the teacup. "Ted, you can be renewed. Psalm 30— weeping may endure for a night, but joy cometh in the morning."

"Open your eyes, li'l Elijah." He gestured out the window, teeth clenched. "Morning never comes up here."

He raised the Bible and came for her.

"Ted, I'm going to have to—"

"She surrenders, her towers fall. Jeremiah 50."

Seri raised the teacup. "You *are* crazy."

"I wish. Oh how I wish I were crazy."

He seized her hair.

"Ted, you're hurting me."

"Always hurt the one you love. Old Testament, right?"

He seized her arm. She yanked free. The teacup broke in her hand. Wham. He smashed the Bible across her head, loose pages exploding. He recoiled, smashed her again. She tripped and hit the carpet, chin knocking, tongue slicing on teeth. Rooke's picture fluttered down, zinc moonlight winking between the burned out eyes of his former friend.

"What is one true thing, baby Jonah?" Rooke kneeled on her shoulders, scarf-end fluttering down. He slapped her. "Forty years in the wilderness?" Slap. "Slavery to Babylon?"

"Ted, please—"

"You're just like your father," he rasped. "Here. Bring this back to him." He stuffed the Bible down her shirt. Then rose, straightening his glasses. "Goodbye, Serendipity. Thanks for the ride."

Seri clenched her teeth, tried to rise. Not Goodbye, Ted. See you soon. See you soon.

See you.

See....

She tried to hear it in Gran's voice, but summoned instead her father's, unremembered for so many years, now clear as prairie sky. She didn't believe the words, any more than he would have.

Her head fell back. She heard Rooke's footfalls, then his heavenly tenor, softly down the corridor—

Our old mal-i-cious foe, is set to work us woe

Both la –dee –da—forgot the words

La –doo –dee –da –da –doo—

† † †

She rolled over and raised herself to her knees, tongue swollen. She believed Rooke now. She had failed utterly on every step of the journey. She had lacked the faith and sinews. She was early Moses, or Abraham's wife, Sarah, who laughed bitterly at God's promise, who did not believe. She was Job's whining friends, or all the weak kings who turned to idol worship. She was Jonah, who ran away. She was the daughter of Pastor William A. Hamm, failed prophet, backslider, coward.

She shook the butchered Bible from her shirt, bookmarked Psalms with the fallen picture. Then she stood and limped to her room, where she ripped open the nightstand drawer and hurled in the Bible. Yes, she *would* be shaken. She kicked the drawer closed, then peeled her clothes and headed for the shower to scrub away the filth of wisdom.

CHAPTER THIRTY

NeEd tO BE TiEd

"Well, 'migo, shall we sit together till we freeze to death?"

Without his glasses, Lor saw mainly blots and blurs. Alistair looked like a wizard halfway to vanishing.

"Think about it," the wizard continued. "We'll unite mystically with the big ice, follow Franklin in a totally different way, a family of annihilation."

Lor wiggled numb fingers. "Wish Franklin were here."

"A true believer." Alistair nodded, blew on his knuckles.

"Wonder where he went."

"Probably on some island blissed out like a Buddha."

"And we're here at a no-show festival, freezing to death, with nothing to eat."

"Shit." Alistair twisted his brim. "Shall we eat your guitar?"

"Don't you touch it."

Alistair stood and coughed a cloud of frost. "W'then, I'm going to look for the night manager one more time, see if we can't rustle up something real around here."

"I'm going to my room. If I can find it."

Alistair strode for the door. "Adieu. We'll meet again."

"Right," said Lor. "Perhaps we'll all meet again. Some sunny day."

††††

Lor passed a darkened alcove where Night Manager Peart perched on an overturned armoire, peering out like an owl. He continued to his room, opened the door to a humid blast. A host of singing candles lit the insides. Bright yellow bananas filled a woven bowl, flanked by a pitcher of ice, a bottle of gin. Shower water pounded the tub in the open bathroom.

His mouth watered. Had he eaten anything since coming to the Agartha? Had he even *been* in his bathroom? The shower stopped. A cloud of steam drifted out, followed by a dripping figure in towels.

Lor reached to grab the doorknob. "What are you doing in my room?"

"This is my room." A woman's voice.

"What number—"

"Close the door. We're losing steam."

He bumped the door closed.

"What do you want?" the woman said, still veiled in shower mist.

Lor squinted, wishing for his glasses.

"Well?" the woman continued. "Speak up."

"What number is this room?"

"Never mind the number," she said. "Who are *you*, breaking in here?"

He had no answer.

"Are you family?"

"No." Lor wiggled his fingers around the guitar case handle, then added, "I don't have a family."

"The way you hug that guitar—"

"Don't touch it," he blurted.

Her face remained hidden as she towelled her hair. "Are you an orphan?"

"Not really."

"Anyone out there you love?" Mist curling between her limbs.

Lor wiggled his fingers. "No."

"When you came in, I thought you were my companion." She paused. Her voice soured. "Coming back to...." One towel dropped from her glistening skin.

"Your companion?"

"He is so cruel, so capricious. And yet...."

Lor peered into the steam. "Someone you love?"

A long pause.

"Forget love," Lor said. "Take it from someone who knows."

"Who are you?"

"My name is Lor."

"Ah!" She clapped, dropping her towels. "The twists and turns of this earthly life. Told you we'd meet again!"

"Oh." Lor squinted. "Shit."

She stepped from steam to candle light, peroxide buzz cut wicking beads of water. "Come in, punky. Out of the cold with you."

Lor turned to flee, doorknob stiff in his hand.

But Darci Shimozowa was laughing, buttoning a long silk shirt. "Little spell of mine. Come in, come in. A little refreshment, in order to finish your journey."

Lor opened his mouth to answer, found only his thickening tongue.

She cracked her knuckles. "Do you know what you are chasing yet?"

He jiggled the doornob. "Something's chasing *me*."

She grinned wickedly. "You're back for more. Always the same story."

"No."

"You men chase orgasm as the crow flies."

"I'm not chasing—"

She frowned. "I'm talking about the *world* of men, punky. Come. Sit with me on the couch."

Lor twisted the doorknob.

She raised an eyebrow.

"You still have my jacket," he blurted.

"Are you cold?"

"I'm hot."

"Take your shirt off." She sat on the couch and crossed her legs. What long toes she had.

Lor closed his eyes, suddenly remembering old lovers. The Jainist, who wouldn't step on bugs, whose utter difference sharpened his attraction. He'd had to leave her. The wet one who soaked his futon through to the carpet. Over the top, he'd had to leave her. The goth girl who begged for unmentionables when she came. God, he'd run from that one, same way he should be running now.

He opened his eyes, found himself on the couch.

Darci licked her teeth. "You still have his dust?"

"Nope."

"Run north. All the way. I've already built the warding."

He shifted. "That snowman out front?"

"Yes. Snowman." Her voice turned bitter. "What kind of thrice-fucked warding can *melt*? There is no real power in this world."

"No."

"Let me hurt you," she whispered. "Please."

"You've still got my jacket." He tried to rise. But she grabbed his hair, yanked him down, bit his throat. He shrivelled like he'd just stepped into the Arctic Ocean.

She let go of his hair and peeled off his belt.

"No," he said.

"Sometimes you need to be tied up to be free."

"Ha, ha." He fought her. "No."

She stood, wrapping the belt around one hand. "We need to cut through this resistance." She opened the nightstand drawer and removed a knife, then tossed him the bottle, a glass, an ice cube.

Lor poured himself two fingers of gin.

Darci plucked a banana from the bowl. "Careful with the panty stripper."

He splashed half of it back, kept his eyes up and open. The ceiling was pasted with flourescent stickers: stars, moons, planets. He looked down.

Darci was peeling a banana with those long fingers, bent way over, knife between her teeth. The handle was jade, the blade wavy like a Malaysian kris.

"Admiring the knife? Belongs to my lover."

She took away his tumbler, still half full.

"Over here." She sat back and patted the couch, biting ice with a crack.

Lor shuffled over.

She sliced banana chunks with the kris and crushed them into the gin, using the blade as a stir stick. Lor leaned closer to look at the mash. Phantom smells twitched his nostrils—lime and lilac, pine bark and peppermint. The knife's blade sucked as Darci pulled it from the mash, sparkled as she set it on the nightstand.

Lor thought it was his watery eyes.

"Here—" Darci spooned banana mud with her fingers. "To cool you."

"No."

She smeared a handful across his face, over his lips. It was cold in his mouth, warm at the back of his throat. Pushing him down with her belted hand, she unzipped his pants and reached for the knife in one musical movement.

"Darci—" He tried to rise.

"Sit down," she ordered.

She sliced off one of her buttons. It hit the nightstand with a click and bounced. Lor could see each bit of broken thread bristling through the buttonhole, each fibre of eyebrow on her face, each lash. She licked a finger and moistened a zigzag line of hairs on his arm. Then slid his own finger between her lips.

"Come on, Lor." Her voice deep, somehow different. "One long, hot, slow honeyfuck is not going to kill you."

"What will?"

She seized his neck.

He sniffed ginger sweat. A sudden fit, a sudden swell.

"Darci. Kiss me."

She bit his lip instead, then grabbed his wrists and cinched them with the belt. When he was tightly bound, she painted his ears with banana mud and inserted her pinky.

"Gentle," he managed. She stroked his ears, eyelids, elbows, prick, too many arms too many arms, why didn't she let him go, let him roll, let him breathe before—

He came like lightning. His orgasm forked, cracked, vanished. The room went with it. Darci too. The bed, the stars, the ceiling.

He saw, in the flash, his hunger for connection. His ache for a single finger of communion, even one night of gently orchestrated illusion. But he was clouds inside.

He opened his eyes. "Let me touch you."

"No." She pointed the knife with pearled fingers. "Lie back. Now."

She sliced off his clothes and sat on his stomach, tracing the knife along his throat.

"I'll untie you," she whispered. "If you promise not to kiss me."

He swallowed. Hands free, he sat up, stroked her arms, and gently pressed her backward, as if they were longtime lovers.

"You must be joking." She pushed him away. "From *behind*."

Through the next half-hour, she didn't once turn to look at him.

"Oh, God...." Lor grabbed her waist, about to come again. "Darci—"

"Watch your tongue," she said. "Tonight you call me Zurah."

"Zurah." He reached to caress her shoulders.

"Don't." She whipped back the belt and cracked him across the neck. He yanked away his hands. Eyes watering.

It was the sting, nothing more.

CHAPTER THIRTY-ONE

The VISITATION

Seri stumbled from the shower and fell still wet into bed.

What's this?

In her room's corner was a wardrobe filled with living trees. Inside a figure crouched beneath an evergreen. Atop the tree sat a magpie, breast aglow with a lantern's radiance.

Her attention was drawn by warm light on her shoulder. She turned in the bed. A cloaked visitor bent over her, face hidden by a cowl.

Seri felt at once the purity. "Who are you?"

He laughed brightly.

She did not recognize him at once, the way she always thought she would. But no matter. Maybe Raphael, guardian of love. Or Sandalphon, keeper of tears. Or maybe even Duma, patron of dreams. The visitor flexed a hand, fingers ringed with white fire. Then she guessed: Sadriel himself, the Angel of Order. The meaning was clear now as it ever was in the Old Testament: do not doubt. Who was she to doubt God?

Seri sat up and extended her hand. But the visitor pointed at the nightstand drawer, as if it housed a forgotten gift or lost possession.

Seri reached down. For *me*?

The visitor dropped his arm and turned, interrupted by a shadow. The dark figure from the wardrobe crouched behind, unweaving the aura strand by strand. The angel waned. No!

"Now a face, soon my heart," he said, voice failing.

Seri reached forward, to no avail. The room quickened to a wheel of darkening motes, caving at the core, spinning faster, smaller, tighter, then imploding with a discharge of golden brilliance.

All her nerves snapped. Who was this wardrobe devil, to destroy her visitation? Night Manager Peart, the freak, Rooke himself? Her father?

She awoke twitching. Three croaking ravens perched outside the window. She clutched the sheets, felt the warm light across her skin. Her first impulse was to smile, but when the ravens croaked again, she frowned. There was something incomplete to this sense of wholeness, as if it failed to reach the deeper cells. She bit her lip. Her face was still bruised. After sitting and listening to her breath, she reached for the nightstand drawer to retrieve the cut-up Bible.

It wasn't there. Only one page of the Old Testament, the Book of First Kings, ripped out. Nestled beside it, a small drawstring pouch.

Seri plucked the page. Of course: the story of the prophet Elijah, disenchanted beneath the broom tree, begging God to let him die. Then his predictable sleep, his visitation, the angel's touch—renewed strength for the final journey. The archetypal prophet's myth. And didn't he get his final strength from food delivered by ravens?

Seri exhaled, slowly. So here were the signs, completely clear at last. A visitation, an inspirational Bible tale, Elijah's ravens at the window. Another chance, a reminder that God did control the world, even its engines of chaos. For good measure, the symbols even mirrored the triadic structure of the journey—Seri, Rooke, and the shadowy apprentice. She cleared her throat. So why did she feel so little heat? Where was the fire, re-lit and stoked to white flame? Why, in fact, did she feel a smitch of disaffection, as if the Elijah tale were some old platitude, and she some jaded pilgrim?

She paused. Hang on, those signs were not triplex, but quaternary: there was also this fourth, this pouch, filled with....

She picked it up. Her fingernails tingled with a strong itch to cast it back and close the drawer. What was inside? Placing it on the nightstand, she slipped on her cotton briefs and sports bra, then her green jeans and sweater, finally her shoes. After staring at the pouch for one long moment, she decided it was not, after all, a sign, and carefully replaced it in the drawer.

She was feeling hollower by the minute. These signs mocked her. She opened the drawer again, dropped in the crumpled, fluttering page. Slowly, with quivering fingers, she reached for the pouch, plucked it, pulled tight its strings. Her fingers warmed. Perhaps then this was the fourth sign.

Still, she did not feel enough crackle or passion to press onward. Where was her damned renewal? Was this her fault? Weren't people who demanded signs without faith? She dropped the pouch. Well, that teaching was in the New Testament anyway. Not *her* book.

She slumped on the bed. The choice was as clear as Augustine: press on with God's plan, or go back. So why didn't she care? She was emptied, bored even, as if lighting and fanning Rooke's fire had cost her own. But maybe that was God's final lesson on this journey, that choice was never a matter of inspiration or heart. Could she hold to faith, complete her calling without the fire? Was *that* the true test?

She plucked the pouch, felt again the tingle up her fingers. Open it. No, pull shut the strings. She held it tightly instead. After one long, deep sigh, she pushed herself to her feet. Yes, this pouch was the fourth sign, opaque, mystical, but with a clarity still. The meaning was, *do not trust to ecstasy.* The meaning was, God's commandments were no glittering Zen aphorisms, but precise declarations written on cool hard stone. The meaning was Seri was no Rooke, and never would be. A good thing, that. Look at the consequences of pure charisma: look at Satan in *Paradise Lost*, or the Green Witch in *The Silver Chair*. Yes, the lesson here was difficult, but clear as virgin ice.

Read the signs. Obey. End of story.

At the door Seri found more signs. Crumpled clothes, a splotch of blood, and, in the middle, stuck in the floor, a knife with a wavy blade. She was surprised to feel so little shock or horror. But there it was. Rooke had killed his apprentice, and left the Bible as his calling card. Now he was heading north.

How much of a lead did he have? She pulled her pocket watch, realized there was no time to search for the body. Mindfully, fastidiously, as if girding with the armour of God to animate her empty core, she slid her notebook in a pants pocket, her watch in the other, and, very carefully, the knife into her sock, point resting on the flat sole of her shoes.

She felt nothing; it hardly mattered. In *The Silver Chair*, Jill and Eustace had heeded the signs at last, and clawed their way up from the underworld, through the labyrinth, to the benediction of a cold winter sky. The Israelites, too, had finally followed God's directions to Canaan. And Abraham, the patriarch, had taken the original strange road, without ever asking questions. God kept the maps: the path of faith was always, finally, the road home itself.

Seri had everything she needed. But, before closing the door behind her, and with only brief hesitation, she dropped the pouch into her shirt pocket, next to her vacant heart.

She could not explain why.

CHAPTER THIRTY-TWO

ThE VISITATION

Lor fell asleep holding one of Darci's fingers.

What's this?

He was inside a wardrobe filled with living trees, gripping Darci's knife, crouched beneath an evergreen from which a magpie gazed gravely, breast aglow with a lantern's radiance. The room outside was dark against the wardrobe's wintry light, but he could see the bed where Darci slept, covers tossed, damp limbs askew. What a relief, to find she hadn't run away. He could hardly stand the thought of—

Damp limbs? He squinted. That wasn't Darci. This woman was too short, too muscular. He clutched the knife tighter. His Buddhist ex? Vandy-Anne Hellemond?

A monstrous cloaked figure materialized over the bed.

"Who are you?" the woman said, rising.

The visitor laughed. Hairs bristled on Lor's neck. He knew that laugh. He'd heard it in the Crystal Room in Lethbridge, in Yellowknife, in every damned town along this river. And he was not going to listen again.

On the bed, the woman reached to touch her visitor, as if he were some lovely angel.

No!

Lor stabbed the knife into the floor, pulled himself forward, stabbed, pulled. In the bed's shadow he raised the knife. Sliced. The blade bit floor.

His finger rolled away. He reached with the stump, trembling, to paint the snowman's hem with blood.

"Kenny!"

The visitor turned. At first Lor thought it was made of moonlight. But no: beneath the cowl the face was dirty snow. The snowman smiled, a stream of quickening features.

"Don't touch her," Lor croaked.

"Ah, Kenny. You gave me life in Lethbridge. A voice in Yellowknife. Now a face, soon my heart."

"Don't touch me." Lor raised his good hand.

"Kenny, Kenny, still not ready?" The eyes smoked out, features whirling. "How many times must I ask?" The snowman laughed again, then vanished in a charge of golden brilliance.

The woman moaned, as if on the cusp of orgasm.

† † †

Lor jumped awake, sat upright. Darci was gone, the sticky stars fallen from the sky. He searched for her clothes. On the bed, on the floor, beneath the sheets. All gone. He bent to sniff her pillow. Nothing. A stray hair? Nothing. Glancing about for something to hold, he hugged himself instead.

Nothing. Nothing would do.

He opened the nightstand drawer and plunged in his hand, grasping for the pouch of dust, grabbing instead a battered book.

He yanked the drawer and stared. His dust was gone, in its place a slashed and severed Bible, from which a photograph fluttered out. He grabbed the picture, found himself staring at himself, flanked by Alistair and Franklin. He flipped the photo over. Dated June 1, ten years ago, in spidery red script. Franklin's handwriting. Franklin's picture.

He flipped back to the photo. Alistair and Franklin looked so much alike. Fuck, did he really know either of them? How many chances had he missed, over the years?

Lor placed the picture on the nightstand and stared at it for a long time. Then he fired his lighter and lit a curled edge. The photo barely flickered. These friends did not burn easily. Lor watched the flames struggle, thin smoke drying his eyes. Finally he stood and rifled all the drawers, but that dust was gone, long gone. It was over. The Weird was going to win.

He stared at the burning picture, just as Franklin's face began to sizzle. Seized with panic, Lor reached into the flames to save him. Too hot—he burned his fingertips, yanked back his hand. Franklin's face curled into a smile before vanishing to ash.

Lor watched the remaining smoke drift up sluggishly, hovering as if too weary to rise further. Finally, it descended into the open drawer. Lor stooped over and breathed it in. Coughed once. Closed the drawer.

All gone. Everything gone now.

After a long span, he stood, pulling himself up with the aid of the night-stand. Time to find rest beneath frozen waters, between stones, behind stars. He would take only the guitar, and these ashes.

The guitar. He had almost forgotten: he still had *some* of the dust, painted across the body. What a relief.

He knelt at the bed. Underneath, beside his shredded clothes, Darci had left him Vandy-Anne's Mackinaw that she had no doubt borrowed in turn from some strange lover in some nameless town. They were all nameless now. He put it on, cased his guitar, scraped the photograph's ashes into his palm.

Ready. He knew where he was going—to a place swept clean, the tip of this crazy island, where he would unravel, and freeze, and sleep forever beneath delicious stars.

PART EIGHT

THE RESTORATION

Faith teaches that there is a right and wrong beyond mere opinion or desire.
—Former Prime Minister Stephen Harper, 2009

CHAPTER THIRTY-THREE

OdiN's HAT

Seri cruised the lobby, mindful of each clean angle where she stopped and everything else began. Every item revealed its own true self—that fire in the hearth, that crack on the tile. She tapped the pouch in her shirt pocket, sipped a black coffee from the lobby perk. Whatever it took to press on.

She smelled burning feathers.

The night manager woman stood at the lobby's centre in a bulky hunter's shirt, squinting through a pair of twisted glasses, tossing pillows into the fire.

Seri stared through the stinky smoke. "Where's the nearest RCMP detachment?"

"Depends where we are."

"We're on Foggy Island."

"Depends where the island is currently floating along the Mackenzie."

Seri deflated. She sipped, tapped her shirt pocket. "Do you know?"

"Directions." Peart waved, then peeled her glasses and licked the lenses, began to scrub them with her shirt. "North, south, five more I can't remember."

"Do you at least have a radio here?"

A bell rang, followed by a male voice. "W'fuck, girlfriends, is there anything real 'round here at all? Holymorphic, nonspectral, to use a couple professor's words? Anything tangible, touchable, true, anything here that might give us a clue?—er . . . corporeal, cognitive, clear-cut, quee, these are all words that begin with a c!—w'cept for the last one, which ain't even a word at all, like it matters up here."

Seri turned to the front desk. She recognized him immediately—tall, thin, silvery hair tumbled to shoulders, the man from Rooke's picture. So he wasn't the dead one. Who was? On his head a tall pointed hat, white and widely brimmed, much like the mad god Odin wore when he wandered the earth hoarding wisdom. But this was no god. This was a man in grave danger.

"It *is* a word," said the night manager.

"Excuse, *'migette*?"

"*Quee*." The night manager replaced her glasses. "Quee is the very last wish you have before you die."

Odin laughed. "Nonsense! But such lovely nonsense, dig?" He rang the bell again. "Comely tommyrot, pop-pee-cock—fetching piffle, winsome tosh—pure ma-lar-kee, fiddle-de-dee—bewitching . . . er, have I used *nonsense* yet?"

"Like it matters up here," said the night manager, squinting.

Seri pointed at Odin. "You're in danger. Do you have companions?"

"All gone. Only one left."

"When's the last time you saw him?"

"A while. Honeypie?"

"Don't call me that. There's a man out to kill you."

"Many men, *'migette*."

"I'm serious."

"Serious?" said the man.

"Tricky concept," said the night manager.

The man rang the bell again and again. "Lord in heaven, *'migettes*, this Arctic makes a man disintegrate."

"No," said the night manager. "It simply attracts those already disintegrating."

She began to unbutton her hunting shirt. Beneath it was a plaid calypso, which she also began to unbutton. The man dinged the bell with both index fingers. The night manager emerged from her two shirts in yet another, this one zippered, not for long.

"Listen to me," Seri said. "What's your name?"

The silvery man stared.

"What are you doing up here?"

He stared.

"Look. The man is going to kill you. He hates you. He's unstable. He's already killed someone."

"Name of?"

"Theodore Franklin Roo—"

"Franklin!" The man stopped hammering the bell. He leaned entirely over the desk. "What does he look like, what, what, what—"

"White beard, used to be neatly trimmed, but—"

"Tall?"

"Very tall. About your height."

"What does he do?"

"CSIS agent. I think."

By this time the night manager was down to a tube top.

"Oh." The man reached up to squeeze his hat. "That is, like, *decidedly* not him."

"Used to be a punk drummer."

"Don't fuck with me!"

"I'm not."

"How do you know?"

"Ten years ago, in Lethbridge, he—"

"Lethbridge! CSIS agent?" The man seized both sides of his hat brim and pulled down. "Un-fuckin' likely—CSIS agents don't even smoke up, and the dude's disappeared for 'zactly ten years...." He stopped to count his fingers, re-counted. "Jumping Jesus."

"You're in real danger here." Seri patted the dust.

Odin gaped at his fingers. "Jumping Jesus, he *is* here, where is he? This is the convergence of the universe! He's where?"

"You don't want to know, believe me."

"Lotta faith, sister." He picked up the bell. "This is the man with the vision, the king of big ice, who has glimpsed through the veil, the *veil*, dig me?—the veil of tears, of fears, of years, of seers and weirs and piers and mirrors, of, of, fuckin', uh, *dweers*...."

"Well, *that's* not a word," said the night manager.

Seri stepped forward. "He's headed for the top of the island. Keep to your room until I've got him under supervision."

"Out of my way!" Odin threw the bell at the wall, one quick ding and a rattle. "He's at the festival."

"There is no festival. Get to your room. I'm law enforcement."

He pushed her aside, boots clomping, hat bobbing. "This man is my father. This is a family re-yoon-yun." He yelled through cupped hands—"Lor! The circus has come to town!"

Lor? The dead one, obviously.

"Indeed." The night manager stood in a laced camisole, skin pinkening, goosebumps rippling her shoulders.

Seri let the man go. He wasn't going to catch Rooke, who had at least a couple of hours' head start. She gathered herself. "How big is this island?"

The night manager squinted. Raised her fingers to her shoulders, began to slide down the thin satin straps.

"Never mind," Seri said. "Do you have a radio, radio-telephone, CB, anything?"

The night manager tossed her shirts into the pillowy fire. "Why not just use our regular phone?"

Seri stared. "You don't have one."

"We *do*."

Good God. Seri's anger flared, replaced instantly by an ache to phone Gran, then by a cold drive. No time for family phone calls, she didn't need that boost anyway. She squeezed her shirt pocket, felt the knife in her shoe. Careful where you step. "You said you've never had a phone here."

The woman began to unlace her camisole. "Where is *here*? And as for *never*, tricky—"

Seri flung up a hand, spilling cold coffee. "Just give me that phone. I have a flight to catch."

CHAPTER THIRTY-FOUR

THE TRUE HALLUCINOGEN

Lor tiptoed from his room. He floated through a frozen tearoom crackled with broken teacups, where twin windows let in beams of honey moonlight, collecting at the room's corners, dwindling to gloom. At the rim of darkness, a small figure with black hair and widow's peak leaned on a room-service cart, creaking the wheels, rattling icy teapots.

"Sir? Ken?"

Lor laughed. Of course, of course. He drifted on. One room dissolving to the next, dark passages unfolding to sunrooms smelling of old smoke.

"Ken?" From the shadows. "Don't go. I beg you. Don't give it to him."

Lor slammed the door.

Hugging his guitar, he marched into moon-scorched snow, until the hotel was far behind, an old ship frozen in arctic waters, turret listing, curtains flapping from broken windows. Soon a winged shadow appeared at his shoulder, and tossed up a cloud of snow, which twinkled down over his head. "Snow, Kenny. The true hallucinogen."

Lor's feet crunched over ice chunks, which he saw now sparkled with blue-green. Wow. They'd been smoking this island itself on Christmas Eve. No wonder everything was fucked up.

An arctic hare zigged by and dove into a fissure, scattering blues and greens, chased by dust devils of snow. Lor unbuckled his guitar case and dumped it in the snow, clutching the guitar to his breast. He moved on, to where his own footprints scored the snow. "You were once the snow angel, right? I dreamed you."

No answer.

Lor slowed. "Are you the same as the snow*man*?"

"Angels appear often as men."

"And demons?"

Blue laughter.

Lor squinted at the sky. "Why do you chase me?"

"Who's chasing who?"

Lor, staring at his feet, saw suddenly that there were two sets of footprints. He slowed. "Tell me what to do."

No answer. Shadow gone.

Lor plucked a long dark coat from the snow. Put it on over the Mackinaw. He walked, black and ragged, until the footprints stopped at a green river, where he mounted a spiny floe frozen to the banks. He kicked at it until it chunked loose and sluiced away.

He floated in darkness, into music—one shimmering note hung with overtones.

Old moonlight, long stored in the snow, released and gathered in clouds at the river's heat. Lor sailed into creeping mist that froze in jewels through his beard. Then into blue forest, light slicing bright nicks and notches before returning to the snow.

The floe crunched to a halt as the river narrowed. All around, spruce bristled with tiny icicles the texture of frozen eyebrows, clinking like countless china teacups trembling in their saucers.

Lor stepped from the floe and slumped down cross-legged beneath a tree. Lay the guitar on his lap. Closed his eyes. How lovely it would be to say a few last words to the guitar. But this forest was a place where words grew too heavy to float.

He felt wind on his eyelids.

Everything here was shedding its skin—love, culture, meaning. The Man was vanished. Lor missed Franklin, suddenly, keenly, as one would miss an older brother. But no goodbyes. He had been right to flee love. He took off his gloves. Reached into his pocket, feeling the photograph's ashes. Closed his eyes.

Now.

Only this.

††††

The cold forced Lor's eyes open. He was wrapped in a tiny mist cloud that bit to his marrow. Knees cracking, he crawled toward the next tree. But the cloud followed him, droplets dancing. Lor stood. The cloud raised with him. He stumbled for the next tree, but the cloud beat him to it, stopping to float beneath blue boughs. He tried to fan it away with his guitar, but it dispersed and gathered again in a misty column.

Fine. Perhaps he was not yet at the island's tip. He would let the cloud lead him north, into increasing cold, where he would complete his calling. But the air warmed; he could feel it at the rim of his nostrils. An apple-scented breeze lit the back of his throat. He thought of birds.

Remembering his purpose, he turned and inhaled the freeze behind him. He dug into his Mackinaw pocket and sifted the photograph's ash. After one step, he turned back to the warmth. The mist danced above a rolling bank, beyond which Lor could not see. The scent of apples again. He remembered climbing an apple tree by a river as a boy, shaking the overhang, ripe red globes dropping to splash and float away. He remembered Alistair.

The mist waited.

Pulling out his ash-blackened hand, Lor got a firm grip on the guitar, then followed the dancing cloud over the bank, across a river, and around a tree, into a summer meadow thick with flowers.

A FEw dEEP BREATHs

"Hurry up." Seri's fingers pressed around the pouch of dust in her pocket.

Constable Rajinder Mohanraj, lone RCMP officer and pilot from the remote detachment in Kivalliq, raised a finger, though not his voice. "Easy. Just go easy now."

"Listen, pencil pusher, you can play policeman later."

Mohanraj removed and bit his sunglasses. "A few deep breaths. Take a few deep breaths. From the diaphragm. Like so." He tapped a pencil against the coils of his notebook, glasses swinging from mouth. "No exaggerations, please. You say you're with CSIS, and this Rooke fellow too. Though he's gone now, correct?"

"The details don't matter." Seri yanked out the mysterious pouch and clasped both hands around it. "This is an emergency. Let's just get in that plane."

"The details always matter." Mohanraj smiled. "Everything is in the details. Police work is in the details."

"Give me that damned ludicrous notebook." She tried to snatch it, missed.

He restrung the glasses around his ears. "The details. You tell, I listen."

"You're hopeless!"

"There is always hope. Hope remains." Constable Rajinder Mohanraj of the Mounted Police slid Seri a tall wooden stool. "Sit down, please. A few deep breaths. Let's make sure everything is in order."

Order. Christ!

"Order," said the night manager, behind her desk, burning peppermint tea bags and unpeeled containers of Cup-a-Soup. "Order is the strange engine of the world."

Mohanraj of the Mounties ignored her. "Sit please," he repeated to Seri.

Was this another tendril of God's final test, to demonstrate patience when all she felt was agitation, to act independently of emotion? Seri sat, pouch in one palm, free fingers knotted in her bangs.

"And if you don't mind," Mohanraj continued, "Please refrain from swearing." He stomped his boots, speedlaced mukluks with thermoplastic outsoles. Then he looked up. "Unlike you, unlike her, unlike *everyone* in this barren land, I am an upright man."

CHAPTER THIRTY-SIX

ENOUGH

STORMS

A painted ocean. Poppies swaying in perfumed currents, pale skies combed with summer clouds and drifting heat. Butterflies flitting in slants of sunshine, the hum of bumblebees.

Lor stopped and stared.

A river flowed up to the sky in misty sheets, pulled by dark clouds to fall back as snow. Sunlight thinned against gloom, the world caught between day and night.

He turned toward the warm half.

He stopped.

A stone's throw away, shimmering in the heat, stood a boy in a top hat and red military jacket. One arm was stuck with fat quills. The other held a magpie.

The boy smiled. A cold smile. "Welcome, thief."

Lor swished through the poppies. He opened his eyes. He didn't remember closing them. He was sitting on the ground, tall stalks swaying overhead.

"Stay awake." The boy held up a palm. "We have a reckoning." At his side, a white cone rose from between poppies. Lor saw the boy's arm was stuck not with quills, but knives.

"Who did you expect?" The boy smiled. Two clean rows of baby teeth. He pulled a knife from his forearm and flung it up spinning. Then another, another. They hung in the air by his head, whirling bright blades.

"Let me pass," said Lor.

The boy's eyes darkened, deep blue to green. "First return my dust."

"Yours?" Lor stared.

The boy laughed. "Come. We have raised enough storms for now." He tapped the white cone at his knees. "I have a family reunion to attend. I need my dust. I will offer you your own life."

"No."

He pointed at the sky. "You think I can't bring winter back?"

Lor stayed silent.

"Give me my dust."

"I don't have it."

The boy's eyes turned from green to black.

"Any more—" Lor quickly added.

"Ah, Theodore." The boy reached to stroke his magpie. "Seems we have a complication."

Theodore squawked.

"Who has it?" the boy said. "Did you offer it to my beloved?"

"I don't know your beloved."

The boy reached to touch the belt mark on Lor's neck. "You do," he said, mouth twisting bitterly. "Tell me. In the morning. Did she stay?"

Lor said nothing.

"Perhaps one of your brothers has it," the boy said, thoughtfully.

Lor touched his neck.

"Or," the boy's eyes sapphire, "perhaps the virgin."

"I don't know any virgins."

The boy stared, tapping the white cone.

Lor shrugged. "I've never known any virgins. I don't have your dust."

The boy squeezed the tip of the white cone, knuckles darkening. The knives clattered and dropped to the ground. Lor's fingers twitched and thrummed the guitar's strings, scattering chords. Sunlight traced the dust glued to the body.

The boy saw. His eyes softened to blue. "Ahhhh. A thief *and* a liar. Well: one bargain for you." He stooped to pick a knife. "Give me the guitar and I'll let you pass."

Lor hugged his guitar.

The boy fingered the knife's thin blade. "You will be alone, finally. It's what you want."

It was what Lor wanted. Wasn't it? Wasn't solitude the point of this long journey?

"No," he said, surprising himself.

The boy's eyebrows arched. The magpie shrilled.

Lor looked down at his guitar, spangled with blues and greens. Thought of his long flight north. All the people he had met. All the people he had fled. Once, long ago, far from this place, in dead summer when chinook winds scorched prairie grass, he had sneaked with Alistair and Franklin down the coulees for a picnic of peyote and 'shrooms, to an unlikely meadow much like this one, where wild roses mingled with dust and prickly pear, and the three of them, connected by filaments of hallucination, had argued and gossiped and laughed like family, and finally passed out, and awakened as strangers to cold shadows and an early evening moon. Franklin and Alistair. Left far behind now.

"A-ha!" A delighted laugh from the boy.

Lor started.

The boy smiled, hands folded prayer-like around the knife. "You're not exactly what you seem, are you? You dream of your brothers, despite yourself."

Your brothers are near.

"Near?" Lor almost dropped the guitar.

I will give them to you. Voiceless words, a melody of air.

"Who spoke?" the boy snarled.

Behind him, a faceless snowman defied the sun.

"Who spoke?" The boy turned. His shoulders jerked up, then slowly, smoothly, descended. "Oh, Theodore. We have an unexpected visitor."

You have outrun all of them, Kenny. But who, finally, can escape what he desires?

"Certainly not you, phantom," the boy sneered. "Get out of my clearing."

The magpie squawked.

One bargain, Kenny.

"I'm speaking to you, daemon." The boy raised his knife. "Listen."

You know what I need, Kenny. Every grain.

Lor plucked a string. "I lost most of it."

Blue chimes, ice cracking.

"I'm speaking to you," said the boy.

Give me what remains. But now I will offer only one brother in return.

"Which one?" Lor said.

"I'm speaking to you."

I will not say.

"What am I, a ghost?" The boy plunged his knife into the snowman and began to carve a face. Wide eyes. A cold nose. A crooked smile. "Forget this visitor, Lor. Give *me* the guitar," chopping chin and cheekbones, "I'll lead you to both your brothers. A reunion. All three of you, together again, at last."

He lies.

"Do not."

He speaks with a frozen tongue.

"Don't you ever melt?" The boy dropped the knife. The magpie bobbed and warbled.

Lor looked at his guitar, and it felt like his last and dearest friend. A reunion? Wasn't that exactly what he was *fleeing*? Searching for a newer, cleaner, colder life?

The boy stared with sapphire eyes. "Give me my dust."

It isn't yours.

"Ah." The boy snapped his fingers. "So you *do* speak."

Don't listen to his voice, Kenny.

"Kenny." The boy smiled. "Is that what your brothers call you? A good name is better than precious ointment."

Don't listen.

"Bah! You will die." The boy again raised the knife. "Daemon. Can you offer him his own life?"

No.

The boy grinned. "Both brothers, Kenny, I promise you. A family at last."

Lor clutched the guitar. He was tempted.

Do not give him what remains of my heart. He will use it for ill. He will sow the seeds of hatred, break the bonds of love, kill his own family.

"No." The boy shook his head violently. "No." His features softened, lost their guile. Then quickened like a child's on Christmas morning. "You have been told the wrong story. Or, rather, you have been told the right story backwards."

Don't listen. His heart is a museum of evil.

"You are too quick to rely on easy myths of evil," said the boy. "*You*, of all creatures. What about *your* story?"

The snowman slicked with ice.

"Does the boy tell the truth?" Lor said.

Kenny, baby, I don't know.

The boy smiled, almost kindly. "Lor. For your kind the dust will bring only sorrow and disenchantment. But for my kind, the dust is a talisman of restoration. If not to heaven, at least to wholeness and love."

Lor's fingers squeaked on the strings. "Then why are you here, alone?"

The boy frowned. "My family is too far fallen. They cannot imagine anything beyond malice, and seek only to checkmate my plans. They are addicted to their own hatreds, truth be told." He extended a hand. "Lor?"

Lor stepped back. "Does he tell the truth?"

The snowman paused. *Who can say? Each tells his own story.*

Four seasons' worth of time drifted down, leaves, soft snow, and cotton-wood. Lor began to thaw inside, bones melting, blood coursing with runoff.

"Okay." His voice was dry and distant. He loosened his tight embrace.

That's mine. Blue chimes and angry wind.

"A fair bargain?" said the boy.

Mine.

As Lor raised his arm to trade the guitar, his shoulder stuck, and his knuckles clenched. The boy laughed, reached, and, one by one, pried Lor's fingers from the neck.

You'll regret—

Just as the guitar changed hands, a distant magpie chattered. Theodore bobbed excitedly, then crouched and flexed his wings. The boy reached with his free hand and pinned the magpie's claws before it could fly. "Dear watch-maker in heaven. Will this tale *ever* end?"

Again the chattering. Lor turned. In a knotty poplar, a second mag-pie cackled, wings raised high, black feathers twinkling. Lor turned again. Theodore struggled in vain against the boy's fingers.

"Yes, Theodore," said the boy. "I know you've suffered. God loves our tears."

The boy laid the guitar by the white cone, then drew a dagger from the heap of fallen knives. Theodore wriggled madly, claws still pinned. The far magpie called. The boy raised the dagger, and said, "One more communion." Lor looked down.

He heard a whizz, a chunk of bone or wood, a broken aye! aye! aye!

He didn't want to look.

He did.

The far magpie was nailed to the trunk, wings spread awkwardly, ribbon of blood tracing the bark's curved corrugations.

Lovely touch, thief.

Lor shifted from foot to foot. His hands felt empty. Digging into the Mackinaw pocket, he gathered the ash from the old photograph of Alistair and Franklin. He pulled it out, sifted it from palm to palm.

Theodore keened.

"Now, Theodore." The boy clutched the guitar once more. "Fly. Find the virgin, who steals my remaining dust."

The snowman glistened. *I will take my heart, Knife Thrower. And I will take you, too.*

The boy chortled. "You're nothing but spirit. You don't even have a real voice."

The magpie drooped, then gathered itself. It sprang from the boy's shoul-der and flapped into the world's dark half, vanished in falling snow. The boy stroked the guitar. When he looked up, his eyes were completely blue, no whites at all.

"*Adieu*," he said.

Lor gripped his brothers' ash. "What about our bargain?"

The boy seemed to consider this, fingers tapping the guitar's dust. Finally he chuckled softly. "Well, if God won't keep *his* promises...."

Lor's squeezed his fists till the knuckles cracked. "You little bastard."

"Please watch your language."

"You goddamned—"

"Shh."

"You goddamned fucking—"

"Tut."

"You goddamned fucking little shit-eating—"

"Hush!"

The boy reached a finger to Lor's lips. "We're not quite finished." Reaching down, peppermint eyes still frozen to Lor's, he grabbed the white cone around the tip. He pulled it from the flowers and tossed it over his shoulder. It landed on the snowman's head.

Lor slumped.

It was Alistair's hat.

The boy giggled. "Too late, now."

Too late for *what*?

"I leave you to your impotent daemon." The boy doffed his own hat, tossed it spinning into the air. His hair was winter white. Then he cracked into a cloud of buzzing flies, guitar shapeshifting with him.

Lor lunged. Clawed at the cloud. Crushed a handful of strings, flies, dust. Held tightly, teetered, fell into the snowman. An ocean of cold poured free, a scent of rain, a sky of sunlight.

The flies tried to buzz south, but were pulled back in a jittering line. They roared once around Lor's head, then winged up and sizzled into the snowman's face. The snow came instantly alive, phantom cloak whirling to existence, features quickening. The snowman, or angel, or demon, or whatever the fuck it was, loomed over Lor, extending its arms, straightening Alistair's hat on its head.

"Ahh, Kenny. Free at last."

Kenny, about to faint, fell forward, just in time to catch the boy's plunging top hat on his own head.

† † †

Seri refused to fill out Constable Mohanraj's Lost or Missing Person Report.

"We're wasting time here," she said. "People could die." Well, that was a slender lie; people were already dead.

"We must proceed with an orderly process." Mohanraj's eyebrows tightened. One thinner than the other. He began to scribble. "I won't lie to you. Search and rescue is not my forte."

"God forbid." She wanted to pull the knife from her sock and cut off his fingers.

He held up the pencil. "God willing, we would have a chopper with infrared and a trained specialist in ice rescue. But the nearest are in Whitehorse. There are none in Kivalliq. Kivalliq is the last post. These are the facts. Please fill in the report."

"I won't."

Mohanraj sighed. He began to fill in the report himself.

"Listen." Seri stood and placed a hand on Mohanraj's shoulder. "Here are the facts. There are men out there on the ice with no survival equipment of any sort. These are not upright men." She hardly cared. She softened her voice for effect. "They could die, completely unredeemed. I tell you in good faith: they are not going to heaven without another chance."

Mohanraj sighed even louder. Poor, pitiful man, with all his vacant certainties. He re-capped his pen and stuffed it in a pocket.

"That was a transparent trick," he said. "And it worked."

Out of the lobby, en route to the plane, Seri saw the snowman draped with Rooke's coat. An out-of-nowhere rage bloomed in her belly, for this creature steadfast in the face of wind and weather.

"You must admire this lovely snowman," said Mohanraj. "So lovingly built."

Seri was already kicking it to pieces.

"What in goodness are you *doing*, Ms. Hamm?"

"Let's go." She knocked the ice from her shoes.

† † †

The Twin Otter winged across dark skies under Mohanraj's capable guidance. Back and forth over the island, though all they saw below was the plane's impossible shadow staining the unlit landscape.

Seri stared down until her sinuses ached. She felt completely emptied, until she raised her head to stare out the window at the endless ice-cracked barrens. Her tongue of fire flickered, then, as they flew across the roof of the world. But the feeling was inappropriate, illicit, more like kissing Ricky, teasing Greg, sniffing Rooke's cologne. She ignored it, spoke to manifest her resolve. "We won't come this far to turn back."

"You know," said Mohanraj. "The Zen masters say that success is a form of failure. Not so different from Christ, who says one must lose life to find it."

Or find it to lose it, thought Seri, grimly.

Mohanraj chattered. "This plane is originally out of Fort Smith. Once it carried Prince Charles from Norway House to Swan River."

"How much flying time do we have?" Seri said.

Mohanraj shrugged. "Can't stay up forever. Some of the parts on this dinosaur are ready to fall apart, scavenged from the old Mountie Air Division—a Beaver that crashed in the Yukon, a Beechcraft burned in a hangar fire in Edmonton, an Otter that crash landed in Newfoundland...."

"A real Frankenstein."

"Frankenstein." Mohanraj nodded. "He's the one with the fangs?"

"No." Seri realized her mistake. "He's the one who created the monster, the one...."

She stopped, fully chilled, every fine hair bristling. Just a minute now: if *she* had summoned Rooke's lightning, if *she* had lit the fire, then given the outcome here, what pray God, what exactly, *what* again was her calling? She had never known God to be fond of irony, that hopeless realm of pagans. What was the sin, what the restoration? What was God's will, what hers? A jumbo jet rumbled high above. For all Seri knew, Gran and Mr. Scott might have been on board, winging their way to Europe. She felt a surprising sting of resentment.

"We'll have to give it up," Mohanraj said, banking steeply. "For now, at least. What in goodness name are you doing?"

Seri realized she had withdrawn the knife, and was slicing off hanks of her hair. She dropped the knife and hair in her lap, heart and sinuses pounding. "Constable, do you know of any text, apocryphal or otherwise, where Satan gets credit for both the fall *and* the restoration?"

"I do not believe in Satan."

"Since one is the source of the other?" Gran had always loved Seri's long blonde locks, said they looked like the White Witch of Narnia's.

"I do believe in Samson," said Mohanraj. "Who of course cut off his hair and lost all his strength. You know this prophetic story, in Judges? I think you had better put that knife away."

Seri pulled the pouch from her pocket, one quick hit of comfort, wondered exactly what was inside, jigged it a few times from palm to palm. "Hold on." She pressed against the window. "What about that little forest down there?"

†††

Lor flung the top hat to the ground and began to stomp it.

The snowman laughed. "Still the same old punk. Yet I thank you."

The sun hazed, mercury dropping. Poppies grew sparkling skins of frost. The snowman blew steam from beneath his cowl, white Merlin hat perched precariously. He gestured widely with one long arm, as if welcoming guests to a mansion.

"Well, Kenny. The time for words is over. Go. Listen for the signs."

Lor's hips tightened.

The snowman fairly bowed. The hat stayed. "You may pass. One brother is the deal. Do not trust your eyes, Kenny. *Listen*. Listen very carefully for the signs."

Lor's buttocks clenched. He listened to his breath, whistling through one clogged nostril.

"Go!" The snowman pointed north. "Follow the moon. Then listen."

The cloak fell away slightly, enough to reveal the snowman's glassy skin. Beneath, deep in the ice, Lor's guitar was cracking into a skeleton—strings stretching to bones, frets bending to ribs, pickups lining a spine. A melody lit the transformation, the most heavenly music Lor had ever heard. If there ever had been a song Fatty was chasing, this was it—smoky chimes, wind through pines, fire and wild violin.

Lor felt like he had chewed and chewed until the tooth itself had fallen out, leaving a vacant ache. He stared at the guitar bones. The dust was long gone. He raised his eyes to the wide white hat, clenching his teeth until they squeaked.

The snowman stepped aside, made a sweeping gesture for Lor to pass. Lor stepped stiffly forward, each footfall turning the ground to snow. He came even with his dark visitor.

"Goodbye, Kenny. I wish you happiness."

"Not goodbye!" Lor lunged and seized the snowman's neck. The snow blackened beneath his ashy fingers.

"Don't touch me!" the snowman gargled. His cowl fell away. His face was a night blizzard. Lor's hands slid up toward the face, toward the hat, ash blackening more snow.

"The time for words is done," said the snowman in a strangled voice. "Release me."

Lor seized tighter. Guitar bones jangled.

"Leave me, Kenny," the snowman croaked. "No one escapes what he denies."

Lor locked his hands and crushed. The snowman's frozen arms encircled him, driving frost into his spine.

"Give me my brother's hat," Lor cried.

"I will not bless you. I will never bless you." The snowman cracked its frozen skin and morphed into a grotesque Frosty sporting an icicle prick. The prick speared between Lor's legs, raised him from the ground till his feet dangled.

"Want a lick?"

Lor hung on. Beyond, the sun melted, summer meadow changing to winter forest—stalks blooming to Christmas trees, flowers to icicles.

The sooty snowman reeled, shaking Lor like a wet towel. "Release me!"

Still Lor squeezed. Ice water poured through his fingers, melting his flesh, freezing his bones. Firing his remaining strength, he flung his head forward and bit out a chunk of snow.

"Give. Me. My. Brother's. Hat."

Then spit it back at the angel's face.

Ashes roared out like a plague of Yahweh, blighting trees, blearing snow, smearing stars, finally choking the moon. The last thing Lor heard was the roar of a plane, then an entire forest of crashing icicles.

† † †

The plane dropped. Mohanraj bit his lip in concentration, patted his jacket pocket. "Would you like a smoke?

Seri almost wanted one. She looked at the knife in her lap. This entire journey she had lacked the keen blade, the Augustine logic to cut through contradictions. She squeezed the pouch. Then, under some new compulsion she could not account for, she loosened its drawstrings and spilled the contents into her palm.

A luscious blue powder.

A thrill danced instantly up her arm, like one touch on the nipple or clitoris. She startled. Something about that sea-blue colour.

She turned to look at the landscape, trees sparkling blue as the dust in her hand, and heard music—snaky violin, chimes in empty canyons, wind and running water. Her arms crackled with goosebumps.

"Can you hear that?" she said.

"Just the wing flaps creaking."

"No. The music."

"Wait! I see motion down there," Mohanraj said. "Good thing you were steadfast."

Seri stared again at the dust in her palms, and was seized with an inexplicable jealousy. She suddenly thought of Gran, with loathing and contempt,
with the kind of bitterness that explodes one day at breakfast with one long
loved—those filthy crumbs, those squeaking teeth and soft inhalations—all
Gran's slobby proverbs, fat platitudes, skinny religion. What a sickening toy
box of consolations.

Seri stroked the knife. "No. Don't land."

"Sorry?"

"We're in the wrong place," she lied. "We've failed. Don't land here."

"We're over the treetops."

"Just climb again."

He turned to look at her, eyebrows tight. His eyes flicked to her palms.

"Climb!" Seri yelled.

She sniffed at the dust. There was only one act she could truly control here
in this dreamland, and that was the extent of her participation. Well, it was
time to take control. Time to withdraw. Rooke and his apprentice could finish
the journey, freeze in Dante's hell for all she cared.

"Ms. Hamm. Why am I climbing?"

"How old is this plane?"

"Depends which part."

"How weak? How corroded?"

"I don't often think about it."

"Could I break this window?"

Mohanraj laughed. "No. That would take a miracle, an angel's strength."

Fine. If she was playing Samson here, failed judge Samson, then God
could complete the story and strengthen her for one final task.

So, Lord? How about it?

She hurriedly sifted the dust into the pouch, tightened the strings, stuffed
it in her pocket. Then grabbed the knife, aimed the butt.

Sniggered. "Lord God, remember me."

One backhand smash to the window. The pane crazed, shattered in
honeycombs.

"Hey!" roared Mohanraj. "That is public property. That is enough. That is
impossible!"

"I know."

Bit by tinkling bit, glass confetti scattered to the night. Chill rushed the
cockpit. The plane dipped.

"This will go in my report," Mohanraj said.

"Just keep circling." She fished her notebook and began ripping out the
pages, pausing only at the last scribble: *I will never be shaken*, Gran's guiding

verse. Seri tore it to shreds, then scattered the pages out the window. She chased them with her chopped hair, tumbling out like wind-blown straw.

"One more pass, Constable."

Finally, she pulled out her grandfather's watch, that antique beauty, that delicate piece, all the springs and wheels. Winding up as best she could, she pitched it from the plane, watched it spin into the dark. "Dear Theodore!" she called after. "A few totems for you!"

"Ms. Hamm, I really must insist—"

"Take me south," Seri said. "As far as we can fly."

"I appreciate your request. But no."

Seri raised the knife. "Constable. It wasn't a request."

"Are you truly threatening me with a knife?"

"Would you prefer a tent peg?"

Moments later, as they winged southward, she patted her shirt to make sure the powder was safe. The ghostly music trailed off, like a choir of falling angels.

† † †

A mist cloud crept through the forest, awakening each detail—each twig, each needle, each barky furrow. A creek murmured over frozen stones.

"Don't drink the water," something said. Then, "Welcome, friend. Difficult to stay awake, isn't it?"

Lor opened his eyes. He was resting against a tree. On the stream's far side, a raven crouched the low boughs, pinned by a moonbeam.

"The Lord provides eternal rest," it said. Then it rose croaking and flapped into the dark.

Lor squinted. A dim figure sat beneath the boughs. "That's a lovely hat," the figure said in the raven's voice.

Lor looked at his hands, pressed around Alistair's wide white brim. He wished for his glasses. His vision here was smoky and blurred.

The man leaned slowly forward, fingers grasping at snowy boughs. "Welcome to the promised land, where we will finally *see*, where the angels will at last be named. Here we will be restored." He coughed. "Here is where time flows backwards, like any good tale or waterway. Here is the pure land. Here we keep our clothes *on*."

"Yeah." Lor leaned forward at the familiar voice. This was his brother, and the snowman had kept his word. "Who are you?" Loudly.

"Shhh. We are waiting to see the signs."

Lor squinted again, collapsed back. No. He did not remember this hoarse voice. Was he deluded by hope, tricked again?

"What is your name, friend?" the man continued.

Lor emptied, felt the distance. "Don't really have one."

"Are you Nebo?"

"No."

"Raziel?"

"No."

"Ah! Of course. One of the sukallin."

"No." Maybe this was a ferryman or gatekeeper. How to decide?

The man paused. "Are you a demon?" He shuddered. "You may not pass."

"No." Lor unblinked, lashes almost icing shut. The stream whispered its cold melody.

His old friend the mist cloud danced just beyond his toes. Here to lead him further on? Lor cleared his throat. But the man seemed to have fallen asleep. Quietly, Lor put a hand to the ground. Just as he was about to push up to wake this brother or stranger, a small silver disc tumbled from the sky, trailing a thin chain. It clonked the sleeping figure's head and bounced to the snow.

"Oh, Serendipity!" The figure started awake. He rubbed his head and leaned forward to pluck the disc from the ground.

"Dear God," he whispered. "The watchmaker himself has awakened me. This is the first sign." He crept into a hollow of bright air. "Friend," voice cold with wonder, "do you see this one true thing?"

Lor peered. The man was wild-bearded as Moses, light hair patched with dark. A pocket watch glimmered in his fingers.

The man peered back. "What is *your* name?"

"I told you."

"He that has eyes." The man fumbled with his shirt pocket, drew a spidery pair of reading glasses. With difficulty, he set them on his nose, wrapped the arms around his ears. "My old friend!" His exhausted features twisted with hunger, and he began to tremble. Then he chuckled, as if infected with long-dormant humour. "My dear old friend. What a strange reunion. The years have been much kinder to you than I."

Lor wondered. He didn't remember either of his brothers being this crazy.

"What name do you go by now?" the man said.

Lor couldn't think of anything. He looked up; snow flittered down through the latticed boughs. He picked a flake from his shoulder, found it smooth and dry. Not snow. Paper shreds, printed with spidery script.

The man plucked another from a branch. "Joshua," he read. "Of course! You are Joshua, and these words are the second sign."

So the man was a stranger after all. One completely mad. If anything, these were signs that Lor had been tricked yet again. He clawed the snow, felt his fingernails bend on the frozen dirt beneath.

The man leaned forward eagerly. "If you are Joshua, then this is not the promised land, not far enough after all. You will enter, where I may never go."

"I'm not going anywhere. I'm finished." Damn that snowman.

The stream darkened. A cloud of bubbles floated by, followed by a school of silver threads. The stranger crept forward and pulled one from the water.

"But you must go. Do you see?" He smiled. "This is one of his hairs, from his hat. The third sign."

Screw the signs, they were all hallucinations. *Listen for the signs*, the snowman had said: well, Lor had listened to that demented voice from Underwood to Inuvik, and where had it gotten him? Lor slumped further against the tree, gritting his teeth.

"Tell me, tell me," the man insisted. "Where is my apprentice? Where is his hat?" At the word *apprentice* his face lit with an almost sacred light, as if his blood ran with fire and could never freeze. Whether it looked angelic or demonic Lor could not decide.

"I don't know." He pitied this lonely apparition. But the thought of spending his final hours like this made his heat rise. To run this far, to the very heart of solitude, only to end up with unexpected company, snared in deranged conversation.

"Tell me, tell me," the man said.

Jesus. Just shut up.

"My apprentice."

Lor inched a quarter way around the tree, looked the other way.

"Joshua?"

Lor clenched his fists, ragged nails slicing palms. He was going to have to cross the river and strangle this stranger, just to get some final peace. He began to rise. A snip of paper fluttered to his lap.

He picked it up and read: *I shall never be shaken.*

Was that old English folk magic? Bible verse? More snowmanic aphorism?

A flush bloomed up his neck, as everything polarized. His attention had lapsed. He had closed his eyes. Here were the snowman's signs after all, three of them, almost missed—

One. A slip of paper, exhorting hope and persistence. Why would he journey this far, only to be shaken from his path? What kind of madness was that?

Two. Hair floating north, to where his brothers were. They would press on, to the North Pole if possible, in keeping with their natures. It was the cunning conclusion to Franklin's original plan: a convergence at the top of the world, where new bonds could be frozen together in a landscape sheared of doubt and despair.

Three. Watch ticking, time flowing. He had wasted too many precious minutes in this sick forest. With a jitter, he noticed that the mist cloud had moved further north, already leaving him behind. His guts pinched. He stood and turned to the man. "I do have to go."

The stranger dropped the pocket watch to the snow and began to furiously twist the hair around his fingers. "Yes, yes. To the promised land." His voice quickened. He pulled nail clippers from a pocket and snipped the blackened skin on his palm. "You cannot remain here. Here is the fruit of our disobedience. Here are the seeds we have planted. We have let our demons run wild. We have thinned ourselves. We are Philistines. We are diminished. We see our mistakes only now, at the final hour. How fitting that it is Christmas Eve." He held more heat than seemed possible in a frozen body. "Where is my apprentice?"

Lor took a step, foot crunching ancient snow. "Really. I don't know."

"Where is your brother?"

"*My* brother?"

"Where is he? It is not too late."

Watch ticking.

Lor considered. There was little reason not to tell. "They're both north. I'm going to meet them."

"Yes, Yes." The madman began to rock. "In the promised land. You will bring him to me."

Lor paused. This was a scene for which he was ill-practised. What did this stranger want? If only Lor had paid more attention to Franklin's social ingenuities, back in the day.

Watch ticking, third sign.

The mist cloud had crossed the river, where it danced among far trees. The madman dropped his chin. Then he snapped up. "Bring him to me!" he barked. "Before midnight strikes to end this Christmas Eve."

He was clearly dying. Lor felt a crumple of sadness. Not like at a funeral. More like watching people eat alone in cafeterias, elderly folk riding the bus alone—faraway stories from the daylight world.

"I have a gift for him." The man's voice hoarsened further. "I have waited for this night."

Watch ticking.

Lor massaged his stomach. Surely a small lie did no harm here. He had to get moving. And a lie might even ease the man's rest. It was not too late to start practicing charity, to start acknowledging the chaos of community, if only with one stranger.

The pocket watch ticked in the snow. The rushing stream grew louder, deeper, colder. The frozen stones chattered. Louder, deeper—

"Okay." Lor dispelled the crescendo. "I will bring him to you. Yes."

"My dear!" The stranger began to scrape snow from the ground. "We will look into the heart of things, the very pith of life. And gather our powder, and renew our journey." His head nodded suddenly, and he dropped into slumber. His hand continued to tap, chattering the nail clippers.

Lor stood, gripping the hat tightly, and padded over the stream. He stopped at the hollow, where black water seeped outward to stain the snow. He squatted to check on the man, who shivered in spite of the hot flush on his cheeks. Lor felt a ripple of loneliness. He had an idea. But he drew back his hands.

No. This was his, his brother's. It could not be given to a stranger.

Still, he loosened his fingers on the brim. Charity, Lor. One act at a time. He could yet transform from snowman to angel—from car stealer to hat giver.

With a light pause he reached forward and placed Alistair's hat on the stranger's head.

When their skin touched, it sparked a cascade of memories. Lor's entire journey unspooled—his long flight from America to the Arctic—not a neat chronology, but a prismatic burst of images. Fatty. Alistair. Dawn Cherry. The strippers. Darcilee Shimozowa. No connections. No points at which he could splice his remembered actions in a chain of consequences. His story had frayed, like this hair still twined around the stranger's finger—thinned, looped, knotted.

The tale would begin again, soon. This time with hope.

Watch ticking.

He tightened Al's hat on the stranger's head, so it would hold fast against the cold. He rose. Smiling for the first time in recent memory, he stepped into the misty curtain, then floated north to the moon's bright country, where both his brothers waited for him, a family at last. He did not look back, to where breezes loosed the hat and sailed it past the treetops.

rEuniOn

Seri always believed that Rooke was still alive, too shrewd
and vaporous to let himself freeze somewhere in the Arctic.
But there were no footprints in the snow. No one in the service
had any memory of T.F. Rooke, not even Pierre Anselm Kanashiro,
who had grown distant, and not a little vaporous himself since
moving to southern Alberta.

One spring night in Vancouver, lost among government documents deep
in the library basement, where the pound of coastal rain diminished to a
distant whisper, Seri discovered an old newspaper article on the McDonald
Commission. She ran into an obscure reference to an A. Rooke, who may
have worked in the late sixties for the RCMP Security Service, I section, the
so-called Watcher service, long since dismantled by the Canadian government for abuses of power.

The story caught her interest, because of the name, yes, but also because
of its strangeness. Whoever A. Rooke was—and the name was obviously
coincidental—he was rumoured to be a special constable involved in a highly
unusual request from D Section, countersubversion, to engage in physical
surveillance of a suspected violent pornography ring that recruited and filmed
under the guise of a travelling circus. This Rooke may have worked with the
FBI in the northwestern states, using a vast infrastructure of informants,

most of them hotel staff. No one knew for sure. The Watchers had never officially existed.

Seri always wished she had made a copy of that story. Years later, travelling alone, talking to no one, she would visit strange libraries to hunt for the clipping. But she could never find it again. Then she would sit, and stroke a finger through her angel dust, until it was long past supper, the traditional time for family fellowship, and she would think of forking paths, and remember a grandmother she had once loved, and a security guard would come to shoo her home. But where was home?

Theodore Franklin Rooke's body was never found.

No one ever looked.

† † †

Soon after returning from the north, Seri had begun to hate Vancouver's misty lullabies. Everywhere she went, a magpie followed.

"Fly," she said. "Go home."

It never did.

She squeezed her dust and dreamed of skies. She wanted to run back to the prairies, maybe the Arctic, renew herself amid thirsty rivers or icy barrens. First she needed to strip her life's old layers: it was becoming increasingly clear that family and friends got in the way. But where to get the fire? She would never pray again.

What she needed was some benediction for the old life. Something to mark the time and start her off. An Old Testament totem, a Rookean ritual. That was it. A ceremony.

Her birthday.

† † †

On her twenty-fifth she sat locked in her room slicing off her hair, fully and evenly this time, with the Arctic knife. The pouch of dust sat on her old toy chest, some of it spilled. Outside was spring—butterflies on the window, bees biting tulips, the familiar magpie. And, impossibly, apples on the tree at the end of the Giant's Bridge. Some were already dropped, as if impatient for summer's end.

She put down the knife, looked out the window. After all these years, the Giant's Bridge still maintained its straightness, north to the porch, south to the bushes. Two directions, a beggar's meal of choices. It was always the same in the Old Testament: Egypt or Canaan, Sodom or the wilderness.

The doorknob clicked. Then a knock. Her mother.

"Seri. Gran's back from Europe. She's hitchhiking home, just phoned from the trucker's cellphone. She's bringing gifts. She sounds so young. Mr. Scott's got a head cold he picked up in the Black Forest."

Seri sat motionless. This was not the time. Her fingers twitched. She grimaced and tried to stay completely still.

"Seri. You're in there, right? By the way, that nasty man from the collection agency called again. Something about your credit cards?"

After many minutes Seri's ribs began to ache. She heard clomping on the stairs, then a sharp rap on the door.

"Pumpkin! Let me in. Wait till you see what I smuggled home for you from this weird hotel in Moravia: a gigantic opus on puppetry called *Casey and Finnegan's Wake: A Tale on How Divers Angels from Heav'n Fell*. Oh, what an intriguing boy's tale. Happy birthday! Let me in. How was the Arctic?"

Another rap. Whiff of lemon perfume.

Oh, Gran. Seri just about rose. The old love flared inside. But then she touched the dust on the toy chest and a deep jealousy surged through her. North or south: a clean Augustine choice. Seri made it. She held her breath, until Gran clomped back down the stairs and whispered with Mum, and then more footfalls and the door slamming.

Seri looked out the window. Down below, Mr. Scott was sneezing into a bright hanky. Mum emerged first, moving to start the minivan. Then Gran, dressed in some weird old-world outfit trimmed with scarves and sashes. She turned to look up at Seri's darkened window, raising the Moravian book. Then crouched to pluck a fallen apple. "We know you're in there, pumpkin-hide! We'll steal you a diet Coke from the pub."

She pitched the apple at the window. It splatted on the glass, scattering bees and butterflies.

"See you soon, Seri."

Seri felt a prick of loneliness, but she chased it with one touch of dust. Her family drove away, while she followed the Giant's Bridge with her eye, all the way to the bushes.

"Not see you soon," she whispered. "Goodbye."

She packed a toothbrush, bank card, and the pouch of dust. Still unsure about travelling to the prairies or the Arctic, she decided to book into the Old Xanadu Hotel on Hastings, where no one would ever look, and she could wait for inspiration.

She cut the last hank of hair, rubbed off all her makeup. Then hoisted the toy chest and dumped it out like a bag of seeds. All the toys tumbled from their childhood hierarchy—Barbie, Slinky, bouncing balls. Sooty ceramic

Gabriel, whose head cracked off and rolled face up, trumpeting. Finally, *The Silver Chair*, pages flapping goodbye. She opened it to the ending, nailed it to the floor with the knife.

Then she dropped the empty box and walked, out the door, down the stairs, into fog-wet morning and a journey's birth. She was twenty-five years old.

She looked like a sick boy, iridescent with joy and bitterness.

† † †

"Get you a drink, sir? Something to chase the heat?"

The hotel bar was dark and empty, except for one bellboy striped with shadows. The smell of hot rain drifted in from windows.

"Just a diet Coke," Seri said.

Ice cubes rattled in a glass. Brief sunlight dashed against them, then vanished.

"Actually." Seri twisted in the chair. "Make it a regular Coke."

A sniff behind the bar. "Sir?"

"Oh, fuck it, make it a vodka with ice. Today's a celebration."

From the shadows the man emerged, cloaked in baggy black uniform and brimmed hat. He bent over her table, eyes hidden beneath the brim, remaining features speckled with lamplight.

"Sometimes a birthday is a dangerous thing," he whispered.

"Oh, for sure."

A day to remember all things lost, every hour and opportunity, every forked path. A pocket watch, a notebook, a calling. A family. Always the choice between two journeys—trust or doubt, damned or saved, broken or renewed, faithful or jaded. But why? Why was it always north or south?

The magpie chattered outside. Seri noticed briefly the iridescent blues and greens among its black and white feathers, flickering in the fitful sunlight.

She ignored it, stared further out the rainy window. "Is that a church across the street?"

"Saint Augustine's."

"You're kidding. You are fucking kidding me." Surely, somewhere, there was a third path. A road travelling east, narrow but not necessarily straight.

"I will read to you from Ecclesiastes, something to suit your mood." The bellboy shifted in the half-light, cracked a heavy Bible.

Seri secretly opened her pouch, poked in a finger. "First let me ask you a question. Do you know of any prophets who were neither faithful nor disobedient?"

"Explain how this is possible."

She trolled a finger through the powder. "Any angels who were neither good nor fallen?"

"I don't recall any, sir. Let me read to you."

"No." She looked out at the church again. "I've changed my mind."

The Bible thumped shut. Seri mashed her dust. Even the smallest choice was a forked path. Bible verse or no? Silence or conversation?

"Okay. Just one," Seri said.

"Sir?"

"Something from the New Testament."

"Ahh."

Seri slid her vodka forward, wiped the cool circle of condensation. She pulled her finger from from the powder. Then neatly folded the pouch and placed it in her pocket. "Yes. New Testament. Just for today. Then never again."

† † †

Summer comes at last to that strange, vast land named Canada. Crows ride the warming west winds, high above towering clouds, eyeing with casual interest the map below.

Far south, in Lethbridge, a magpie shreds the pages of a Bible on the walk. The words blow north.

Far north, in the Arctic, a raven nips the strings of a smashed black guitar. The notes blow south.

Far west, in Vancouver, the flies hatch early.

No one on the map pays much notice. There are barbecues to light, beers to chill, phones to tap. The circus is in town again. The days are long and elegant. The sun blares. The children sing. Afternoons the knives fly.

In each realm a hotel looms above, silent and watchful. Most of the rooms are booked—to families, to lovers, to friends on shared journeys. But some rooms remain locked and unlit until summer's end. Behind their empty windows the fires dance like falling angels, waiting for the snowmen, and the moon's return, and the long winter night.

THE END

AfTErWorD

ARCTIC SMOKE could only have been set in the 1990s. For one, it was probably the last decade in which characters could self-identify as anti-establishment while refusing to virtue-signal in ways that became common after 2007, when social media and the mobile device crashed together and began to accelerate nascent cultural trends. More importantly, it was the decade in which the Seattle Scene actualized the final death of punk. At the risk of offending those who hated British cultural critic Mark Fisher ("K-punk")—indeed, CELEBRATED his suicide—I have to acknowledge his strong influence on this book. Fisher, in a vivid analysis of Kurt Cobain's "dreadful lassitude and objectless rage," argued that grunge gave voice to a youth culture of total frustration, in which rebellion was no longer a real option. And then grunge itself committed suicide.

Nineties rebellion was no longer that brief hot connection to alternative community, the way it was in the sixties, the seventies, and episodically in the eighties. Pre-nineties, the habits and symbols of punk had a grace period where they truly were disturbing and oppositional. Those habits and symbols were always soon-to-be captured by the machine, of course, and sold back to the posers, latecomers, and hangers-on. But there would always be a little lead-time for the true believers to flee and start the next fire. Sadly, by the nineties rebellion was *prefigured* by the machine. Punk could only exist as a weird spectre without any legible history: it was anticipated, produced, marketed and sold by the machine as a *precondition* of its own existence. And so, at the close of the millennium, we had gone from the MC5 to Blink-182. Could a true punk feel anything other than despair?

I was never a true punk. I wanted to be. Some freak friends I knew in the nineties asked me what I thought would happen to the scene if it were transported out of its historical context, that of densely populated, culturally exhausted cityscapes. One friend enthusiastically proposed a thought experiment: "Like, what if a punk band had to tour the *Arctic*?" What a great premise, I thought, and immediately stole it. Years later, as I began to write, the doubts tumbled out. What *was* the Arctic for my friends, symbolically? Did it function as a repository for fetishes and projections, the way the "Orient" and "Africa" and "The New World" did in so many works of British Imperialism? I had already been to the High Arctic—a boyhood fantasy realized—but the question was just as urgent when directed at myself. After all, my adventures on that Arctic trip were downright hallucinogenic, and probably romanticized in both my immediate experience and retrospective memory.

So I began to consider the projections of "northerness" so common to generic fantasy. In maps of Narnia and Middle Earth, south is generally the geography of the swarthy and diminished human. East, in Narnia, is the geography of exploration and the unrevealed or redeemed. West, in Middle Earth, serves much the same function. But north—north is consistently the embodiment of wonder, mythological power, and romanticized "wildness" (is there Galadriel fetish porn? Probably).

Northerness—especially its ethnocentricity and "medievalism"—has seeped out of its literary precincts into a variety of subcultures, some more toxic than others. One florid example is Scandinavian Black Metal, a scene that has often borrowed from Tolkien's lore and iconography. Some Black Metal, especially the traditional Norwegian variety, shares a racist and xenophobic bent with neo-nazi strains of punk. Other forms of punk—anarchist, straight edge, vegan—are perpetually at odds with both their racist kin and the "Viking" melodrama of northern Black Metal. Some forms of punk share with some forms of Black Metal the stage antics of cutting and self-mutilation. It's complicated. The turf wars over what even *counts* as authentic "punk" or "black metal" will likely never end. But what almost all punk and black metal scenes share is an excruciating drive to burn down what are perceived as asphyxiating cultural norms. Churches of Norway, anyone?

Speaking of churches, I went to a one at least three times a week growing up just north of Montana, in the small city of Lethbridge. Some American tourists dropped by our church one Sunday, and described Lethbridge as "*Twin Peaks* North." I couldn't have agreed more. What a perfect setting for a surreal story. The town is sliced down the middle by a phantasmagorical river valley filled with cottonwoods, cactus, and rattlesnakes. It's the type of valley that suddenly, surprisingly, plunges down out of the otherwise flat landscape. It was the site of the last great "inter-tribal" battle in Canada—the Battle of the Belly River—between the Iron Confederacy and the Blackfoot Confederacy.

Lethbridge was a famous brothel town in the early nineteenth century, as referenced by Timothy Findley in his novel *The Wars*. The high-level train bridge that spans the valley is the largest of its kind in the world. Many have plunged to their deaths attempting to climb it. Supposedly, one of my childhood friends was tied to the tracks in a drug-deal gone bad, crushed to bits by the train. Chinook winds howl out of the west to drive everyone crazy, sometimes raising the topsoil and creating the infamous and so-called "black blizzards." It's crazy dry. Many are infected with Chinook madness: the rates of suicide and divorce are supposedly high.

Lethbridge isn't all bleakness and weirdness. It counts many Japanese Canadians among its population, the descendants of racist internment and evacuation policies during WWII. They've enriched the culture tremendously. Smack in the middle of this prairie town we have a wondrous Japanese garden, where one can attend a tea ceremony unlike anything at the local saloon or coffee shop. There are many Buddhist temples; I first learned to meditate in one of them. I was lucky enough to grow up with the Tamayoses next door, the Shimozawas around one corner, the Okamuras around the other, and the Kanashiros down the street. Some of them are great guitar players.

Until the nineties, anyway, Lethbridge culture was a cheek-by-jowl concoction of rednecks, farmers, fundamentalist Christians, Mormons, Buddhists, bikers, old hippies, young goths, immigrants, Hutterites, Káínawa folk and their confederates, the Piikani and Siksika (whose traditional territories Lethbridge occupies), and the perpetually hopeful and disappointed "university types." The mix could be visually striking on a bustling Thursday afternoon. A family friend immigrated to Canada from Iran, and, after his flight, caught a bus from Calgary. As it rolled into the Lethbridge station, downtown, he looked out the window and burst into tears. He thought he was in the wrong country.

So it all went into the mix—punk, Lethbridge, fantasy, nineties, northerness. I tried as best I could to write a formulaic novel in the genre tradition of urban fantasy. How'd that work out for me? In the documentary *Gimme Danger,* James Williamson, guitarist for the Stooges, said of the *Raw Power* era: "it was our best effort to make hit records ... but the thing about us is, we're so delusional about what is popular, because all we really care about is what we like." Enough said.

Without the Stooges, could there ever have been the Ramones? Without the Ramones, could there ever have been a Nirvana? Trick questions. When writers and musicians note that they "could not have done it alone," they are not simply being gracious or indulging false modesty, but expressing an indelible truth of interdependence. We may experience ourselves as the main characters in our own stories—with our discrete motives, clear desires, and choices that spring from our inner "selves"—but life's not really like that. They don't call fiction "fiction" for nothing. I didn't cook up, *ex nihilo,* an idiom that nestles the sagacious with the jejune. Bugs Bunny taught me that. An old girlfriend accidentally offered me the name Dawn Cherry. The Right Honourable Stephen Harper loaned me his speeches without even knowing it. On and on go the imprints and influences, forever rippling.

So a big Lethbridge thank-you to NeWest, the small press with big designs. Matt, Claire, Michel, and the rest of that gang are producing consistently wonderful and beautiful books. To my original readers: Rosemary Nixon for a magpie's eye; Candas Jane Dorsey for a raven's brain; Timothy J. Anderson for a crow's nose. Speaking of birds, special thanks to Kit Dobson, who agreed to be my final editor despite what must have been his better judgment. While I'm at it, thanks to Bill Bunn, Mike Thorn, and all my friends at Calgary's S.A.W. Workshop for hot tea, warm wishes, and cool advice. And to Calgary's IFWA, surely the *least* hard-drinking writer's association in history. These folks are accomplished writers. They sure ain't punks.

While writing, I read a lot. It would be shifty and shiftless of me not to acknowledge my humongous debt to other writers. First, to the books that deeply inspired me: Katherine Dunn's *Geek Love,* Mark Helprin's *Winter's Tale,* and Angela Carter's *Nights at the Circus.* All three are built of language that is so supersaturated it becomes palpably hallucinogenic. Second, to secretive old Thomas Pynchon himself. In *Gravity's Rainbow* and *The Crying of Lot 49,* he shows how one can take conventional story craft and push it so hard that it comes apart at the seams: too much causality, chronology, agency—all the familiar elements of story can, with enough overdrive, actually zip themselves inside-out to create a bewilderment much better than plain old chaos ever could. Third, to the incomparable Flannery O'Connor. In her collection *Mystery and Manners,* she celebrates a kind of fiction that frustrates our hardwired urge to connect with character and groove on plot. I aspire to that.

A cheerful shout-out to the Bible, surely the wildest anthology of weird tales ever collected. That's because New Weird is actually very old. It's part of many story traditions in many cultures.

Nothing could be less punk than scholarship. I have to do some for my day job; I don't have to like it. But I have to admit that sometimes a rare beast—scintillating, vibrant academic work—sneaks up and bites me in the ass. In a good way. So my enduring thanks to the narratologist H. Porter Abbott, who has investigated the interface between storytelling and human evolution in a fabulous book called *Real Mysteries*. Abbott gives a great evolutionary explanation for the compulsive human desire for story. But he also supplies compelling research that serves as license to engage in storytelling *misbehaviour*. Certain kinds of stories can jam our evolutionary repertoire of reading strategies; such tales create a haunting and humbling resonance, where the human mind is suddenly aware of itself, caught in the very act of failing to impose standardized narrative order and clarity. Abbott demonstrates how such weird tales can gift the reader with a spooky perception of what lies outside of language and story.

Speaking of the outside of language, thank you and apologies to all the drummers I have stolen from in the attempt to enliven my prose, including "Pretty" Purdy, Steve Ferrone, John Bonham, Ian Mosley, and "Death Metal" Dave Mills. The delicious ways in which they hear time have found their way into this book. Stories dry up, and words lose their sense, and meaning withers. But rhythm *remains*.

Lethbridge
June 2019

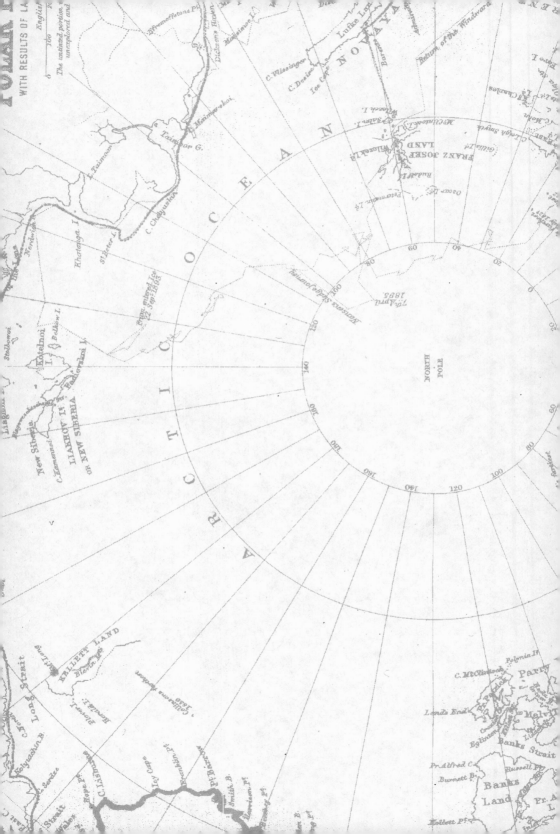